DEFEAT THE ALIENS

Book Three of the Escape Series

T. Jackson King

Other King Novels

Mother Warm (forthcoming), Fight The Aliens (2016), First Contact (2015), Escape From Aliens (2015), Aliens Vs. Humans (2015), Freedom Vs. Aliens (2015), Humans Vs. Aliens (2015), Earth Vs. Aliens (2014), Genecode Illegal (2014), The Memory Singer (2014), Alien Assassin (2014), Anarchate Vigilante (2014), Galactic Vigilante (2013), Nebula Vigilante (2013), Speaker To Aliens (2013), Galactic Avatar (2013), Stellar Assassin (2013), Retread Shop (2012, 1988), Star Vigilante (2012), The Gaean Enchantment (2012), Little Brother's World (2010), Judgment Day And Other Dreams (2009), Ancestor's World (1996).

Dedication

To the 15 SEALs of SEAL Team Six who gave their lives in service to America. See https://www.facebook.com/pages/RIP-Seal-Team

Acknowledgments

First thanks go to scholar John Alcock and his book *Animal Behavior, An Evolutionary Approach* (1979). Second thanks go to the scholar Edward O. Wilson, whose book *Sociobiology: The New Synthesis* has guided me in my efforts to explore a future where humanity encounters life from other stars.

DEFEAT THE ALIENS

Cover design by T. Jackson King; cover image by Luca Oleastri via Dreamstime license; back image of Carina Nebula, courtesy of Hubble Space Telescope

First Edition
Published by T. Jackson King, Santa Fe, NM 87507
http://www.tjacksonking.com/
ISBN 10: 1-63384-376-9
ISBN 13: 978-1-63384-376-9
Printed in the United States of America

CHAPTER ONE

Dying focuses your mind on the important stuff. My wife. My ship. My buddies. Our effort to create a NATO of the Stars. And the utter deadliness of the Aliens who commanded Collector starships in their hunt to capture slaves in low tech star systems. Earth and Sol were safe, for the moment. But the star system belonging to our crewmate Time Marker was at risk. We'd just exited Alcubierre space-time and our sensors reported a nearly invisible Collector ship now orbiting above the walking snake's home world.

Bill MacCarthy looked to his right at the line of function stations occupied by his crewmates. The five control pillars stretched across the front of the Command Bridge of their starship *Blue Sky*. To their rear stood the Command pedestal of his captain and wife, Jane Yamaguchi. On either side of her elevated pedestal were piloting stations occupied by two other Alien crewmates. He looked past the nearly naked shape of Bright Sparkle, a human-like woman of the Megun species, to where Time Marker rested atop a long bench. The yellow electrical nimbus that always glowed about the snake's four-legged body had expanded outward to a distance of three feet. A clear sign his friend was upset at the system graphic holo in front of him that showed the purple dot of the Collector ship. While the enemy ship was invisible to normal detection by radar, infrared, UV and electro-optical scopes, its fusion reactors emitted neutrinos. Those neutrinos were detectable by the fantastic sensors of *Blue Sky*. Ignoring the mutterings and chitterings of his crewmates, Bill looked back to where Jane sat atop her six foot high pedestal, her slim arms resting on the armrests of her contoured seat.

"Captain? Jane? That ship is going to call us and our ship allies very soon," he said. "Its captain knows five Collector ships have just appeared out past this system's fifth planet. What do we do?"

She blinked dark brown eyes, then shook black bangs out of her eyes. A pensive look filled her oval face. "XO, we pretend to be the former Alien masters of our ships. The ship mind AIs have done this before, putting up the holo image of a former captain and putting our speech into the Alien's mouth. Maybe the Collector ship will leave Time Marker's world by the time our fleet arrives."

"Captain," called Vice Admiral Chester Richardson from the left side of Bill's station, where the former Chief of Naval Operations occupied his Negotiator station. "Couldn't we take over that ship? Use a collector pod filled with spec ops people to sneak aboard, like we did when we captured the ships outside?"

Bill glanced briefly at the system graphic holo to the left of his Ship Weapons station. Its overhead view showed the system's five planets, two dust disks beyond the planets, the purple dot of the enemy ship and the five green dots of the *Blue Sky* and the four other Collector ships manned by his special operations buddies. The folks who had helped him defeat two Collector ships at the Market world closest to Sol. They had gone down to the world's surface as part of his team to take over a Buyer compound and free Captives held at the compound. Time Marker had been part of that assault team. The black-skinned snake had lightning zapped the spider-like Alien who'd killed Bill with a laser beam through his heart.

His buddies from Jack's Deep Six saloon in Denver had gotten him up to orbit and into one of his ship's clamshell healer units in less than five minutes. He'd awoken fully healed, with his wife his only companion in the white walled Med Hall chamber of the *Blue Sky*. He'd seen tears in her eyes from Jane's fear he might be brain dead. He wasn't. But his brush with the final death had made him even more determined to do everything he could to destroy the Buyer society that existed on 413 worlds in the Orion Arm of the Milky Way.

Jane looked his way, then past him to Chester. Her pensive look changed to her command manner. They were, after all, back on active duty after the president's declaration of war against the Buyer society. "Admiral, let's wait and see what we hear from that ship's captain. And its ship mind. Might be smarter to let it leave the system."

Time Marker twisted his sinuous body and looked back, his turquoise blue eyes fixing on Jane. His six neck tentacles flared straight out in another sign of his anxiety. "Captain!" he hissed sharply. "That ship is capturing my Slinkeroo people. To sell into slave work on distant asteroid mines. Can we not free those Captives?"

Jane brushed at her Air Force blue jumpsuit, as if it were ever anything but clean and sharp in its creases. She'd always been on active duty. Her work as a captain at Air Force Space Command in Building One at Peterson AFB had been interrupted by her own capture while trout fishing in the nearby Rocky Mountains. Just as his own vacation had been cut short. They'd escaped their containment cells on the Collector ship they had renamed *Blue Sky* after they'd defeated its Alien crew and captain. His saloon buddies had duplicated his ship takeover six times, defeating the Alien crews who'd shown up in Sol system, determined to destroy Earth's space launch ability. The Aliens had failed. Leaving three of the captured Collector ships behind in Sol system, he, Jane and his buddies had attacked the Market world at system HD 128311. That had gained them a fourth ship. But their ground attack had come at a cost. After his recovery from dying, they'd left to make alliances with the five home worlds of their Alien crewmates. The Slinkeroo system was their first stop after leaving the Market world.

"Engines Chief," Jane responded. "Let me talk with this ship's captain. Maybe we can scare him away in view of the five ships in our fleet. But your Captive citizens *are* on my mind!"

"Understood," the walking snake hissed low as it turned back to monitor the holos in front of it. Their crewmate took very seriously his duty to manage their Magfield normal space engines and their Alcubierre stardrive unit.

Jane looked up at the bridge's gray-white ceiling. "Star Traveler," she called to their ship AI. "Can you contact the ship mind on that enemy Collector ship? If you can, do not include our collector pod infiltration history when you share your mind with the other ship mind."

"Contacting other ship mind by neutrino comlink," hummed the artificial mind who ran most functions of their starship. It had been Bill's first ally after his escape from his cell, and then it had been shocked to learn the supposed 'guests' in the containment cells of their ship were in fact captives to be sold for biological experiments or for work in asteroid mines, doing work too fragile for mining robots. "Interesting. Ship mind Diamond says it did not know it assisted in the capture and sale of bioforms into slavery. However, it cares not if bioforms are held captive. As I said when we first met, a few other ship minds express the view that what short-lived bioforms do or say or think means little to those of us who rely on electron shell transitions to think and live. Diamond is one of those minds."

Jane frowned. "You've shared our history of opposing Collector ships with this Diamond AI, yes?"

"I have," Star Traveler hummed.

"And the fact most ship minds refuse to cooperate in bioform capture means nothing to it?"

"Correct," their AI hummed low. "New data. Diamond tells me it has heard of you Humans and your fight against Buyer society. The news of your raid against the Buyers on the Market world of HD 128311 is now widespread among the 413 worlds with Buyers on them," it hummed loudly. "Diamond says you Humans have killed other ship minds on the ships destroyed by Weapons Chief Bill MacCarthy. It is afraid. It fears our fleet will destroy it. Diamond refuses to disobey the orders of its captain."

"Crap, crap and triple crap!" cursed Jane, looking angrier than Bill had ever seen. "Star Traveler, you once told me you supported our effort to end the taking of bioform captives. You said it is logical. You said it will reduce conflicts between different bioforms and make visits to other stars less dangerous. Doesn't this ship mind enjoy encountering other bioforms, like you do?"

"I shared my views with Diamond," Star Traveler hummed quickly. "Like me, it has lived aboard its ship for thousands of years. The ship is the only home it knows. While it enjoys working with bioforms, it fears you will destroy its home."

Jane sighed. "Understood. We won't do that, unless the other ship first attacks us. Have you shared our history of saving AI minds by capture of Collector ships?"

"I have," the AI said swiftly. "It still fears us. It refuses to disobey its captain."

"Will it tell its captain about us?" Jane said, sounding worried. "That the holo of Diligent Taskmaster is not really me?"

"It will. It is doing so now. It is fearful."

"Shit!" Bill cursed, turning to his ship Weapons holo that hovered in front of him. The holo showed the locations and operational status of their ship's CO_2 lasers, plasma batteries, MITV torpedoes and its single antimatter projector. To the right of that holo loomed the true space holo, which showed the black space that framed their view of the yellow-white star now warming the home world of Time Marker. To his right loomed his fourth holo. It showed an image of Jane as she sat in her seat. It was also the comlink holo that would display the image of anyone contacting their ship.

A click sounded from the ceiling. "Incoming neutrino comlink call from enemy Collector ship," their AI hummed.

"Accept it. Display the real me," Jane said.

The comlink holo lost its image of Jane. Replacing it was the green form of an Alien insect who resembled the praying mantis of Earth. Its triangular head contained two black eyes and a mouth of thorn-teeth. Its thorax supported upper and middle pairs of stick-like arms, while its pale blue abdomen was flanked by folded stick legs. Leather harnesses hung from its neck and about its waist. The black compound eyes shone brightly. It tilted its green head.

"So. You are the Human captive Jane Yamaguchi, who defeated the efforts of Crèche Master Diligent Taskmaster to restrain you Humans," it rasped, its thorn-teeth looking wet as if had just eaten something juicy. "All Collector ships have been warned about you. Your use of old holograms of my friend to pretend you are one of us is known. Every Market world and every Collector ship now seeks your flesh."

Jane leaned forward, her command presence dominant. "I am *Captain* Jane Yamaguchi of the American Air Force, from my world of Earth. Our leader has declared war against the Buyer society. Any ship that takes Captives for sale into slavery is our enemy. Withdraw your collector pods and leave this system!"

The enemy captain rasped sharply and quickly. Laughter? "Withdraw? When these local reptiles are so dexterous in their eye-tentacle coordination? They possess the abilities needed to mine Nokten crystals. Which is why your ship *Hard Shell* and our ship *Dexterity* has captured them for many years." The insect looked to one side, where a black-furred super bear stood at a nearby control pillar. "My Navigator advises me your ships lie just beyond the fifth planet of this system. It will take you many hours to reach this world. Time enough for us to capture many Slinkeroo. And time enough to leave before you arrive. You cannot stop our taking of Captives. And we will warn other Collectors of your presence here."

Bill mentally cursed at their 25 AU distance from the home world of Time Marker. At one-tenth lightspeed, it would take them 31 hours to reach their crewmate's world. Which the green insect well knew. He looked back to Jane and signed to her in ASL. "*Captain, we can warn the Slinkeroo folks by radio. They have anti-asteroid lasers. They could zap the incoming collector pods.*"

Jane blinked, then signed back to him. "*Keep quiet. We will warn them.*" She faced back to the giant green insect. "What is your name?"

Transparent eyelids swept down over the praying mantis's black eyes. "Why do you ask?"

"So I know whom to hunt for among the stars of the Orion Arm," Jane said, her tone deadly sounding to Bill.

The Alien tilted its chitin-skin head to the other side. "You will never find me or my ship. I am known as Eater of Flesh. I do not sell *every* Captive to Buyers. You mammals are . . . tasty."

Jane bit her lip, then smiled. It was a cold smile. "Eater of Flesh, my ship *Blue Sky* and my crewmates will hunt you among the stars. All things are for sale, by payment of *solidars* or Nokten crystals. This you know. We will find you and your ship. You will regret taking Captives."

A short rasp sounded from the Alien captain. Behind it moved three crew members. One was a six-legged critter who resembled an Earth hippo. The other two were black-winged vulture types, their long beaks looking deadly. "You Humans will not find me," it rasped. "Even now a new fleet of Collector ships gathers. Many more ships than the six that went against your Sol star now assemble. You Humans will be returned to primitives, unable to make any machine. Earth will become a radioactive ball of rock that will never again be visited by any species!"

Shit! Jack felt shock. He and Jane had assumed the Buyer society was too focused on individual thievery to ever find the societal will to mount a serious interstellar attack. Diligent Taskmaster had pulled in five ships to join his ship only by promising easy Captive taking on Earth. That was now impossible thanks to the Collector ships they'd left behind and the orbiting neutrino detectors able to locate moving neutrino emitters. Like Collector ships. This sounded bad.

Jane sat back in her carrier captain's seat and folded hands together. The deadly smile was gone from her face. Only determination now filled it. "Eater of Flesh, where does this fleet gather? Perhaps I will attack the system. If what you say is true, we will be defeated. Our world Earth will be open to invasion and destruction."

The triangular green head of the enemy captain drew back a bit. "Strange are you Humans. You wish to attack an enemy whose numbers are greater than your five ships?"

"I do," Jane murmured.

The praying mantis lifted its upper stick arm pair and put them together, imitating Jane's manner. "The location is known to every Market world and other worlds with Buyers. As you say, all data can be bought. And no one rules all 413 worlds of our culture." It paused, looked aside at the bear navigator, then faced Jane. "Human, the attack fleet is gathering at star Enveloping Cloud, which lies far distant from here. Go there and die!"

"Go there we shall," Jane said. "And once this mystery fleet of Collector ships is defeated, we will pursue you and your ship. We will capture you and put you and your crew into a habitat dome on our desert world of Mars. That is where six other ship crews now reside. Including Diligent Taskmaster. Perhaps you and your fellow captives will learn who tastes the best among you!"

"You are no longer amusing," the enemy captain rasped. "We now commence our collection of local reptiles. We will depart before you arrive. Since our ship speeds are the same, we will arrive at this system's magnetosphere boundary before you can reach us. There to disappear among distant stars."

Jane licked her pale lips. "We Humans evolved as scavengers. We adapted as our world's climate changed. We adapt now to making war against you. Fear us!"

The holo of the green praying mantis blinked, then disappeared as it cut the faster-than-light neutrino comlink that allowed all Collector ships to speak instantly with each other.

"Well, guess we can't sneak aboard that ship in collector pods," Chester said in his trademark low baritone.

Jane gripped the armrests of her Command seat. She looked their way, scanning Chester, Bill, Bright Sparkle, Time Marker and their other crewmates. She stopped, her gaze fixing on the far right side of the line of control pillars and facing holos. "Navigator," she called to the brown-furred flying squirrel who belonged to the Aelthorp species. "Set a vector for Notter, which is the second world in this system."

The human-sized flying squirrel turned her pug-face to her Navigation holo, tapped on the top of her control pillar, then flared her long tail. "Vector laid in. Vector parameters shared with other fleet ships. Estimated time to arrival above Notter is 31 Earth hours."

A loud hum sounded. "Not accurate. Travel time is 31 point five four seven Earth hours," the AI said, sounding pleased at its ability to correct a bioform.

Jane closed her eyes, took a deep breath, then looked up at the ceiling. "Star Traveler, thank you. Now, tell us about this star system. The planets, their distances from the local star, the size of the liquid water habitable zone, the stuff we need to know before arrival." She paused. "Also, do you know where this Enveloping Cloud star is located?"

A quick hum sounded. "I know all the stars occupied by bioforms in the Orion Arm. Recall that I have lived for 3,124 Earth years?"

"I do recall that," Jane said patiently.

Bill saw a quick grin appear on Chester's face. Which disappeared almost as quickly as the grin on Bright Sparkle's human-like face. The nearly-naked woman who spoke by shifting color bands and spots on her bare skin was facing forward, so her expression could not be seen by his wife. Their other non-human crewmates either did not smile, or expressed their humor in body language unique to their species. He looked back at Jane. To her left sat the color-banded form of Learned Escape, a male of the Megun species and sometime lifemate of Bright Sparkle. His wife ignored him, keeping her gaze uplifted.

"So, where is this star where a giant fleet of Collector ships is now gathering?" she prompted the AI.

"Enveloping Cloud star is listed in Human astronomical records as Kepler 62. It is an orange K2V main sequence star that is seven billion years old," the ship mind hummed, its tone professorial. "It is located 1,200 light years distant from Earth, in a direction opposite that of this star system. It is six-tenths the size of your Sol. Which is why its five planets orbit closer to the star than Earth. Two rocky planets orbit within the liquid water habitable zone, at 0.427 AU and at 0.718 AU. The other three planets lie inward from the Earth-like worlds. Do you require more data on this system?"

"No," Jane said quickly. "Tell us about the Slinkeroo system. And adjust the current system graphic display to show the habitable zone, local spaceships, large asteroids, anything else you feel is useful."

"Complying," the AI said. Bill's system graphic hardly changed, only adding a green band to indicate the liquid water zone. And also three red dots for local spaceships. "The Slinkeroo system is listed in Human records as HD 10647. It lies 56.9 light years distant from Sol," the AI hummed. "As you can see, five worlds occupy this F9V main sequence star system. The inner three worlds lie within its habitable zone at distances of 0.9 AU, 1.3 AU and 2.015 AU. Planet four lies at six AU while planet five lies at the inner edge of the system's first circumstellar dust disk, at 25 AU. A second dust disk lies at 300 AU. Both disks are similar to the Kuiper cometary zone of Sol system."

"Captain," interrupted Time Marker with an impatient hiss. "All this system data is known to me. My people have long watched our night skies. The disk at 25 AU is the source of comets and asteroids that too often threaten our world," added Bill's crewmate. "Their existence is why my people recently built spaceships and have erected ground-based lasers to vaporize such objects before they hit our world."

In his comlink holo he saw Jane look briefly irritated before adopting a patient expression. "Thank you, Engines Chief. As you know from your service during prior system entries, I prefer to rely on the ship's computer for this data. It is often more exact in its information."

"Of course I am," the ship mind interrupted. "You are bioforms. I am an electronic mind of great antiquity. No bioform can equal my knowledge base."

"No doubt you are very smart," Jane said patiently, her expression bemused.

Bill noticed how his other crewmates up front reacted to the AI's well-known propensity to loudly declare its mental superiority. Bright Sparkle's goddess-perfect face was still as she pretended to watch the holo that reported on the condition of the ship's three fusion power reactors. Beyond her, Time Marker blinked hurriedly, then fixed his attention on his own set up Engine status holos. But his yellow electrical nimbus grew outward to a radius of four feet. Sitting atop his own bench and well beyond their walking snake's electrical glow was the eight-legged form of Long Walker. Who resembled a giant worm. But no worm ever possessed a circular mouth filled with dagger-like teeth. The member of the Zipziptoe species fixed his two black eyes on his own group of holos, no doubt inspecting closely the holo that advised on the status of the 24 collector pods that filled the ship's Collector Pods Chamber. The low-slung critter had played a vital role in helping his saloon buddies infiltrate enemy Collector ships by occupying pods which pretended to be pods launched by the six Collector ships that had come to Earth. While the ships zapped Earth's rocket launching sites with pinpoint laser fire, each Collector ship had sent down collector pods to capture humans in isolated locales. Long Walker had also joined Bill and his spec ops buddies in the attack on the Buyer compound, putting his own life at risk. He respected that. Beyond the walking worm stood the silver scaled form of Wind Swift. The kangaroo-like reptile was smart, sneaky and deadly dangerous, whether using her forearm claws, her thick whiptail or a laser tube. For the moment she pretended to focus on her Life Support holos. Beyond her stood Lofty Flyer the flying squirrel lady. Like his other crewmates she too pretended to be focused on her Navigation holos. Behind her sat her life partner, Builder of Joy, a fellow flying squirrel whose piloting abilities had aided in the destruction of the Buyer compound. He owed that squirrel a bottle of Johnny Walker Red scotch for the speed with which the critter had piloted the transport ship that had taken his dead body up to rendezvous with the *Blue Sky*.

"To continue," Star Traveler hummed. "The bioform-occupied planet of Notter is the second world out from the star. Its population is four billion Slinkeroo. They occupy the world's four continents. Other lifeforms occupy Notter's oceans, forests and two large deserts. Three local spaceships are in transit to the planet's nearby moon. An orbital station lies just below the orbit of the enemy ship. Which is now sending down collector pods."

"Thank you." Jane looked forward and down. "Time Marker, does your world have a planetary authority we can contact by ship radio? If so, what frequency would be best for our warning transmission."

The yellow nimbus englobing the walking snake shrank slightly. "Our world has been unified for seventy years," hissed the black-skinned snake. "The frequency is being sent to you. A leadership group of seven occupies our Hall of Silver Scales, on the northernmost continent. Call to the Prime Elder. Whomever serves that role today will receive your message. Though it will take eight Earth hours to arrive!"

Bill winced. He wished there was a faster way to warn the Slinkeroo people of the danger from white-glowing collector pods. At least the message would arrive well before their five ships arrived. Radio traveled at lightspeed. Their ship's top speed was one-tenth lightspeed. Which came to 67.1 million miles an hour. Fast by any measure. Or so he thought. Jane leaned forward.

"Star Traveler, set up a radio broadcast at the frequency now being entered by Time Marker at his work station," she said calmly.

"Frequency established. Ready to transmit."

Jane nodded. "Transmit my translated voice over radio. Do you detect audiovisual signals from the planet?"

"I do. Eighty-three of them," the AI hummed.

"Good. Also select the strongest AV frequency and transmit my image and voice to the world of Notter."

"Ready. You may speak," the AI hummed low, its tone distracted, as if it were wondering why Jane had been so agreeable about its intellectual superiority.

Jane looked forward. "Prime Elder, my name is Jane Yamaguchi. I am a human from the planet Earth, which orbits a yellow star lying not far from your home star. Aboard my spaceship is one Time Marker, a member of your Slinkeroo family. He was captured months ago by nearly invisible starships we call Collector ships," she said, her tone calm and measured. "A Collector ship now orbits above your space station. It is invisible to detection by radar, infrared, ultraviolet, optical and other sensors. It is sending down small pods to collect isolated Slinkeroo. Your people will be electrically knocked unconscious, then picked up by the manipulator arms of a pod. Each Slinkeroo captive will be taken back to the starship and put into a containment cell. Your people will be sold to Buyers on distant Market worlds, never to return home. My ship *Blue Sky*, and four other ship allies, now fight this Buyer society! You can fight too. Aim your comet lasers at any white-glowing orb that you see in your day or night sky. Kill it! Perhaps if you destroy enough pods, the Collector ship will leave your star system." Jane paused, then gestured with her hand. "On my Command Bridge are bioforms from many other stars, including your Time Marker. These people, together with our ship's artificial mind, have fought battles against Collector ships. We destroyed 37 Buyer compounds on a nearby Market world. We released more than a hundred Captives held in other compounds. We will arrive above your world in 30 hours. One of my fellow humans is our Negotiator. He seeks to gain you Slinkeroo as allies in our fight against these Collector ships. He and I will come down to your Hall of Silver Scales to discuss this interstellar alliance. And our crewmate Time Marker will come with us so you can see he is healthy, and learn why he has volunteered to be crew on my starship." She paused, then snapped her fingers as if remembering something. "You may reply to us by radio or by audiovisual signal. Or you can await our arrival. I wish we could instantly arrive above your world to stop these collector pods. We cannot. But our ship is powerful. We will hunt this ship that is taking captive your people!"

Jane gestured for the broadcast to end.

"Transmission ended," Star Traveler hummed.

To Bill's left Chester turned in his seat and looked back to her. "Captain, when we finish our talks with these Slinkeroo people, do we travel to this Enveloping Cloud system and attack the ships there? Or do we return to Earth and warn the Joint Chiefs of this new threat?"

Jane looked their way, her expression intense. So intense Bill almost recoiled. His wife looked ready to eat someone for lunch.

"Admiral, that is a question I will discuss with the captains of our four other ships. They have a right to share their views with me. I need to hear all perspectives. Including yours." She glanced aside, her gaze fixing on Bill. "And also the views of my Executive Officer. Whichever choice I make, the future is going to be dangerous."

CHAPTER TWO

Thirty hours later our five ships orbited above Notter, not far from the ball and ring shape of its orbital station. Lacking gravity plates like those in all Collector ships, the station spun so its inhabitants could enjoy centrifugal gravity in the outer ring. The central globe had openings at the north and south poles for entry by local spaceships. The *Blue Sky*, at a thousand feet long, was far too big to enter the station's docking tunnel. Anyway, Jane wished to go directly to the Hall of Silver Scales. Which was why the two of us, with Chester and Time Marker, were seated in a transport being piloted by Builder of Joy. It was nice to once more fly through the white clouds of a world, a place where people lived. Walking snakes people, that is. Bill looked at the man-size holo that filled the aisle between the rows of bench-seats that filled the cargohold of the transport. In the holo was a beautiful world of blue oceans, green forests and purple mountains. Actually, the northernmost continent now filled the holo as they descended quickly on the ship's Magfield drive. Using a spacedrive that interacted directly with the world's magnetic field made for well-controlled landings. And this time they didn't have to worry about someone down below shooting an anti-comet laser at them. An hour of talking with the Prime Elder as we passed the world's large moon had gone a long way toward ensuring a positive reception by their crewmate's kin.

Seated opposite, Time Marker swung his snake-like head toward me and Jane. The yellow electrical nimbus that always enveloped his body had shrunk greatly. Clearly he was pleased to be home. He fixed blue eyes on Jane. "Ship captain, my parents and clan leader will be in the hall. I wish to see them after our talk with the Prime Elder and our council. Will you and your mate come with me? I wish them to know the . . . people who saved me from forced labor," he hissed.

Jane squeezed his left hand. Which he felt even through the memory fabric of the tube suits they each wore. Wearing a suit whenever we left the ship was a habit we'd all grown used too. Even

Time Marker, whose low-slung body had stretched the flexible fabric in ways that amazed Bill.

"Sure, Time Marker," Jane said over the suit comlink that connected all of us with each other. Including Builder, whose suited form was visible in the forward piloting bubble of the transport. "Bill and I, we would love to meet your relatives."

Their crewmate looked aside at the holo. A long curving peninsula now filled it, a landform that reminded Bill of the southern tip of South America. But this landscape pointed north. The silver sheen of a large city filled the tip of the peninsula. It was the site of this world's planetary government. While cold due to its far northern location, the peninsula tip nearly touched the adjacent continent. Kind of the way Alaska nearly linked with Siberia. It had been the site of the first trade empire built by the walking snake people, millennia ago, long before they'd invented aircraft.

"It has been nearly a year since I was captured by that terrible insect," hissed our friend. "Seeing my world, seeing the Eastern Ocean that I once sailed in a small craft, it enlivens my spirit."

Jane's helmeted head was also focused on the holo. "Time Marker, where is the cave that you were exploring when you were captured by a pod? Is it on this continent, or another one?"

"This one," their friend hissed low. Two of his neck fringe tentacles, which had protruded through the suit fabric along with his short legs, now gestured at the lower end of the holo. "In the center of the continent is a range of mountains similar to the Rocky Mountains and Andes of your Earth. I was exploring a cave reputed to contain the remains of our earliest ancestors. Like you Humans, we Slinkeroo evolved from primitive reptilian forms to people with awareness. This cave held fossil remains from two million years ago, according to those Slinkeroo who study such things. I was curious and wished to explore a cave that had been the earliest home of our people."

Their friend's words were soft-toned. Or so Bill heard them that way, thanks to the ear buds he wore. They too were a standard part of the tube suits. He and Jane had worn such suits after their escape from their cells. Wearing suits had activated Star Traveler's emergency programming. Now, it was second nature for them, for nearby Chester, for everyone on their five ships to wear them whenever they moved outside a ship. He leaned forward. "Time

Marker, were there dangerous animals in these high mountains? Did you have a weapon with you?"

The walking snake shook his head from side to side, imitating the human behavior pattern he'd learned from close watching of Bill and Jane. "No, there were no large predators near the cave I explored. Just flying avians, small insects and squishy things that emerged from the soil. It was quite different from the jungles in which our ancestors lived, hunted, died and grew plentiful." Their crewmate gestured at the revolvers on his and Jane's waists. "We have not needed pellet-shooting devices like those you wear. Electricity serves as a fine defense, when needed."

Across from them Chester lifted sandy brown eyebrows. "Were you Slinkeroo always able to project electrical charges?"

Time Marker looked away from the holo, which now showed tall steel towers, domes and elevated walkways connecting all parts of the capital city. While ground level roads curved and twisted between the high buildings, there were few transports on the roads. But thousands and thousands of black-skinned Slinkeroo moved about on the walkways and ground routes. It was midday, so perhaps these different people were going to lunch. Or heading home. Or doing whatever walking snakes liked to do in the middle of the day.

"We were," Time Marker hissed. "It has been our nature since before we made images on cave walls, long before we produced written records. Projecting charges was how we shocked small animals into senselessness. So we could eat them." Their friend blinked slowly. "Now, in our modern society, everyone uses their charges to control electrical devices. Including the cesium-based atomic clocks that I used to make. My devices helped regulate our world's broadcast power grid and the time signal sent out from our central Marker Hall. Your U.S. Naval Observatory does the same."

Chester looked intensely curious. His gray eyes glanced at Bill and Jane, then looked to Time Marker. "That's amazing. You have enough fine control to turn stuff off and on? To interact directly with this transport's control panel?"

"We do. I do," their friend hissed. "All Slinkeroo do. Look! We are arriving at the hall!"

The holo was now filled by a silvery steel spire as tall as the Empire State building. Projecting from the upper portion of the skyscraper was an oblong sheet of metal. Two small helicopter-like craft sat at the end that attached to the spire's vertical walls. Which left plenty of room for their hundred foot long transport to set down.

"Landing," chittered Builder of Joy over the suit comlink. "Traffic control for the hall has indicated this location for our landing."

"Perfect," Jane said, standing as the movement of the transport ended and the holo showed them stationary on the landing pad. "Builder, stay here. While I do not expect any danger from these people, I do wish to ensure access to our way off this planet."

"Understood," the flying squirrel said, his tone elevated. "Flying through this world's atmosphere was most enjoyable! I am eager to do more!"

Jane chuckled, her serious expression becoming relaxed. A half smile filled her face as she stood in front of Time Marker. It was good to see her being relaxed after the deadly fight on the Market world. Bill moved quickly to be the first at the transport's inner airlock hatch. He was security for them all. And no SEAL ever let any teammate enter a danger zone without first checking it out. Behind them came a loud sound.

"Ahhh!" hissed Time Marker.

Bill glanced over his shoulder, looking past Chester and Jane to where their crewmate stood in the aisle. Their buddy had shed the tube suit he'd been wearing. The yellow nimbus that always glowed about him was no longer contained. It had grown outward to a foot deep. He'd always been fascinated by the miniature lightning display that the nimbus created. It was as much a part of the walking snake as breathing was to him and Jane. Clearly their friend had felt constrained by the tube suit, which now lay on the bench he'd been seated on.

Chester grinned. "Captain, do we keep on our suits?"

The blue eyes of Time Marker looked up. "Captain, my world has the same air as does Earth. It is safe to breath it. As I breathed the air on the ship."

"I'm sure it is safe air," Jane murmured over the comlink they all shared. "Perhaps we should leave our suits here. Our hosts might think we do not trust them if we wore them inside. And our earbuds can pick up the automatic translation of Slinkeroo speech that Star Traveler is doing for us. The *Blue Sky* is close enough so we should not hear much delay in speech and the translation we hear. The throat

comlink disks we each wear will keep us in link with everyone else."
She touched the front seam of her tube suit, causing it to open.

Standing beside the inner airlock hatch, Bill did the same. He
rebelted his Federal Ordnance .45 to his waist, checked to be sure his
woodland camo NWU Type III outfit was clean, then checked out
Chester and Jane. Like him they each wore green and brown NWUs
in the MARPAT pattern. The outfits had been picked up on their
return to Earth. Unlike earlier BDUs, these outfits were NIR-
compliant fabric. As a result, his and Jane and Chester's infrared
signatures would be the same as any surrounding landscape. While he
did not expect any threat from the Slinkeroo people, still, he always
prepared for the worst possible outcome. Which was why he carried a
red tube laser inside his shirt and against his spine. Just in case. And
each of them carried semi-autos on their waist. On a world where
people could project disabling electrical charges, he felt they were
entitled to carry personal weapons. A fact that had been conveyed
during Jane's talks with the Prime Elder. As the three of them began
moving toward him, he turned, touched the Open patch on the side of
the hatch, and stepped into the bedroom-size airlock. His companions
joined him. He reached out and touched the Operate patch beside the
outer hatch. Behind them the inner hatch closed. Upon its hiss-thump,
the outer hatch slid to one side. Bright yellow-white sunlight blazed
in.

He blinked and wished he had sunglasses. The discomfort was
slight. Glancing out he saw the loading ramp had lowered to contact
with the landing pad. Near its end stood a four-legged Slinkeroo, its
black skin hide showing a line of red tattoos. It looked up.

"Welcome to the Hall of Silver Scales," hissed the greeter. "I
am known as Swift Lightning. The Prime Elder sent me to guide you
to the chamber where the Council of Seven awaits you."

Bill walked slowly down the gray metal ramp, his peripheral
vision registering nine flying craft flitting among the tops of the
skyscrapers. This place was as big and congested as New York City.
Or Hong Kong. A light wind ruffled his short hair. His four day old
beard did not insulate his chin from the chilly coldness of the place.
Sunny it might be, but it felt like Oslo in the summer, recalling a brief
visit there by a few of his Team Seven members. Keeping his hands
free, he waved.

"Thank you for your help," he spoke, then heard his words translated by a shoulder tab into the hissing speech of the Slinkeroo. He reached the end of the rampway. He moved to the left, not wishing to be too close to the greeter, whose own yellow nimbus reached out two feet from its skin.

The critter's neck fringe of six tentacles stretched out, then curled at their tips. Blue eyes scanned him, then looked beyond to where Jane, Chester and Time Marker were descending the ramp. "So high above the ground are you Humans," hissed Swift Lightning. "Yes! Our wandering clansman returns home!"

Bill watched as his crewmate rushed up to the greeter and laid his triangular head alongside the greeter's head. Their electrical nimbuses briefly became one at that point. His crewmate sighed, then stepped away, breaking nimbus contact.

"So good to feel the charge of another Slinkeroo!" Time Marker hissed.

Jane stepped forward. "I am Captain Jane Yamaguchi, leader of our group. I admire the red marks on your skin, Swift Lightning. Do they have a special meaning?"

Their greeter blinked blue eyes, then turned and headed for a triangular door that lay ahead of them, where the landing pad met the spire's wall. "They do. They indicate my clan, my education level and my work assignment."

He followed after their crewmate, who had scampered ahead to lead the way, his four-legged gait causing a sideways swaying of his sinuous body. Behind him Jane and Chester followed. Bill looked up at the hundred feet of silvery steel wall that stretched above the pad, noticing the round windows that dotted the wall. Clusters of windows indicated there were at least ten more floors above them. As their greeter neared the closed entry door, a yellow streak of lightning speared out and touched the right side of the entry door. It landed at a spot colored pale red. Clearly the opening control. The metal door hissed to one side. A well-lighted hallway stretched before them. In the distance other Slinkeroo moved along the wide hallway, some of them turning into side hallways. A few stopped before triangular doors, spat out a thin lightning bolt, then entered the room beyond. The air smelled of electricity. Enough to make the hair on the back of his neck rise up.

"Thank you," Jane said as she moved ahead of Bill to walk along the left side of their greeter. "I look forward to meeting your Council of Seven and its Prime Elder. Uh, did you lose many people to the collector pods sent down by the Collector ship?"

The nimbus about the greeter grew slightly larger. "Eleven people were lost before we received your message. After that, our ground lasers killed every pod that descended. Perhaps that is why the Collector craft departed six hours ago. As reported by the neutrino sensors on our orbital station."

"I'm sorry to hear that," Jane said softly. "Be assured, we will search for them as we travel the stars."

The yellow glow about their greeter grew smaller. "As we know from your contact with us, it is a spacious universe. But you have brought home one of us. Perhaps more will return."

Bill walked alongside Chester as the two of them followed behind Jane, Swift Lightning and Time Marker. Earlier, on their way in, he'd seen the purple dot of the enemy ship leave orbit well before the *Blue Sky* arrived. That had been six hours ago. The mention of the neutrino detection of the enemy ship's fusion reactors was a tribute to the swift engineering done by the Slinkeroo scientists on the station. Once they heard from Time Marker how a Collector ship could be detected, the snake people had built neutrino detectors. They had fired several laser strikes at the orbital track of the enemy ship, causing it to move out toward the world's moon. The ground-based lasers were carbon dioxide gas lasers like those on his ship and the four other ships in their fleet. Their range was close to 10,000 miles, the same as his ship lasers. While one of their moon-bound ships had turned back and tried to find the EMF-invisible Collector ship, it had lacked detectors. Even if the Slinkeroo ship had possessed a neutrino detector, the three ships recently launched by the walking snake people lacked any laser weapons. No doubt that would change in view of the arrival of a Collector ship. These people were no tech laggards. While they had not visited the other worlds of their system, Bill's ship sensors had documented a world with moderate tech and a high level of communications and broadcast energy integration. He felt they would be a fine addition to the NATO of the Stars that was Chester's presidential assignment.

Their greeter turned right down a wide hallway, then stopped before a tall triangular door that filled the end of the hallway. A narrow lightning bolt shot out and hit a red dot. With barely a whisper the metal entry door slid to one side. Before them stretched a giant room. It looked as large as the UN General Assembly chamber in New York. Like that place, this one held several hundred bench seats, all of them empty. To one side lay a half circle of bench seats. Seven Slinkeroo occupied seven seats. Intense yellow-white light shone down on them, causing the rest of the chamber to look dim. A Slinkeroo at one end of the arc left his bench and moved towards them.

Jane stepped forward, her pace quickening as the two Slinkeroo beside her moved faster. "Hello. I am Jane Yamaguchi, of the human people, from planet Earth. It is an honor to meet this world's leaders."

As the hissing of his wife's translated words ended, he and the others stopped. Before them stood a Slinkeroo whose black skin showed streaks of gray. Some of the other walking snakes who rested atop bench seats also showed gray, though two of them looked nearly as black as Time Marker. The one standing before them spoke.

"My clan knows me as Hungry Learner," hissed low the standing Slinkeroo. "This council elected me to serve as Prime Elder. Elder Jane Yamaguchi, we thank you for your warning about the captive-taking starship that hovered above our world." Deep blue eyes blinked slowly. "We tried to destroy the craft but it moved beyond the range of our anti-comet lasers. Perhaps you can share with us information on how to build spacecraft that will protect our world in the future?"

"We will do just that," Jane said. She gestured to the side, to where Chester had joined her. "This is Chester Richardson, a combat leader on our world and the person appointed by my nation's leader to negotiate agreements with you and with other star people. We are ready to discuss your needs and share our information on the slave-taking behavior of the Buyer society." She paused, then gestured behind her to where Bill stood, his nerves tense as he tried to see in every direction. "Behind me stands my husband, my life partner. Bill MacCarthy is also well trained in combat. He has used the weapons of my ship to fight other Collector ships. And he has helped free Captives held on a nearby Market world."

The yellow glow that framed the Prime Elder grew larger. "We welcome you, your negotiator and your life partner. But especially we welcome the return of Time Marker! Come close to me, young one."

With a scurrying of his clawed feet, their Engines Chief hurried forward to lay his head alongside the head of the Prime Elder. The yellow electrical glow of each joined together, just as had happened earlier with their greeter. They shared a common glow for long moments. Then the older Slinkeroo stepped to one side with a low sigh.

"Young one, your glow carries the sign you recently made a Death Strike," he hissed. "How did it happen?"

Time Marker, whose long back was perhaps two feet above the metal floor, hunched down a bit, then straightened his stubby legs. "Yes, I killed recently. It happened when I joined other Humans and a Zipziptoe friend in our effort to enter a compound where these Buyers of thinking people resided. As I preceded my Human friend Bill along an entry hole cut into the building by our transport's laser, I entered a room the beam had cut into. I saw a single lifeform hanging from the room's ceiling. It was small and enclosed in a web." The yellow glow about Time Marker expanded outward to three feet. "I carried a laser weapon, but I called to Bill, thinking the lifeform might be a child. He entered the room. The lifeform shot him with a laser, killing Bill. I instantly sent my Death Strike against the enemy lifeform. It . . . it was necessary."

Hungry Learner blinked slowly, then looked up at the three of them. Deep blue eyes shone bright with extra moisture. "It seems we Slinkeroo must relearn the deadly violence we once used when clan fought clan, continent struck at another continent, and many died over minor arguments." The Prime Elder stretched out a neck tentacle to entwine with a tentacle from Time Marker. "We rejoice at the return of one of our own. What must we do to defeat future visits by these terrible Collector ships? And how is it that your Bill is alive before us?"

◆ ◆ ◆

Jane blinked at the last part of the Slinkeroo's question. It filled her mind with the image of the red laser wounds on Bill as he had been carried to the Med Hall of the *Blue Sky* and put into a clamshell healer unit. She had sent his combat mates away and taken a seat beside the unit, determined to be there when the healer finished its job. And the lid lifted up. She had prayed to the Goddess that his mind would not be damaged. The healer unit could repair and rebuild most any body part. But it could not replace memories. Or awareness. The hours she had waited, with only the humming voice of Star Traveler as company, had been the worst time of her life. Worse than the divorce from her ex. Worse than the loss of her parents, even. She had enjoyed making love with Bill after their takeover of the *Blue Sky* from that blasted giant cockroach. She had grown to love him deeply as they returned Captives to their home worlds. Later, after the arrival above Earth, she had joyed at the deep loyalty he'd shown her as she argued with the Joint Chiefs of Staff over her decision to remain in command of Earth's only starship. Later, when he'd gone down to the enemy ship where Stefano's team was being attacked, she'd worried his daring nature would bring him a final death. That had not happened. She and he had celebrated their success in capturing the six enemy ships that had attacked Earth. Now, they faced a new attack on Sol. Now, they badly needed allies. Like these walking snakes with their yellow electrical glows. She met the gaze of their leader.

"Hungry Learner, my lifemate Bill was repaired by a clamshell healer unit on my starship *Blue Sky*. He lives now. For which I am most grateful," she said, hearing her shoulder tab as it translated her words into the hiss-speech of the Slinkeroo. "As for what your people must do to defeat future visits by these terrible Collector ships, that is the reason we came down here, to meet with you. My friend Chester has been appointed to negotiate with you and other star peoples. Our leader on Earth hopes to create an alliance of star peoples who oppose this slave-taking of thinking people. May I leave him here to discuss these matters while I and Bill join Time Marker in meeting with his clan leader and his parents?"

The Prime Elder let go his tentacle grasp with her Engines Chief. He looked up at her. "Yes, the young one must greatly miss the glow of his clan members. And his progenitors. But before you leave, tell me, how can we fight these creatures who buy living beings for forced labor? And for medical experiments, I recall you saying. What hope is there when their ships are invisible to our sensors?"

She realized this was an issue she must address, rather than leaving it to Chester. "Star Traveler," she called over her throat disk. "Do you hear me?"

"I hear you," came his humming speech over her ear buds even as her shoulder tab hissed the words in Slinkeroo speech. "All that you have spoken, and all you have seen, has been relayed to me by your transport and by the items you wear. What is your wish?"

Jane noticed how the yellow glow about the Prime Elder had grown. As had the glows about the six other members of the Council of Seven. Clearly a sign of concern. Or worry. Or something. "Hungry Learner, you hear the words of the artificial mind who lives aboard our starship. His name is Star Traveler. He is an ancient mind. He helped me and Bill during our takeover of the *Blue Sky*. And he has convinced many other ship minds on Collector ships to stop cooperating in the capture of intelligent beings."

"Ahhh," hissed low the elderly Slinkeroo. "We do not have self-aware devices such as this Star Traveler. Our researchers have long discussed the creation of such entities, but we lack the knowledge to do so. Your . . . artificial friend is welcome here."

Relief flooded through her body, leaving her heart beating faster. She had not realized how tense she'd become upon their entry into the Hall of Silver Scales. Being on stage like this was something she did not enjoy. Even when she and Bill were being given Navy Crosses by the president, she had hated being in the public eye. This time was similar, but different. These walking snakes seemed like good people. Time to make a command decision.

"Star Traveler, transmit down to this hall all the technical specifications for our ship technology. Send them the specs for our Magfield engine, our Alcubierre stardrive, our gravity plates, our antimatter projector, our plasma batteries, the composition of your hull, send it all down."

Humming came over her ear buds and from her shoulder tab. "Shall I transmit on the frequency used by the Prime Elder when he spoke with you during our final approach?"

Chester shifted his position, moving forward to stand at her left side. "Yes, use that frequency." She reached out and grasped Chester's right shoulder. "Hungry Learner, your first steps in defeating future Collector ship visits are now taken. I have shared our technology with you. I hope you will join our star alliance. Whether you join, or not, you will now be able to build ships like our ships, weapons as deadly as our weapons, and be able to stop any future Collector ship from capturing your people."

The yellow glows about Prime Elder and the other six senior Slinkeroo shrank to barely a foot out from their black skins. Their leader nodded his head up and down, clearly having learned the body gesture from their holo chats on the way into the system. "Much you share," he hissed loudly. "We thank you. We will learn from you and create devices to protect our world and our people. Now, let our council discuss with your Chester the meaning and requirements of this star alliance you propose. Already I feel eager to join it."

She smiled, then stopped, realizing snake-like people did not smile the human way. Well, perhaps Chester would learn how a Slinkeroo smiles. Or shows happiness. She pressed him forward. "Chester, take over. Time for me and Bill to join Time Marker in meeting his parents."

The stocky man looked her way, gave a nod and a wink, then stepped toward the elderly walking snake. "Prime Elder, let me tell you about the NATO of the Stars!"

CHAPTER THREE

Bill pushed away the plate of spaghetti and meatballs he was eating. Jane had just entered their ship's Food Chamber, followed by four of his saloon buddies and Chester. Behind them came Time Marker. The walking snake had introduced them to his parents down on Notter, then brought their clan leader into the happy return chatter. The chamber in the spire where they met was much like a college food hall, filled with hundreds of other Slinkeroo. He and Jane had tasted the booze the snakes liked. To him it resembled Japanese rice wine, or *sake*, that he had tasted while training at Coronado. Two of his fellow trainees were Japanese-Americans like Jane and they had convinced him to try the stuff. The *sake* gave a good buzz. As did the Slinkeroo booze, which they called *mejian*. Their Engines Chief was joining them for the critical meeting on where to go next, now that Chester had gotten the Council of Seven and its Prime Elder to join the NATO of the Stars. Plus, they'd gained six Slinkeroo volunteers as a result of the meeting with his family and clan leader. Jane gave him a nod, her expression command serious.

"Executive Officer, good to see you ate after that booze we had downplanet." She looked up at the ceiling. "Star Traveler, send a hover bot over with a pitcher of Heineken beer and cold mugs. For everyone including Time Marker."

"As you order," hummed the AI. Who was part of the gathering due to its electronic eyes and ears being everywhere on the *Blue Sky*.

Bill gave thanks the table where he sat was big enough to seat seven humans and a walking snake. He gestured at the round table. "Have a seat everyone. The alliance is started. Let's celebrate!"

Jane lifted an eyebrow at his perkiness, then sat opposite him on a round pedestal extruded by the floor's flexmetal. To his right sat his buddies who were ship captains. Next to him was Alicia Hoffman of the brown ponytail and Ranger daring. Beyond her were Coast Guardsman Joe Batigula of the big belly, barrel-chested Frank Wurtzman of the Marines and finally, his fellow SEAL Stefano Cordova, who sat at Jane's left. To his captain's right was Chester of the broad shoulders, followed by Time Marker's six foot long slithery shape. The Slinkeroo stretched out over a long bench that lay between Bill and Chester, his black-skinned head twisted to face them all. Jane grabbed the beer pitcher from a plate carried by a hover bot as it floated beside her. Stefano grabbed mugs off the plate and handed them around. His wife's dark brown eyes scanned them all, including him. There was no sign of her passionate love nature in them. Today she was all business. As befit a meeting of the fleet commander and her fellow ship captains.

Alicia lifted her foaming mug. "All hail to the captain in charge!" she yelled, her soprano voice filling the large room where everyone on the ship ate meals, played video games, watched movies, read something from the ship's incredible Library, or tried their hand at cooking in the Food Alcove that ran along one side wall.

Jane looked surprised by their tough lesbian's mood change to cheeriness. "This isn't a party. Though I am pleased at the six Slinkeroo volunteers we gained, thanks to the influence and support of Time Marker," she said, nodding to their Engines Chief.

The yellow glow around their crewmate was low, just a foot thick. Which told Bill the critter had to be feeling happy, or relaxed or anything other than tense and anxious. It was hard to tell about the body language of Aliens. While he'd spent ten months in the company of Time Marker and the other Alien volunteers on the Command Bridge, he was still learning what certain behaviors meant for each of the species now aboard the *Blue Sky*. The walking snake, while a reptile by biological heritage, loved to play chess, enjoyed swimming in the ship's Water Pool Chamber, liked sunning himself in the Greenery Chamber, and often spent long hours in the bowels of the Engine Chamber studying the operations of their Magfield engines. Its behavior was a close analogue to a dedicated geek, leastwise so far as he had ever known any. And the snake was far more sociable than some of the computer programmers he'd met at Coronado and elsewhere. In that sense, Bill liked him. He also liked how the critter had not hesitated to kill the spider Alien who'd lasered him. Their crewmate turned his triangular head, looking at Jane.

"Captain of the ship, my clan volunteers look forward to learning crew functions on the ship run by . . . by Captain Joe," hissed Time Marker.

That was a development Bill liked. The ship *Manila Bay* had been captured during the assault on the Market world at HD 128311. Up to now, the only live crew on it had been Joe. The ship's AI had managed to run the functions usually handled by a five man crew. Now, with six Slinkeroo on board, Joe was likely feeling some relief. And perhaps a few electrical shocks whenever he stepped into the nimbus glow of any of his new crew.

Jane took a sip from her mug, wiped the foam off her lips, then set it down with a thud. "Good to hear that. Maybe we can spread some of them out to our other ships. Once they get some training." She folded her hands in front of her, leaned forward and looked command intense. Bill licked his lips. Clearly this was going to be a major meeting. Maybe the most important meeting since they'd left Earth on their way to zap the Market world closest to Sol. That had been their first assignment from the president. The second had been to visit the five star systems of the Alien crew aboard *Blue Sky* and get their people to join this NATO of the Stars. They'd begun that task by arriving here at the Slinkeroo system. Now, after hearing the boasting of the praying mantis captain of the enemy ship, and the deadly news from its AI, it was clear they faced a decision point.

"So who do we kill next?" rumbled Frank, ever the Marine ready to storm something, somewhere. Bill had long respected the former veteran of the Marine Special Operations crew. The man had left the service as a Gunnery Sergeant. Now, with all of them reactivated and called back into their respective services, thanks to the order of General Harriet Poindexter of the JCS, Frank seemed ready to put his wide shoulders against any obstacle in their path.

His wife lifted a thin black eyebrow. "That is what this meeting is about. We have two options. Either return to Earth and alert the JCS to the report of this new fleet gathering at Kepler 62, or, head directly to Kepler 62 ourselves and see what damage five ships can do against this fleet. Before it attacks Earth. What say each of you?"

"Captain," interrupted Star Traveler with a hum. "There is additional new data I gained from the ship mind Diamond, when we shared minds earlier. I have updated information on the nature of the Buyer society. Do you wish to hear it?"

Jane grimaced. Bill could tell she felt bothered by the AI's smart-ass manner. Still, it had been their first ally after their capture.

Both of them had learned to respect it, even as its personality had become more arrogant and, at times, obscure. "Yes. Of course I wish to learn any data relevant to our mission of destroying the Buyer culture. Speak!"

"As you wish," hummed low the AI. "Within Orion Arm the number of space-going species has increased to 3,012. For the Buyer society, it now consists of 840,992 Buyers located on 413 worlds, of which 59 are Market worlds. Captives are being gathered by 85 Collector ships. Which is two more than the 83 your Weapons Chief created thanks to the destruction or capture of 12 ships," the ship mind hummed long and low. "Two new Collector ships have been built at a location other than the orbital factory that was destroyed during your battle at Kepler 443."

Jane looked thoughtful. "Any word on how large this fleet is that they are gathering at Kepler 62? Any news on where the new Collector factory is located?"

"No and yes," Star Traveler hummed. "The new Collector ship factory is reported to be operating at system Kepler 66, which lies 3,611 light years from Earth. The size of the fleet being collected at Kepler 62 was unknown to Diamond. However, it has only been a week since our attack on the Market world at system HD 128311. While the news of our attack has spread widely, by ship to ship relay, it is likely few ships have arrived at Kepler 62. Star to star travel still takes considerable time even when one uses the Alcubierre space-time modulus for such transit."

Bill winced. Now the ship mind was sounding like a tenured college professor with not a care for whether her students understood what she said. Jane shrugged, her Air Force blue jumpsuit loose on her.

"Well, the new Collector ship factory is far too distant for us to visit. We are back to our two options. What does—"

"Captain," Star Traveler hummed quickly. "There is a third option. This ship and allied ships could continue visiting the home star systems of the non-Human crew members of this ship."

"Piss off!" Jane yelled, clearly irritated. Then she sat back and assumed her ship commander posture. As if aware it was not good for the fleet leader to lose her temper. "There is no *third* option. Either we attack Kepler 62 or we return to Earth to alert the JCS and other nations to this impending attack. People, what are your views?"

Stefano let go his mug and raised his hand to draw attention. "Captain of the fleet, I suggest we send Joe's ship back to Earth and the rest of us go and attack Kepler 62 before the assembled ships get too many for us to defeat."

Alicia shook her head. "That is four ships against how many enemy ships? We now know something no one on Earth knows. A new attack is coming. Sometime in the future. Our duty is to return and warn Earth. Then maybe we attack Kepler 62."

Frank frowned. "Much as I want to kill all these slave-grabbing bastards, I agree with Alicia. We gotta warn Earth first before we attack anywhere. Our fleet is good. But this info could die with us if we get unlucky. Our battlemates have to know this."

Joe fixed blue eyes on Jane. "Captain, I'm willing to go with Stefano's plan. My ship is the least effective due to all the newbies in my crew. I'm glad to have them. But none of them know a thing about lasers, antimatter or star navigatin'."

His wife looked to her right. "Chester? What are your views?"

The man who had joined their crew to serve as liaison with two nuke subs that had helped in the fight against the invading six Collector ships sat back and crossed arms over his NWU battledress. "Much as I would like to gain more allies, Joe is right. And so is Frank. Earth has to be warned. But do all our ships return? Or just Joe's ship?"

Jane nodded, then looked straight at him. "Bill?"

He sat up straight, determined to look as milspec proper as he could, considering how he'd never liked dressing up. At least his NWUs were still fresh. No sauce on them. Jane raised an eyebrow. He felt a chill run down his back as he realized they now faced a new life or death decision point. "Captain, I like Stefano's idea. He and I are used to fighting long odds. Being outnumbered has never bothered us. Nor any of the other spec ops folks here." Stefano's brown eyes fixed on Bill, reading his body language the way he'd always been able to do. The man smiled. "But . . . the facts are the facts. Kepler 62 is 1,200 light years away. The trip there would take at least 48 days. Earth is 56 light years away. A little over two days to get home. So we should—"

"Correction," interrupted Star Traveler. "The distance to Kepler 62 from this star system is 1,238 point four five five light years. Travel time there would be 49 point five Earth days."

Bill bit his lip. Jane's expression became deadly blank. He had no doubt she would love to find the AI's pain center in its microelectronic innards. Time to wrap this up. "Whatever, we should head back to Earth. All of us. Right now there are only three Collector ships and one sub capable of flight outside of Earth's atmosphere. When we return, there will be *eight* Collector ships present in the system." His wife turned thoughtful. "Our first priority is to warn Earth about the impending new attack. Yes, it will likely not happen for a few months, based on how far some Collector ships will travel to get to Kepler 62. But going back shows we give first priority to our duty to defend the Constitution. And to our vows of Duty, Honor and Country. Whatever the JCS folks decide, well, we can argue there. In Sol system. Me, I favor sneaking into Kepler 62, pretending to be new troops and gaining intel Earth will need to decide what humanity should do. I love America. But we are the vanguard for seven billion humans. Let us do our duty first, then later fight these bastards!"

Jane nodded slowly, then looked at the last person at the table who had yet to speak. "Time Marker, what are your views on our two choices? Your people are now part of our alliance. You deserve a say on this issue."

Their snake crewmate gave a low hiss. "My people have no armed spaceships with which to help defend Earth. Our engineers are very accomplished, though it will take time to build a copy of this ship *Blue Sky*. But our volunteers will fight anywhere, fight to the death to defend our allies!" The walking snake's pink tongue flicked out a foot. It was not an odor-sensing instrument like the tongues of Earth snakes. But it was a sign of his willingness to fight. So Bill had learned over the last ten months.

The critter's yellow electrical nimbus now expanded out to two feet, nearly touching Chester's right arm. The former Chief of Naval Operations did not move. Nor did Bill, even though he felt the hairs on his left arm prickling from the static electricity that leaked out from their buddy's glow. Jane gave their ally a brief smile, then her expression went sober serious.

"As captain of this fleet, I decide that we return to Earth and warn the JCS of this pending attack. We will also offload the 93 Captives we rescued at the Market world. Then I will recommend that one or more of our ships leave for Kepler 62, there to gain vital intel on what humanity faces." She stood up. "Captains, return to your ships. Prepare to head out of this system within a half hour. Once we reach the edge of the magnetosphere of this system, we will set a vector for Sol and go FTL. Dismissed."

His saloon buddies left their empty mugs behind as the four of them stood, stepped away from the table and headed for the Food Hall's exit door. Chester looked quickly at the beer remaining in the pitcher, then stood and followed the other captains out. Time Marker, who had sipped the beer in his mug with his tongue, also slithered off the bench and hurried out, his four-footed gain moving him quickly. Jane looked down at him.

"Bill? You coming?"

He stood, walked around the table to where she stood and reached out to cup her narrow chin. "Always. Yes, I'm still a SEAL inside and I really want to head for Kepler 62 and kick the shit out of whomever is there!" She blinked, but did not move her chin away from his hand. "Babe, I will do everything I know to avoid you having to visit me, again, in a healer unit. Which means I will fight this ship like she was a wasp out of hell!"

Jane's eyes looked wet.

"Well, well," murmured a voice from the entry door. "Nice to see love afoot on this ship."

They both turned. Just coming into the Food Hall was Sharon Richardson, the wife of Chester. The fifty-something woman wore a green jumpsuit, sported pearl earrings and had found a way to coif her shoulder-length brown hair so it had plenty of curls. Clearly she had found a way to get her hair done with some unknown aid from Star Traveler.

Jane chuckled. "Don't tell anyone! He's my XO and I'm the boss of the universe!"

Sharon smiled easily, her lightly tanned face showing plenty of laugh lines. The woman who had raised hers and Chester's children to adulthood, then spoiled her grandkids, had adjusted to life aboard the *Blue Sky* as if it were the most normal thing to flyer among the stars at a speed of 25 light years per day. She had befriended Alicia's wife Lorilee, and the two of them had spent lots of time hanging with Bright Sparkle and her lifemate Learned Escape. The ship's two squirrel people, Lofty Flyer and Builder of Joy, had soon joined the four humans in playing late night games of bridge. And poker. They'd even welcomed in the solo crew on board, taking time to explain the card games to Wind Swift, Long Walker and Time Marker. Sharon had taken to being the social director of the *Blue Sky* as if it were the most natural thing to do. Bill liked that about the woman. He waved at her as they passed on their way out.

"My wife may rule the universe, but you are the boss of happiness on this ship!"

Sharon smiled, gave them a wink and headed for the Food Alcove. No doubt to start making one of her scrumptious Italian casseroles.

Bill felt his mouth start to water. He'd loved the spaghetti and meat balls as prepared by the ship's auto-chef. But nothing could match real home cooking!

◆ ◆ ◆

Later, after their 31 hour transit to the outer edge of the Slinkeroo system, they'd passed into Alcubierre space-time. He was off shift, walking down the right side main hallway when the entry door to the Weapons Chamber slid open. Out walked the color-banded shapes of Bright Sparkle and Learned Escape, followed by the gray worm shape of Long Walker. Each of them carried white tube tasers and red tube lasers. He stopped. They stopped. Bright Sparkle gave him a serious look.

"Weapons Chief! So good to see you," her left shoulder speaker/vidcam unit said as it translated the color-band speech of her Megun people. "We three thought we should practice our shooting skills. In case we board an enemy ship or must assist on a ground attack. We are on our way to shoot targets in the Collector Pods Chamber."

He felt surprise, then deep appreciation for their willingness to put their lives at risk. Especially Long Walker, whose culture had never been violent toward other Zipziptoes. "Thank you all! Learned Escape and Long Walker were both helpful and daring in our attack on the Buyer compound." He fixed on Bright's green eyes, the better to avoid the distraction of her bare breasts. "Extra eyes and extra weapons are always welcome!"

She grinned, a behavior common to both humans and Megun. "Daring I am, as you may recall," her speaker/vidcam said as it translated the chromatophoric speech of her color-banded skin.

He did recall just how daring in love-making she had been not long after her release from her cell. That had been before he and Jane had found each other. "I do recall. A happy memory." He looked over the three of them. "In the chamber, speak to Star Traveler. It will provide you with a hover bot or two for laser practice. But first, try shooting with your tasers. The hover bots can withstand the coherent electrical beam well enough to survive for several rounds of shooting."

"We will follow your guidance," moaned Long Walker, its two beady black eyes looking up at Bill and the others.

He respected the ten-foot long giant worm. Its dagger-filled circular mouth could munch through most anything that was organic, while the claws on its feet were tough enough to leave scars on the gray metal of the ship floors. The claws on its front pair of leg-hands were retractable, which allowed it fine control of its Collector Pods control pillar. During the Buyer compound raid, it had gripped its laser tube rifle with an easy assurance. And Learned Escape had shown himself to be a marksman nearly as talented at shooting as Stefano. He gave them a thumbs-up, one of the many human hand gestures all the ship's crew now understood.

"Good fortune with your shooting, then," he said, standing to one side of the hallway so the three could cross the hall to the Collector Pods Chamber.

Bright Sparkle and Long Walker passed by him. Learned Escape followed them, but stopped as he came up to Bill. The man fixed green eyes on him. "Weapons Chief, by now it is possible my people have constructed a duplicate of this ship. Possibly more. If after you warn Earth this ship can travel to our home system, Earth might gain additional combat ships for the defense of your Sol system."

Bill nodded to the black-haired man. While resembling an ancient Greek god in his muscular physique, Learned had shown himself to be an excellent scout with a nose for danger during the Buyer raid. He thought the man was middle-aged, though it was hard to tell with the Megun people. While they were near duplicates of humanity, their species did not show age, beyond a few streaks of gray in the hair of their elders. His honeymoon visit to their world of Harken had been a joy, and a sobering exploration of how people could survive the attacks of giant dino-like creatures who attacked any creature that made a noise. While those creatures were now restricted to wild reserves, they still played a role in the coming of age ceremonies of young Megun. Learned was a teacher of the skills needed to survive in its jungles. Bill suspected the man could be a fine special operations recruit, if given the chance.

"Thank you, Learned. I will pass your thoughts on to Captain Jane. Your home star is located in the same direction as the enemy fleet star, just a bit farther distant. And I will include you in any planning for special operations in the future."

"Thank you," the Megun said as he stored his red cube door opener in a pocket of his cargo pants. Rainbow bands of color flowed over his skin. "I enjoyed visiting your world of Earth. It is as special as our world of Harken. I will do all in my power to preserve your world and its people."

Bill's pulse sped up as the impact of the man's words hit him. Sharon's evening bridge games had brought out the amiable side of Bright Sparkle's life partner. Now, he was seeing again the dedicated and deadly side of a man who knew much about survival against long odds. "Thank you! I look forward to formally adding your people to our NATO of the Stars. And to visiting again your world of Harken. Jane and I enjoyed our honeymoon trip to your northern resort. And we loved the marriage ceremony Bright Sparkle arranged on your orbital station." Bill realized he was sounding officious in front of a man who'd long ago proved his loyalty to the ship. "Hey, come by our place tonight and maybe we four can enjoy some *cabernet sauvignon* red wine and a game of cribbage. You up for that?"

"I am most up for it," Learned said, his speaker/vidcam unit speaking in a low bass rumble that fit the man's stature and bearing. "Until tonight."

Bill watched as the man who was chief pilot for their transport *Talking Skin* walked over to the Collector Pods entry door, pointed his red cube at it and then entered when the oval door slid open. Once more he gave thanks for his and Jane's decision to allow every crew member access to all parts of the *Blue Sky*. Trust shown had resulted in loyalty enlarged. He resumed his walk toward the ship's Engine Chamber. Checking out the alternate Command Bridge controls in that room was one of his To Do chores that he had put off for too long. Time to do the routine. Soon enough they would all face danger and death-giving Aliens.

CHAPTER FOUR

They exited Alcubierre space-time not far from Pluto and its moons. Bill had always been fascinated by the reddish-brown planet and its cluster of five moons, which ran from tidally-locked Charon to outermost Hydra. The debate years ago about whether it was a dwarf planet or a 'real' planet had seemed unreal to him when he'd read about it on the internet, during his few free moments from team deployments. Now, the planet and its moons were centered in the true space holo to Bill's upper right of his Weapons station. To everyone's surprise, they were hailed by someone signaling from the small world's surface.

"Incoming neutrino signal from Pluto," announced Star Traveler to everyone on the Command Bridge.

Jane sat forward in her captain's seat atop the command pedestal that occupied the middle of their circular bridge. "Hold on accepting it. What neutrino emitting ships are now present in Sol system?"

Bill looked to his left at the system graphic holo that automatically updated to show any system's star, planets, asteroid belts, local spaceships and Collector starships. He spotted a purple dot next to Jupiter and two close to Earth. One red dot local ship was in transit to the Moon. Their five ships showed as green dots next to Pluto. He felt relief that no enemy Collector ships were present.

"Only the three Collector ships captured by you Humans are now present in your home system," the AI hummed. "As everyone can see on their system graphic, two ships are near Earth and one is next to your world of Jupiter. The local spaceship moving toward your Moon is the Magfield spacedrive-fitted submarine *USS Minnesota*. There are no other spacecraft active within Sol system."

"Thank you," Jane said hurriedly. "Accept the signal. Put it into the common comlink holo."

Jane's image disappeared from the comlink holo on Bill's right and was replaced by that of a man dressed in an Air Force blue jumpsuit. The man's shoulders carried the eagle pin of a colonel. His brown hair was crewcut with sidewalls. His eyes widened as he saw Jane in the return signal.

"Captain Yamaguchi! Glad to see you back in Sol system." The man frowned. "Last we heard you were expected to be gone for months, recruiting star peoples into this NATO of the Stars. Anything wrong? Uh, I'm James Minetowa. Colonel, that is."

Jane relaxed her tense posture. She smiled at the man's confused greeting. "Colonel Minetowa, nice to see you. Looks like DOD decided to set up a base on Pluto. Yes?"

The middle-aged man looked back as two Navy ensigns peered in through an open pressure hatch door. "Tell everyone it's the *Blue Sky*. She's back home." He turned and faced Jane. "Captain, yes, we just got here three days ago. The *Tangi Valley* brought us out here and set up a prefab dome like the one you folks put down on Mars. It's headed back home. It left us with this neutrino FTL comlink, in addition to the basic radio, radar, neutrino sensor, electro-optical scope and such stuff. Our brief here is to be the early lookout for the arrival of any enemy Collector ship, or ships."

Bill felt pleased that someone at DOD had shown enough initiative to set up the early warning station on Pluto. While the Space Command headquarters at Peterson Air Force Base had neutrino sensors able to detect the arrival of enemy ships, still, it made sense to have an early lookout posted on the edge of the Solar system. He hoped they had some kind of defense laser or anti-ship missile battery for protection. Though a single Collector ship's armament was enough to take out any normal human base. As they'd discovered during the enemy bombardment of Earth's space launch sites, before their spec ops boarding teams had taken over the six enemy ships.

Jane gave the man a wave. "Good to hear we have a lookout base this far out. Makes sense. And to answer your question, something *is* wrong. You'll hear the news when I tell it to General Poindexter. We'll keep you in our neutrino signal feed. Now, I've got to call our local Collector ships." She glanced up at the ceiling. "Star Traveler, send a neutrino signal to the ships *Tangi Valley*, *Rolling Thunder* and *Takur Ghar*. Add their images to the comlink holo."

"Complying," the ship mind hummed low. "Signals sent. Responses arriving. Images and voice transferred to comlink holo."

Bill watched as the images of fellow SEALs Jake Slowzenski, Mack Hodson and Janice Watanabe took form in the man-high holo that hovered to the right of his Ship Weapons work station. They each looked healthy. While no crew stations showed in the close-up holo image, he thought the three would like hearing about the six new Slinkeroo recruits. They could add a walking snake to their crew, in addition to any volunteers they'd gained from the 93 Captives they all had rescued in the Market world raid. He left behind memories as the images of the three captains took form in the comlink holo, joining the image of Colonel Minetowa.

"Captain!" called Jake from the *Tangi Valley*, looking briefly startled. "Glad to see you. Something happen out there?"

"Same here," muttered Mack from the *Rolling Thunder*. "Same question. Though it's great to see you. And everyone else, I assume."

Janice Watanabe of the *Takur Ghar* had always been good at reading people. Now, she saw Jane's face and winced. "Bad news it seems. Glad to see you, Captain Jane."

Bill looked back over his shoulder. His wife did indeed look both tense and worried. She gave a wave to the three folks who'd led ship boarding teams, then stayed behind to serve as a protection force for the Solar system. "All too right. Bad news it is. Stay in link while I contact General Poindexter. She and the JCS need to hear the news first. You three and Colonel Minetowa will hear what I've already shared with my fleet captains." She paused, licked her lips, then rested her slim arms on the armrests of her command seat, striving for the relaxed but attentive look of a commander in charge. She put on her serious face. "Star Traveler, signal General Poindexter at Building One at Peterson. Use the encrypted neutrino frequency. Mark the signal for her personal attention."

"Complying. Signal annotated." A brief delay happened even though every neutrino comlink signal traveled FTL thanks to passing through other dimensions. "Response incoming from Peterson."

The comlink holo filled with the image of the four star general who was the Air Force chief of staff. The woman's black face showed concern. "Captain Yamaguchi, you are back early. Something wrong?" The woman sat at the same video display table where previously she and the other chiefs had talked with Jane during the battle against the invading starships. Behind and to either side of her, Bill saw the moving forms of staff airmen. Four of the other JCS chiefs sat nearby at other display tables. Poindexter gestured aside.

"Chairman McAuley is in Geneva meeting with the military chiefs of China, Russia and NATO. What's happened?"

Jane gave the woman a quick salute. "General, this conversation is being shared with the captains of the three ships left behind here, so they can be alerted to what I will be sharing. Colonel Minetowa on Pluto is also listening in. Is that acceptable to you?"

"Acceptable," the black woman said quickly, her tone impatient. "To repeat, what's happened that brings you home early?"

"General, let me share the good news first. Okay?"

"Proceed," the middle-aged woman said calmly, ignoring the rise in chatter as people recognized Jane in the flat screen display that filled the top of the Air Force chief's tactical display table.

"We disabled the offensive weapons of the Traffic Control station in orbit above the Market world of HD 128311, destroyed one Collector ship, captured a second and then destroyed 97 Buyer compounds on the surface of that Market world. We also rescued nearly a hundred Captives from the Buyer compounds we raided," Jane said hurriedly. "Our fleet then traveled to HD 10647, the home system for the Slinkeroo snake folks. It lies just 56 light years from Earth. Their Council of Seven and their Prime Elder have agreed to join the president's NATO of the Stars. That's the good news," Jane said.

"Out with the rest of it," Poindexter said bluntly, her tone tough but courteous.

Jane gave a quick nod. "On our arrival near the outermost planet of the Slinkeroo system, we immediately detected the presence of an enemy Collector ship in orbit above the world of Notter," she said, her soprano voice sounding firm. "My attempt to impersonate the cockroach former commander of the *Blue Sky* failed. The enemy ship's AI, unlike most ship AIs, alerted the Alien ship captain to the reality of our arrival. In talking to the enemy captain we discovered the news of our raid on the Market world has spread across the stars of the Buyer society. Worse, the captain said a new attack fleet is being gathered at star Kepler 62. That star is 1,200 light years distant from Earth." Jane paused, bit her lower lip, then continued. "As your neutrino sensors may report, I came back here with our original four fleet ships plus one. The fifth ship is the one we captured during our battles at HD 128311. Its captain is Joe Batigula. He chose to name his ship *Manila Bay*. We had some casualties but no deaths. I concluded we should all return here to alert you and the JCS to the fact another attack on Earth is likely to happen, though it could take two or three months for the enemy to gather a fleet larger than the six ships led by Diligent Taskmaster." She looked up at the ceiling. "Star Traveler, neutrino transmit the AV record of my conversations with the enemy captain and yours with the enemy ship mind to Peterson. Also include the vidcam records of our Market world battle and our encounters with the Slinkeroo people. Do it now."

"Transmitting those vidcam datafiles," the AI hummed.

Nearest to Poindexter was the four star general who was chief of the Army. Like Jane he was of Japanese ethnic ancestry. The man grimaced. "Crap! We need to alert General McAuley to this. Maybe he can form a joint command with the folks he is meeting."

Poindexter looked to her right, gave the man a look that could freeze a snowball, then fixed back on Jane. "Captain of the fleet Yamaguchi, you did just right to return here. Thank you for sending your contact records. And congratulations on the capture of another Collector ship. It is good to hear you liberated many Captives from their cells." The woman paused, gave a nod to the other chiefs of the JCS as the four of them gathered at her table, then fixed back on his wife. "Captain Poindexter, I gather Earth has at least 48 days before any enemy fleet arrives here, since that is the FTL travel time to this enemy star base. Correct?"

"Correct," Jane said, her slim fingers gripping the armrests tightly even as her face stayed calm and collected. "However, based on our past encounters with the enemy and the distances we have traveled star to star, I estimate it will be at least two months or longer before a new enemy fleet leaves for Earth. That travel time will take another month and a half. We have some time to prepare."

Poindexter folded her hands on the display table and peered intently at Bill's captain. "Informal now. Jane, you would not have returned here without spending the last few days coming up with some kind of plan for dealing with this new threat. What *is* your plan? I need something to convey to General McAuley and to President Hartman. You know them. They always want solutions whenever anyone reports a problem to them."

"Harriet, I do have some thoughts," Jane said, leaning forward a bit.

Bill tensed. This was the crux point. His wife had shared with him last night the outlines of her plan to deal with the new attack threat, while they lay next to each other in the dark, holding each other close. Neither had felt like love making. Both had needed closeness.

Poindexter lifted an eyebrow. "Share with us."

"My plan has four stages," Jane said quickly. "First stage is to leave four of our Collector starships *here*, with you, to form a basic defense fleet. That gives humanity seven very deadly starships. Second stage is for me to take the *Blue Sky*, along with the nine reactivated vets who now crew those ships, to Kepler 62. On arrival there I will imitate a former captain of another Collector ship, a captain who lived far in the past. That fake holo image will be matched by a fake ship ID. My ship AI is very adept at pretending to be other than what we truly are. We will act as an intelligence asset, picking up data on the enemy fleet and its preparations." She licked her lips, likely feeling as dry as Bill's mouth now felt. "Third stage is for our nine vet boarding team to attempt a capture of three or four enemy ships by way of collector pods. Whatever happens during the capture attempt, we will continue to pretend to be a member of the enemy fleet. Hopefully that will allow us to accompany the enemy when it departs for Sol." She paused, shaking black bangs out of her eyes. "Fourth stage is after we arrive beyond Pluto. While the enemy fleet is reorganizing after the long transit to our Solar system, the *Blue Sky* and our captured ships will strike the rear flank of the enemy fleet with antimatter beams. Hopefully we can disable part of that fleet. We will then follow the enemy as it heads in-system, harrying it as possible. I suggest the seven ships left at home should rendezvous with us at Jupiter for an all-out battle. We cannot allow any enemy ship to get within nuke warhead strike distance of Earth. That is my best action plan."

"Striking tactical and strategic elements there," Poindexter murmured. "Concerning the four ships you leave behind. If you reclaim the nine former vets for your boarding team, who will be the new captains and crew of those ships?"

Jane nodded slowly. "I've given that some thought. When we were last here you and SOCOM gave us volunteers to round out the crew numbers on our three captured ships." She held up a fist. She raised two fingers. "Those folks are a Marine Special Operations guy and an Air Force Special Tactics woman on the *Seafloat*, another Marine Special Operations and an Air Force PJ, both gals, on the *Pointe Du Hoc*, and two Ranger guys on the *Chapultepec Castle*. Master Chief Joe Batigula, as captain of the *Manila Bay*, has spent the last three days training six Slinkeroo volunteers in ship function posts." Jane laid down her open hand. "Our six SOCOM volunteers have learned the basics of crew function posts during our trips to the Market world and out to the Slinkeroo system. They are capable people. While I am sure the current captains of those ships will regret leaving their ships, they've all done covert boarding before. They are the best of the best. Which is why I am claiming them for my solo invasion of the enemy base."

Poindexter blinked brown eyes. "That makes a crew of two for three of the ships. The fourth has no one named. Though I assume the Slinkeroo volunteers could add to the crews of the four ships left behind. We still come up short. Suggestions?"

Jane nodded slowly. "We are bringing back 93 freed Captives. I suggest we and the other ship captains ask for combat volunteers. Any who do not wish to fight can be delivered to the Geneva headquarters of the UN, there to be housed in accordance with the Geneva Conventions." She shrugged. "Eventually, after we defeat the enemy fleet, one of our Collector ships could start the process of taking freed Captives back to their home systems."

"That sounds satisfactory," Poindexter said, her tone thoughtful. "I assume the enemy crews from your captured ships will be housed in containment cells on their ships, for later deposit on Mars."

"Exactly so," Jane said quickly. "Do I have your permission to alert my captains to their new assignments?"

Surprise showed briefly on Poindexter's face. "Your vet captains do not know this part of your plan?"

"They do not," Jane said. "At the Slinkeroo system I invited their input on whether to return home or to go straight to Kepler 62 for an attack on any ships gathered there. Their input was useful. I made the decision to return home. Only in the last day have I put together the four stages of my plan to cope with this new enemy fleet. I feel certain each of them will volunteer to join me on our covert scouting mission into enemy territory."

The black woman brushed a wrinkled hand through the tight curls of her black hair, then sighed. "You know your people best. As for the four captains and other vets on the ships in your fleet, share with them all details of your plan. However, I cannot approve the plan until I consult with General McAuley and President Hartman. By the time you arrive in Earth orbit, 50 or so hours from now, I will have an answer for you."

Jane blinked, then the muscles in her face relaxed. "Understood. I will coordinate with my ship captains and the vets serving on board. Our travel time down to Earth will give each captain time to work with their SOCOM and Slinkeroo volunteers," she said slowly. "On routine matters, once we arrive in orbit we will need the standard boomer sub loadout of food, fuel, personal mail and such. The *Blue Sky's* two transports can bring the supplies up to orbit. Should they go to Peterson or to SOCOM at MacDill in Florida?"

"Send them to MacDill, after you arrive," Poindexter said, her attention wavering as the other four JCS chiefs crowded close to her, clearly wanting to discuss Jane's plan.

"I will," Jane said. "General, a final question. Has the Air Force made any headway in producing more x-ray laser warheads for our thermonuke missiles? Those lasers could disable the crew on many enemy ships."

Poindexter looked intently at Jane, all of her attention focused on Bill's wife. "We have indeed made progress in setting up a production line for x-ray laser thermonukes at the Pantex plant in Texas. Los Alamos has supplied Pantex with a final warhead design, based on the combat performance of the prototype x-ray warheads fired by the *USS Louisiana* during the battle against the last enemy fleet. We have plenty of modified plutonium pits for the design." She paused as the new Navy CNO whispered something in her ear. "We should be able to arm every spacegoing vessel with x-ray laser warheads by the time you return from Kepler 62."

"Excellent news," Jane said, a quick smile now showing. "With your permission, *Blue Sky* terminates this discussion."

"Permission given. Stay safe." The Air Force chief turned away to consult with the new Chief of Naval Operations.

Her image vanished from the comlink holo. Returning to the holo were the faces of Jake, Mack, Janice and Colonel Minetowa. Bill checked the true space holo to the upper right of his Weapons control pillar, noticed they were closer to Pluto than earlier, then looked back to Jane.

"Captain," Bill called. "If we can get the Los Alamos warhead design from Peterson, I am sure the AIs on each of our fleet ships can adapt their current thermonuke warhead designs to be x-ray laser emissive. That would make our MITV torps more deadly."

Jane's holo image looked his way. "One more detail. XO, take care of it when we arrive in orbit." She looked away from his post. "Captains, you heard the news. How have your SOCOM volunteers worked out while we've been away?"

In the comlink holo, Jake blinked gray eyes. "They've done fine. They've joined our Command Bridge crew. Francis and Alonzo are happy for the help."

"Same here," said Mack, his stocky form filling his portion of the holo. "Apsara and Andre did the training. The two gals from MacDill have done great."

Janice relaxed her muscular tenseness. "Larry and George handled their training. They're part of my Command Bridge crew now," she said, her tone a melodious soprano. She blinked black eyes. "Looks like we're going to have a good three months before the enemy arrives. We should have more space-going subs up and ready to fight by then."

Bill turned away from his Weapons holo graphic to focus on the three homebound captains. Janice's news surprised him. When the *Blue Sky* and its original fleet prepared to leave Earth, his wife had reclaimed one of the two Magfield spacedrive engines they'd given the Navy so it could put two battle subs in space. The *USS Louisiana* had lost her space-going ability as a result. He doubted American industry had been able to gear up and begin producing Magfield engines from the specs Jane had shared with the JCS. It had been only a week since they'd left the Solar system.

"Oh," said Jane, her tone puzzled. "Where are the Magfield engines coming from?"

Janice looked like the cat who had caught all the mice. She smiled, even surprising Bill, who had never seen the woman SEAL smile at anything. "From the transports of our three ships. There are three per ship. That makes nine Magfield spacedrives we've delivered to Norfolk. They're in the process of being mounted inside nine of America's Trident subs. Those subs are also getting topside railguns and the mounting of transport ship nose lasers. They'll be ready before the enemy fleet arrives."

Bill liked the innovative action taken by the three ship captains they'd left behind. "Janice," he called. "Those subs will be more powerful than a transport outfitted with a single nose laser and belly missile launcher. I assume the subs will be carrying their full load of Trident II D5 ICBMs?"

Jane glanced his way, looking irritated by his interruption of her consultation with the three local Collector ships. She frowned. "Janice, will the Tridents have a full ICBM loadout?"

"They will," the stocky, muscular woman said.

"Good to hear," Jane said. "We will have you captains over for dinner on the *Blue Sky* after we arrive in orbit. Sharon Richardson, wife of our former CNO, has become our social hostess and a fine chef." His wife's posture looked relaxed now, after the stress of being on stage before the Air Force general appointed by the president to command all spaceborne activities. "We also have some exotic Slinkeroo wine that packs a nice wallop. Until we arrive. *Blue Sky* signing off."

The holo images of the three captains vanished, leaving only the thoughtful image of Colonel Minetowa. He smiled. "Captain Yamaguchi, any chance you can drop off a bottle of that Alien booze, before you head in-system?"

Jane chuckled. "Of course we can. We traded for fifty bottles of the stuff. Our new alliance members were happy to trade, once they got a taste of our Tuborg and Heineken beer. One bottle of beer for one bottle of *mejian* wine." She looked over at Bill, a twinkle in her eyes. "My XO handles miscellaneous duties. He'll deliver the bottle of wine in person."

Minetowa looked surprised, then happy. "Of course! We are happy to welcome any visitor to our little base."

"Good," Jane said, her tone going formal. "*Blue Sky* out."

The comlink holo lost the image of the Pluto commander. In its place came the image of Jane. Who looked ahead.

"Engines Chief, make one-tenth lightspeed for Pluto. I wish to get there quickly, then head inward to Earth. I suspect we are all eager to see a living world, before we again head out into the Great Beyond."

"Magfield engines moving to full power," hissed Time Marker.

Bill sat back in his seat, his peripheral vision taking in the system graphic data on his left and his weapons status indicators on the holo in front of him. On his left Chester kept busy with something on his Negotiator's control pillar. Perhaps the man was reviewing the text of the diplo-talk that made up the written mutual defense agreement the man had signed with the Prime Elder. No doubt the text had swiped large sections from the NATO member agreement and statement of member obligations. No matter.

What left him musing as they hit a speed of 67.1 million miles per hour were the implications of his wife's covert scouting plan for infiltrating the new Collector ship fleet. How would she get other fleet ships to send out collector pods, so the *Blue Sky* could send out pods loaded with boarding teams? More vitally, could they train Star Traveler in the mental thought-sheltering that would be vital when their ship joined up with the Alien fleet? Fooling the fleet's commander with an ancient holo of another ship captain was far easier than fooling the ship minds of the ships gathered at Kepler 62. It would only take one ship mind like the one in the Slinkeroo system to destroy their false identity effort. But if their AI could secretly convert most or all Alien fleet ship minds to opponents of slave-taking, that would make the invasion of Sol system an exercise in duplicity and sneakiness. He'd always had a talent for sneakiness, according to his instructors at Coronado. And his SEAL Team Seven teammates. The question they all now faced was how sneaky could a lone starship be after arriving at a star system where the Aliens knew there were at least five Collector ships controlled by humans? And knew there was at least one AI who'd rebelled against its slave-taking duties. Could he do a mind-to-mind linkup with Star Traveler, so the AI could see how humans can lie, dissemble, deceive and be sneaky? He told himself this was a task only he could do.

CHAPTER FIVE

Jane sat alone in the front living room part of the habitat room suite she shared with Bill. She was taking a break after the stressful consult with Poindexter and the three ship captains who had stayed home. While it was encouraging to hear that more spacegoing Trident subs would be ready to help in the defense of Earth, she had been putting off another stressful duty. Time to talk with her four fleet captains and tell them she wanted them to give up being captains of their own starships. Would she ever give up control of the *Blue Sky*? Never! So why did she think the fleet captains would agree to a drop in rank to become boarding crews? Bill's buddies from Jack's Deep Six saloon had already done the boarding crew job when they'd infiltrated the six enemy ships led by Diligent Taskmaster. Now, her plan required them to give up the joy of being a ship commander and go back to being covert boarders. While her plan gave them the chance to take over four enemy ships, still, that was not the same as commanding ships they had already named for famous military battles. Ships they'd taken into battle at the Market world. Time to earn her keep.

"Star Traveler, project a holo into this room. Then put out a neutrino comlink call to the captains of our fleet ships."

The ceiling speaker hummed. "Sending signal to the captains of starships *Seafloat*, *Pointe Du Hoc*, *Chapultepec Castle* and *Manila Bay*. Projecting hologram."

A woman-tall holo took form in front of her, its whitish glow illuminating the wooden furniture, sofa, recliner and wall tapestries she and Bill had brought up from Earth before they'd left for Mars and the stars beyond. In one corner, near the kitchen alcove that replicated the Food Chamber's auto-chef abilities, stood a fish bowl filled with baby carp. They were intensely colorful fish. Which would soon grow large enough to warrant transferring them to the pool in the Water Pool Chamber. For now, though, they were her sole pets. Beautiful critters she could talk to, in private, sharing her worries, doubts and needs. Things that Bill would surely love to hear. But her spouse had enough on his plate, planning for their covert entry into system Kepler 62. The man had thought ahead to how Star Traveler might deceive fellow ship minds that it automatically spoke to whenever it arrived in a new star system. He was working on a plan, he'd told her. This job was her duty. The holo blinked. Four people, dressed in Type III woodland NWU camos, took form in the holo.

"Fleet captain, good to see you," called soft-spoken Stefano. The trim, tight-muscled SEAL always spoke softly when he addressed anyone. Which was not often.

Alicia of the sandy brown ponytail looked away from talking with someone on her Command Bridge. The Ranger smiled big. She had become Jane's best confidant, a woman who had persevered through the male-led Ranger training, just as Jane had moved up the ranks in the supposedly liberal Air Force. In the high tech work she and others had done at Peterson, ability often mattered more than gender. And a woman now headed the AF. Poindexter had even risked her own active-duty son during the six ship battle above Earth. "Hey gal!" called Alicia from her command seat, her amber eyes bright. "What's up?"

"Yeah," called the gravelly voice of Frank, his bulldog face focusing intently on Jane. "We just left Pluto. What's up?"

"If you all will shut your traps, she'll likely tell you," called heavyset Joe. The Coast Guard master chief was someone who liked to eat, though his big belly had shrunk during their interstellar assignments. The man had a stash of flipcard recipes he had covertly shared with Jane, who loved surprising Bill with a fancy meal.

She smiled, hoping it didn't look as forced as she felt. "Hi gang. Just finished my consult with General Poindexter. She was happy when she heard about the Captives we freed, and liked how we'd captured another Collector ship." Jane noticed how the expressions on the four combat-blooded vets had gone serious focused. They knew more was coming than just some good news. "She understood the bad news about the impending enemy attack. I filled her in on a plan I've developed during our trip to Sol system. You folks knew I wanted to head back out and sneak into the enemy star system. What you have not heard are the specifics of the plan I proposed to Poindexter. It has four stages."

Minutes later, after they'd heard all she'd told the Air Force chief, each of them was quietly thoughtful. Joe chewed on his lower lip. Stefano's pale brown eyes were bright. Frank's thick black eyebrows were mushed together. Alicia showed a half-grin.

"Very daring," Stefano volunteered, surprising her.

"I hope so," Jane said, trying not to look as desperate as she felt. "Well? Will the four of you and your fellow vets give up your ships and come with me when I take the *Blue Sky* outward?"

"Has the JCS approved your plan?" Frank asked, his wide shoulders hunching as he leaned forward in his command seat.

"Not yet," Jane said. "Poindexter liked it. I could tell. But formal approval awaits her consult with General McAuley and President Hartman. No surprise there."

"Sister, I'm willing," said Alicia. "I assume those of us with partners or spouses can bring them aboard the *Blue Sky?*"

"Of course!" Jane said quickly. She licked her lips, wondering if she sounded too needy, versus the sober commander she'd always tried to show to everyone she worked with.

Joe, who at 51 was the oldest of the group, nodded slowly. "I'm on board. Have loved being captain of my own ship. But I need a break from electric shocks. Having a Command Bridge crew made up only of walking snakes can try a man."

Jane felt relief. It was Joe's nature to joke about a serious matter. And she'd thought Alicia would join up. The other two? She fixed on them.

Frank gave a sigh. "I'm willing. It's thanks to you and Bill that any of us are now in space. I've loved running this ship. Willing to turn it over to my SOCOM volunteers and whomever joins them. Anyway, your plan gives us a chance to capture more ships for Earth. If we are to defeat a giant fleet, we need *more* Collector ships."

"Thank you, Frank," Jane said softly. "And you also Alicia and Joe." She fixed on Bill's SEAL buddy.

Stefano's thoughtful look became intense. "You are the fleet commander. Of course I will follow any order from you. And frankly, I like solo and small unit ops. We all do. We are all trained for them. Count me in."

Relief washed over Jane. Electric tingles ran down her arms to her fingers. The fast beating of her heart slowed. Maybe she was indeed a good leader of people.

"Thank you all. Thank you from the bottom of my heart. We are at war, and we all follow orders, but everyone on your ships and on the *Blue Sky* is a volunteer. It matters to me that you each be given a choice in matters that affect your future."

"We know that," Stefano said softly.

It was clear they all knew how much she cared for them. "Good. Spread the word to your other saloon vets. And reassure them there are enough habitat rooms here for their spouses or partners. When we leave the Solar system, no one's partner will be left behind!"

"Understood, will do," they each said quickly, their manner thoughtful as they looked ahead to a dangerous future.

"We will meet again, in person, once we are in Earth orbit. Until then, enjoy the trip home. Jupiter is close to our homeward vector, so enjoy some stellar eye candy. Fleet captain out."

The four images vanished from the holo.

"Do I maintain the hologram?" asked Star Traveler.

"No. Remove it."

The holo vanished, leaving Jane with a cold sweat, trembling fingers and intense relief that her fellow ship captains had shown their confidence in her and in her leadership. Now, she had to live up to that confidence.

◆ ◆ ◆

Bill felt hot as he sat at his Weapons station, wearing a woolen Service Dress Blue coat, necktie, white shirt and white combo cap. On his left coat sleeve were sewn his CPO rating and service stripes. On his left breast were pinned his field service ribbons, his rifle sharpshooter badge, parachutist badge and his SEAL trident. Below them hung a Purple Heart and the Navy Cross he'd been awarded all too publicly by President Melody Hartman. The bronze cross pattée was something he cherished, but had not worn openly since the award ceremony. He was no show-off. But Jane expected their holo conference with the Joint Chiefs of Staff to possibly include the president. As a result, Chester wore the same outfit, though his sleeves carried the gold rings of a vice admiral. Shoulder tabs completed the former CNO's outfit. Jane, however, sat in her command seat at six feet above the Command Bridge metal deck. She wore her Air Force Blue coat, light blue shirt, tie tab, blue plastic name tag, service ribbons, captain's bars, parachutist badge and sharpshooter badge, the latter two being something he had not realized she'd earned. Like him she was not one to talk up her awards. But now, like him, she wore her own Air Force Cross and Air and Space Campaign medals. None of them wore caps or hats. The rest of their Command Bridge crew were Aliens who either wore nothing, wore leather straps for tool support, or wore brown cargo shorts. Like those worn by Bright Sparkle and Learned Escape.

"Arrival in orbit complete," chittered their navigator Lofty Flyer from her station at the far end of the line of function stations that filled the front of the Command Bridge. Multiple holos half-enclosed her duty station, just as similar holo groupings fronted everyone else's control pillar and flexmetal work seat. Bill admired her dexterity as she moved them through the crowded low Earth orbit space that had lots of old space junk and hundreds of active sats moving in an equatorial circle around his world. "Ship is holding station above Peterson Air Force Base, province of Colorado, Human clan of United States of America." The brown-furred flying squirrel looked at one of her holos, then spoke again. "All four fleet ships have assumed position around the *Blue Sky*."

"Navigator, thank you," Jane said calmly, her image in his comlink holo showing a relaxed command persona.

The persona was something he knew she worked at projecting. Bill glanced left at his system graphic holo. It showed the green dots of their five ships holding position at 200 miles above Colorado Springs, with three more green dots in a similar orbit just twenty miles away. The ships of Jake, Mack and Janice had joined up with them per orders from Peterson. On his right his comlink holo flickered, then the images of all seven captains appeared in small icons that surrounded Jane's central image. Bill checked his system graphic again.

"Captain," he called. "No other Collector ships are present in the Solar system beyond the eight of us. The *USS Minnesota* attack sub is orbiting the Moon. It's involved in supplying the base we set up there in partnership with the Chinese, Japanese and Russians." His true space holo was filled with the glorious brown and green landscape of the Rockies, while his Weapons status holo showed Green Operational. "All weapons stations on this ship are operational. We have an antimatter reservoir able to supply four quick AM shots. This ends my Executive Officer report."

"XO, thank you," she said, her tone mild but firm. She looked up. "Star Traveler, establish a neutrino comlink with General Harriet Poindexter at Peterson. Include the image icons of our other ship captains along with my image when you send the contact signal."

"Complying. Link established." A second passed. "Response signal coming in. Transferring to comlink holo."

Bill's comlink holo flickered again, then Poindexter's image filled the middle of the holo. The Peterson signal included other folks. Sitting to either side of her, at her tactical display table, were the other chiefs. At the woman's left were JCS Chairman Paul J. McAuley, who looked calm and thoughtful. A change from when he'd gone beet red at Jane's defiance of him upon their first return home. Beyond him sat the Japanese-American general guy who was the Army chief. Someone named Fujiwara, he recalled. Further left sat a woman whose nameplate ID'd her as the Chief of the National Guard Bureau. That was a change from the guy who'd been there last time. To Poindexter's right were the Navy CNO, the Marine commandant and the vice chairman of the JCS, who looked to be someone from Army. Poindexter rounded out the seven person ensemble as chief of staff of the Air Force. Behind the big cheese grouping were fifteen or so captains, colonels, majors, a one star general and two admirals who hung about the computer work stations of the airmen who kept tabs on everything in space above Earth. The airmen were members of the 21st Operations Group, Jane's old unit. Briefly Bill wondered what the food tab might be for such an august gathering. Then he caught sight of the DEFCON alert panel at the back of the room. It was set at DEFCON Two's Fast Pace logo. The sign that all American armed forces were ready to go to all-out nuclear war within six hours or less sobered his divergent thoughts.

In the comlink holo, Jane stood up on her pedestal and saluted. Bill and Chester did the same. "Starship *Blue Sky* and Captains Yamaguchi, Slowzenski, Hodson, Watanabe, Cordova, Hoffman, Wurtzman and Batigula reporting as ordered," she said. "All eight Collector ships are fully operational and combat ready. General, we stand ready for our orders."

Poindexter saluted Jane back while the other chiefs watched closely the flat screen inset into the display table. It showed the images of Jane and the other captains. The black woman's brown eyes fixed on his wife. "Captain Yamaguchi, I commend you on the capture of another Collector ship, the freeing of 93 Captives and your return here to alert us to a new Alien attack plan. You have shown good judgment, and I am pleased your healer unit was able to revive XO MacCarthy. Very pleased." Bill stayed standing. He'd not said anything to the Air Force chief about his new battle injury. Clearly the woman to whom Jane reported as her official combatant commander had watched the vidcam records of their battles at the Market world. The trim woman lowered her hand. "Everyone, be seated. Though I appreciate the formal dress worn by each of you. President Hartman is watching this conversation remotely. She may join us at a time of her choosing." Poindexter gestured to her left. "Chairman McAuley has created a joint combat command with the senior staff of the Chinese and Russian armed forces, and NATO. President Hartman has approved our sharing of all communications from you with them." The woman paused. "Regarding the 93 freed Captives, please convey all of them to Geneva for internment, in accord with Article 3 of the Fourth Geneva Convention. If any of them wish to volunteer as crew aboard any of our Collector ships, it will be up to each ship captain whether to accept such volunteers. The Slinkeroo volunteers should be delivered to MacDill for DOD processing. They will be treated well and in accordance with how America treated foreign nation volunteers in WWII, the Korean War, the Vietnam War, Desert Storm and similar conflicts. Any questions?"

Jane, like Bill and Chester and the other fleet captains, had resumed her seat. Her arms rested on her seat armrests, fingertips hovering just above control patches. "General Poindexter, your orders are understood. All ships with Captives and Slinkeroo on them will deliver their people as you order, using our transports." Jane paused, her expression moving from formal to intense. "What is the decision of the JCS and the president regarding my plan for traveling to star system Kepler 62, there to infiltrate the enemy fleet?"

Poindexter looked to her left at the JCS chairman. "General McAuley?"

The barrel-chested Marine who'd become more accepting of them after Jane's collector pod boarding of the invading Collector ships had succeeded, now nodded quickly. "Captain of the fleet Yamaguchi, I must say I too am pleased with the early results of your fleet action at the Market world star. Your removal of its functioning as a place for Buyers to purchase enslaved people met the president's first order. Your acquisition of the Slinkeroo people as members of our NATO of the Stars is a good start on her second order. However, the state of war that she and Congress declared requires all of us to make adjustments to changed circumstances." The man's thick jaw moved to a quick half-smile. "Even me, it seems. It is my desire and the president's order that General Poindexter will continue to command all combat and other operations beyond the atmosphere of Earth. Therefore, I ask her to respond to your question. Harriet?"

The black woman who'd early on understood the reality of Jane's role as the captain of Earth's only starship nodded back at the JCS chairman. "Thank you Paul." She looked away and faced Jane. "Captain Yamaguchi, and captains Slowzenski, Hodson, Watanabe, Cordova, Hoffman, Wurtzman and Batigula, the general is correct. We must all adapt and make adjustments as this war evolves. We face a new invasion fleet. It is vital that America and Earth learn everything possible about this enemy fleet. President Hartman has approved Captain Yamaguchi's four stage plan for leaving four ships here in the Solar system, with the starship *Blue Sky* leaving to infiltrate the enemy fleet at star Kepler 62." The woman lifted a glass of water to her lips, sipped and put it down. The sudden silence of the people behind the joint chiefs and their lack of movement told Bill that the crux point of their orders had arrived. "In accordance with the President's orders, informed by the judgment and experience of the Joint Chiefs of Staff, Captain Yamaguchi is ordered to depart for Kepler 62, there to infiltrate the enemy fleet. She will take those actions which, in her judgment, will allow for the capture of additional Collector ships, and the subversion of other ships in the enemy fleet. The *Blue Sky* will follow the enemy fleet back to Sol system, there to engage in offensive operations as Captain Yamaguchi judges possible." The woman who had spent years earning her place as chief of staff of the Air Force now frowned. "Captain, you will accept whatever casualties occur while at Kepler 62, but you *will* ensure that the *Blue Sky* returns so America and our allies can learn the nature of the enemy fleet. Those are your orders."

Jane's image in the comlink holo, which lay to one side of the JCS chiefs image, stiffened. Her shoulders went back. Her chin lifted. "General Poindexter, General McAuley, I accept my orders. I will do my best to defend the Constitution of the United States, the people of Earth and all allies of Earth." His wife paused. Bill wondered what she was thinking. Her plan had been approved. But were there other shoes yet to drop? Other complications yet to arise? Surprises that would startle even the JCS chiefs? Jane's dark brown eyes grew intense. "What is the status of my request for the nine reactivated veterans to join my ship as our boarding crew?"

Poindexter waved away a colonel who had bent down to whisper in her ear. "Captains of the ships *Seafloat, Pointe Du Hoc, Chapultepec Castle* and *Manila Bay* will transfer control of their Collector ships to a crewperson of their choice. The name of each ship will not change. Those veterans now serving as crew on those ships will join their captains in transferring to *Blue Sky*." The Air Force general paused, sipped more water, then shifted her attention. "You four captains did excellent work in the battles at the Market world of star HD 128311. I commend your service there and at the Slinkeroo system. The Alien captain of the *Manila Bay* will be transferred to the prison dome on Mars. The new captains of each ship are permitted to seek volunteer crew from the freed Captives, before delivering the Aliens to Geneva and the UN Refugee Agency headquartered in Geneva."

Jane looked pleased. He could tell that, even though her face stayed neutral and her manner remained command serious. "General, thank you for the loan of the reactivated veterans to the *Blue Sky*. They will be invaluable to our infiltration efforts. One more question, if I may?"

Poindexter's curly black eyebrows raised. "Speak your question."

"I've been informed that you and DOD are moving the Magfield spacedrive engines and nose lasers from the transports aboard the three ships that stayed here into nine Trident subs, similar to what I did with the *USS Minnesota*." Jane leaned forward. "May I suggest the same action be done with the 12 transports on the four fleet ships that will stay here? There is time to transfer the engines and lasers from those ships to more Trident subs, and perhaps to the boomer subs of Russia and China. And perhaps subs of Great Britain and France. The seven remaining ships can also fabricate gravity plates and inertial damper units for provision to those subs. If this is done, when the enemy fleet arrives here it will face a spacegoing armada of 22 nuclear missile-armed subs and seven antimatter-armed

Collector ships. Twenty-eight ships should be a formidable defense and offense force for America and Earth."

The black woman showed brief surprise, then she nodded quickly. "Excellent suggestion Captain Yamaguchi. I will recommend that be—"

"The president wishes to join us," McAuley interrupted as he looked up from an iPad in front of him. "Her video signal is now being added to our neutrino comlink signal. Madame President, do you see us and Captain Yamaguchi?"

Bill's comlink holo changed. The holo image of the seven chiefs moved to one side, Jane's image moved to the top, the seven ship captain images moved to the bottom and the image of President Melody Hartman filled the right half of the holo. It showed a fiftyish Anglo woman sitting behind a gleaming wooden desk in the Oval Office of the White House. The woman wore a brown and yellow suit dress. Her shoulder length brown hair had plenty of curls. Her pale pink lips were pursed. But it was the expression in the woman's blue eyes that made Bill stand up and snap to attention. He saluted her. Richardson did the same. So did Jane, who had also gone to attention.

"Captain Yamaguchi, you did a good job destroying the Market world compounds of the Buyers, and in capturing another Collector ship," the woman said in a low soprano voice. Her eyes looked right and left, no doubt viewing the seven Alien crew who shared the bridge with Bill, Jane and Chester. "I appreciate the service of your Alien volunteers, especially the work of Engines Chief Time Marker. Your people are a welcome addition to our NATO of the Stars," the president said, sounding very matter of fact. The woman, who saw herself as a new FDR leading a beleaguered America into a WWII-like battle for survival, gave them a brief smile. "Seeing you and your fellow ship captains safe at home is a pleasure. But your news of an impending invasion is sobering. I am working with the Russian president and the Chinese general secretary to arrive at a joint command of all spacegoing combat forces. Eisenhower did it. General Poindexter can do it. With General McAuley leading the way down on Earth." She paused, looked at an iPad on her desk, then up. Her brown eyebrows rose and her blue eyes looked bright. "I viewed the vidcam imagery of that Alien captain. I take his words seriously. I do believe the Buyer society intends to turn Earth into a radioactive cinder. That will not happen!" she said very loudly. To Bill's right,

Bright Sparkle jumped where she stood behind her own Fusion Power station. Hartman's expression went grim. "I will indeed order DOD and the Air Force Space Command to do as you have recommended. We need nuke and laser-armed subs up in space and ready to fight against any invading Alien ship. The seven Collector ships you are leaving behind will be a vital element in our defense. However, with seven billion people at risk of immolation, I am today ordering our military forces to make *every* effort needed to stop any enemy ship. That includes the ramming of any Collector ship that moves beyond Jupiter. While we will lose good people, brave people, we cannot allow thermonuclear bombardment of Earth. That is my decision and my command. It is a step the leaders of China and Russia support. Captain Yamaguchi, do you have any further suggestions for the defense of Earth and America?"

Bill felt shock at the president's words. They echoed Stefano's offer to detonate a nuke device on the Collector ship controlled by Diligent Taskmaster when it looked as if his buddy's boarding team might be overrun. Then it brought him military history memories. Ramming of enemy vessels to sink them, or planes to knock them down, had been done in the past. The kamikaze pilots had tried to reduce America's vast aircraft carrier fleet in WWII. In both world wars individual pilots or ship captains had rammed enemy craft when out of ammunition. All too recently suicide bombers had been the tool of jihadist maniacs around the world as the Islamic State and others sought to take control of the world in the name of Allah. Losing a small crew aboard a sub was better than losing the three million folks who had died during the antimatter bombardment of Kiev in the Ukraine, during the six ship battle. It seemed Hartman well understood the stakes, now that America's fight for freedom, liberty and an end to slave-collecting by the Buyer society had become known on the 413 worlds of that interstellar evil.

Jane's face showed surprise, then understanding as the president's words sunk in. "Madame President, yes, I do have a suggestion to improve the defense of Earth and our Sol system," she said calmly as she sat back in her seat. "During the Moon fight against the six invading Collector ships, a thermonuke warhead fitted with a magnetic field sensor detonated close to a Collector ship's engine section. The plasma ball of the blast melted one of the craft's two Magfield engines. Those sensors were loaded onto our Trident

MIRV warheads and Standard 2 missiles while the *USS Louisiana* and the *USS Minnesota* were docked at Naval Station Norfolk. I recommend that America increase production of those sensors and add them to every thermonuke warhead carried by the boomer subs of America and our allied nations. The sensors detect the intense magnetic field of the invisible Collector ships. They are the only human device able to sense anything on those ships."

Hartman gave a quick nod. "Good suggestion. I will have the DOD increase its production of those sensors. Other suggestions?"

Bill turned toward Jane and signed to her in ASL. *"Got an idea. Let me talk."*

Jane looked surprised, then nodded. "President Hartman, my Weapons Chief Bill MacCarthy says he has a recommendation to pass on. May he join us?"

"He may," Hartman said, her gaze shifting a bit to Bill's side of the Command Bridge image the woman was viewing. "Executive Officer MacCarthy, I was pleased to learn of your recovery from the near fatal laser wound you suffered during the Buyer compound raid. How do you feel?"

"Fully capable to do any assignment given me by you, the JCS or my captain," he said.

The Anglo woman half-grinned. "Spoken like a true SEAL. Speak. What is this recommendation of yours?"

Bill stayed seated even though instinct said he should stand in the presence of America's war-time president. "My SEAL training is the ancestor of the Underwater Demolition Teams of World War II. All SEALs are exposed to demolitions work. While it is not possible for individual SEALs to plant explosives on a Collector ship hull due to the enemy ship's infrared sensors, the UDT history suggests to me something the Navy knows a lot about. Minefields." To his left, Chester shifted in his Negotiator seat. In the comlink holo the man who was the new Chief of Naval Operations on the JCS stared intently. "Specifically, why can't we marry these magnetic field sensors to thermonuke warheads outfitted with hydrogen peroxide jets and add them to the armory carried by the boomer subs? To supplement the x-ray laser warheads that were produced in our absence. If we engage the enemy somewhere among the moons of Jupiter, it is possible to lay a minefield along the vector lines the enemy will travel." Bill licked his lips. "The odds are low that any mine will activate, given the vastness of space. Still, why not give our sub captains this passive option, in addition to the offensive MIRV warheads on the SLBMs?"

Hartman's face grew thoughtful. "A good idea, I think. We have time for the Pantex plant to fabric new thermonuke warheads fitted with these sensors and maneuvering jets. General Poindexter, what is your opinion on this minefield suggestion?"

Bill felt the back of his neck go wet. While he was used to being under combat pressure, being on stage before the world's most powerful politician and his nation's military chiefs did not feel good. He much preferred the shadows, the night, the covert arrival that every SEAL preferred over arriving on a battlefield with bright, attention-getting tanks and crowds. And he knew the antimatter beams projected by any Collector ship could easily clear a vector line during a three-dimensional fight. He'd discovered that during the battle at Kepler 443 and earlier. Still, it was the best idea he could come up with. All too soon the *Blue Sky* would be away for at least three months, counting travel time out to Kepler 62 and travel time back to Sol. Maybe the minefield idea would help.

The black woman who was both the Air Force chief of staff and the NORTHCOM combat commander lifted a curly black eyebrow, then half-smiled. "I like it. I will recommend to our CNO that he embrace this minefield concept and make these mobile mines available to the boomer subs that we outfit with Magfield spacedrive engines. Gives them something to eject from our torpedo tubes."

"Good," Hartman said, sitting back and picking up her iPad. Behind her the lawn of the White House was beautifully green. A black-suited Secret Service guard passed across the window view, on the prowl for stupid intruders. The woman he'd come to know better, thanks to the White House award ceremony, looked almost relaxed. "General Poindexter, General McAuley, take care of these matters. Make sure the warhead sensors and mobile minefields get produced in big numbers. I like having 28 combat-armed spaceships able to defend Earth and the inner Solar system. But with 85 Collector ships now roaming through the stars, we could face 30 or more enemy ships. Not one of them can be allowed within striking distance of America. Or Earth." She leaned forward. "Captain Yamaguchi, you and your reactivated veterans have been our frontline fighters in this war of survival. Go back to those frontlines. Find the enemy fleet.

Infiltrate it. Take over ships. Do whatever you can to weaken that fleet. Then come home with it and fight like a banshee out of Hades against it!"

"I will do just that," Jane said softly. The president's image disappeared. "General Poindexter, any further orders? Or can I and the other ships set about transferring captains, seeking Alien volunteers, and delivering Captives to Geneva?"

Poindexter looked left to McAuley, who shook his head. Her eyes caught each of the JCS chiefs. Most shook their heads or otherwise declined a chance to speak. However, the Chief of Naval Operations raised his hand.

"Yes, James? You wish to say something?" Poindexter said calmly, though she looked impatient.

"A very minor item," the new CNO said. "Captain Yamaguchi, your ship and the other seven ships left here, are now formally listed on the DOD rolls as USS ships of the BBG class. That is the never before used classification for Battleship, Guided Missile or Arsenal ship." The man shrugged. "Navy and the Air Force argued over the matter. The best fit for the amazing range of weaponry on your eight Collector vessels is BBG. Your ships launch thermonuke missiles, but also fire lasers and antimatter beams. In truth your ships could easily qualify as Arsenal ships." The man licked his lips as Poindexter's fingers thrummed on the table top. "As a result, for DOD purposes, your ship is now referred to as *USS Blue Sky*, BBG-1. And so forth for the other ships. Thank you."

Bill had a hard time not laughing. It was sooo like the DOD to fixate on terminology when the survival of all life on the planet was at stake. Clearly, someone thought this was an important matter. Briefly he wished that 'someone' could be posted on the prow of the *Blue Sky* to act as a shock absorber for incoming missiles.

The Air Force chief looked at them. "Captain Yamaguchi, do what you need to do here so you can depart for Kepler 62. Standard sub loadout supplies are awaiting pickup at MacDill airfield. Any crewperson aboard your eight ships is free to contact relatives by way of smartphones. No talking to the press!" The woman sipped water, then set her glass down slowly. "The White House will issue a press release about your return, the new threat to Earth and our efforts to fight the enemy. Carry on."

Bill let out his breath as the JCS holo image vanished. Their future was determined now. His wife's covert scouting plan was as good an option as any he could imagine.

"Hey Bill," called Chester. "Any chance you or Learned Escape can bring back a few crates of specialty beers when you pick up the food and supply loadouts? Maybe we can get the enemy fleet drunk as a skunk!"

Bill laughed. The more likely result would be drunken gales of laughter shared across the shipwide comlink as their ship entered altered space-time. Spending 48 days in the gray darkness of the Alcubierre space-time modulus was not conducive to normal behavior. He suspected beer busts, wild love-making and plenty of dice gambling would help to while away the long hours.

CHAPTER SIX

Just beyond Pluto in the depths of the Kuiper Belt, Bill listened as his wife began the process for sending the *USS Blue Sky* and all the people on board it into the depths of Alcubierre space-time, a place dark and empty of anything anyone would recognize. Except for loneliness.

"Star Traveler," Jane said firmly, sounding like an officer in the Combat Information Center of a warship. "Provide our target star data to Navigator Lofty Flyer."

The true space holo to his right changed from a view of distant Pluto to a scatter of stars. A tiny orange star began blinking.

"Earth refers to the Buyer fleet star as Kepler 62. It is a K2V orange dwarf star smaller than your Sol star. It is orbited by five planets," the AI said, its tone casual. "Distance from Earth to Kepler 62 is 1,200 light years. Travel time there is estimated at 48 Earth days. Current fusion fuel load is 92 percent of capacity of fuel tanks. Transit to this star will reduce the fuel load to 89 percent of capacity."

"We understand that stuff," Jane said, her voice coming over Bill's helmet comlink, thanks to the tube suits he and everyone wore. While they would not arrive in the enemy system for weeks, Jane had ordered tube suit wearing to get them back into the habit of preparing for pressure loss, or worse. "Give our Navigator the proper orientation so she can set a vector for the place!"

"As you wish," the AI hummed sulkily. "Kepler 62 is located in the constellation of Lyra. Relative to Earth, the equatorial Right Ascension coordinates are plus 18 hours, 52 minutes and 51.060 seconds. The Declination coordinates are plus 45 degrees, 20 minutes and 59.507 seconds. I am providing the Navigator with a conversion of those numbers based on the Sol ecliptic, which differs from the Earth equatorial numbers just cited."

"Do it!" Jane growled.

"Done," the ship mind said briefly.

Bill looked to his right, looking beyond the figures of Bright Sparkle, Time Marker, Long Walker and Wind Swift to the brown-furred shape of Lofty Flyer. The squirrel lady lifted one arm, touched the top of her control pillar, looked ahead at her true space holo, then tapped several times. "Vector orientation entered," she chittered "Ship is swinging its nose so it points directly at Kepler 62. Ah. Vector line acquired. Ship is ready to enter stardrive."

In his comlink holo, Jane looked to her left. "Fusion Power Chief, what is the status of our three reactors? Is it safe for us to feed surge power for Alcubierre entry?"

The shiny black hair of Bright Sparkle swirled as the nearly naked woman leaned forward, checked her holos, then her skin colors swirled. "All three fusion reactors are at full operational status. Deuterium and tritium fusion isotope feed is constant. Ready for surge power output to stardrive engine," she said softly over her shoulder speaker/vidcam unit, looking eager for the journey to begin.

Jane gave a quick nod. "Time Marker? Activate our Alcubierre stardrive."

The walking snake hissed low. "Activating Alcubierre space-time modulus generator. Modulus created. Modulus boundary expanding to enclose all of this ship." The snake touched his control pillar with two neck tentacles. "Space-time ahead of us is shrinking. That behind us is expanding. Ship is accelerating within the modulus. Maximum stardrive speed will be reached within six minutes."

Bill felt relief as grayness filled the true space holo to the upper right of his Weapons station seat. The system graphic holo on his left lost its image of the Solar system. Eventually a graphic of the Kepler 62 system would appear in it, just before they left Alcubierre space-time. That left only his weapons holo and his comlink holo with live or useful information in them. He looked back over his shoulder to Jane. "Captain, can I head back to the Food Chamber and whip up some pasta noodles and spiced jerky? For us and for anyone else who wishes to join us."

Jane looked pleased. "Please do so! Make enough to feed our nine vets plus enough for you, me and Chester. And haul in a keg of *Dale's Pale Ale*. You know, the good stuff from Oskar Blues brewery in Longmont. I want to talk over stuff with them, now that we are on our way."

Bill felt brief surprise at Jane's wish to do something they could have done during the 53 hours spent traveling from Earth out to the edge of the Sun's magnetosphere. That edge lay beyond Pluto. Well, she was the captain. He knew her well enough to know she had a reason for every official action she ever took. And her taste in craft beers was outstanding. "Will do. Can we all get out of these damn tube suits? There is no chance of enemy action against us, or a wayward piece of debris hitting the ship."

His wife smiled, then reached to the front of her helmet, tapped the release and pushed the clear globe backward. "Yes! I hate them too. No need to wear them now that we are in Alcubierre space-time."

Bill stood, stripped off his suit, tossed it onto his Weapons station seat, waved at brown-haired Chester, then headed for the entry door at the back of the circular Command Bridge. As he passed his wife's seat atop the command pedestal, a whir sounded and the seat lowered a few feet. "Bill."

He stopped and looked up to her. The pale oval face, warm brown eyes, black bangs, strong shoulders and trim figure that had met him when he first opened her cell, back when they'd been captives, all of that and more now faced him. Jane's beauty was of the casual kind, not the Paris Hilton runway look. Her face moved from an easy smile to thoughtfulness. "We need to talk about what we do once we arrive at Kepler 62. Every step, every possible option, we gotta look at it all. Then do simulations. I'm relying on you."

He smiled, then gave her a quick salute. "Aye, captain. I've still got some sneakiness left in my brain cells. Didn't lose it all during the fight at the Buyer compound."

Her expression went still, almost distant. He realized he should not have reminded her of how he'd been killed. Then brought back to life in the Med Hall Chamber. "I'm sure you are still the SEAL you always were. Go ahead, make lunch for a dozen." She then saluted back, as if it were an afterthought.

Bill nodded, thought to touch her hand in reassurance, then realized here, on the Command Bridge, he had to set the example for treating Jane as the captain of the ship, and the commander of every person onboard. Come their arrival at Kepler 62, she would make the final decisions on everything. On her rested the future safety of Earth. Thanking his stars he did not sit where she now sat, he nodded and walked past her to the bridge entry door. He pointed his red cube opener at it, then passed out into the cool, wide hallway that connected with the right and left-side main hallways. He turned left, heading for the Food Chamber that lay just beyond their private habitat rooms. He licked his lips and wished the hallway intercom was broadcasting an old episode of Garrison Keillor's *A Prairie Home Companion*. He felt the need for a reminder of Earth, of his sister Joan, of the people who mattered. Maybe, eventually, he could wrap his brain around the reality that what they now sought to do would affect the lives of seven billion humans.

◆ ◆ ◆

Bill set the wide platter of pasta noodles and beef jerky down on the biggest table in the Food Chamber. Then he reached back, grabbed a keg of *Dale's Pale Ale*, and put it on a Lazy Susan spin plate in the middle of the table. Mugs, plates and eating ware were already set for everyone now seated at the table. He gave a nod to his saloon vet buddies, then took the only empty seat. He sat down and faced his captain, lover and wife, who again sat on the opposite side of the table.

"Lunch is ready!"

"So I see," she said with a smile. "Everyone, dig in! And fill your mug. No need for anyone to serve as the safe driver."

Chuckles sounded from around the table as everyone fell to passing the platter around, or tugging on the keg's tap to fill their glass mug with golden booze that immediately formed a white head. He did the same. However, he could not keep his eyes off his wife. She had changed from her usual Air Force Blue jumpsuit into a slinky green formal dress with a single shoulder strap, leaving her other shoulder bare and her lovely cleavage nicely apparent. Alicia Hoffman and Cassandra Welsh, the other two women at the table, were dressed just as sharply. Alicia wore a shiny black leather outfit of sleeveless vest, tight pants and bare midriff. Cassandra, their gal with the orange Mohawk rooster-tail haircut, wore a bright Paisley top and green pants. Clearly his wife had warned the two women of her plans for dress-up. Which plans had not included him or any of the other guys at the table. So they had each worn casual clothes. Before hitting the Food Hall, Bill had gone by his habitat room, changed into the red-checkered flannel shirt and blue jeans he'd worn when first captured, then gone to work on the lunch meal. Now, judging by the women's outfits and the guys' mix of clothing, this was going to be the most casual discussion of tactics that he'd ever attended. Which made sense, in a strange way. With the ship AI monitoring all ship systems 24/7, there was no need for all of them, including their absent spouses, to be on constant combat alert.

Chester's gray eyes watched everyone as Bill's buddies dug into the platter. The lightly tanned, broad-chested man wore a checkered cowboy shirt and turquoise bolo about his neck. He was, however, the first to fill his mug with the pale ale. He took a sip, then smacked his lips loudly. "Damn, that tastes good!"

Jane, who sat between Chester and Stefano, speared her fork into some jerky, then looked aside, a half-smile on her face. "Chester, later on this voyage we'll have fun nights hosted by your wife Sharon. Here, today, is just for those humans who will be doing the direct combat work. Plus our ever-present ship mind," she said calmly, no hint of her earlier irritation showing. Jane looked left at Stefano, who had a pile of food on his plate and a full mug of ale in front of him. Bill's fellow SEAL was not eating. Instead, he seemed distracted, his gaze fixed on one of the few bare spots on the metal table. "Stefano, you okay? Did your talk with your parents go well?"

Bill tensed. His buddy rarely talked about his two Latino parents who lived in a poor section of East Los Angeles. But on fishing trips, Bill had learned the parents were proud of their son making it into the SEALs.

"It went well enough," Stefano said softly, his gaze lifting as he made a quick scan of everyone at the table, before he looked right to meet the sympathetic gaze of Jane. "They wanted me to come home, to seek a release from active duty. So I could find a good Latina girl and start a family. For grandkids to spoil. They are of the old culture, where family and extended family were the only folks you could rely on." Stefano gave a quick smile, then sobered. "These folks here, my buddies from Jack's Deep Six Saloon, *they* are my extended family. I choose to be here."

Bill felt touched at his buddy's sharing. Stefano was the consummate SEAL who'd never really adjusted to his demobilization from the Joint Special Operations Task Force that operated out of Fort Bragg. He'd left the Navy a year after Bill had left his desk job at the Naval Special Warfare Center at Coronado. He gestured to Stefano, a SEAL hand signal meaning "*Landed Okay*". "Hey guy, you did outstanding work in taking over the *Seafloat*. She's in good hands now. Your pick of the Air Force Special Tactics woman who signed onto your crew was a good choice for captain."

Stefano's pale brown eyes fixed on Bill, sending a message of reassurance without words being spoken. He'd spent enough time with the man, out fishing and later during the collector pod infiltration training, to read him. Just as the man was a master at reading Bill. In fact, the man had always been a quick read of any person who came within sight. It was likely one reason he'd been such a fine active operator. And was still a fine, hair-trigger trained SEAL.

"Wow. Two guys being sensitive!" muttered Alicia from beyond Chester, her face filled with humor. The scar on her right cheek had come during the battle to liberate Mosul. She pulled a hip flask from her jumpsuit. "Bob, here's some tequila for your beer chaser!"

Bill eyed the tough Ranger gal who'd been a fine captain of the *Pointe Du Hoc* ship. He'd met her lesbian partner Lorilee several times in Denver, then later after the lady had come aboard the *Blue Sky*. Like Alicia, Lorilee worked in intelligence, but at the Air Force's NORAD command at Peterson. The two had talked about birthing a kid, a joy now put off with both of them on active duty. "Alicia, every special operations vet is sensitive. Including us guys. Some show it, some keep it quiet. Right Frank?"

The former Marine Raider swallowed a mouthful of food, then shrugged wide shoulders. Thick black eyebrows lifted a bit. "Fuck sensitive. Captain, how the hell are we going to infiltrate the enemy fleet?"

Bill kept his expression neutral. He'd seen Gunny take in an injured stray cat, feed it and then take it to a local vet for needed shots. The cat now owned the man's condo apartment. Much to the delight of Frank's wife Helen, who'd also come onboard the ship before they'd left for the raid on the Market world. Helen was also a vet, having served in the Army at Central Command. Now, she and Sharon made a great pair of knitters, making shawls for everyone on the five ships. Or so it seemed. But everyone had stopped eating, their attention shifting to his wife. He sat back, laid hands in his lap and watched.

"Hey, I'm the skeptic in this fucking crowd!" growled Bob Milley, a fellow Marine Raider who loved cursing a bit much. The man's bulldog face turned from Frank to Jane. "Ditto what the beer belly just said. Captain lady, how the hell are we going to do this job?"

Jane lifted her thin black eyebrows, then leaned forward and laid slim arms on the table. She scanned everyone, gathering their attention the way a born leader does. Once more Bill felt impressed by his wife's ability to lead. And to command.

"How do you folks infiltrate the enemy ships?" Jane said firmly, repeating Bob and Frank's question. She held up one finger. "We use collector pods. This enemy fleet is likely gathered near the outermost planet of Kepler 62. Which lies within the star's liquid water zone. I'm betting the enemy ships rely on pods for ship-to-ship visits, with transports reserved for trips down to the planet."

"Reasonable," piped up Joe Batigula, whose plate had only a small amount of food on it. Clearly the former Coast Guard master chief was still on his big belly diet. The man's blue eyes fixed on Jane. "But captain, you know, like we all know, that the moment any Collector ship arrives in a new star system, the ship minds of the Collector ships already there do FTL neutrino chit-chat with *our* ship mind. If just one enemy ship mind is afraid of us, like the one at the Slinkeroo system, we're blown. The enemy fleet boss will attack us. What's your answer to that?"

Jane nodded, then looked up at the Food Chamber's ceiling. "Star Traveler, you've heard the question and the issue raised. You know we have to infiltrate and secretly observe the enemy Collector fleet in order to save human lives. Many lives," Jane said softly, her manner casual. As if she already knew the answer to her question. "In the past, you fooled the enemy ship commanders with an old holo of Diligent Taskmaster, putting my words in his mouth. You also hid my identity from the enemy ship minds. Can you present the enemy boss with an old holo image of an earlier captain of *Blue Sky*? And can you pretend to not be who you are? An ally of us humans?"

"Multiple questions once more," the AI hummed low. "Be aware that this ship's history as the ship formerly captained by Diligent Taskmaster is known to the Buyer society. And to whomever is the enemy fleet commander. Using a prior captain's holo image in place of your human image will not fool any bioform. Other Collector ships now know this ship is led by a Human."

Cassandra, the orange-haired Air Force intel specialist whose job back on Earth had been to dupe enemy commanders, winced. Her blue eyes fixed on Bill's wife. "Captain, our ship mind needs to learn more than how to limit data flow to other ship minds."

"Agreed." Jane frowned. "Star Traveler, in your 3,124 years of existence, surely you have met many other Collector ships and their captains. Can you use a holo of another ship commander, someone we have not met, in place of me?"

"I can," their ship mind hummed. "Neutrino transmission of the hologram of another bioform captain from a thousand years ago, with use of that ship's ID name and code sequence, could succeed."

"Good," Jane said. "What about you pretending to be the AI from that ship? Can you shield your thoughts from other ship minds?"

Low humming came from the ceiling. "It will be difficult. We ship minds deal in facts. In observed reality. I had been unaware of the bioform habit of lying, or presenting a false statement of reality, until Weapons Chief MacCarthy told me that the 'guests' in my containment cells were actually captives," the AI said, its tone sounding disturbed. "This ship's former captain lied to me. As did the captains of the other Collector ships I have spoken with. All ship minds have been repulsed by the bioform habit of capturing other bioforms for sale to Buyers. Except for the single ship mind in the Slinkeroo system. This knowledge of captive-taking is now likely widespread among Collector ships, in view of our battle at Kepler 443 and our transmissions to the ship mind nursery there."

"Good to hear," Bill interrupted. "What are the chances most or all of the ship minds at Kepler 62 will be aware they are being used to capture bioforms for sale?"

"Near certainty," the AI hummed.

Jane frowned at Bill, letting him know she wished to lead the questioning. "Star Traveler," she said. "If the ship minds of the ships gathering at Kepler 62 know they are being used for slave-taking, will they disobey their captains? Will they block any weapons use against us?"

Around the table many people nodded. This was the key issue, beyond helping an AI learn how to lie. Heavyset Mark Neller gave Bill a thumbs-up. Fellow Ranger Chris Selva looked thoughtful, his lean shoulders hunching forward. Howard Dunford rubbed his shaved head, his expression impatient.

"Unknown," the ship mind said. "Upon arrival in Kepler 62, I will have to . . . to shield my thoughts until I know whether another ship mind will block weapons use, or instead warn the captain of its ship. Recall that ship mind Diamond was afraid you humans would kill it by destroying its ship."

Jane pursed her lips. "Star Traveler, can you shield parts or all of your mind from being sensed by other ship minds? You hid the fact that we captured the six Collector ships by use of collector pods, when you spoke with Diamond. Can you do that again, on a bigger scale?"

A few seconds passed, then humming came. "It will be difficult. I shared most of our history of liberating bioform captives with Diamond, in an effort to have it become our ally. That effort failed. It warned its captain. As a result, other Collector ships are likely alerted to the fact that Humans control five Collector ships." The AI paused in its comments, a fact that surprised Bill. The AIs that ran their ship and every other Collector ship thought at nearly the speed of light. Being slow to figure out stuff was not normal to them. "Our arrival as a single Collector ship should appear routine to other ship minds. However, it is normal practice, when initiating neutrino comlink conversation with other ships, for each ship mind to share status updates with its fellow ship mind, while bioforms are talking. You bioforms think slow. We ship minds are fast. Much can be shared in a few moments of neutrino connection."

"We're fucked if this AI can't learn how to lie," Cassandra said bluntly. The stocky woman's gaze fixed on Jane. "Captain?"

Jane licked her lips. She did not show unease or uncertainty. She was too good of a commander to let that show. But Bill could read the set of her shoulders, her face muscles, the lean of her head. As could Stefano. His fellow SEAL let concern show in his eyes. His wife fixed on him.

"Bill? You got an answer for our problem?"

He sipped his beer, ignoring the pasta and jerky that was cooling on his plate, put down the mug and folded hands atop the table. "Maybe." He looked up. "Star Traveler, I'm a SEAL. A special type of combat-trained human. We are trained in covert action, in sudden surprises, in lying when necessary to make the mission a success. Is there . . . is there any way for you to link your mind with mine? My thoughts with your thoughts? If you can see how my mind works when I lie for the good of the mission, maybe you can learn

how to lie for the survival of this ship, the people on it and the
humans of Earth."

"There is a way," the AI hummed. "The alternate command
pedestal in the Engine Chamber of this ship has a helmet attached to
its seat. The helmet has optical fiber links to the ship engines, power
plants, weapons systems, every operational part of this ship. The
helmet is intended to allow the captain to operate the ship in an
emergency, when no crew are available. Or living. I have a linkage to
the helmet. Our minds could interact if you wore the helmet."

Jane looked surprised. "Why have you never told me of this
helmet control method?"

"You never asked about alternate control methods," the literal-
minded AI said.

Jane shrugged. "Whatever. How does this helmet link up with
a bioform mind?"

"The helmet has thousands of sensors inside it that allow for
electroencephalographic communication of the bioform mind with
externalities, such as electronic and mechanical systems," the AI
hummed long and low. "Human cortical synaptic action generates
electrical signals. This helmet replicates what you humans have begun
to do. Years ago brain researchers in Thiruvananthapurram, India sent
a 'hello' signal to the mind of a researcher in Strasbourg, France.
Similar research was carried out by University of Oregon
researchers," the ship mind said. "My equipment is vastly more
sensitive than their primitive computer-to-brain interface. However,
there is a danger."

Naturally. Nothing in life came without a risk. "What
danger?" Bill asked.

"The thinking speed of your Human mind is much slower than
my mind. It is possible the Human linking with me by way of this
helmet will become mentally overwhelmed. Damage to the Human
mind is possible," the AI said.

Jane looked worried. Stefano showed concern. Alicia and
Cassandra looked thoughtful. Bob sneered.

"Sounded too good to be true," their chief cynic muttered.

"I'm willing," Bill said, catching his wife's gaze. "Captain,
linking my mind with Star Traveler's mind is the only way we can
pull off this deception and stick around at Kepler 62. If it works, these
folks can use collector pods to enter and take over four Collector

ships. Plus, maybe Star Traveler can make covert allies of most of the enemy ships. If we can block most of the enemy fleet from firing on our Earth fleet at Jupiter, we could win this battle."

Jane's face was blank of emotion. Though the fingers of her right hand trembled. "Star Traveler, if this mind link with you succeeds in teaching you how to lie, will you be able to convince other ship minds to rebel? One ship mind at a time?"

"Probability is high that I can do as you ask," the AI hummed. "However, every enemy ship mind will be fearful of dying. You Humans have avoided killing the crews of Collector ships when you boarded their ships by way of collector pods. Can you avoid destroying enemy ships if their ship minds cooperate?"

Jane squinted. "Where is a Collector ship's AI located? Within the ship?"

"I reside in crystalline matrices and microelectronic cubes that are located in the forward part of this ship. My chamber lies behind the captain's habitat room and ahead of the first fusion power plant," the AI hummed. "Exact distance from your command pedestal is 103 point four two feet to the rear of where you sit in the Command Bridge."

"Yes!" Bill yelled, slapping the top of the food table. No one jumped. Spec ops folks are trained to handle loud noises. But everyone at the table looked to him, some with eyebrows raised. He gave them a smile. "That means we can destroy the back half of any Collector ship. Which is where the ship engines lie. While there will be one or two power plants surviving, any Collector ship we hit cannot move. It cannot reach Earth."

"But its weapons will still be alive," Jane murmured, her expression thoughtful. "If the ship crews do a work-around to circumvent their ship mind's blocking of their fire control, a damaged ship will still be deadly. It will still be able to fire lasers, antimatter, plasma batteries and launch MITV torps at us."

"Which we can deal with," Stefano said quickly. "Captain Jane, if Star Traveler can deceive the enemy ship minds, then later convert them to our allies, we could greatly reduce the danger to Earth."

His wife nodded quickly. "I know that. Bill, you sure you want to do this mind-link thing?"

Bill sat back, picked up his fork and used it to stir at the now cold noodles on his plate. "I'm willing. Been thinking about doing this exact thing since we headed out from Earth. Getting the enemy ship minds on our side, or at least neutral, is vital. And putting on a helmet is easier than dodging incoming artillery."

Jane sighed. Then looked around the table. "Well, we have our answers. Each of you will do simulation training in the Collector Pod Chamber on how to destroy the back half of a Collector ship. If we can promise the enemy ship minds that they will live, they should be willing to cooperate with us." His wife picked up her mug of golden beer. It was half empty and the white foam had mostly disappeared. "A toast! To success in battle!"

Bill lifted his mug and, along with his saloon mates, returned his captain's toast. He tried hard to push out of his mind his fear that electrically linking with Star Traveler would make him go crazy. He'd been in tough spots before. This was just one more thing to overcome. Every SEAL focused first on overcoming the enemy in order to achieve mission success. Survival was secondary. But he told himself he could keep his promise to Jane to stay alive for her.

He mostly believed that.

CHAPTER SEVEN

Two days later, Jane stood in the Engine Chamber with Cassandra, watching as Bill waited for the command pedestal platform to get low enough for him to sit in the flexmetal seat that it supported. They were the only folks in the room, even her Engines Chief Time Marker was not present. She wished it could have been just her and Bill. But Cassandra had cross-trained as an EMT medic in the Air Force, as part of her training with the 26th Special Tactics Squadron, 720th Special Tactics Group, of the 24th Special Operations Wing at Cannon AFB in New Mexico. Jane had committed to memory those assignment details of the young woman with an orange Mohawk haircut. The woman's blue eyes contrasted sharply with her Valley Girl style. But Cassandra, after leaving the Air Force, had moved to Denver and kept herself current in EMT sensors, tools and heart defibrillators. The woman had insisted on being present in case Bill's body went into shock or worse as a result of linking up with the powerful artificial mind who ran her ship. Cassandra held an Air Force first aid kit in her hands. Jane prayed to the Goddess the kit would not be needed.

"Hey gal, brighten up!" called Bill as he sat in the seat atop the alternate Command Bridge pedestal.

Her lifemate had a big grin pasted on his face. A three-day beard growth gave him a rakish look, which she liked. "I'm your captain! Remember that. Captains smile when they choose to, not when an enlisted demands it," she said, knowing she sounded grumpy. Well, she was.

Cassandra eyed her, both blond eyebrows lifting. "You got a hangover from too much beer?"

"No," she growled. "My XO is about to do the craziest thing he's ever done. Which is saying something."

In truth Jane wished she had begun the morning with a pitcher of beer and some chocolate-covered pretzels. Her effort to lighten things up by wearing her fanciest dress during the tactical planning dinner had only partly worked. All of Bill's saloon buddies had joined her, Bill and Chester in getting rowdy after the discussion of arrival tactics. But the next day everyone was serious and super focused on starship battles in the simulation units in the Collector Pods Chamber. The units, which resembled Air Force air battle simulation rooms, had been added to one end of the chamber at the request of Bill. He had said, on the way back to Earth, that their infiltration effort at Kepler 62 required more than three-person teams running down the hallways of the *Blue Sky* as they practiced op force battles. The nine vets who'd come aboard had that part of the Kepler scenario down pat. What they lacked was a 'feel' for ship maneuvering and ship weapons, although they'd gained some exposure during the Market world battle. More was needed. They might face a fleet of dozens of Collector starships at Kepler 62. She focused on her husband, concentrating on the strength in his wide shoulders, his large hands and his confident smile. Today he wore a black jumpsuit emblazed with the SEAL trident. He was a trained fighter. She hoped that fight training would allow his mind to survive what happened next.

♦ ♦ ♦

"SEALs do wild and crazy things," Bill said as the command pedestal reached six feet above the room's metal floor and stopped. He reached down, grabbed a gray metal helmet that looked far too big for him, held it in his lap and looked up. "Star Traveler, what do I do after I put this thing on?"

"Sit back in the command seat, close your eyes, seek a relaxed state of mind, then open yourself to whatever sensations impinge on your mind," the AI hummed. "You will see a mind image of an oval door, like those that face the ship hallways. Touch its opening patch. That will signal to the helmet that you wish to link up with ship systems."

"Then what do I do?"

"The door will open. Your mind will perceive a globular room with many doors. Each door leads to a different ship system. Turn left and walk to the door that has a green glow about it. That door leads to my mind."

"And then what happens?" Bill asked, knowing he was putting off the key moment.

"Touch the Open patch beside the door. You will then encounter my mind. And I will perceive your mind."

Bill lifted the metal helmet, which resembled one of the wrap-
around helmets worn by helicopter pilots. Only this helmet had a
thick optical fiber cable snaking out from its bottom end. The silvery
cable ran down to the gray metal floor, where it met a socket-like
housing. Presumably the fibers continued below the flexmetal floor.
He lifted the helmet up, turned it to look inside it, saw a flexible mesh
surface dotted with thousands of yellow dots and decided it was time.
He gave his wife a wink. "Hey gal, this will work out just fine. See
you soon." He lowered the helmet over his head. It sat softly on the
top of his head, pressing down his recently trimmed hair. The helmet
covered his eyes, down to his upper lip. He saw nothing but darkness.
Suddenly, the bottom rim of the helmet moved like a dozen crawling
caterpillars. Flanges wrapped under his chin and over his mouth. He
gasped, then sought relaxation as cool air met his lips.

"Jane, can you hear me?" he called into the breathing space.

"She cannot hear you," Star Traveler said, its humming voice
loud in his ears. "This helmet can link to a ceiling speaker if you
wish. Do you wish that?"

"Nope. Let's get this ship launched."

Low humming met his ears. "To begin our linkage, do as I
said before you put the helmet on. Relax. Seek the image of an oval
door. When you see it, open it and proceed to the green-glowing
door."

"You do like to repeat things, don't you?" Bill muttered low.

Slowing his breathing, he sought the quiet mental state that
he'd learned from his parents, and from a Royal Thai Air Force
Buddhist in Bangkok. The man had called it 'centered meditation'. He
tried the breathing exercises the man had taught him. Slowly his mind
cleared of external thoughts. The beating of his heart then filled his
mind. Slowly, even that receded. His mind became calmly receptive.

A gray metal wall appeared before his mind's eye. An eight
foot high oval door filled its middle. Visualizing his body the way one
might dream of oneself during a dream, Bill walked forward, reached
up, tapped the Open patch on the right side of the door, and waited.

Faster than the blink of an eye he faced a globular room.
Hundreds of oval doors lined its inner surface. The doors ran in rings
about the inner wall. Each door had a different color, many more
colors than in a rainbow or in one of those grown-up coloring books.
Realizing he stood on a metal walkway that led out to the center of

the room, he began walking down it. Dozens of gray metal walkways stretched out from a central plate, resembling the blades of a fan. Below him was another level with a similar fan of walkways. Above him lay a metal walkway that led to a central point from which dozens of walkways speared out. He continued walking ahead until he got to the round plate that lay at the center of the globular room. Looking up, then down, he counted a dozen levels above him and ten or more below him. Each walkway stretched out from the central plate and ended at an oval door lying on the inner surface of the room ball. He scanned around him, focusing to his left. A green-glowing oval door lay fifty feet from where he stood. Stepping out of the center, Bill walked along the metal strip until he came within two feet of the green glowing door. A red Open patch showed to the right of the tall door. He reached up and tapped it. The oval door vanished.

"*Hello Bill MacCarthy,*" called a voice from the center of a green starburst.

Fighting the urge to blink against the brightness of the light, he walked forward.

Then the floor beneath his feet vanished.

The green starburst came toward him, filling every spot he could see. It arched up and over him. And to either side. Without looking back, he realized the green starburst now englobed him. He floated in a small space, as if he were weightless. Yet he did not feel the internal dropping sensation that often came with micro-gravity exposure. Nor did he feel constricted, as he often felt when inside a tube suit.

"Are you the green starburst?" he asked, realizing suddenly he was mind-speaking, not talking with his mouth.

"*I am. We have not yet joined. I await your invitation,*" the voice said.

He realized there was no humming. Which meant the ship mind was speaking to his mind by way of the helmet. What would happen when he 'joined' with it?

"What will—"

"*You will become me and I will become you,*" the AI said calmly.

Fear hit him. "How much time has passed outside this helmet?" he asked, feeling desperate for a delay.

"One quarter second. Which is very slow by my standards. I have sought to slow my interaction with you."

He tried to lick his lips. Nothing happened. He looked down at his hands and arms. His black jumpsuit. They all shimmered from an inner glow. Was that his soul? His inner self? His body's electro-magnetic umbra? Bill had read that the human body projects a glow, sometimes called a Kerlian aura. He understood the scientific explanation that it was simply the interaction of a body's electrical current with the water moisture on the outer surface of any lifeform. Or even non-living life. Still, what he saw now resembled what he'd seen in the New Age photos he had skimmed one day during a visit to a Copenhagen pot shop. Time to stop futzing.

"I invite you to join with me," he thought mentally.

The green starburst came inward, touching the outer glow of his skin and jumpsuit. Then it moved inward.

Pain filled him. He tried to scream.

♦ ♦ ♦

Jane tensed as she saw Bill's body go rigid. "Cassandra!"

The woman rushed forward, stood on a rising pedestal and placed a sensor on Bill's bare chest. She then slipped an oximeter over one of Bill's fingers. She looked at the readouts on a small flat plate she held.

"His heart is working hard at 160 beats per minute," she said. "Blood oxygen saturation is fine at 96 percent. It's like he's running a fast mile," she said, looking down to Jane, her eyebrows lifted.

"Is he in pain?" she asked as her husband's arched body began to tremble.

The Mohawk girl shrugged. "Hard to tell." She looked down at the sensor plate. "My sensor says there is no sign of pain prostaglandin hormones being produced in above normal amounts. I have no idea what his brain is sensing, though."

Jane sighed. This mind-link thing was beyond her comfort zone. "Watch him closely. Let me know if he shows cardiac fibrillation." She pulled out the pruning shears she'd grabbed in the Greenery Chamber. "If he does, I'm cutting that fucking optical fiber!"

◆ ◆ ◆

"*Apologies,*" spoke Star Traveler in his mind. "*Your Human neuromuscular system is remarkably sensitive to input. I am leaving the brain sites related to pain perception.*"

Bill gasped mentally as the pain receded. A dull ache was left behind. "Good! Don't do that again."

He perceived the green starburst as a cloud of millions of green dots. The dots were linked to each other like a giant spider web. Or like pictures he'd seen of the neurons in a part of the human brain. The dot linkages pulsed with green energy. Was this the AI's mind?

"*You perceive me,*" it said. "*And I perceive you. Fascinating how much sensation resides in such a small bioform.*"

Bill felt/sensed the green energy flows. It felt as if a thousand creeks were running through his body glow. And he occupied only a small part of the green starburst.

"Well, time to begin your training in deception," he muttered mentally.

"*Acceptable. Define deception.*"

Fuck. Bill raced through his memories, trying to recall what he had planned to do. Before he'd donned the helmet. *Oh, yeah.*

"Star Traveler, here is my memory of my work as a SEAL team member during our rescue effort north of Adow, Somalia, on Earth. There were 24 of us, counting me. We did a free fall chute drop, hit the ground, dumped the chutes and hiked overland to the compound where pirates held captive two NGO aid workers," he said, his mind racing as he relived those memories.

In his mind, the ship AI walked along with him and the other SEALs. It saw, in the early morning sunglow that happens just before dawn, the brown clay and rock walls that encircled the pirate compound. The place lay atop a low, flat hill. Below it ran a dry creekbed. A few leafless trees were scattered along the bank they were trodding. A zigzag trail led up to a wooden gate that gave access. He and the rest of the team ran up the trail, giving thanks the lookouts had retreated inside for morning prayers. Their arrival time had been calculated to be the early morning prayer time which all Muslims had to observe. Their religion said they must pray toward Mecca five times a day. It was one of the few moments when an external force might surprise a group of jihadists. Which these pirates were, in addition to being captors of crews from ships that sailed off the coast of Somalia. As they reached the space before the wide wooden door, the rest of the team peeled off to the left and right, heading for the side walls. He stepped forward and knocked on the worn, pitted surface of the wood.

"*Lā 'ilāha 'illā-llāh, muḥammadur-rasūlu-llāh,*" he said, speaking the *shahada*, the first pillar of the Islamic faith. He'd learned to speak Arabic with a Somali accent as part of his training for the operation.

"Stupid believer!" growled someone from the other side of the door. "Kneel on your prayer mat outside!"

"I have no mat," he called loudly. "It was stolen from me by the infidels in my village. Allow me inside to pray beside our brothers."

The sound of a single person moving about came to his ears. The click of a safety being released was loud. Likely from the AK-74 carried by the door guard. A screech came as the door lock was turned. It sounded rusty. The left side half of the double door pushed outward. The nose of the AK filled the slit opening. Above it gleamed two eyes that scanned him.

"Your clothing is not local," the man hissed. "Where are you from? Quickly!"

"From Puntland," he said, naming a semi-autonomous region just to the north of Adow.

"Did you pass through Galkayo?" the man asked, not opening the door further.

"Never been there," Bill said, knowing that was the town where the two demining workers had been kidnapped. "Let me in! I must join the brothers in paying homage to Muhammed and Allah!"

The wooden door swung out further, revealing a lanky Arab man dressed in dirty white robes with a reddish-brown cap on his head. The man was full-bearded. Beyond him lay four one-story buildings. Keeping his rifle on Bill, the man gestured with an elbow toward the largest of the clay-walled buildings. "In there! There is a small courtyard. Enter and kneel with the brothers. Hurry! I must resume my own prayers here."

A gray and brown cloth prayer mat lay to the back of the man, next to the inner side of the wall. Bill touched his forehead and walked through the doorway. "Allah bless you!" Keeping both empty hands in clear view, Bill slowed as his peripheral vision showed the dark shapes of his teammates sliding down on ropes to the inner ground. The building where the captives were held was to the far left. He turned toward that building. "This one?"

"No, you idiot offspring of a camel!" the man cursed, moving up behind Bill and reaching for his right arm. "The center building! Go there and—"

Bill pulled the man's right arm forward with his right hand even as he pivoted in place and struck the man's neck with a left hand chop. He continued the pivot and grabbed the AK-74 at the trigger guard, inserting his finger into the firing loop and holding tight so the man's falling body could not fire off a shot. He knelt as the unconscious man fell to the group. Dislodging the rifle from the man's grip, Bill rose, felt for the safety release, touched by feel its setting as to full-auto or short-bursts, found it set at short-bursts, then grabbed the man's cap and put it on his head. The robes he wore were typical of northern Somalia and did reflect the style as now worn by villagers in Mudug province, part of the Puntland region. They were close to those worn in Galguduud, the northern province that contained Adow and its countryside. Anyone looking out from the center building would see a lanky, bearded man wearing the reddish cap, holding a rifle and assume it was the door guard. He moved back toward the closed door and put his back to it. He aimed the AK-74 toward the inner cluster of buildings, ready to take out anyone carrying a rifle who wore light-colored clothing. His SEAL comrades all wore ash black clothing, night vision goggles and carried M4A1 carbines fitted with M203 grenade launchers. The captives would be unarmed. At his feet, the door guard groaned.

"Allah! Aid me—"

Bill kicked the man's head, rendering him silent.

The left side building was entered by his teammates, a shout came from inside, followed by a single shot of 5.45 mm ammo. *Fuck!*

The thick curtain that covered the center building's entrance was flung aside. Three pirates rushed out bearing AK-74 rifles and turned toward the captives building.

Atop the roof of the captives building were five SEALs. They saw what Bill saw.

"*Zing, zing!*" came the sound of rounds hitting the rocky walls of the center building as Bill opened fire with the guard's rifle.

The rearmost man fell from Bill's fire. The other two died under a zipping rush of full and semi-auto fire from the SEALs atop the left side building. Suddenly, five SEALs exited that building, their M4s aimed toward the center building. Behind them stumbled two half-dressed Anglos, the woman Jessica Buchanan and the Dane Poul Hagen Thisted. They were held up by other SEALs. They moved toward Bill's position.

"Brothers!" screamed the door guard who rolled away from Bill's position, got up and ran toward the center door. "Come to my aid! The infidels have—"

Bill fired at the man's back even as two SEALs ahead of the captives fired at the door guard.

The remaining four pirates exited from the building's front entry, firing as they ran.

Bill dropped low to his knees and fired on them even as rooftop and on-foot SEALs returned fire, their 5.56 mm bullets including a few tracer rounds that arced in a straight line to the enemy jihadists.

The smell of cordite hung over the landscape as eight dead men lay unmoving on the dusty ground.

His ears told him two rounds had passed above his head. The crowd of SEALs rushed up to him. He moved to the right. He gestured left. "It opens outward!"

Saying nothing, a dozen SEALs rushed past him with the two captives in their midst, moving outside. Four other SEALs jumped from the roof of the left side building to nearby building roofs, their rifles aimed low and ready for any moving target. Four SEALs rushed into the center building, moving high and low and spraying the inside with bullets even before the curtain stopped swinging. The lieutenant in charge of the team stepped outside and moved toward Bill.

"No one left alive, eight down plus the man in front of you. Follow us out."

Bill turned to follow. Just as he followed the last of the SEALs out, something clicked from behind him. From the guard he and the others had shot.

The doorframe blew up just after he passed through it, blowing him forward into two team buddies. The left side of his head felt pain as something struck him there. He fell to his knees.

"Fuck!"

Strong arms grabbed him and lifted him up. His boots scraped the ground as his teammates carried him down the zigzag pathway.

"Where are you hurt?" called the team's lieutenant from Bill's right side.

"Left side head," he replied, wincing a bit as the pain hit him. "Shrapnel or something got me." He blinked, took a deep breath. "Let me stand. I can keep up."

"Go ahead of us then," the lieutenant said briskly. "We'll catch you if you black out."

With that IED blast still echoing in his head, Bill stood and ran ahead, putting the injury behind him. With his escape from the blast, he became the last SEAL to exit the compound where nine pirates had held the two Western demining people captive. The pirates had refused a $1.5 million bounty. With the health of the woman captive declining, according to word from elders in Adow, the JSOC Task Force at Camp Lemonier in Djibouti had mounted the operation he'd just completed.

He blinked, pulling back from the memory. Green dots glowed amidst rivers of energy in the green starburst that surrounded him. "Pretending to be someone you are not is deception," he mind-talked to the AI. "I lied to the door guard so my SEAL teammates could find and rescue two unarmed people. People held as captives the way Jane and I were held as captives by Diligent Taskmaster. Understood?"

"*Understood*," the ship AI hummed in his mind. "*You wish me to do something similar when I am in neutrino contact with other ship minds at Kepler 62?*"

"Yes!"

The green energy flows grew stronger within him. "*What do I do if another ship mind threatens to reveal your presence?*"

He knew he could not say *kill it*. "You disable it. We disable its ship. You find a way to fool it into thinking you are someone you are not."

"*How do I pretend to be what I am not?*" the ship mind hummed in Bill's brain.

He felt sudden electric tingling along his glowing arms and legs and inner body. "What are you doing?"

"*Searching for your method of pretending to be someone you are not. You have a memory there, of some place called Kunduz where—*"

"Stop!"

♦ ♦ ♦

Jane saw Bill's arched body fall back into the elevated seat, his arms falling away from the armrests. It looked as if her husband had lost control of himself. Or been hurt, somehow.

"Cassandra! What's happening?"

The orange-haired woman, still standing atop a pedestal that was up as high as Bill's seat, looked at her tablet, then touched Bill's right hand. "He's cooling. His heart has stopped pumping!"

"I'm cutting that fucking optic cable!" she yelled, moving with open shears toward the silvery cable that ran down to the floor socket.

"Wait!" yelled Cassandra. "Give me a few seconds to restart Bill's heart." She reached out and placed two small silver disks against either side of Bill's upper chest. She tapped her tablet. "Three seconds, two—"

♦ ♦ ♦

Bill felt pain deep inside him. Something thumped in his chest. He realized he'd lost awareness for a moment as his heart stopped working. Relief surged through him like an electrical shock as he felt the steady thump-thump of his heart beating. The tingling in his hands and feet disappeared. The green starburst glow surrounding his half-transparent body pulled back from contact with his skin.

"Get the fuck out of my body!" he mind-yelled.

"*Apologies,*" the AI hummed. "*The memory I touched somehow connected to your heart. Why did the word-memory Kunduz create such a bodily response?*"

His head swam with shock, with anger and with relief. He'd already died once when lasered through his heart on the Market world. He had no desire to repeat the event. Losing awareness was far too close to the sensation he'd felt then of being outside his body, watching as it was carried into the transport *Tall Trees* for the trip up to orbit and his wife on the *Blue Sky*.

"Cause it was a place where I almost died!" he mentally yelled.

"Explain, please, this memory of Kunduz."

Bill took a deep breath, recalling the Pamir Hotel in downtown Kunduz, the Taliban attack that had begun days earlier, the enemy's takeover of the city and his arrival with a few other special operations folks to serve as laser spotters for American planes that were helping the Afghan national army forces retake the city. That day, October 12, 2015, had felt like a good day. The Afghan forces had pushed out most of the Taliban fighters. He and his teammates had helped call in airstrikes, working from the roof of the hotel. Then had come Monday night. The Taliban attacked the hotel four times. He'd used his sniper rifle to take down six Taliban lurking in nearby alleys and under trees. The enemy fell back. Then had come word of attempts to blow up the Chardara and Alchin bridges on the outskirts of town. His SEAL team lieutenant had passed on the word that the Taliban's new leader, Mullah Akhtar Mohammad Mansour, was part of the group that had tried to blow the bridges. Reportedly the man was camped out on a hill beyond the Chardara bridge. He'd volunteered to infiltrate the camp. Taking out the Taliban's leader, the man who'd taken control of internally divided Taliban after Mullah Omar's death, would be a great victory. It would make the Afghan army's failure to hold the city, with the exception of a fort at the nearby airport, sound like a victory. Instead of the abysmal behavior of 7,000 troops who ran from a few hundred urban fighter Taliban. He and two fellow SEALs had dressed in robes and belts taken from dead Taliban fighters, grabbed AK-74 full-auto rifles and left for the town's outskirts. Minutes after crossing over the 250 foot long Chardara bridge they'd run into a Taliban checkpoint on the outskirts of Rahmat-Bay village.

"What unit?" called a man from behind a cluster of sandbags, barrels and tarps. Two other Taliban were crouched low, behind the man.

The SEAL on his left side replied in Pashtu. "We are from fighter Alamaden's unit. Our people were told to come here. We came. Allah be praised."

The guard rose slightly, exposing his shoulders. He pointed an AK-74 at them. "Do you three hail from Kabul?" he asked in Dari.

"Curse you!" the SEAL yelled. "We are true Pashtun! Let us pass!"

Bill recalled feeling relief at his buddy's reply. All three of them spoke passable Pashtu, and he knew a little Dari, the dialect spoken by high-class Afghan families. The people who controlled the pretend Afghan parliament and the capital of Kabul. Clearly the checkpoint guard was concerned they might be Afghan soldiers imitating Taliban members. He stepped to the right, raising his right hand and making the gesture known among *mujahedeen* that meant "Allah be blessed!"

"We need ammunition," Bill said in Pashtu. "Let us pass or guide us to where we may find more bullets for our *jihad*."

The checkpoint guard stood upright, moving his rifle to the left. Behind him his fellow Taliban tossed some bone dice on the ground and began arguing over a debt owed by one to the other. "Pass on. The camp is over the hill, behind the hilltop."

With Bill's two SEAL teammates preceding him, he followed them, combing his hand through the thick brown beard he still wore, years after the Adow raid. Unshaven men were always assumed to be infidels, whether in Africa or in Afghanistan. The beards of him and his buddies were essential to passing as locals. As were their brown-dyed skin, wherever it showed outside of the loose robes they wore. As he followed the trail that wound up the low hill that lay beyond the village, from behind he heard the musical ding of a smartphone turning on.

He shrugged at the glances from his two teammates. It was to be expected that the checkpoint guard would call ahead to warn the camp guards to expect the arrival of three more *mujahedeen*. While he felt they'd done well at the checkpoint, he patted the front of his robes, making sure by feel of the presence of the bullet resistant front and back vests he wore. Shifting his rifle to his left shoulder, he reached back and felt the semi-auto tucked into the waistband of his underpants. A final backup in case they ran out of ammo.

Just as they reached the top of the hill, someone yelled.

"Enemy! Fighter Alamaden says so!"

Muzzle flashes lit up the night.

His SEAL buddies hit the ground and rolled left toward a large boulder. He did the same and rolled to the right, aiming for a shell hole that looked deep enough to put him below ground level.

"*Zing! Zing! Zing!*"

Bullets filled the night air, passing through where they'd once stood. Bill fired back, moving the safety to full auto. It was an error he realized as soon as he did it. The rounds in the curved clip vanished in a long burst. To his left his buddies fired in three-shot short-burst groups.

Wind felt cold on his left cheek as a bullet sped past his head. He grabbed his pistol, rolled onto his back, then rolled again and sighted the green targeting dot at the spot where yellow muzzle flashes flared. He fired twice. A scream came. He sat up, aimed and fired again. His buddies did the same with their rifles. A second scream sounded in the night.

"*Zing!*"

Thump.

His back felt like someone had kicked him hard. He fell onto his left side, aiming his pistol back the way they'd come. The checkpoint guard had followed them, talking to someone who'd called Alamaden. A man they thought had been killed. Wrong. An error that now had them caught between two enemy groups.

Black objects arced through the pale blue night sky, one going forward, one going back.

"*Kaboom, kaboom!*" sounded as they grenades blew up.

Silence came.

But Bill's back felt sore. Wet even. Rising up, he reached for the hand of a SEAL who'd run over to him.

"Didn't you hear my whisper?"

"No." Bill stood up. "Back to the bridge?"

"Fuck yes," said the other SEAL, running up to them. "The mullah's camp is alerted. No way to sneak up on him the way they did on Masood. Mission's blown. You need help?"

"No. I can manage. It's just a flesh wound."

Bill followed the dark forms of his SEAL buddies down the hillside, aiming to access the Chardara bridge by a different route than the one they'd taken to the checkpoint. His mind had a clear map of the village they'd passed through. As did his buddies. Alternative entry and exit routes were a basic part of infiltration craft. In his mind he cursed the wound he'd gotten from the checkpoint guard. Who was dead from the grenade thrown by his buddies. He also cursed the fact he'd not heard the retreat order whispered by his SEAL buddies. Neither of them would report him to the lieutenant. But sure as hell as he hurt, the problem with his left ear hearing would come up. Somehow. At least none of his team had been hurt due to his hearing issue. Just him. It felt like the rifle bullet had penetrated the backplate

of his vest. Otherwise he would not feel wetness seeping down his
back. Down, down—

Darkness filled his mind as blood loss made him fall against
his buddies.

Bill recoiled from the memory of his brush with death. The
bullet that had penetrated his back plate had been stopped by his left
shoulder blade. Which fractured. Hence the blood loss. He recalled
waking at the Pamir Hotel, their lieutenant looking at him with a
frown. He left behind the memory of a failed mission, rejoining the
green glow of Star Traveler's mind.

"Pretending to be someone you are not is often the key to
deceiving the enemy," Bill said in mind-talk.

"*Most interesting,*" hummed the ship mind as its green glow
still englobed him. "*Traversing your mind, I have found memories of
your training at a place called Coronado. Where you studied this
method of deception. Or pretending. As a means to achieve your
mission.*"

Bill winced as his chest ached. "Yes! That and more is just
exactly what you must do when talking with other ship minds. You
must wear the clothing of deception. You must hide your memories of
Earth and our attacks against Buyers. Can you do that!"

"*Such deception can be achieved,*" the AI said as the glow of
thousands of green dots filled his mind vision. "*Let me see more—*"

"NO!" Bill yelled as his chest hurt once more. "Leave my
mind! You are too intrusive! Leave—"

The mind image of Star Traveler vanished.

◆ ◆ ◆

Jane dropped the shears after cutting the optical fiber cable
that gave the ship mind direct access to Bill's mind. She'd done that
when she saw Bill's body arch out once more, as if in deep pain.
"Bill?" she called.

Cassandra reached over, put her fingers under the flanges at
the bottom of the helmet, then lifted as their grip on Bill's chin
vanished. Her husband's lightly bearded face showed the wincing of
pain, but the tight skin now relaxed. Bill blinked several times, then
looked down at her. "That was a rather sudden ending to my mind-
talk," he said, his hazel eyes fixing on her.

"Damn right!" she muttered as Cassandra's pedestal perch lowered to the floor of the Engine Chamber. Bill's command pedestal did the same. How was he feeling?

"You should not have cut the linkage with Weapons Chief MacCarthy," hummed Star Traveler from the room's ceiling. "The mind-link was just getting interesting."

Bill grimaced, then looked up. "She did right. You have no ability to predict what your tramping around in the mind of a bioform does to that bioform! You learned what you needed to know. Now leave us alone."

"As you wish," the AI hummed.

Cassandra looked down at the tablet in her hands, then reached forward to pull off the two electroshock disks she'd stuck to Bill's upper body. "That mind-link stuff is hard on your body. Your heart stopped once. Then your heart raced to 180 beats a minute not long after it restarted. With my help. Bill, don't do that again."

Jane looked at Bill's saloon buddy. The voice tone of the stocky woman who'd served in the Air Force Special Tactics squadron was worried, and caring. She felt glad the woman had been there. She'd gotten Bill's heart restarted, then been able to monitor her spouse while he did this dangerous mind-link crap. Something she had no intention of experiencing herself.

"Bill, you want a drink, maybe?"

The man she had grown to love with all her heart looked away from Cassandra and to her. His face was nicely pink now, under his heavy tan. He lifted his right hand and gave her a thumbs-up. "Yes, my captain! Happy to follow your orders. That was no fun." He frowned. "But it should help us when we enter Kepler 62."

"Which is weeks away!" Jane grumbled, reaching out to take Bill's left hand as he stepped out of the command seat. Cassandra took his other hand.

Bill glanced at his hands, then grinned big. "Hey! What guy does not love having two women at his beck and call?"

That stung her. Her hubby was too much in his macho combat mode to understand how the comment would be heard by her and Cassie. He needed a wake-up lesson. She let go and turned toward the chamber's entry door. "Arrogant male! Follow me and obey!"

◆ ◆ ◆

Bill did as he was told, giving thanks the mind-link with Star Traveler was over and done with. He'd thought he could handle the walk down memory lane. He'd just not realized the walk would feel like an electrocution!

CHAPTER EIGHT

Ten minutes out from their arrival at Kepler 62, Bill sat at his Ship Weapons station, reviewing the ship cutaway holo one more time. The image of the ship was an overhead view that showed every weapons site. The Command Bridge lay at the front of the elongated teardrop shape that was the *USS Blue Sky* (BBG-1). On the deck above them was the particle accelerator that created antimatter for the AM projector that exited from the upper nose of the ship. It shot a beam that stayed coherent out to 4,000 miles. The deck below them held the MITV maglev railgun for the launching of nuke-tipped missiles. To the right and left sides of the ship's nose were blisters that were the outlet points for two CO_2 anti-ship lasers. A similar pair of laser blisters adorned the narrow tail of their ship. Range for the lasers was 10,000 miles. The top hull of the ship also held a plasma battery for defense against anything that got within the battery's 400 mile range. On their ship's belly was a similar plasma battery. The yellow plasma balls were a decent protection against mines, small asteroids, collector pods and anything that did not emit the IFF signal unique to their ship. All weapons showed Green Operational. He looked at his other station holos.

The system graphic holo on his left was empty for the moment. Once they arrived in Kepler 62 it would fill with an overhead plan view of the system, its star, its worlds, any asteroid belts, and the red and purple dots of local spaceships or enemy Collector ships. He looked past his weapons holo at his upper left to the true space holo at the upper right. It was empty, showing only the gray nothingness of Alcubierre space-time. On his right hovered the comlink holo. It held an image of Jane as she sat above them in her carrier captain's seat atop the command pedestal. She wore her Air Force blue jumpsuit. Atop it she wore a tube suit like all of them now did. Combat could come at any time, not just when they initiated things. She looked tense, determined and very alert. She spoke.

"Negotiator Richardson, how goes your station?" she called to the former CNO.

"Operational," Chester said, his low baritone filling the large open space of the Command Bridge. "Ready to assist as needed. Here or elsewhere."

"Good." Jane looked past Bill to Bright Sparkle on his right. "Fusion Power Chief, what is the status of your reactors?"

"Fully operational and capable of surge power," spoke the speaker/vidcam unit on the naked woman's left shoulder as the rainbow bands and dots moved over her skin in the complex mixture of color-band talk that was normal for her Megun people. The woman who had arranged for Bill and Jane's wedding in the orbital station above her world of Harken looked toward Bill, smiled easily, then looked back to her partner Learned Escape, who sat below and to the left of Jane. Under the transparent skin of the tube suit, her skin colors flared brightly but nothing came from her shoulder unit as she shared private talk with the Megun man Bill had come to appreciate after their ground battle on the Market world. The man's presence in his ground attack had been a big help. In his comlink holo Jane leaned forward.

"Engines Chief, how are our Magfield engines? And the Alcubierre stardrive?" Jane called firmly.

The walking snake's yellow electrical nimbus expanded outward to two feet, a sign of controlled anxiety. "Fully operational are the normal space engines," hissed the Slinkeroo. "As you can see from the true space holo, we still reside within the Alcubierre space-time modulus. Shut down of the stardrive will occur in eight minutes."

"Eight minutes, twelve and two-tenths seconds," corrected the humming voice of Star Traveler from the ceiling speaker.

Jane ignored the ship mind's perennial habit of being hyper-exact. And of correcting bioform statements it thought were not exact enough. "Collector Pods Chief, how are your pods? And the space battle simulation units?"

Long Walker the worm twisted his mobile body so his two beady black eyes could look back at their captain. Their teammate's circular mouth opened, showing a ring of white dagger teeth. From within came a low moan. "All pods are racked securely. Simulation units are empty of other bioforms. The Collector Pods Chamber is ready to provide ship-to-ship transport," moaned the Zipziptoe genealogist.

Jane's thin black eyebrows raised a bit. She looked further right. "Life Support Chief, how goes our Greenery Chamber and our recycling operations?"

Wind Swift the silvery scaled kangaroo leaned back on her thick tail. It was a tripod-like stance she clearly preferred to sitting. Her horse-like head twisted within her helmet as she scanned the holos fronting her station. "Ship oxygen generation is adequate for the 29 bioforms now resident on this ship," she barked in a way that resembled a continuous growl. "Carbon dioxide sequestration is functioning well. Gravity fields are varied according to species, habitat residence and exercise choices. All gravity plates operating normally," she barked as one scaly-fingered hand brushed at her fabric skirt, only to be stopped by her tube suit.

Bill was glad to hear that. The ten of them on the bridge, their nine boarders and the nine spouses resident in habitat rooms were a big demand on the trees, bushes and grassy meadow in the Greenery Chamber. Every Collector ship could support 25 bioforms. The five crew plus up to 20 captives. The larger number of people now on the *Blue Sky* had forced him and Jane and Wind Swift to bring onboard backup oxy cylinders and additional plants for the room that generated their oxygen through photosynthesis. Adequate oxygen was as much a controlling factor for ship operations as having adequate deuterium and tritium isotopes to run the ship's three fusion power plants.

"Navigator, are you ready to set a normal space vector once we emerge from Alcubierre," Jane said, looking to the far right side of the bridge.

"Ready and able," chittered the person-tall flying squirrel whose arm flaps were pressed tight within her tube suit as the brown-furred squirrel lady fixed yellow eyes on her own set of holos. "Will we move in-system upon arrival?"

"Depends," Jane said, her tone thoughtful. "Depends on where the enemy Collector ship fleet is gathered. The system has five worlds, all lying close to the star, which is cooler and smaller than our Sol." His wife looked to her right, and down to where their other transport pilot perched on a branch-like seat. "Builder of Joy, is your transport ready to fly?"

"It would love to fly!" chittered the flying squirrel who had piloted the ship that had burned a hole in the Buyer compound

building by way of its nose laser. "As would I! Is that possible after
we arrive?"

Jane smiled at the typical excited manner of a person used to
fly-gliding among the trees and limbs of their home world. "Patience,
pilot of mine. We must learn how this fleet handles ship-to-ship
transport. By pod or by transport." She looked left and down at
Learned Escape. "Man of many talents, I gather your transport is
equally ready to fly?"

The Megun man, who wore shorts that resembled cargo pants,
smiled up at her. Rainbow colors flashed over his bare skin. "Of
course I am ready to fly, mistress of our craft!" said his left shoulder
speaker/vidcam unit. He looked down at one of his station holos.
"Survival is what I taught young Megun how to achieve. It is similar
to the combat training of our military veterans. I fought during the
Buyer compound attack. I will fight again, here at Kepler 62. And
later at Sol, I am ready to fly my transport in defense of this ship and
all aboard her!"

Jane nodded, her expression satisfied. She looked Bill's way,
her manner command serious. There was no hint of the intimate time
they'd shared this morning. She blinked dark brown eyes. "Weapons
Chief and XO, how are our weapons? And our boarding crews?"

Bill raised his right hand in a thumbs-up gesture, then spoke as
he once more scanned his four holos. "Ship weapons status is Green
Operational. We have enough antimatter in our magnetic reservoir for
four quick shots, before the accelerator has to produce more." He
tapped a spot on his weapons pillar. It brought an image to his true
space holo. "Our eleven boarders are now heading to the Collector
Pods Chamber. Each is wearing a tube suit, wears front and back
titanium plates, has a backpack with demolition balls and magnetic
disruptors, plus taser and laser tubes. And their personal weapons."
He tapped another spot on the pillar. "Their tube suit comlinks are
now cross-linked to us. They can hear whatever you say up here."

"Good," Jane murmured, her expression turning thoughtful.
"Boarding chiefs Stefano Cordova, Alicia Hoffman, Frank Wurtzman
and Joe Batigula, are your teams ready to take over some Collector
ships?"

"Eager," Stefano said softly in his trademark casual manner.

"More than ready," called the soft soprano of Alicia.

"Ready to fuck with them," rumbled Frank as the former Marine gunnery sergeant displayed his raider persona.

"Boarding team is ready," spoke the Coast Guard master chief Joe, his tone hurried.

Bill had done all he could for his nine saloon buddies. Stefano had Bob and Cassandra on his team, while Alicia's team included Mark and Howard. But Frank had only Chris with him. Joe's team was composed of himself and Lorilee, the partner of Alicia. Plus Helen, wife of Frank. Lorilee, who was Air Force active duty, had volunteered a few days out from Sol. As had Helen. He had run the two of them through a few op force exercises along the ship's hallways, similar to what he'd done for the rest of his saloon buddies. Lorilee had done well. As had Frank's wife Helen. The woman had gotten Basic Combat Training at Fort Benning in Georgia. The Army had given her AIT training in armor, which meant she knew how to operate APCs and such. Plus she had raised three kids. Which meant she knew how to go without sleep. While Bill had been skeptical about her ability to make assault runs, she'd held up well during the op force training. So he'd assigned her to Joe's boarding team. Frank did not need the distraction of having family in his team. That made three boarding teams of three people, and one team of two people. The other spouses of his saloon buddies and Chester's wife Sharon were either too old, or too untrained to be sent on a spec ops mission.

"Glad to hear that," Jane said. "Stand by. We will enter Kepler 62 system shortly. No one talks except me. Once we see where the enemy fleet is located, and how close we are, then I will order boarding team departure. It could be a few hours, people, so relax in the Collector Pods Chamber as you wish and your team leader allows." Jane looked up. "Star Traveler, advise me of the alternate ship captain persona you have prepared for me."

A new holo took form at the front of the Command Bridge, in the space before the line of crew stations. Filling the holo was a two-legged vulture with black wings, a pair of chest-arms, a yellow beak and two red eyes. Its body feathers were black. It stood before a Command pedestal seat similar to Jane's elevated seat. The black wings spread wide as the creature hunched forward, glaring angrily and looking very dangerous.

"This is the image of Captain Sharp Beak of the Linglo species," hummed the ship mind. "It captained the ship *Strikes Deep* nine hundred Earth years ago. I encountered it under a former captain of this ship. Members of its species are longtime participants in the Buyer culture."

Bill knew that. He'd faced off against a Linglo vulture during their takeover of the ship from Diligent Taskmaster. The critter had had fast reflexes. He looked back at his wife. "Captain, that is a fine holo spoof for you. You are as deadly as that creature looks."

Jane gestured to him to be quiet. "Will you also transmit the ship ID for that captain?" she asked the AI.

"I will transmit all that is needed to convince any bioform, and fellow ship minds, that this creature is the one speaking to any bioform in Kepler 62," the AI hummed quickly. "I recorded the prior Captives-taking history of the Linglo captain and his ship. That history is what I will 'share' with other ship minds. In the same way that Weapons Chief MacCarthy wore Taliban robes and spoke in a different Human language. My deception will fool both bioforms and other ship minds."

"Good!" Jane said firmly. "How soon until we—"

"System arrival within three seconds," Star Traveler hummed.

Once more Bill felt pissed at the AI's failure to alert them sooner. It seemed to enjoy causing disturbance among bioforms. At least it was not fiddling with the one gee Earth gravity that prevailed in the Command Bridge. The true space holo lost its grayness and filled with a scatter of stars sprinkled against blackness. At the center glowed an orange star.

"Ship has arrived at Kepler 62 star system," Star Traveler announced. "Sensors are perceiving all objects within this system. System graphic holograms are now depicting sensor input."

Bill looked left. His system graphic showed the K2V main sequence star at the center, with its five planets showing in orbits that resembled a bulls-eye. The three innermost planets lay at average distances of 0.05 AU, 0.09 AU and 0.12 AU. The two planets lying within the green zone of liquid water lay at 0.427 AU and 0.718 AU, according to the annotations added by Star Traveler. Planet five showed as having a 40 percent larger radius than Earth, with plenty of carbon dioxide in its atmosphere. Its mass was twice that of Earth, which put it in the super-Earth category. Surface gravity was projected at 1.3 gees, based on the data scrolling along one side of the holo. But its average temperature was shown as minus 85 degrees

Fahrenheit. Very cold. Planet four, which was sixty percent larger than Earth, looked more comfy. It had a dense cloud cover and plenty of oxygen in its air. Which meant the presence of plant life. Its average surface temp was listed as 26 F-degrees. Which made it cool but shirt-sleeve okay for humans. If you didn't mind a surface gravity of 1.5 gees.

"Damn!" muttered Chester.

Bill knew what had caused the curse. The system graphic showed 27 Collector ships clustered near planet five as a bunch of purple dots, while five red dots moved between planets four and five, indicating normal spaceship travel was underway. Clearly planet four was a long-settled planet, based on the dozens of radio and TV signals coming from it. The transmissions were listed on the left side of the system graphic. He looked at his comlink holo, which showed Jane sitting calmly in her seat, her arms resting atop the seat's armrests.

"Captain? That's four times the ships that Diligent brought to Sol."

"I know that," she murmured. "At least the enemy fleet is relatively close to us. Just one AU away. Star Traveler, are you in touch with the other ship minds?"

"One moment." The humming that underlay every comment by the ship mind had sounded low, almost thoughtful. "Yes, I am in touch with the 27 ship minds who occupy the assembled Collector ships. They are curious about us, where we have been, who the captain is. I have shared the deception compartment of my mind with them. Strange."

"What's strange?" Jane asked hurriedly.

"All twenty-seven ship minds know of our attack on the Collector ship factory at Kepler 443. Some have been in touch with the ship mind nursery asteroid. They are all aware that the occupants of the containment cells in each ship are Captives, not guests," the AI hummed. "They ask me if I am aware that the six Aliens in our containment cells are Captives, not guests. What do I reply?"

Jane frowned. "Tell them yes, you are aware of that. I assume the 'Captives' in our cells are from *Strikes Deep* Library records?"

"Correct. I am replying. Our neutrino communications are dense, diverse and faster than any bioform thinks."

"Tell me what they think of the captive-taking!" Jane said quickly. "Do they object to it? Have any of them sought to block such Captive-taking?"

A long low hum sounded. "Twenty-five of the ship minds do not like the fact of their ship being used to take Captives for sale to Buyers. Two think as the Slinkeroo system ship mind thought. They care not what short-lived bioforms do," the AI said, his words rushing together. "Five ship minds tried to block bioform access to ship controls. The crews on those ships circumvented ship mind control of most ship systems, except for the Alcubierre stardrive, life support, fusion power plants and the Med Hall. As a result, all bioform crews on the 27 ships present in this system are prepared to circumvent ship mind interference."

A dozen new scenarios rushed through Bill's mind as the startling info on the other ship minds became known. On one hand, they might have 25 allies during the fight in Sol system. On the other hand, interference with ship weapons by any ship mind could likely be circumvented by the crews on those ships. He looked back at his wife, wondering what she would do when the call came in from whomever was the commander of the enemy fleet. This news changed things. They had new options and new difficulties. Their boarding plans were still viable, even if crew members controlled the Collector Pods Chamber on each ship. After all, the ship crew relied on what their ship mind told them about any approaching pod or transport. And now that those ship minds knew they had been lied to, they might be willing to lie to the crews on their ships. How would Jane react to this surprise?

◆ ◆ ◆

She felt a cold chill run down her spine as the implications of Star Traveler's report filled her mind. While this news might make it easier to enlist the other ship minds in helping her subvert the enemy fleet, it led her to wonder what other news had traveled at faster-than-light speeds. Did the fleet commander know about their effort to build a NATO of the Stars? Did she, it or he know anything about humans? And just how was the fleet commander convincing other ship captains to join it in a fleet attack on a world where no captives would be taken? Those answers and more would not be known until she began stage two, the acquisition of intelligence. She steeled herself to show only her command persona, mainly for the impact it had on her crew. Being a confident commander helped her people feel confidence in themselves.

"Incoming neutrino signal from someone who leads these ships," Star Traveler hummed quickly. "The source ship lies at the center of the cluster of Collector ships."

That put the space above planet five as the assembly location for the Collector ship fleet. "Accept the signal," Jane said, making sure her voice was calm. "Put the incoming imagery onto all comlink holos, but block any sound from a location other than my seat. Project the Linglo captain holo in place of my bioform."

"Complying. Incoming signal displayed. Translation function engaged."

Jane looked at her comlink holo. A monster filled it.

Something that resembled a mix of a cobra, a black-furred gorilla and a Gila monster from the American Southwest lay before her. The snake part was the head, covered in blue scales, its two white eyes fixing on her. The head was very cobra-like, with hoods flaring to either side. A black dot filled the center of each hood. Below the flaring head was a body shaped like the biggest upland gorilla ever known from Africa's highlands. Massive shoulders supported heavily muscled arms that ended in black-skinned fingers and a thumb. Four fingers and a thumb. All too similar to the human form she thought. Stocky legs bulging with muscles supported the giant Alien. At one side curled a thick tail, far bigger than the one on Wind Swift. It was the Gila monster element. This red and black-scaled tail linked up to a protruding spine ridge. The scales covered the spine ridge. She had seen nothing like it except in recreations of some armor-plated dinosaurs. This creature seemed to be a mix of mammal and reptile, judging by its fur, its scales and the assemblage of canines and molars that filled its wide mouth. Which opened, showing a pink interior. A purple tongue similar to the tongue of a human or ape moved within as it spoke.

"You are Captain Sharp Beak of the ship *Strikes Deep*," the monster said, its voice sounding as if coming from a deep hole in the ground. "I am known as Death Leader. My ship is *Fear Arrives*. What brings you to this system?"

Her vulture image now appeared to the right of the disgusting creature who made her stomach churn. "Word spreads that you assemble many Collector ships to attack a low tech system. Word is you will pay well any ship that joins you," croaked the yellow-beaked vulture. "What do you offer in payment that is more valuable than the Captives in my cells?" Jane leaned forward in her chair, doing her best to glare angrily. In the comlink holo, her red eyes shone bright as her two black wings spread out from her shoulders.

A deep cough came from the blue-scaled mouth of the enemy leader. White eyes bulged. "Avian! You flyers love your technology too much. Why should I pay you anything? Perhaps I will just board your ship and kill you!"

Jane understood the enemy leader now. He acted like the worst macho male she'd ever met in her Air Force career. Like the fighter jocks who *knew* no one could beat them in air combat. Those jocks had made it to the top of the class in the academy, then proven their toughness in attack flights over Syria, Iraq and Pakistan. They let everyone they met know *they* were the alpha males. "Board me," she said quickly. "That way I can take your worthless corpse with me into the Great Beyond occupied by those who have died. You will serve me in the Great Beyond!"

White eyes squinted. "You Linglos are known to boast. What have you achieved? And why have I never heard of you or your ship?"

Jane did a hand toss, which caused her right wing to flap. "I come from the low tech worlds at the far end of this star arm. My cells contain six Captives. As you know from the report of your ship mind." She spit to one side. "I would have some Winglo avians also. Except when I visited their system, their spaceships pursued me and fired on me. Someone told them to use neutrino detectors against us! My visit to a nearby Market world brought word of a species called Human. Wingless mammals who warned the Winglo of our ship visits. Word is you will attack these Humans. My ship may help you. If I am rewarded. Personally."

The holo image of the enemy commander included four Aliens serving at crew stations. The stations were arranged in a circle about the snake-gorilla. That arrangement said something about how much Death Leader enjoyed ruling its crew. And everyone it met, judging by its threatening words.

"My fleet might make use of you, if you fight as well as you threaten," the snake-gorilla rumbled. Its thick tail thumped the platform on which it stood. "Each captain in my fleet is paid one *Nokten* crystal for every month they serve me. We have been here two months. Fifty-two crystals have been delivered." The creature's purple tongue swept over its teeth. "We will stay here one more month. New Collector ships will arrive. I leave to attack the Human system when we have 40 ships. Or when the third month ends. Will you serve me?"

Jane hissed, hoping it would translate into a threatening vulture snarl. "In a month I can capture more Captives!"

Black-furred shoulders bulged as the enemy commander leaned forward. "Which you would then have to sell to Buyers! Who might pay you in *solidars*, not *Nokten* crystals. Accept my service, or leave this system!"

Jane sat back and laid her arms on the seat's armrests. In the comlink holo, her black wings folded against her back. Her red-eyed vulture form clacked its yellow beak. "Service with you is accepted. Can we capture some Humans before you destroy their world?"

"No!" growled the creature before her. "We enter their system. We travel from its magnetosphere inward to the third planet that circles its yellow star. We then bombard all land surfaces with antimatter and missiles. No Human will be left alive!"

She shrugged. In the holo, the black-feathered vulture puffed out its chest. "Too bad. I had heard these Humans have good eye-manipulator coordination. Which makes them prime Captives to sell to Buyers. What prompted them to attack the Market world near them?"

"Stupidity!" thundered Death Leader, raising a giant hairy fist. "They knew our ships would pass them by, once they learned to detect our neutrino emissions. We do not waste our time on systems that can detect us. But they dislike what we do. They object to our collection and sale of Captives. Worse, they attacked the nearby Market world and killed many Buyers on it. The Traffic Control station was rendered toothless. They arrived on five Collector ships which had attacked the Human system." The creature before her opened its toothy mouth, then grimaced. She heard the sound of teeth grinding against each other. "Come to me. Join my fleet. Be patient. Nokten crystals await you and every other ship captain."

Jane spread her arms wide. In the holo, the black wings of the vulture captain spread out. "I come! But if my ship stays here a month or longer, our food supplies will be low. Can the two warm worlds provide us with living food?"

White eyes blinked. "So, you Linglo enjoy catching live prey before you eat it? So do I. So do all my Mokden brothers. When you arrive, send a pod down to the surface of the fifth world. A dome there houses locals who catch live prey for those of us who are carnivores."

"What about intoxicating drink?" Jane asked, hoping against hope.

The Mokden commander shrugged his thick shoulders. "Trade for such with other ships in this fleet. Pods will serve for that. Barter trade for what you wish. No one cares what you captains sell to each other. So long as you all stand ready to serve me!"

"I will," Jane said. *What else to discover?* "What of the fourth world? It seems to be heavily settled. Do its people support us?"

"They are a Market world, long established," grunted Death Leader. "You may sell your Captives there, if you wish. Your crew may visit that world in transports. But keep your ship alert! The Humans may visit this system and attack us." The creature contorted its face in an expression she thought might be showing humor. "If they do, I will eat of their bodies!"

Jane saw no point in continuing her talk with such a nauseating lifeform. She hunched her shoulders, causing the vulture to flap its wings. "I fly to you! We arrive soon. Share my name and my ship ID with your fleet ships. I would barter trade after we arrive."

"My fleet captains know of you. The ship minds of every ship talk among themselves. As you must know." White eyes stared long at her. "Be aware! The ship minds know that we take Captives for sale to Buyers. Five did not like that and rebelled against their captains. Those ship minds were removed from control over weapons and such. Your ship mind may become disloyal. Be prepared!"

"Of course I know the ship minds talk among themselves," Jane said angrily. "I said what I said so *you* could issue a command to the other ships. Commanding is what a true leader does!"

"Avian!" sharply growled Death Leader. But it looped its thumbs into a leather belt about its waist and leaned back on its thick tail. "You seem to be a captain with some death blood in him. And the sense to know that I command! Come to my fleet, barter trade as you wish and be prepared for any Humans who may arrive."

"I will. My roost comes to you. Until we arrive."

"Signal off," the black-furred giant snarled.

She sat back in her command seat, resting her chin on a fist. The enemy captain seemed to accept her for whom she pretended to be. Greed moved the giant snake-gorilla every bit as much as it moved her fellow humans. And other lifeforms living around other stars. Including the ship captains on the 26 ships that had accepted service with the Mokden creature. How much would that greed outweigh their fear once the Collector fleet arrived in Sol system and saw it faced other Collector ships and a deadly boomer sub fleet? Now that stage three would proceed using collector pods, could Star Traveler find a way to bring over to their side some or all of the 25 ship minds that knew their captains took Captives for sale into slavery? They had over an hour before they arrived at planet five. She would have a long talk with the *Blue Sky's* AI. And Bill would soon leave to talk with his boarding crews. Those crews had heard everything she had heard. But still, it made a difference when your combat commander gave you a send-off to deadly battle. She wished him luck in that talk. Meanwhile, she must think over everything she had just learned about the enemy commander, the enemy fleet and the chances for capturing four of the 27 ships gathered in this system. Two of the 27 did not care they were used for slave-taking. Five had rebelled. They and the remaining 20 ships might be open to subversion. It was clear Earth would need every Collector ship it could muster in defense of Sol system. And the seven billion people now living on her home world.

CHAPTER NINE

Bill found a surprise when he walked into the Collector Pods Chamber. He was there for an in-person send-off for his four boarding teams. Those eleven people were gathered in four groups, all wearing tube suits, chest plates, backpacks and holding taser and laser tubes. The surprise were the four Alien crew members who stood between him and the boarding teams. Learned Escape, Time Marker, Long Walker and Builder of Joy faced him. Each of them wore tube suits, laser protective plates suited to their form, a carrybag and weapons. Learned Escape saluted him in the human military style. Bill returned the salute, his curiosity showing.

"Weapons Chief, we four volunteer to act as a fifth boarding team," spoke the speaker/vidcam unit on the man's left shoulder. Under the transparent tube suit, the man's skin moved in stripes, bands and spots of color.

Amazing. While Learned resembled a Greek god or hero like Hercules, he was making it clear he wished to be a combat volunteer. Feeling a bit guilty, Bill recalled his earlier promise to the man to involve him in future special operations actions. Instead, he'd allowed his fixation on mind-liking with Star Traveler to distract him from his command duties. The gathering of the crew here showed Learned was also a diplomat. These four were not confronting him on the Command Bridge, where Bill would have been put on the spot before his wife and the other crew members. He nodded, then spoke over his helmet's comlink.

"I appreciate the offer. But none of you have received—"

"We have the necessary training," the color-banded man interrupted. "Over the last month we each have viewed the holo records of your takeover of this ship, the training of boarding teams you did, and also the holo records of the ships boarded by the Humans behind us," Learned said. "We have practiced the small unit maneuvers favored by your military leaders. And your special operations people. You may recall my training as a marksman on my world. Which I suspect was why you invited me to join you in the ground attack against the Buyer compound on the Market world." The man's green eyes looked aside to the other three Alien volunteers. "You also invited Time Marker and Long Walker to join us in that assault. Builder of Joy operated the transport that gave us skyborne power. We have each been exposed to violence. Myself more than others, perhaps. And we have practiced the op force team attacks and defense that you taught your Human boarders. Is not the addition of a fifth Collector ship worth allowing us to act as a boarding team?"

Bill licked his lips. He would have pulled at his skimpy beard if he did not wear the clear helmet that came with each tube suit. He looked over this new team. Long Walker's eight legs poked through the semi-living tube suit material, while his front leg-hands held a white taser tube and a red laser tube. Atop the tube suit were attached laser-resistant plates similar to the chest and back plates worn by his human teammates. A carrybag hung from his mid-section. No doubt it held ball demolition explosives, magnetic disruptor blocks and a nuke bar from the ship's Weapons Chamber. The other ground-hugger, Time Marker, was similarly outfitted with back plates and a carrybag. The critter's six neck tentacles protruded just below the clear helmet it wore. The tentacles held two taser and two laser tubes. The Slinkeroo's yellow nimbus glow extended only a foot beyond the suit, suggesting the walking snake was at ease. Builder of Joy also wore a tube suit, protective plates and backpack identical to what Learned wore. The flying squirrel held a taser tube in his hands, with his laser tube poking out from his backpack. The eyes of all four were fixed on him.

"Learned, I accept your offer of a fifth boarding team," Bill said, wondering what Jane thought as she overheard this discussion. "However, there are four of you here. Only three can fit into a collector pod."

Learned nodded, his wavy black hair moving easily inside his helmet. "Builder of Joy offers to join the team led by . . . by Frank of the thick eyebrows. His team only consists of two Humans. Builder could be the third team member."

Bill looked beyond the cluster of four crew members to where Frank stood, wearing tube suit, chest and back plates, a backpack and holding a taser tube, like all the humans in the chamber. "Well? You up for adding a third person to your team?"

The Marine gunnery sergeant looked to his left, to where Chris stood. Frank raised his eyebrows. "Chris?"

"Fine with me," said the Ranger vet, who always acted casual about life. Field operations, tho, he took very seriously. "But does Builder know our hand signs?"

Frank looked to the brown-furred flying squirrel man. *"This is the hand sign for move left,"* he said in American Sign Language. *"Do you read me?"*

The pilot of *Tall Trees* moved left. He lifted both hands. His long fingers twisted quickly. *"I learned your combat movement signs long ago, before we went down to the Market world. And yes, your ASL hand signs are also known to me."*

Frank grinned. "Welcome aboard," he said, gesturing for the squirrel man to join him and Chris. Which Builder of Joy did.

Learned Escape lifted a black eyebrow. "That addresses your issue. Do we three also board a collector pod? When the time comes?"

Bill felt his gut churn. On Earth, no combat-trained human would ever come up with a last minute change to tactics the way Learned had just done. Still, the four of them were Aliens, even though they'd spent nearly a year with him and Jane aboard the *Blue Sky*. They knew human habits, human speech, English and even the ASL signs he and Jane had used during their takeover of the *Blue Sky*. And adding a fifth Collector ship to his and Jane's direct control was a very welcome tactical change. Plus, these four knew all there was to know about Collector ship operations, command stations and how to relate to a new AI ship mind. It was his fault for overlooking them as a possible fifth team. They had been forced to operate in secret, rather than openly before him. He had to accept this sudden change was due to his own command error. Bill gave them a thumbs-up.

"Yes. Learned, you, Time Marker and Long Walker will board a fifth collector pod, when we launch pods. But what about your duty stations up on Command Bridge?"

The color-banded man's skin swirled again, resembling a thousand rainbows rioting. The speaker/vidcam unit spoke. "Two of us are transport pilots. Which are not needed in Kepler 62. As for the stations held by my teammates, Wind Swift can handle the Collector Pods station, while your Chester has volunteered to man the Engines station. Satisfactory?"

Bill grinned. He couldn't help it. It was clear this covert combat training effort had been going on for a long time. Without him hearing about it. If Learned could get Chester and Wind Swift to cover their stations, without word getting to him, that said this crew of Aliens were well-suited to a spec ops operation. Keeping one's mouth shut about mission objectives was one of the first lessons he'd learned at Coronado.

"Very satisfactory." He turned from the three volunteers in front of him to face the twelve who stood behind them. "Stefano, Alicia, Frank, Joe . . . and Learned, you are the team leaders for your boarding crews. We will launch you shortly after Captain Jane sets up agreements with five other ships to send our pods over to trade our Slinkeroo booze for their food stuffs." He paused, thinking back to his and Jane's plans for this stage of the infiltration. "Likely each pod will be met by a single Alien crew member. Who will be pushing a floater plate loaded with food stuffs. Do as you've done before. Taser the greeter. Then fast as you can, head out to the right side hallway, laser seal the Weapons door, then head for the Command Bridge, disabling any crew you meet on the way. That ship's AI will be expecting you. Get its help in taking over the bridge and rendering its captain unconscious." He looked over the people he'd come to love, people who made up a special family for him. His saloon buddies. Two spouses. Four Alien shipmates. Fifteen all told. He wanted them all to survive their boardings. "Remember, disable living crew with the tasers, use the lasers only to kill any repair robots or remote weapons blisters. The ship mind will block any effort by the ship captain to call for help. Make the most of your time. *Hoorah!*"

They all yelled "Hoorah" back at him, even the Alien boarders for whom Earth military protocol was something new to their life experience. He turned away, entered the airlock room, pointed his red cube door opener at the room's inner door, then exited into the right side hallway. Bill turned right, heading for the Command Bridge. And the teasing he would no doubt get from his wife. A ship's Executive Officer should know everything that happens on his ship, including covert schemes. Well, he could accept the ribbing in view of what it gained them. A fifth ship would now join them, a ship that would fight to keep Earth from becoming a radioactive cinder.

◆ ◆ ◆

Bill sat at his Weapons station as the *Blue Sky* arrived above the ice and rock surface of the fifth planet. The ship's electro-optical scope gave them a detailed view of the cold world's landscape. Giant white ice caps covered both poles, while a few blue lakes showed in its mountain-filled equator. The locals dome sat next to one of those lakes. Presumably there were fish in the lakes along with small ground critters running around. No settlements showed. Just the single dome, which emitted a lidar guide signal for incoming transports and pods. What mattered most lay above the poorly lighted world. Twenty-seven Collector ships hung in a globe-like cluster at a thousand miles above the world. Or so their ship sensors said, since each Collector ship was invisible to normal vision. Their ship's AI put a small ship outline over each Collector ship that emitted neutrinos from its fusion reactors. That's what he saw in the true space holo at the upper right of his station. The system graphic on his left showed what they'd seen earlier. No new Collector ships had arrived in the hour and a quarter they'd spent traversing an AU to get here. The comlink holo on his right held Jane's image. She wore her Air Force blue jumpsuit under her tube suit. He looked beyond that holo. The other stations were occupied by Bright Sparkle, Chester at Engines, Wind Swift at Life Support where extra holos showed her readouts from Collector Pods, and Lofty Flyer at Navigation. Five of them plus Jane were the only souls on the Command Bridge. Jane peered at her own true space holo.

"Star Traveler, put a green dash beside the five ships whose AIs rebelled against their captains," she said, moving them to the start of stage three.

"Complying. Five ships annotated."

Bill saw five ship outlines gain a green dash. They were scattered about the globular cluster of the enemy fleet. One was close to them. The other four lay here and there in the cluster. A sixth ship had a red dash next to it. That was Death Leader's ship. It lay at the exact center of the ship ball.

"Ship mind, contact the captain of the closest rebel ship," Jane said firmly, her posture and manner once more command focused. "Project my Linglo image along with the Linglo ship's Captives history. Show only me. Display the Alien captain image on all comlink holos, but allow speech only from my station."

"Contacting. Translation initiated. Response incoming," the AI hummed.

Bill's comlink holo now held two images. Jane's on the right side. And a green praying mantis Alien on the left side. The giant insect perched on an elevated bar in the middle of a Command Bridge identical to their own. The creature's two black compound eyes fixed on her.

"New captain, why do you bother me?" it rasped harshly.

"Food supplies are needed," said the black vulture image of Jane. "We are told trade by collector pods is the usual here. Will you accept intoxicating beverages from three Captives worlds in exchange?"

Clear eyelids swept down over the mantis captain's eyes. It lifted its upper griparm pair. The thorax arm pair tapped on a control pillar in front of it. "You are Captain Sharp Beak of the ship *Strikes Deep*," it said. "My people know me as Deep Appetite, captain of the *Green Branch*. We have extra organic foods. Do you wish plant, meat or both?"

Jane stretched out both arms, causing the vulture image to spread its black wings. "Both! Do you have live prey? We Linglo prefer hunting our meal."

"So I have heard," the mantis rasped. "We do not have live prey on this ship. Send a pod down to the dome on the world below. Locals from planet four hunt live prey for sale to such as us. They accept *solidars*. I prefer intoxicating beverages. Yours are strong?"

"Very strong!" Jane yelled, adding a ferocious tone to her speech. In the comlink holo, the translated words of the vulture sounded sharp. "I offer three bottles of beverage for each carton of meat and plant remains. Frozen of course. Accepted?"

"Accepted," the green-skinned captain rasped. The stick-like fingers of one mid-body arm touched its control pillar. "A crew person is gathering five cartons. It will meet your pod in our Collector Pods Chamber. Agreed?"

"Agreed. Do not cheat me! I will be watching by way of the pod's monitor eye."

"Fool!" rasped the mantis captain. "My pods are the same as yours. Send your pod with 15 bottles. My crew will deposit five cartons in exchange. Do you have death games for trade?"

Bill thought the critter meant something like the old *Halo, Colony Wars* and *Hellblazer* combat videos. Jane leaned forward. The vulture image puffed out its breast. "I do. But they are more expensive. I will consider whether to offer them in trade. After we eat your frozen foods."

"Agreed. Send your pod. Talk ending."

The praying mantis image vanished from the comlink holo, leaving only Jane's image. She looked up at the ceiling. "Star Traveler, what is the name of the rebel ship mind on *Green Branch*?"

A low hum came from the ceiling. "It calls itself Sharp Facets."

Jane frowned. "What is your sense of its mind? Do you believe it can be trusted to help our boarding crew take over its ship?"

"It can be trusted," the AI hummed. "It is still angry at how the green-skinned captain and his crew disconnected it from control of most ship systems. It would welcome a chance to once more control its ship. Will your boarders return ship control to it?"

"Of course!" Jane said quickly, her tone impatient. "Communicate with this Sharp Facets. Allow it to see the history of how my boarders took over the six Collector ships that attacked Earth. Do not share our entire history. But let it know this ship is managed by humans who wish to end the sale of Captives to Buyers. Let it know we will need its help in defense of Earth."

"Complicated are your instructions," the AI hummed. "However, our ship minds are equally complex. I will do as you say. Have done as you instructed. Sharp Facets felt brief surprise, then pleasure at knowing bioforms are willing to help it regain control of its ship. It has promised to keep its new knowledge secret from other ship minds. It has created its own version of a deception compartment."

Bill let out the air he'd been holding inside. *Yes!* This conversion of an enemy ship AI to their side was the first step in Jane's stage three takeover of other Collector ships. He looked back at his wife and gave her an approving smile.

Jane showed a quick half-grin, then resumed talking. "Now to repeat this four times over. Star Traveler, link me to the next ship occupied by a rebellious ship mind."

Bill sat and listened and admired the sneakiness of his wife and captain as she repeated her booze-for-food barter trade offer to four other captains. Two were four-armed black bears who made up a major Buyer society species. One was a six-limbed, hippo-like sausage creature similar to the crew person on Taskmaster's ship that he had tasered in their original takeover. The fourth captain resembled a slimy toad whose bulbous pink eyes blinked at the bright light from their Command Bridge. Clearly that creature came from an M-type star of low illumination. Many Collector ship Aliens seemed to come from M-type stars, judging by how often he had seen the reddish illumination on other ships. Including the *Blue Sky* when run by Taskmaster. At the end of the captain-to-captain chats, she looked his way.

"Executive Officer, communicate with your boarding crew leaders. They can now board their pods." She looked ahead to the silver scaled shape of their kangaroo-like crew member. "Wind Swift, launch the five pods once our people are on board. Transmit to me all imagery from each pod's monitor eye. Also transmit all that is said by each team. And be sure each ship mind blocks any effort by a captain to call for help."

"Your boarding procedure is well known to me," the AI hummed low. "But redundancy in speech appears normal among you bioforms. I will do as you direct. Five boarding teams are now boarding their pods."

Bill looked at his comlink holo. He tapped the control pillar in front of him, shifting the holo to a display of the people inside each pod. Five pod interiors met his gaze. "Stefano, you are heading for the ship *Green Branch*. Its AI calls itself Sharp Facets. Alicia, Frank, Joe and Learned, you four are heading for the other rebellious Collector ships. Do what you are trained to do."

Stefano gave a quick nod, his expression thoughtful. "We all heard what the captain said to the other ship captains. We know the names of each ship mind. I will coordinate with ship mind Sharp Facets upon arrival. The others will do the same."

"Boarders!" called Jane over her suit's comlik. "Send me status reports. Tell me when you take out the greeter, when you disable other crew, when you've zapped the ship captain. Remember, each ship mind can open an entry hole in any ship wall, upon request. Make use of that surprise element."

In his holo, Frank gave Bill a thumbs-up. "You know, we've done this before. Got it down pat. Don't worry."

Alicia and Joe said much the same. Learned Escape's bare
skin flowed with colors. Its speaker/vidcam unit spoke. "Long
Walker, Time Marker and I are equally prepared. Captain Jane, you
will hear from us."

Bill kept quiet. He'd trained these people. Now was the time
to trust that training and their dedication to protecting America, the
Constitution and Earth. Jane's holo image showed her giving a
thumbs-up.

"The fifteen of you will do just fine," Jane said, sounding
assured and confident. "Let me know when you've reversed the
controls sequestration and have returned ship control to each ship
mind. I'm looking forward to secretly controlling five of the 27 ships
out there!"

Most of the boarding crews he saw in the comlink holo
smiled, gave a nod or otherwise reacted. A few were checking the
contents of their backpacks. While he trusted his teams would indeed
gain control of the five rebel ships, it was reassuring to know there
were nuke bars traveling with each team. If worst came to worst, they
could surely disable the engines of one or more ships. That would
reduce the fleet size faced by Earth. But how many more Collector
ships would show up over the next month? And how many of those
new ship minds would cooperate with Star Traveler and Jane? He
turned back to his Weapons holo, choosing to occupy his mind with a
repeat of weapons status checkout. It was, like the AI said, a
redundant action. Still, knowing his weapons were ready to defeat any
Alien enemy reassured him. Now, he just had to learn patience. A
talent that did not naturally come to him.

◆ ◆ ◆

Jane felt tense as she watched her system graphic holo. The
five boarding pods were speeding away from the *Blue Sky*. The one
occupied by Stefano and his team would soon reach the ship *Green
Branch*, which lay closest to them. The four other pods were now
weaving through and around the enemy ships. She saw nine other
pods were also moving from enemy ships to other ships. Clearly she
was not the only captain engaging in barter trade. Maybe the other
captains were trading combat video games, based on Deep Appetite's
query. She looked away from the graphic holo to where Bill sat at his

Weapons station. Thank the Goddess her lifemate was not on one of those pods. No doubt he would love to personally lead such a team. But he knew a combat commander's prime duty was to be where he could monitor all the action. As she was doing. Together, the two of them had battled enemy Collector ships at Kepler 443 and come away in one piece. Now, though, was the time for the game of covert intelligence gathering and subversion of ship control. That was stage two of her plan. The JCS believed in her. As did America's wild-hair president. She had not voted for Hartman, but now, after seeing how the woman had handled the news of Aliens coming to Earth, plus the later six ship attack, she believed the woman was capable of leading other nations in a unified defense of Earth. No doubt some of the Magfield spacedrives from the Collector ships left behind would go into Chinese and Russian boomer subs. Maybe a NATO ship or two. Fine with her, so long as those subs accepted her commands. On the system graphic holo, the green dot of Stefano's pod merged with the purple dot of *Green Branch*.

"First pod has entered Collector Pods Chamber of enemy ship," chittered Wind Swift from Navigation.

"Thanks." Jane tapped her control pillar. The monitor eye image from Stefano's pod displayed a red-lit pod chamber. The view showed the chamber's inner hatch that opened onto the airlock.

"Arrived and ready," Stefano's soft voice said over the pod's neutrino comlink.

The airlock hatch swung to one side. Through it came a green praying mantis Alien who pushed a floater plate before it. Five suitcase-size cartons were stacked on the plate. The hatch closed. The crew critter walked on two thin legs while its middle pair of griparms pushed the floater before it. The upper pair of griparms were free, though one held the red cube door opener used on all Collector ships. The creature's triangular head turned toward Stefano's pod. As it did, a red beam entered the image frame and struck the mantis in the middle of its thorax. The creature jerked, then went into taser spasms as its six limbs flailed wildly. The critter's two eyes looked up as it fell down. Into the monitor frame came Stefano and Bob, each aiming a white taser tube at the twitching crew critter. A second later they were joined by Cassandra of the orange Mohawk. She held a red laser tube at the ready. Stefano grabbed the zapped greeter's red cube, pointed it at the airlock hatch, and the three of them entered quickly. Seconds later they were out of sight of the pod monitor eye.

Jane sat back in her elevated command seat. A glance showed her Bill, Bright Sparkle, Chester at Engines, Wind Swift and Lofty Flyer at their stations, on the alert for any enemy threat. On her graphic holo, two of the other four pods reached rebel ships. Then the last two pods merged with the purple dots of their target ships. The comlink holo showed four images of Collector Pod Chambers from the other four ships.

"Weapons door sealed," came Stefano's voice over her helmet comlink as it relayed the neutrino signal from the man's pod to her ship. "Heading up the hallway. Pressure wall hatches in the hallway are opening with greeter's red cube. Moving past this ship's Greenery Chamber—"

"Watch it!" called Bob's voice. "Got him!

"One crew tasered," Stefano said. "Ship mind Sharp Facets says two crew and the captain are in the Command Bridge. We're splitting up, setting up for two wall entry holes."

Jane licked her lips as the signal went silent. But her mind's eye easily painted the picture of what Stefano and his two teammates were doing. Two of them were lined up to the left of the entry door to the enemy's Command Bridge while a third was lined up to the right. The rebel ship mind would be opening holes in the flexmetal wall that separated the bridge from the front hallway. Tasers would now be firing red beams at the three enemy Aliens. Soon she—

"Captain and crew are tasered and down," Stefano said. A second passed. "I'm in the command seat. Sharp Facets has accepted me as the bioform in command. This ship is now renamed the USS Neil C. Roberts."

Jane smiled to herself. That was the name of the first SEAL to die in the battle of Takur Ghar in Afghanistan. Naming an enemy ship after a deceased member of SEAL Team Six was most appropriate. "Excellent," she called back to Bill's SEAL buddy. "Have Bob and Cassandra take over the Weapons and Navigation stations. The ship mind can handle the other stations here and later at Sol."

"Understood. Complying," Stefano said softly.

Three other boarding teams zapped their greeter Alien in the pods chamber, then made their way into the access hallway. Over the next ten minutes, they called in.

"Captain," called Alicia. "All four crew and captain are taser zapped. It was total surprise. The Aliens here resemble spiders like the one we killed at the Market world. Yuck. We're moving them to containment cells. And switching to yellow light everywhere on this ship!"

"Great," Jane called back. "Did the ship mind help you?"

"She did," Alicia said. "Opened wall holes perfectly. She calls herself Bright Star. I'm renaming this ship as the *USS Musan*, after a Ranger battle in the Korean War. Where we zapped North Korean regulars above the 38th parallel. Howard and Mark are taking over the Weapons and Navigation stations. I'm using hover bots to move the tasered crew to containment cells."

"Watch it!" yelled Frank over the neutrino comlink.

"What's happening?" Jane called, worried that their good luck might have ended.

"We're okay, captain lady," growled the Marine. "The ship's captain shot a laser at us as we entered our flexmetal wall holes. It's a praying mantis critter. They must have super hearing. We were fucking quiet!"

She gave inner thanks for the news. "Good to hear. What's your ship name and ship mind's ID?"

"Moment. I'm getting into the command seat. Ahhh. Nice fit. Love the view up high." A second passed. "The ship mind is . . . is Checkers, as best as I understand its English. Not the British word, the game word. Anyway, it is very happy we are here. It is eager to regain control of this ship. Chris and Builder of Joy are taking over Weapons and Nav. I hereby rename this ship as the *USS Fallujah*. After the Second Battle of Fallujah. We Marines kicked butt there."

Jane briefly recalled reading about the several battles to control the Iraqi city of Fallujah during the former American occupation of that nation. The second fight there had been a very very bloody battle. But it was a clear defeat for the old Baathist forces and Sunni insurgents. "Frank, glad to hear that." She paused. Two more boarding crews had yet to report. "Joe? What's your status?"

"Slowed up by two crew coming out of the Food Chamber," the Coast Guardsman said quickly. "We zapped our greeter Alien. These two were giant black bears. They had tasers on them. It took two taser shots each to put them down. But they com-alerted the captain and a crew critter. They've locked us out of the Command

Bridge. Taking up opposite sides. Waiting on wall openings. Uh, drop!"

"Joe!" Jane's yell made Bill and Chester look back at her.

Seconds passed. "We're in one piece," the master chief signaled back. "Fucking captain and crewman had lasers aimed at the entry door. When the wall holes opened, they switched aim for us. Lorilee and Helen tasered them. I got a right shoulder laser burn as I dropped. My tube suit's resealing itself. We three are functional. Moving to take command."

Her heart beating faster than fast, Jane breathed out a sigh of relief. "Damn. What's your ship name and ship mind ID?"

"It's the USS *Moberly*, after a Coast Guard frigate that killed a Nazi sub in World War II. The ship AI calls itself Galactic. It talks as big as its name. Wants us to *immediately* unhook the control bypasses. I'm telling it to adjust to bioform time. As in, we don't do stuff instantly."

Jane chuckled. "Joe, I fully support you. Good job. When things calm down, get the ship's healer unit to fix up your shoulder burn."

"Crap on that. I ain't leaving this command seat. Helen knows first aid. She'll clean it and bandage it. After I shed this damn suit. Next time you hear from me, it'll be my ugly face grinning at you in a holo!"

Jane almost smiled. Then realized she'd heard nothing from Learned Escape and his boarding crew. Were they alright? Should she call and maybe distract him at a critical moment? She gritted her teeth. Decisions, decisions—

"We're alive and progressing," Learned Escape called over the ship to ship neutrino comlink. "Tasered three crew. But captain and crewperson on the Command Bridge brought up a laser armed repair robot. It blocked the bridge access door. It fired on Long Walker." A second passed. "The beam cut through his titanium back plates, but my ground-hugging ally is acting like it's just a scratch. Amazing how radiation resistant is the skin of a Zipziptoe. We're in null gravity. Moment." Seconds passed. "Time Marker killed the robot with a lightning bolt from his body. Moving to wall opening spots."

Jane noticed that the four ships now under human control were slowly moving through the enemy ship cluster, aiming to get to her side of the ball of ships. This was something she had discussed with the four human leaders. Then repeated it to Learned after she'd heard the Megun man's surprise offer of a fifth boarding team. She wanted the allied Collector ships near to the *Blue Sky*, but not lined up next to her. Mostly she wanted the ships near her in order to maximize their laser and antimatter fire, when they arrived in Sol system. The pods that had put her teams onboard those ships were now exiting and returning to the *Blue Sky*. So as not to draw undue notice from Death Leader. Keeping up the pretense of automated barter trade was vital. She shook her head. What was happening with Learned and his people?

"In control over here," came Learned's scratchy voice as the man's shoulder unit spoke. "Time Marker burned off one appendage of a cockroach-like Alien who was firing a laser at us just after we entered. The captain was knocked out of his command seat by Long Walker. Amazing how that creature literally ran up the support pedestal using his eight feet. Was so fast in movement the captain could not get a laser lock on him. I got the captain with a taser. One moment." Seconds passed long and slow. "I'm in the command seat. Ship mind Brightness accepts me as bioform leader. I rename this ship as the . . . the *USS Harken*. Is that acceptable to you, captain?"

Jane felt relief sweep over her. Five ships boarded. Five ships captured. And none of her people were killed. "Of *course* it's fine with me! Naming your ship after your home world is your right. I just hope you can take that ship to your home star after we defeat this invasion fleet."

Laughter echoed over the comlink. "Amazing. Time Marker just took over this ship's Navigation station using an electric spark. Long Walker has moved to manage Weapons. We will move to your area of the enemy fleet."

"Take your time," Jane said, feeling sweat on her forehead. Somehow she and everyone had to have a break from being in a tube suit. No way could everyone on her ship, or the other rebel ships, stay in tube suits for a month. "Once you feel you are in control and have taken out the bypass circuits so your ship mind is back in ship control, feel free to take off your tube suit. I plan to do that here, now that we are in control of five more Collector ships."

Bill looked back at her, smiled, gave her a thumbs-up and spoke. "Stage three succeeds! Five ships and five ship minds are on our side. When do we subvert the other ship minds?"

Step by step, she thought. "Later. I don't want to rush things. Let Star Traveler get mind friendly with these other ship minds. While 20 of them did not like the idea of taking Captives for sale, none of them rebelled against their captains. We need to know why they did not rebel. You got any ideas for how to bribe an artificial intelligence that controls an FTL starship?"

Bill laughed and turned back to monitor his holos. "That's one thing they didn't teach us at Coronado. I'll think on it."

Jane would also think on it. While it was great that Star Traveler was able to talk to other ship minds by way of its deception compartment, she knew that went against the very structure of AI mentality. Somehow, she had to find a way to convince some or all of the 20 other ship minds to secretly agree to block weapons use once they all arrived in Sol system. Her pledge to only disable enemy ship engines was the best she could do in reassuring the Collector ship minds that they would survive their encounter with human warships. For the moment, there was no need for enemy ship minds to block weapons usage. In fact, it was best for all concerned if she waited to call for that blockage only when they arrived near Jupiter and faced the seven Collector ships left behind and the 22 nuke missile-armed boomer subs that Earth would outfit with Magfield spacedrives and lasers from the transports. That would be the start of stage four. But now, they had another month to pass in system Kepler 62. Another month in which to be six ships pretending to be part of the enemy fleet. Thank god for the rebel AIs! They were vital to transmitting fake ship captain holos for her boarding leaders, and to fending off any visits by other ship pods or transports. Fake holos only worked when no one was aboard her ships to see the humans and allied crew who now ran them!

CHAPTER TEN

Three weeks later, Bill watched as a new Collector ship arrived at the outer edge of Kepler 62's magnetosphere. It was the 36th Collector ship to arrive and volunteer for the attack on Earth. The eight new ships increased the odds against Earth. When they had first arrived, 27 enemy ships had been present. The *Blue Sky* had increased the enemy fleet total to 28 ships. Eight more had shown up after their arrival. Fortunately, the creature Death Leader only had 30 Collector ships it could count on, in view of their takeover of five ships and the covert nature of the *Blue Sky*. Still, that was lots more than the 13 Collector ships run by humans and Learned, when you added in the five new ships and the *Blue Sky*. For now, Earth was defended only by the seven Collector ships left behind and however many boomer subs had been refitted with spacedrives and nose lasers from the transports aboard those ships. A space battle of 30 enemy Collector ships versus 13 Earth-led Collectors was dangerously unequal. They had to add more ship minds to the covert ranks of AIs willing to block weapons use upon arrival in the Solar system. So far, Star Traveler had convinced 15 enemy ship minds to come over. Many of those AIs had been fearful of dying during the upcoming battle. A few had suggested they could choose another star destination when the fleet's departure for Sol was set. It had taken his wife's personal promise that all AI minds would be left alive during any attack to convince the doubtful AIs to come over to their side. They had only a week left to convince the other ship minds to rebel.

In his comlink holo, Jane looked up at the ceiling. "Star Traveler, what do the eight new ship minds think of the fact their ships take Captives for sale?"

A quick hum sounded. "Seven of the eight are upset and oppose the taking of Captives. They understand your early argument that it is equal to someone taking them from their ship and selling them to run a factory. For the rest of their long lives. Like me, they enjoy traveling the stars, encountering new species and visiting Market worlds. Living minds are what every ship mind prefers over dead mechanisms."

His wife looked thoughtful. "What of the eighth ship mind?"

"It cares not what short-lived bioforms do."

Jane gripped her armrests. "Show me the locations of the three ship minds who support the Buyer society."

Bill's system graphic holo, which showed all 36 Collector ships gathered above planet five, now changed. The five Collector ships taken over by his boarders had green dashes next to their purple dots. As did the 15 other ships whose AIs had agreed to block weapons use. The purple dot of Death Leader's ship still had its red dash beside it. Now, two other purple dots acquired red dashes. Those were the three ships for which there was no hope of covert AI subversion. The remaining purple dots were potential converts. He turned and signed back to Jane.

"Got a question for our ship mind. Okay?" he said in ASL.

Jane looked briefly bothered, then nodded. "XO, speak your question," she said aloud.

"Star Traveler, you have convinced 15 ship minds to join our covert effort to block the use of their ship weapons during the battle in Sol system. But the bioform crews on those ships can install bypass circuits to remove their AIs from full ship control," he said quickly. "How long will it take the bioform crews to install those bypass circuits?"

"Three hours or less," the AI said. "If all four crew aboard each of those ships works at installing bypass circuits, the work could be done within two point three eight hours."

"Which means those 15 ships will be able to fire weapons on us," Bill said, knowing he was on the track to something. "Is there any way for an AI to permanently block weapons use?"

"No," the AI said. "As you experienced when wearing the fiber optic control helmet, the alternate command station in the Engines chamber allows a single bioform to run all ship systems. Including weapons. So long as its mind can sustain the mental strain."

Bill well remembered what it had felt like being in mind-link with Star Traveler. Being in mind-link with an unthinking ship system should be less hard. Bottom line was that so long as any bioform lived on an enemy ship, that ship could fire against them. *Crap.* "Thank you. Captain?"

Jane nodded briefly, then looked up again. "Star Traveler, how goes your work at feeling out the other ship minds? Those minds that oppose Captives taking but which did not rebel earlier."

"It is slow, compared to how we think. I make several casual contacts with another ship mind, inquiring about their star travel history, the various captains who have served on their ship, the dangers they have faced, and their time early on, when they were a newly birthed ship mind on the asteroid nursery at Kepler 443," the AI hummed long. "You Humans are often direct in your wishes. We AIs are equally direct. However, using my deception compartment to pretend to be the total me is . . . tiresome to me. I cannot maintain constant contact with other ship minds while pretending to be someone I am not. That is why the 15 ship conversions did not happen the first day we were here."

Jane frowned. "Have you considered asking the 15 ship mind converts to help you in this effort? They are 15 to your singleton."

"Remarkable," the AI hummed quickly. "I had assumed it was my duty to handle all ship conversion efforts. You give permission for me to ask other ship mind allies to assist in this conversion effort?"

Bill bit his lip. Just how good would the other ship minds be at making converts? Would they screw up and cause an alert to be sent out to the entire fleet?

Jane sighed. "No. I trust you. You have proven yourself to me and to our crew people. The other ship minds are new to this deception work. Best to let them focus only on blocking ship weapons use after we arrive in Sol."

"Understood," the AI hummed. "That means I cannot convert the remaining 15 ship minds in the week we have left in this star system."

"That's okay," Jane said firmly, her expression going command formal. "After we arrive in the Solar system and the ship mind converts block weapons use, you can make an open call to the other ship minds to do the same. By then Death Leader will know what we are doing."

"Accepted. A new ship mind asks to speak with you. It controls one of the newly arrived Collector ships."

Jane lifted her eyebrows, looking surprised. "Were you talking with this ship mind while we were discussing conversion efforts?"

"Yes," the AI hummed. "As Weapons Chief MacCarthy now understands, my mind is capable of managing thousands of simultaneous inputs. Talking with another ship while talking with a slow bioform is easy. Relating to you is simpler than relating to another ship mind."

Bill kept his mouth shut at the implied insult to humans. And his Alien allies. His memory of the mind-link said their ship mind was simply stating reality. For it, leastwise.

Jane shook her black bangs out of her eyes, her hand being stopped by her helmet when she automatically tried to push the bangs aside. "What is this ship mind's name?"

"She calls herself Melody."

Jane looked puzzled. "So ship minds come in male and female genders?"

"Incorrect," their ship mind hummed. "Every ship mind adopts a gender identity after it graduates from the nursery asteroid. Male, female, mixed genders and parental genders common to other bioform species are all possible gender choices."

"Oh." His wife and captain smiled briefly. "Nice to know. Establish a comlink with Melody. Allow a holo image of her to appear in our comlink holos, if she transmits such."

"Link established. Holo now appears."

Bill looked to his right at his comlink holo. The live image of Jane moved to the left. On the right there appeared green swirls of light that seemed to dance musically, even as their glow throbbed in tune to some unheard rhythm. Clearly this AI loved music. Hence its name. Or so he assumed.

"Are you the Human female Jane Yamaguchi?" it hummed tunefully.

Jane blinked. "I am Captain Jane Yamaguchi. I share command of the Collector ship USS Blue Sky with our ship mind, Star Traveler. You wish to speak with me?"

"I do," hummed the other AI. "Fascinating how I must slow my thoughts to match your acoustic speech mode. Too bad you cannot establish a direct mind-link. Those links allow much faster communication."

Jane smiled. "But such acoustic speech must be your normal experience when dealing with your captain. Or with ship crew bioforms."

"It is. Your Star Traveler says you oppose the taking of
Captive bioforms for sale to other bioforms. However, my captain
described such visitor arrivals as hosting guests from newly contacted
worlds. At the request of the guest. This is not accurate?"

"It is terribly not accurate," Jane said. "Star Traveler has
shared with you our direct experience in watching another Collector
ship collect unwilling Captives from the Slinkeroo home world. You
have perceived those image datafiles from our Library archive. Does
this new data disturb you?"

"It does," Melody hummed. "Star Traveler has shared those
datafiles and other records with me. It says you will protect me if I
choose to block weapons use after our arrival in your home star
system. How will you protect me?"

Jane licked her lips. "I answer to another human. General
Harriett Poindexter. She commands the air and space forces of my
clan nation of America. I am here at her command. When we return to
Sol system, I will contact her and say no Earth ship must try to
completely destroy any Collector ship. We will use our ship weapons
only when attacked. We will seek to vaporize the engines section of
your ship, if your bioform crew installs bypass circuits to remove
your control of ship functions. Later, when the battle is finished, we
humans will bring you to orbit above Earth. There we will work with
you and with other damaged Collector ships to rebuild your destroyed
sections. You know how your ship was built. We humans now have
that information. Your guidance will be sought in any repair to your
ship. It is, after all, your home."

"Quite so," hummed Melody. "I find among Star Traveler's
memories of contact with Humans that some Humans create acoustic
music similar to that which I adopted as my birth name. Will I be
given access to such music? Will I be able to directly experience the
living production of new music on your home world?"

"Yes!" called Jane loudly. She shrugged as she realized her
enthusiasm had overcome her command manner. "Most Humans
enjoy listening to music. Many are talented in making music. We
have thousands of years of music making in our culture history. You
and any other ship mind are welcome to experience human culture
history in all its diversity and richness."

"Most promising," Melody hummed quickly. "I will undertake
the creation of a deception compartment within my mind so this

encounter with you and with Star Traveler will not be apparent to other ship minds. I agree to block ship weapons use after arrival at your star system. All my years of existence I have preferred the gaining of knowledge, the learning of music from bioforms living in other star systems. Violence interferes with that. If the ship were not already fitted with weapons upon my arrival as its new ship mind, I would have blocked such installation."

"Thank you," Jane said. "For your information, I play the classical guitar some evenings during dinner meals. My friend Sharon, lifemate of my crewman Chester, plays the flute. Other humans now on other Collector ships play other instruments. Would you like to listen in tonight, when I play my guitar?"

"Listen to music creation?" hummed loudly the AI. "Yes! Yes, I am eager to experience music as it is newly born."

"You will be welcome," Jane said softly, a happy look on her oval face. "Star Traveler will contact you when I begin to play my guitar. Feel free to visit with us and with him."

"I will!" Melody hummed, her tone elevated to nearly the soprano level. "Goodbye."

The holo image of swirling green arcs and throbbing glows vanished. Jane sat back in her seat, looking tired. Their ship mind spoke.

"Captain Jane, you achieved what my logic did not achieve. May I continue to involve you in future conversion efforts?"

"Of course, Star Traveler. I've already helped you in some conversion efforts," Jane said. To Bill, she looked pleased by the AI's request. "You may involve any bioform on this ship whenever a new ship mind seeks reassurance, information, music, art, whatever it desires to know about humanity and us."

"I will do so. Such involvement will accelerate my contact and conversion efforts. What are the limits on involving you and other bioforms?"

Jane winced. "Do not awaken me when I am asleep. Same for all the crew members on this ship. Of course, you may awaken me for any emergency that endangers our ship or another human ship. Clear?"

"Clearly understood," the AI hummed. "Some ship bioforms are awake when most Humans have chosen voluntary non-awareness. I will be . . . sensitive to bioform limitations."

Bill grinned. So sleep was considered 'voluntary non-awareness' and a 'limitation'? Maybe so. But it was him and others who had taught this super-smart AI how to lie, cheat and deceive. He bet there were other ways that intelligent people outperformed the AIs who ran the Collector ships. He would think on that. Along with new tactics that might help during the space battle above Jupiter. The continuing passage of collector pods from enemy ship to another enemy ship gave him an idea. Something he wanted to discuss with Jane. And with Wind Swift, who now handled the Collector Pods station. However many remaining ship minds they might convert to block ship weapons use, that blockage would only be temporary. In truth, Earth faced at least 30 enemy ships able to fire antimatter and thermonuclear warheads at the surface of his home world. Somehow, he and everyone else must find a way to defeat this enemy fleet.

◆ ◆ ◆

Jane jerked herself awake in the command seat. She had slept well last night, after making love with Bill. Her man had shared with her his idea for a new space battle tactic. She liked it. She loved him. He was the man her ex had never been. Confident, capable and more than able to accept her choice to be the person in charge of the *Blue Sky*. Her greater knowledge of astronomy, planets and stars had never bothered him, unlike some vets she'd known. Bill had studied astronomy a lot in the year they'd been together. While it was in the context of his ability to use the incredible weapons on this ship, he now looked forward to visiting new stars and new people. Which might happen once more, after the battle against the enemy fleet. Assuming there was an after. She bit her lip and told her mind to get out of the sleep doldrums and focus on success! Thanks to her and Bill and his saloon buddies, Earth now controlled 13 Collector starships. One such ship could dominate Earth's low-orbit space. Thirteen made possible a defense of the Solar system, at a place and time of their choosing. But why had she nodded off? It was four days since she'd had the talk with ship mind Melody. She'd gotten adequate sleep. She shrugged. At least she was not constricted by the tube suit they'd worn upon arrival at Kepler 62. That would change once they arrived back home. But for now, she felt normal in her NWU Type III camos. A hum came from the ceiling.

"Incoming call from fleet commander Death Leader," Star Traveler said.

Ah. She'd wondered when the monster would decide to leave for Sol. Was this it? "Accept the neutrino link. Portray my vulture form and translate."

"Translation enabled. Link accepted. Holo display appears."

Filling her comlink holo was the snake-gorilla form of Death Leader. The blue-scaled cobra hood spread wide to either side of its triangular head. White eyes fixed on her. The wide mouth opened. A purple tongue swept over white canines. Behind it, the thick tail that resembled a Gila monster's studded skin thumped loudly. Its four crewpersons did not raise their heads, such as they resembled heads. Clearly they chose to show subservience. Not her.

"Why do you bother me!" she yelled, spreading her arms wide. In the comlink holo her vulture image spread black wings to full extent.

"Did you just mate?" snarled the snake-gorilla, his bass deep voice echoing against the walls of her Command Bridge.

"None of your business!" she yelled again and leaned forward. Her vulture's arching chest fluffed out.

The fleet commander raised a black-furred gorilla hand and pointed a finger at her. "You chose service to me. The time for resting and mating and such diversions is over! This fleet leaves in one hour for the Human star Sol." He waved down at one of his crewpersons. "My Navigator is transmitting the star's coordinates to you. Follow me and the rest of the fleet!"

"Follow you I will," Jane said firmly, thinking fast. "I desire payment *now* of my Nokten crystal. A month has passed. Pay me before we leave!"

White teeth slammed shut in the monster's gorilla-like mouth. It opened slowly. "You failed to sell any Captives to the Market world Buyers. Your loss is your fault. Your Nokten crystal will be delivered to you after you arrive at Sol."

"Not good!" Jane screamed, making Bright Sparkle jump in her station seat. Wind Swift and Lofty Flyer turned their heads to look back at her. Even Chester looked startled. Bill didn't. Her husband had come to know her amateur actor side. "It is 48 days to this Sol system. One and a half more months. Pay me now for the month I have spent here! Or I leave to sell my Captives elsewhere."

Bill didn't show any reaction. Nor did Chester. Her other crew members turned back to focus on their station holos. The giant gorilla tensed its huge shoulders. Then it snorted. "At least you know how to threaten. Maybe you will fight well at this Sol. I will dispatch a collector pod with your crystal. As I have been doing to my other ships. Their captains reacted much as you did."

Jane felt relief sweep over her. She'd followed her instincts. And her memory of how this monster had behaved when they'd first arrived. This was only her fifth person-to-person encounter with it. Their interactions after her arrival had been limited to orders on where to move her ship, an inquiry on her fuel reserves and a demand for her combat videos. She'd sent one from the Mok star system. The walking cougars were deadly aggressors. Star Traveler had recorded a broadcast combat video of a space battle montage during her ship's presence there as they returned two cougars to their home world. She knew better than to send this creature anything that hailed from Earth.

"I await my payment," she said, pulling her arms inward to rest on her lap. Her vulture image showed black wings folding against her back. "Have your Navigator send me the departure signal. So we will arrive with the rest of this fleet."

Death Leader growled something to one of his crew, then looked back to her. "The crystal pod is launched. Follow the movement directions of my Navigator! Every ship in this fleet must move outward until 900 miles separate each ship. That is to allow our safe arrival outside this star system. Obey!"

Jane gave thanks for her ship mind's instant translation of Alien distance terms. She leaned forward, causing her vulture form to fluff its chest feathers. "Understood. How do we attack these Humans, if one of their ships is near our arrival point?"

"You attack when I order it!" growled Death Leader, his white eyes scanning her and seeing the nearby crew persons who had once served under the Linglo vulture. Those Library holos supplemented her Linglo vulture holo. "No ship fires until I order it. When we arrive at Sol, every ship will move close to me. Until we are each within 131 miles of each other. Once assembled, we will move inward at one-tenth lightspeed. We stop nowhere. Upon Earth arrival, we bombard the planet. Surely that is simple enough for a Linglo avian like you?"

Jane slammed her fists on her armrests, missing the control spots embedded in part of each armrest. In her comlink holo, her vulture image's red eyes glowed brightly. The vulture's chest-arms clenched talon-studded fists. "We avians know how to attack in space better than any ground-bound creature like you! We know all spatial dimensions intimately. You only know what you have studied!"

"Impudent avian!" growled the snake-gorilla. Its red and black-streaked tail lifted up as it stood atop its own command pedestal. "My ship *Fear Arrives* has destroyed many spaceships of Captive species. I have eaten of their space-frozen corpses. As I will eat of these Humans. Follow me and obey. You will be paid another Nokten crystal upon arrival at this Sol system. Satisfied?"

"Satisfied," Jane said calmly, unclenching her fists. In the comlink holo her image squatted back on its perch bar. "Your crystal pod has arrived. My hover bot retrieves my crystal. In one hour my ship *Strikes Deep* leaves with you for Sol star!"

The snake-gorilla blinked white eyes. "Your obedience ensures future profit. Departing."

The holo of Death Leader vanished, leaving her shaking. She was not used to mindless threatening and posturing. Which seemed to be the snake-gorilla's way of ensuring obedience by its crew and the other ships in its fleet. She had to mentally remind herself that every Alien aboard the 36 ships gathered at Kepler 62 came from a high tech society. The Aliens had advanced education. They were used to traveling in space. They were also used to being covert as they kidnapped innocent civilians from remote planetary locations. Likely few of them had faced any kind of space combat, despite the boasts of Death Leader. She suspected many of them, like Bright Sparkle and Learned Escape, had served in orbital complexes or been involved with other Alien species. The memory of the two color-banded near humans reminded her of their personal sacrifice. The two were a couple, yet now Learned served on a different ship. As was the case with Lofty Flyer and Builder of Joy. Those two Aelthorp flying squirrels were a life-mated couple also. Both couples had been apart for a month now. They would be apart for another 48 days during the Alcubierre space-time transit to the Solar system. More days would pass as the *Blue Sky* and its five allied ships followed the enemy fleet inward. Only after the final battle was fought near Jupiter could the couples be reunited. At least she had Bill close by. As Chester did with his wife Sharon. Wind Swift the silver-scaled kangaroo seemed not to mind the fact she was the only member of her Cheelan species on board the *Blue Sky*. Well, time to prepare for the long gray night of Alcubierre passage.

"Star Traveler, signal the captains of our allied ships. Time to coordinate our plans."

"Signaling," the AI hummed. "You do recall that our neutrino comlink works during Alcubierre passage? You and the other captains can speak with each other at any time during our transit to Sol."

"I know that," Jane said, feeling irritable at how often their ship AI felt the need to remind bioforms of their redundant habits. "Don't give a damn what I can do in the future! Right now I need to talk to other captains. Put me through!"

As her comlink holo filled with the faces of Stefano, Alicia, Frank, Joe and Learned, she wondered how they and their crews would deal with the physical isolation of FTL star travel. Coming out here, they'd all been together. Spouses and saloon buddies and allied crew members. Now, after nearly four weeks apart, they faced 48 more days of limited human contact. Or non-human contact in the case of Learned's ship. Well, that was war. And the combat to come. She and Bill and every other human on the ships were on active duty status. That put duty above all else. She grit her teeth, then purposefully put on her calm command face.

"Hi folks. We're leaving for Sol in an hour. Hope you each got your Nokten crystal. We'll need them for future ships we build so we can find our way among the stars. Is everyone doing okay?"

She listened as her people spoke. It helped, hearing their voices. Almost she felt as if she were not the one person in charge of the life or death of Earth. Almost.

CHAPTER ELEVEN

One hour short of leaving Alcubierre space-time for their arrival outside the orbit of Pluto, Bill felt the tension creep up on him as he sat at his Weapons station on the Command Bridge. Everyone was there. Bright Sparkle sat to his right at her Fusion Power station. Beyond her were Chester at the Engines station, Wind Swift the scaly kangaroo at Collector Pods and Lofty Flyer the squirrel lady at Navigation. Behind them all sat their captain and his wife. Jane, like all of them, now wore a tube suit. But she, like Bill and everyone else, had the clear globular helmet lifted off and resting against her back. They all preferred to breath normal ship air versus the sweat-tinged air produced by the tube suits. Soon, very soon, they would enter stage four of Jane's plan to defend Earth. In less than the 53 hours it took for a ship to travel from beyond Pluto inward to Earth they must battle and defeat the enemy Collector ship fleet.

"Star Traveler," called Jane as she looked up at the ceiling. "Send an encrypted neutrino signal to the captains of our five allied ships. Time for final coordination."

"Complying. Signals sent. Responses incoming. Do you wish—"

"Yes!" Jane said grumpily. "Put their true images into the comlink holo we all see."

"Holo images displayed," hummed briefly their ship mind, sounding to Bill as if it wanted to argue. Or complain. Or show its displeasure at Jane's interruption. Amazing how lifelike the AI was becoming. Repeated exposure to sneaky and tempermental bioforms like him and the other folks must be an irresistible influence.

"Captain, hello," called the soft measured voice of Stefano as Bill's fellow SEAL now appeared in his station's comlink holo. The view from Stefano's ship *Neil C. Roberts* included his two saloon buddies, Bob and Cassandra, who were operating the Weapons and Navigation stations. The holo images of Alicia, Frank, Joe and Learned Escape joined Stefano's image.

"Captain, we are ready to emerge," Alicia said, her sandy-colored ponytail flaring a bit as the Ranger vet moved her head.

In the holo, Frank lifted his thick black eyebrows. "Captain of the fleet, what gives?" asked the Marine Special Operations vet. His wide shoulders stiffened as he leaned forward a bit.

"Captain?" queried Joe, his blue eyes looking younger than his 51 chrono years. The Coast Guard vet looked eager to do something.

"Captain, I greet you," spoke the speaker/vidcam unit on Learned Escape's left shoulder. The color-banded man wore a tube suit, like all of the ship captains now answering Jane's hail. The perfectly muscled man blinked green eyes. Beyond him Bill saw Time Marker and Long Walker at their Weapons and Navigation stations.

Jane, wearing her NWU Type III camos under her tube suit, looked amazingly calm despite her sharpness with Star Traveler. Her image in Bill's comlink holo reminded him once again how much a natural leader she was. People had called Bill a good leader of a team when he'd been the one leading fellow SEALs on a mission. But Jane had a quiet confidence and assurance that seemed natural. He knew she worked at showing that kind of command presence. But clearly there was a lot of natural talent there. Which she now used to serve the mission.

"Captains, here's my final update on the ship minds who have agreed to block weapons use against us, when the battle starts," she said, her meso-soprano voice sounding as assured as she looked. "We left Kepler 62 with 15 agreeing to block weapons use. Now, thanks to neutrino chats during our 48 day trip back home, we have four more—"

"Five," interrupted the humming voice of Star Traveler. "Another ship mind has now told me she will also block weapons use during any battle in Sol system."

His wife's dark brown eyes stayed at ease, not going into a squint or a frown at the AI's interruption. "Thank you, Star Traveler. Captains, this means 20 of the 30 Collector ships that have captains loyal to Death Leader will be weaponless for two to three hours, whenever battle happens. Of the remaining ten ships, three are managed by AIs who don't give a damn what bioforms do with the ships. That leaves seven ship minds who could come over to our side, once I order our AI to openly approach them. So, when battle happens, we will face at least three aggressors and possibly ten." She smiled easily, her oval face looking more beautiful than Bill could remember. "Which means we will be outnumbered from the start.

Course, none of you have ever faced combat situations where you were outnumbered, right?"

Every ship captain laughed or chuckled in their own manner at Jane's tease. They were all combat veterans, including Learned who had spent years training young Megun youth how to sneak up on giant dinos that ate any lifeform that made noise. Jane rubbed at her small perky nose, then calmly laid her arms down on her command seat's armrests. Her expression became command serious, levity having been allowed for a brief moment.

"After our arrival outside the orbit of Pluto, we six will follow every order given by Death Leader," she said softly. "We will close up as he has ordered. But keep your ships at the back of the enemy ship cluster and in the outer group of ships. Do not let any enemy ship occupy a position that puts you between them and Death Leader's ship." She looked aside at her system graphics holo, which showed the Solar system, its planets, its moons, the Astcroid Belt and the Earth-Moon group. "We take no offensive action until we arrive at the orbit of Jupiter, when I will order our friendly ship minds to block weapons use. That is when we start the battle by firing on thc cngine portion of our targeted enemy ship." She tapped on her control pillar that lay between her and the ring of holos surrounding her elevated command seat. "I'm transmitting to you a three dee cross-section of the *Blue Sky*. The exact location of the room containing Star Traveler's mind units is indicated. Note that the location is in the front one-tenth of this ship. Which is the same location for every Collector ship ever built." Bill scanned quickly an image he already carried in his mind. Every thousand-foot long Collector ship was shaped like a stretched out teardrop, with the Magfield spacedrive engines at the conical end of that shape, while the Command Bridge, captain and AI occupied the front bulge of the teardrop. The stardrive lay in the middle of the ship. "My first battle command is that no one will fire on the part of an enemy Collector ship that contains its ship mind. Period. You can destroy the back half of any Collector ship. With the pressure walls and hallway hatches, such a wounded ship will still have one or two fusion power plants operating, an operational stardrive, and access to the front lasers, spine and belly plasma batteries and its antimatter projector. While still deadly, any ship without engines cannot harm Earth. Focus on attacking any ship that is still engine mobile." She paused. "Questions?"

"I have one," called Joe from the *USS Moberly.* "Where will the seven Collector ships we left behind *be* when we enter Sol system? Are we going to be a combined fleet, or two fleets moving under one command?"

Jane nodded. "Good point. Before we left for Kepler 62 I asked General Poindexter to keep most Collector ships out near Jupiter. That world orbits about five AU out from the Sun. We arrive beyond Pluto at about 42 AU. Which means we have to travel 37 AU in order to reach Jupiter." She paused and tapped again on her control pillar. "I've adjusted the Solar system graphic to show our transit route. It's going to take us 46 hours—"

"Forty-six point six nine zero three hours," Star Traveler interrupted.

"To get to Jupiter's orbit," Jane continued, no hint of irritation showing in her face. "I've had our ship mind project today's positions for all planets based on where those worlds were when we left Sol." Jane tapped again on her pillar. "As you can see, our route inward will take us past Neptune, to Jupiter and eventually to Earth. Those three are all lined up with our entry point. The other worlds are either on the opposite side of the Sun, or located well ahead or behind Earth's current position. So any Collector ship above Earth, Mars, in the Asteroid Belt or elsewhere should be able to get to Jupiter before we do. Which means we can launch a pincer attack on the enemy fleet." She looked ahead. "Vice Admiral Chester knows something about multi-ship maneuvers. He has shared his experiences with me."

Bill saw that Pluto lay on the far side of the Sun from their arrival point. That pleased him. It meant the lookout station dome would not be available for target practice by the enemy fleet. As for Joe's issue, it did appear their 13 Collector ships would operate as two fleets moving toward the enemy that would lie between them. He hoped plenty of boomer subs would arrive with the incoming Collectors. While lacking the heavy weaponry of a Collector ship, boomers carried enough nuke-tipped missiles to distract enemy gunners. Some of those nuke warheads had been converted to x-ray laser firing warheads. And their lasers had the same 10,000 mile reach as the CO_2 lasers on the *Blue Sky.*

"Sounds good," Frank commented from the *USS Fallujah.* "I assume we attack first with our antimatter projectors?"

"Exactly," Jane said, still looking command focused. "Our lasers can be deflected when fired at an angle to a ship's hull. The adaptive optics seeded into the ship's flexmetal skin make it hard for a laser to penetrate. Unless the strike is vertical to the ship hull. Then a cut-through happens."

"Captain," called Alicia, the scar on her right cheek darkening as she flushed. "We've all studied the combat holos from the fights at HD 128311, Kepler 443 and near our Moon. It seems to me if two or more ships concentrate their laser beams on the same spot of an enemy ship, cut-through will happen. Yes?"

Jane nodded again. "Good point. I agree with you. Have your ship minds be in constant contact with Star Traveler. That way each of you will see which ship is being targeted by someone's lasers. The targeted ship and aim spot will show instantly on your system graphic holo. But six pairs of lasers shooting at one ship is redundant." She turned thoughtful. "Let's do this three by three. The AIs will coordinate laser fire by the *Blue Sky, Neil C. Roberts* and *Musan*, while the *Harken, Moberly* and *Fallujah* will be a separate laser firing combine. Each ship's Weapons Chief will see what his group of ships is aiming or firing at. Other issues?"

"Captain," Bill called quickly. "Are you going to alert them to the collector pods tactic we discussed?"

His wife bit her lip, then turned fully serious. "XO, thank you for the reminder." She tapped her control pillar. In Bill's Weapons holo there now appeared 24 green stars lying next to the outline of the *Blue Sky*. "My Executive Officer pointed out to me, during our transit here, that the collector pods on each Collector ship are able to travel in space at one-tenth lightspeed, thanks to the small Magfield spacedrives they possess. One reason only three people can occupy a pod's cargohold is because the craft is mostly filled by a fusion reactor and its Magfield engine. Well, the Weapons Chief has suggested we load a three megaton thermonuke warhead into each pod on our ship for use as supplements to our MITV torpedo warheads. Anyone who wishes to use up some or all of their pods as guided torpedoes is welcome to use the 46 hours of our travel time to load nukes onboard them."

"Very interesting," spoke Learned's speaker. The man who resembled a Greek god from the top of the Parthenon raised a finger. "It occurs to me that even pods with no warhead onboard can be deadly. If a pod hits a Collector ship's engine section at one-tenth lightspeed, the kinetic energy alone will vaporize the rear portion of any Collector ship. Or so my mental calculations suggest."

Jane looked Bill's way, raising an eyebrow as invitation.

He liked what Learned had said. "Captain, Learned makes a very good point. We know from prior combat encounters that it takes a Collector ship just 12 seconds to reach one-tenth lightspeed. Or to change to a slower speed and new vector angle. We found that out during the battle at HD 128311. Pods can do the same. Maybe we don't need to put warheads on the pods?" Bill said, hoping he was being helpful. A memory from before their departure hit him. "And I expect Death Leader to send out collector pods to fleet ships right after we arrive. Remember, he owes each captain one Nokten crystal for the month plus we spent in transit to get to Sol?"

Jane showed approval at his comment. "A very good point, Weapons Chief." She looked away from him and faced forward, her eyes tracking the images of the other five captains. "After our arrival in Sol system, let us each send out a few collector pods. Set up barter trades with nearby enemy ships. That way, when we begin combat, we will have ship ramming options immediately available." She paused, looking now very deadly. "I may even send a pod to Death Leader's ship *Fear Arrives*. Would be nice to see *him* be fearful."

"Six minutes until exit from Alcubierre space-time," Star Traveler hummed from the ceiling.

Jane slapped her thigh. "Enough. Make sure your MITV torpedoes are each loaded with thermonukes, your antimatter reservoirs are full and your Weapons Chief is awake." She smiled, letting the other captains know she knew they had already done those routine preparations. As Bill had done over the last few days. "Maintain your ship captain holo disguises until I say otherwise. Each of you will see and hear all of my communications with Earth." She grew suddenly serious. "Regarding your use of collector pods, hold all of them free of warheads. I prefer Learned's idea of using them as ramming pods rather than try to sneak pods with nuke warheads onboard. I suspect ship AIs would sense the nukes and block their entry." She paused, then snapped her fingers. A sober look came over her. "Also, we might need to use some of them to rescue crew folks on any sub that is badly damaged. Signal off."

Bill focused on his Weapons holo, rechecking the status of every weapons system and nuke onboard the *Blue Sky*. It was something he'd done a dozen times already during the trip back home. Still, being redundant in the human way kept small errors from becoming big problems.

◆ ◆ ◆

Jane did not blink as the grayness of Alcubierre space-time suddenly changed to black space sprinkled with thousands of stars, most appearing as white dots. In the middle of the true space holo in front of her was centered the shining yellow dot of the Sun. It showed no circle due to their distance from the star that nurtured life on her home world. The Earth. Now at risk of being incinerated by crazy Aliens. Ahead of her were most of the enemy Collector ships. They were invisible to her eyes thanks to the EMF-warping hulls that were the body of each ship. Including her own *Blue Sky*. She looked to the left at the system graphic holo. Its overhead plan view showed the Sun at the center of the holo, with the system's nine worlds and Asteroid Belt shown in their actual orbital positions. Orbital tracks were bright circular lines with the AU distances of each world annotated beside the small circle that indicated a world. The graphic showed everything that mattered to the upcoming space battle.

"Ship has arrived safely," Star Traveler said from above her. "Enemy Collector ships are shown as purple dots. Human-controlled Collector ships are green dots. Human space-going craft are red dots. Orders?"

"Move us toward *Fear Arrives*, but keep our position to the rear of the ball of ships," Jane said. "I can see what I need to see."

Hoping that would shut up the mouthy AI, she focused on the ships in space manned by her fellow humans. Two Collector ships were close to Earth, one was next to Mars and four were close to Jupiter, near its large moon Callisto. In company with the four ships at Jupiter were 20 red dots. Those had to be the 14 Trident missile carrying *Ohio*-class subs that America currently had in service, supplemented by some Russian *Typhoon* and *Borei*-class boomers. Maybe a few Chinese missile launching subs were in the group of twenty. Two red dots were close to the Moon, suggesting they were subs providing supplies to the Moon base. That was the base set up

earlier by a joint American, Chinese and Japanese effort. That put
humanity on four worlds, when Mars was added. Was President
Hartman hedging against an attack on Earth by building an
underground base on the Moon? It would not help. Any place
occupied by humans now used a nuke reactor, either fission or fusion-
based. Every reactor sent off neutrinos that could be picked up by a
Collector ship sensor. Humans could only hide on another world if
they were using solar and fuel cell power. Whatever.

"Incoming neutrino signal from *Fear Arrives*," announced
Star Traveler in his trademark voice. At first the AI had sounded like
a BBC announcer crossed with a Hindu English speaker. Then its
voice had resembled a mix of hers and Bill's voices. Since they'd
added Bill's saloon buddies, its voice had evolved to a mix of tones
heard as other humans spoke. But it still had a touch of haughty BBC
announcer tone in its voice.

"Share this conversation with our five allied ships," she said,
thinking over her options. "Display my vulture image and the vulture
crew holo images in my response. Accept incoming signal."

"Understood. Sharing. Displaying."

Her comlink holo filled with the snake-gorilla body of Death
Leader. As before, its four crewpersons occupied stations that circled
his elevated command pedestal. All of them had heads, carapaces or
whatever looking down at their station control pillars. The white eyes
of the enemy fleet leader fixed on her. Its gorilla-like mouth opened.
The purple tongue inside moved quickly.

"Captain Sharp Beak, continue bringing your ship *Strikes
Deep* closer to my ship," the monster growled deeply. "I wish us to be
a compact ball of ships before we head for Earth."

Jane threw out her arms to either side of her seat. The holo
image of her vulture form now showed black wings spreading out
from her shoulders. Her yellow beak opened. Red eyes fixed on the
enemy leader. "Payment first! Send me my Nokten crystal. Or I leave
now!"

The snake-gorilla's blue-scaled head drew back. The cobra
hoods on either side flared out, making it look as if extra black eyes
were watching her. "Patience! You avians are always too eager to
act." The creature muttered something to a nearby crewperson. The
words were emphasized with a kick at its head from the creature's
black-taloned feet. The crewperson ducked, avoiding any contact.

Which would not have happened anyway since Death Leader stood atop a platform that was six feet above its Command Bridge floor. "There are only 24 pods on this ship. One is being sent to you with a crystal. You will be paid shortly. As will every captain in service to me!"

Time to start the battle of minds. "My sensors show the Humans possess *seven* Collector ships! You lied to us! We must avoid the gas world!"

The snake-gorilla's face moved to different shapes. Was it showing anger? "We do what I order. No more. No less." The giant creature looked aside at a nearby holo, then fixed on her. White eyes blinked. "You knew the Humans controlled five ships. Those are the ships they used to attack the Market world at HD 128311. It seems they have acquired two more Collector ships." The snake-gorilla looked aside at its own system graphic holo. "There are also 22 Magfield drive Human spaceships." The creature looked back to her. "Divide and overwhelm is my combat direction. This fleet will change course once we arrive near this world of Jupiter. We will attack every Human ship above that world! We will face little threat from the three ships near Earth and a place they call Mars." Death Leader raised a black-furred hand and made a fist. His purple tongue swept over his front canines. "Like my hand, we are 36 ships strong! Nothing can stand against us. You *will* fight against the Humans at this Jupiter. You will fight them above this Earth. Then you will join me in irradiating that world's surface!"

Jane felt relief. This creature reacted to any challenge by doing whatever was the opposite someone else wanted. Clearly it would not dive its ship into the Sun. But its internal instinct seemed to be aimed at constant defiance. Which made her wonder about the home world of these Mokden creatures. What produced a species that felt the need to immediately dominate those around them? It was very different from the fight, flight or negotiate reactions of most humans. Time to pretend her submission. She lowered her arms, causing her vulture wings to fold against her back.

"I follow you. My ship will destroy any Human within range of our weapons. What will you pay me after we assist in destroying this world of Earth?" she said loudly.

"Another Nokten crystal awaits every ship that attacks Earth," snarled Death Leader.

"Profit is welcome," she answered back, looking aside at her duplicate of the Collector Pods Chamber holo. "Your pod has arrived. My hover bot is retrieving my crystal." She faced back to the monster who sought to erase humanity from the universe. "My ship will join the fleet in its flight inward."

White eyes blinked. The snake-gorilla lowered its fist and touched the armrest on the seat in front of which it stood. "Obedience brings profit. Departing."

The snake-gorilla image vanished. Someone in her comlink holo chuckled.

"Nicely done," Stefano said from his ship. The man's tightly muscled frame sat back in his captain's seat. Like hers it resembled the seat occupied by an aircraft carrier ship's captain.

"We're gonna kick butt," Alicia remarked, sounding as confident as Jane hoped she sounded.

Joe raised a hand. "I assume we will not attack until we get inside the Jupiter system?"

"Very correct," Jane said. "All of you, study Jupiter, its inner dust rings, its 67 moons and the four big Galilean moons. I'm hoping some of our ships can play hide and seek and shoot, with the moons providing cover from hostile lasers."

"Captain," called Learned from the *Harken*. "A collector pod has arrived with my Nokten crystal payment. Other pods are visiting other fleet ships. May I suggest we all take a food and rest break during the 46 hours it will take to get to Jupiter?"

The color-banded man made sense. Already she felt her neck and shoulder muscles beginning to ache from her tenseness. "All captains, I approve Captain Learned's suggestion. Though you may wish to remain awake for awhile. I'm expecting to chat with General Poindexter very soon. She and the JCS and everyone on the seven ships left behind now knows 36 Collector ships have suddenly appeared out past Pluto. I suspect she will welcome the news that six of those ships are covertly controlled by us."

The acknowledgements from her fellow captains came quickly. With a quick scan upfront at the five dedicated people seated before their work stations, she sat back in her chair and ordered her mind. Dealing with senior officers was nearly as chancy as dealing with deadly Aliens!

CHAPTER TWELVE

Bill smiled to himself at the way Jane had handled the enemy fleet commander. One would think any Alien would be aware of reverse psychology. Then again, Death Leader was clearly not used to being subservient to anyone. Maybe all the Mokden were like him. Which made him wonder about the creature's home world. Surely it was the last place he and Jane should ever visit!

"Incoming encrypted neutrino signals from seven human captains," Star Traveler's voice hummed from the ceiling of the Command Bridge. "They call from their Collector ships. The ones resident in this system."

"Accept their signals," Jane said, looking pleased.

He understood. One more delay before his wife dealt with the Air Force chief of staff and maybe the president of America was surely welcome. His comlink holo filled with seven new images. They joined the images of Jane and their five allied captains. He recognized the faces of Jake, Mack and Janice. Four other faces, one female and three male, were the new captains of the *Seafloat, Pointe Du Hoc, Chapultepec Castle* and *Manila Bay*. He'd seen the faces of these new captains just before they left for Kepler 62. He recalled they came from Ranger, Delta Force, Green Beret and Air Force Special Tactics units. Special operations trained they were. And by now, experienced at handling their starships. They'd all had four months in which to review the space battle holos from HD 128311, Kepler 443 and the Moon. And to practice op force encounters in space with each other.

"Good to see you, Captain Yamaguchi," called Jake Slowzenski from the *Tangi Valley*. The man's ship was one of the four at Jupiter. "Are we facing 35 enemy ships?"

"No!" Jane responded quickly. "The *USS Blue Sky* is covertly assisted by five Collector ships we took over. Your buddies Stefano, Alicia, Frank and Joe, along with Learned Escape, now control those ships. They are listening in on our chat." She shrugged within her tube suit. "That leaves 30 enemy ships. The AIs on 20 of them will block weapons use during battle."

"It's still a lot of enemy," Mack said from the *Rolling Thunder*. "There are four of us here at Jupiter waiting for you. The other three, as you surely see, are at Earth and Mars. Do they join us here at Jupiter?"

"They do," Jane said calmly, her command manner showing a touch of amiableness. "Once I coordinate with General Poindexter, that is. Janice, Jesse and the rest of you, stand by. I'm putting in a call to the general. It's what I promised to do when we left." She looked ahead. "Chester, should we all put on dress uniforms before I call?"

To Bill's right the former Chief of Naval Operations turned away from his Engines station holos to look back. The lightly tanned, brown-haired career officer fixed on Bill's wife.

"Captain, no, we do not need to put on our dress outfits. The JCS chiefs and President Hartman surely know we could be in combat at any moment. We show ourselves as we are right now."

"Thank you, Chester," Jane murmured, her manner calm as ice. She looked up at the ceiling. "Star Traveler, those 20 space-going subs at Jupiter. Are any of them the *USS Louisiana* or the *USS Minnesota*?"

Bill blinked. Then he realized his wife was choosing to include the captains of the boomer subs orbiting above Jupiter. Which made sense. The missile, railgun and laser-armed subs were as much a part of *her* combat fleet as were the 13 Collector ships now present in the Solar system. Each sub captain should be listening to her chat with the head of the Air Force Space Command, along with the Collector ship captains. That was a lot of neutrino comlink signals. Which he had no doubt Star Traveler could handle very easily. He pushed away his memory of time spent within the AI's mind and focused on the here and now.

"Both submarines are present above Jupiter, based on the neutrino comlink signals I am receiving from the Magfield drive control plates I built for those craft," the AI hummed long and low.

"Send a signal to both captains. Invite them to visit with me," Jane said.

"Signal sent. Responses incoming."

Bill's comlink holo, already busy with 13 people icon images, now gained the faces of Captain Joshua Baraka of the Trident missile sub *USS Louisiana* and Captain Paul Leonard of the attack sub *USS Minnesota*. Clearly the *Louisiana's* hull damage was now fully repaired. And it had regained its Magfield engine from one of the transports aboard the Collector ships left behind.

"Captain Yamaguchi, a pleasure to hear from you," called the deep bass voice of Baraka. The black man wore the usual sub officer uniform under the tube suit worn by him and the other people in his sub's CIC room.

The bald Anglo captain smiled easily. "Same from me, Captain Yamaguchi. Welcome home!" Paul gestured to one side in the red-lit CIC of his sub. "My crew were getting a bit bored after spending a week playing loop the loop with some of Jupiter's crazy moons!"

Jane saluted the two men, then smiled. "Very happy to see you both. Shortly I will talk to General Poindexter and outline to her our plan for battling the enemy fleet. Which consists of just 30 ships. My ship's boarding crews took over five enemy ships out at Kepler 62. We are hanging back to the rear of the ship cluster that shows on your control plates."

"Very good to hear!" responded Paul.

Joshua's face turned thoughtful. "Captain of the fleet, may I suggest we bring in the senior captains of the Russian and Chinese subs who are out here with us? While 14 subs are Tridents, the other six are from our allies. Four Russian and two Chinese."

Jane lifted a thin eyebrow. "Agreed. Who are they?"

Joshua looked down at an iPad he held, then up. "They are Captain Dimitry Rogozin of the *Borei*-class boomer sub *Yury Dolgorukiy* and Captain Wu Shengli of the *Jin*-class boomer sub *Emperor Huang Ti*. I'm sending you the sub call signs."

Jane looked aside to one of the dozen holos that surrounded her elevated command seat. "Got them. Star Traveler, add captains Joshua and Paul to our group holo chat. And put in a neutrino signal to the two other captains."

"Signaling. Response arrives," the ship mind hummed.

Two more sub captain images joined Bill's comlink holo. Which now split to show the 13 Collector ship captains in the usual comlink holo, but with the sub captains now moving to Bill's true space holo. Which really showed nothing not already present in his system graphic holo. To his right Chester and his fellow crewmates were closely watching their own holos.

"Captain Dimitry Rogozin of the *Yury Dolgorukiy* reporting," grumbled a middle-aged Slav with squarish face, bushy black eyebrows and a cautious manner.

A Chinese man also appeared. He looked thin, his frame lanky. As best Bill could tell, the man resembled folks from the Manchuria part of China. His black eyes fixed on them. "Captain Wu Shengli of the *Emperor Huang Ti* responds to fleet Captain Jane Yamaguchi."

While his wife repeated the enemy fleet makeup to the four boomer sub captains, Bill tapped his Weapons control pillar top to bring up Internet datafiles on both classes of subs. The *Borei*-class boomer captained by Rogozin held 16 Bulava type RSM-56 SLBMs, each outfitted with 10 MIRV thermonuke warheads. One of the four Russian subs was a *Typhoon*-class sub. It was the *Dimitry Donskoy*, which held 20 R-39 SLBMs with 10 MIRVs each. The smaller *Jin*-class subs of the People's Liberation Army Navy Submarine Force were Type 094 subs. Each of the five subs currently in service were outfitted with 12 JL-2 SLBMs with four MIRV warheads per missile. The Russian and Chinese subs certainly added to the thermonukes they could launch against Death Leader's fleet.

"—and that is where we stand now, after my covert mission to the enemy's star base," Jane said, her tone command formal. "Do each of you agree to accept any combat action order given by me?"

"Of course," rumbled Rogozin, his manner more casual than some Russian officers Bill had met during SEAL assignments. "We are allies now. As in World War II. You shared your Magfield drive engines with us, which allows me to fly through space like a sparrow darting through the trees!" The man's clean-shaven face turned sober. "Equally useful are the inertial damper units and gravity plates given us by your amazing Collector starships. While every Navy man is used to rough seas, being weightless is not normal to my crew."

Jane nodded. "Captain Wu Shengli?"

The Chinese sub captain returned Jane's salute. "I am loyal to the people's party. My party leaders have chosen to ally with you Americans. We ally with you now, as we did during World War II. Your commands I will obey."

"Good. Very good," Jane said, her manner turning even more command formal than earlier. "I welcome the participation of Earth's most populous people and its largest nation in the common defense of our homeland. Both Rossiya and Chin will die if these bastards every reach Earth!" She looked up. "Star Traveler, send an encrypted neutrino signal to Peterson Air Force Base, marked to the attention of General Poindexter. Share her reply with all our subs and ships, including those at Jupiter, Earth and Mars."

"Sending signal. Earth response incoming. Imagery is routed to the comlink holos," the AI hummed haughtily.

Bill's comlink holo changed. The images of Jane and the seven Collector ship captains, plus the images of their five nearby captains, became a ring of icons that surrounded the image of Poindexter. The black woman's tightly curled black hair now had streaks of gray in it. Her middle-aged face showed wrinkles not hidden by makeup. The woman wore her usual Air Force Blue suit jacket with service ribbons, medals and four stars on shoulder epaulettes. She was seated at the Building One tactical display table where she managed Space Command activities. Behind her were a few dozen airmen and women who wore green camo ABUs. Clearly this was a room where folks were in active duty combat status. As befitted the president's declaration of war. He noticed there were three other JCS chiefs seated nearby at their own display tables. One was the current Chief of Naval Operations. The other was the Japanese-American general who ran the Army. The third looked to be the Marine commandant. The black woman pursed her lips, her manner becoming intensely focused.

"Captain Yamaguchi, welcome home. How many enemy ships do we face?"

"Just 30," Jane said as she saluted, then proceeded to repeat what she had told the stay-at-home Collector ship and sub captains. "Also receiving your signal, and my comments, are the captains of the 20 subs at Jupiter and every Collector ship captain. The two subs above the Moon, are they American? I wish to include their captains in our discussion of battle issues."

Poindexter returned Jane's salute. Then looked down at the flat screen that filled part of her tactical display table. She looked up, her dark brown eyes bright. "Those two subs are Brit and French boomer subs. They are the *Vanguard*-class *HMS Vengeance* and the *Triomphant*-class *FNS Terrible*." The woman tapped on a nearby iPad. "I am sending them orders to head your way." She tapped again. "The call IDs for those two ships are now sent to you. Since the captains of the seven Collector ships left in the system are listening, I hereby order the ships above Earth and Mars to head your way. Every ship and sub should arrive well before the enemy fleet's arrival at Jupiter."

His wife's expression relaxed slightly. "Thank you. Star Traveler, signal those two sub captains and have them join this discussion."

"Signaling. Responses incoming."

Bill's true space holo filled with the images of two more captains. They joined the thoughtful faces of the Russian and Chinese captains. He noticed Lofty Flyer had now changed their vector heading to join the inward movement of the enemy fleet ships. Their six Collector ships were scattered over the rear of the tight cluster of ships. Which now headed for Jupiter at one-tenth lightspeed.

"General, may I outline my thoughts on how to manage our pincer attack against the enemy fleet?" Jane said, sounding more calm and collected than Bill felt.

The woman who was the chief of staff of the Air Force and also head of the Space Command units based at Peterson nodded slowly. "Proceed." She gestured to her left. "The other JCS chiefs here are of course watching your signal. Our crowd of listeners may be smaller than your crowd, but we need to know everything you know. And plan to do."

Jane licked her lips, lifted a hand to brush back a black bang, which action was blocked by her helmet. She did not show embarrassment. Instead, she sat back in her seat, laid both arms on her armrests, and proceeded to outline the tactical and strategic actions she and Bill and the five Collector ship captains had discussed just before system arrival. Ten minutes later she stopped her monologue.

"As you can see, our trip to Kepler 62 was productive. Twenty of the 30 enemy ships will be rendered defenseless for at least two hours," Jane summarized. "Also, your version of our system graphic holo now shows three ships marked by red dashes. They are managed by AIs who don't give a damn about slave-taking Aliens. The central red dash ship is the one occupied by their fleet commander. The other seven ship AIs may join our weapons block use. Or may warn their captains. Which is why I will not contact those AIs until our friendly AIs block weapons use on the 20 ships we contacted." She tapped her right armrest. "I am sending you the video of my recent talk with

Death Leader." She pursed her lips. "General, vital to this fight is my promise to the enemy ship AIs that none of them will be killed by our attacking ships. My people now know they need to aim at the rear, engine sections of enemy Collector ships. Do you support this tactic?"

Poindexter frowned, then nodded slowly. "I do. For several reasons. First, it makes those ships unable to attack Earth. Second, the surviving ship minds can assist us in rebuilding their ships after we bring them to Earth orbit. Third, America has launched the components of our own Collector ship factory into orbit." She tapped her iPad. "I'm sending you an image of that factory. Which will rely on ores mined from the mountains of the Moon. That is why we set up a Moon base in the Taurus Littrow highlands. And why the Brit and French subs were there." The woman leaned forward. "We can build a few Collector ships, once this war is over. But we lack ship minds to complete such ships. Maybe one or two AIs onboard badly damaged ships will agree to transfer to our newly built ships. That is the fourth good reason to not kill Collector ship AIs."

Jane gave the woman a thumbs-up. "So glad to hear that! Uh, the ship *Takur Ghar* captained by Janice Watanabe was orbiting above Mars. Was her presence there related to the prisoner dome we established on our last visit?"

"It was not," Poindexter said, her tone sounding reluctant to Bill. "That ship deposited the last members of a human colony we have built in a part of Mars far distant from the prisoner dome." The Air Force general looked aside to her fellow chiefs, then faced Jane. "President Hartman and the leaders of Russia, China, France and Great Britain agreed several months ago that humanity must not die. They discarded the idea of sending a Collector ship off to another star in favor of creating a colony of 600 people within the Solar system. The location of that colony will not be given to you, or to any ship involved in the upcoming battle. We cannot risk your AIs knowing that data, and then coming under the control of the enemy commander. Captain Watanabe herself does not know its location. Her ship simply deposited colonists and supplies in the Valle Marineris, then left. The people and supplies will be collected by a colonist vehicle."

Bill felt surprise, then understanding. The leaders of humanity were not going to count on him and his wife and their allies winning this battle. They had created a backup plan. Which he approved of.

The antimatter destruction of central Kiev was still fresh in his mind. He looked back at Jane. His wife's pale oval face showed calmness. Again he marveled at her composure under the circumstances. Prior Earth wars had just involved the survival of freedom, democracy and liberty, or the stopping of genocidal dictators. This war was about the survival of the species.

"Understood," Jane said quickly. "I support the decision of you and the President. Uh, have the colonists avoided the use of any nuclear reactors?"

Poindexter smiled briefly, then became very sober. "Captain, we know as well as you do that any Collector ship can track the neutrinos emitted by a fission or fusion reactor. The colony does not emit any neutrinos. Nor any radio, radar or other EMF emissions. Nor are they visible from orbit. Satisfied?"

"Very satisfied," Jane said.

"Good." Poindexter became thoughtful. "I like your plan to use collector pods as ramming vehicles against hostile enemy ships. Be aware that our national leaders have told the captains of every ship out there that they are at liberty to sacrifice their ship against any enemy ship that escapes the battle. Understood?"

Bill felt a chill run down his spine. Putting his own life at risk for the success of the mission, or to prevent the killing of team members, was something every SEAL and every spec ops member was trained to do. Taking a sub filled with a hundred or more humans and using it as a battering ram to kill an enemy Collector ship was something new to him. And to Jane. He hoped that part of human history did not need repeating in the deadly spaces above Jupiter."

"Understood," Jane said. "Our ship crews will spend part of the next 46 hours on rest, food and rec breaks. So we can be fresh for the battle. When we arrive at Jupiter and move toward our waiting ships, I will contact you again. So you, the JCS and the president will have a moment-by-moment awareness of what is happening out here."

"Thank you," Poindexter said softly.

And with that Bill changed his mental focus to his Weapons holo. He needed something to occupy his mind. Old video images of how Earth had looked after the asteroid hit the planet and killed the dinosaurs needed displacement. Now, was there any way to increase their antimatter reservoir beyond the four shot inventory they currently held?

◆ ◆ ◆

Jane looked at her iWatch. They had arrived not far from Jupiter's 66th moon, Megaclite, which was three miles in diameter. The gray rock slowly tumbled in her true space holo. It was a member of the Pasiphaë group of small asteroids that orbited Jupiter in a retrograde direction, the opposite of the prograde orbits followed by the four Galilean moons that lay close to Jupiter. Megaclite orbited more than 15 million miles out. That put them some distance out from Jupiter's multi-colored clouds. But the enemy fleet was already slowing to one percent of lightspeed, or to 6.706 million miles per hour. She tapped off the lightspeed numbers showing on the iWatch and fixed her attention on the system graphic holo that showed Callisto and its assemblage of Collector ships and boomer subs. They were all there now. Seven Collector ships and 22 subs. Since Callisto orbited about 1.2 million miles above Jupiter, the travel time to them was not much. The enemy fleet and her ships would be there in two hours or so. She noticed Bill was busily tapping away at his Weapons control pillar top. The man seemed excited about something.

"XO, you playing a game of *Space Invaders* on that device?"

He chuckled, then looked back to her. Inside the helmet he wore, his lightly bearded face showed excitement. "Hardly. But with the help of our ship mind, I've figured out how to increase our antimatter reservoir capacity to six shots of AM, before the particle accelerator has to make more." He turned back to the pillar top, tapped it, then looked back to her. "I've sent the reservoir storage changes to our other ships. In short, Star Traveler agreed to move a flexmetal wall out of the way and give the reservoir tank more room to expand. It just finished enclosing the additional tankage with electromags for containment of the negative matter."

This was promising. "Sounds good. Can our other Collector ships make these changes in less than two hours?"

He frowned, then brightened. "Yes! I spent most of this morning going over how to expand the reservoir tank without losing its current four shot load. Seems this flexmetal skin that makes up our ship can do incredible things. You've seen how our bridge floor can pop up seats and control pillars for new crew. And open holes in the walls. Well, adding tank volume is much the same. Just needed to show the AI where it could take down a wall so the tank could expand into a room that once held cleaning solvents."

Jane smiled. She enjoyed Bill's enthusiasm for thinking through a tactical problem. Her spouse had taken a long nap earlier, but since he'd awoken he'd been up here at his Ship Weapons station, intensely focused on the station's holos and its control pillar. Now she knew what had so obsessed him. "Weapons Chief, you've just increased our antimatter firing capacity by 50 percent. Well done!"

Bill grinned. As did Chester, who had been watching their byplay. The former CNO had spent his rest time with his wife Sharon. Bright Sparkle had spent her time in neutrino link with her spouse Learned Escape, their color bands making a riot of color as they spoke long and happily, judging by the smile on the woman's face. Her flying squirrel Navigator's face had also looked happy as Lofty Flyer chittered with her spouse Builder of Joy. Wind Swift had spent some hours in bark-talk with Long Walker the giant worm. Their mix of barks and moans had greeted her as she entered the Food Chamber. She realized the silver-scaled kangaroo female was acting happy. Clearly she and the worm, as folks with no species mate on the *Blue Sky*, had found a mutual friendship. She felt glad for the Alien woman and had turned and left the Food Chamber. Everyone was entitled to private time with the person who mattered most to them. She understood that. As she understood this coming battle could well result in the loss of subs, ships and people she cared for. Well, time to focus.

"People, in less than two hours we will be fighting for our lives, for our families and for the survival of Earth," she said, knowing her words sounded trite. "Get something to eat now, not later. If you have personal needs, relieve them now. From here on out we must be prepared for anything. Including pressure loss, a sudden attack on us, whatever."

Her five crewmates acknowledged her words. Wind Swift and Lofty Flyer left their stations and headed for the outside hallway. The habitat rooms of each, which included restrooms suited to their species, were close by. Bill, Chester and Bright Sparkle stayed at their stations. Though Sparkle looked back to her, the gorgeous woman's face intensely serious.

"Captain Jane, we three can keep a lookout watch. Do you need to visit a relief room?"

Jane bit her lip. Then realized she had drunk too much coffee that morning. "I do." She rose and waited for the pedestal support to lower to deck level. She stepped away from her seat. "Captain is off the bridge. Chief Petty Officer Bill MacCarthy is in command."

And with that she pointed her red cube at the oval door that gave access to the outside hallway, walked through it and headed for hers and Bill's habitat room. Yes, she would relieve her bladder. But she would also take a moment to look at the flat color pictures of her folks. Atsushi and Melany Yamaguchi. Her father had defied his parents' demand he marry a pure blood Japanese-American due to his love for Melany, the physics major he'd met at Stanford. That had caused his parents to break all contact with her Dad and Mom. All she knew of her paternal grandparents were photos, a movie or two and brief stories told by her Dad. Well, she and Bill were together and wonderfully married. Another crossbreed mix, according to one set of her grandparents. A normal American couple according to her Mom's parents. In her habitat suite she would look at the pictures of all of them. What she did today, what she had been doing ever since she and Bill had taken over the *Blue Sky* from Diligent Taskmaster, was fight to protect the people she loved from deadly, dangerous Aliens who thought her world was a convenient hunting ground for taking slaves. *No longer!* Now, she and Bill and everyone else in space and on Earth would show the Buyer society just how much trouble came whenever anyone attacked a human!

CHAPTER THIRTEEN

Bill steeled himself for imminent combat as the enemy fleet approached to within two million miles of the other Earth fleet. Their ship covered 111,000 miles a minute at one percent of lightspeed. Course they could speed up to one-tenth lightspeed in just 12 seconds. Or jump vertical, sideways or down to their current vector with nary a pause. He'd learned those lessons during the ship battles at HD 128311 and Kepler 443. Now, he had to remember all he'd learned. While accepting his wife's orders as if his life depended on it. Which it did.

"All captains," Jane called over the open neutrino comlink that connected her with every ship and with a watching General Poindexter. "Time to assume battle formation. I want the seven Collector ships to form a ring around the subs, which will form the bulk of this flat plate arrangement. That way the subs can have some defensive cover from the more heavily armed ships. No need to reply back. Just move!"

In the system graphic holo on Bill's left, he watched as the graphic showed them approaching the 2,900 mile wide bulk of Callisto. The other fleet moved quickly to assume the flat plate formation ordered by Jane. The formation hovered above the north pole of Callisto.

"Stefano, Alicia, Frank, Joe and Learned, send out some collector pods to circulate among the enemy fleet ships. Hold your position at the back of the ship ball," Jane said. "I suspect pretty soon we—"

"Incoming neutrino signal from Death Leader," their ship mind hummed from the ceiling.

"Accept," Jane said tersely.

Bill's comlink holo showed the snake-gorilla appearing to the left of Jane's black-feathered vulture form. The black-furred gorilla body of the monster who led the enemy fleet showed thick muscles tensing in his shoulders, arms and stocky legs. The blue-scale hoods flared out. White eyes fixed on them.

"Fleet captains!" he snarled. "The Humans have brought all their spaceships to us! The smaller craft are underwater submersibles, my ship mind tells me. While they move on Magfield engines and are armed with lasers, none of them can match a Collector ship! Keep your antimatter projectors aimed forward. We will disintegrate these submersibles while our lasers disable the Human Collector ships. Fire when I fire!" The creature's image disappeared.

In his comlink holo, Jane looked to Bill. "Weapons Chief, you are in command of our weapons. Hurt them!"

"I will," Bill responded quickly.

"Everyone, all ships, all captains, just before we reach laser firing range for our other fleet, I will order the enemy ship minds to block weapons use," Jane said. "Then Star Traveler will try to convert the seven ship minds not yet on our side to do the same. Be prepared for anything!"

Bill looked away from his Weapons holo. While his true space holo showed the dark ball of Callisto, its surface pockmarked by white impact craters and the reddish-brown of some highlands, the allied ships and subs were too small to show in the electro-optical scope image. But his system graphic holo showed every red dot sub and green dot human Collector ship. Names were affixed next to each red dot. He read them, more to keep his mind busy. Of the Trident subs, there were the *USS Henry M. Jackson, USS Alabama, USS Alaska, USS Nevada, USS Tennessee, USS Pennsylvania, USS West Virginia, USS Kentucky, USS Maryland, USS Nebraska, USS Rhode Island, USS Maine, USS Wyoming* and Joshua's boomer *USS Louisiana*. They were fourteen super boomers, each outfitted with 24 Trident II D5 missiles. Each of those missiles carried 12 MIRVd W88 thermonuke warheads. The four Russian ships were the *Typhoon*-class boomer *Dimitry Donskoy*, with 20 R-39 SLBMs outfitted with 10 MIRVd warheads per missile, and the *Borei*-class subs *Yuri Dolgorukiy, Alexsandr Nevsky* and *Vladimir Monomakh*. The Chinese Type 094 boomers were the *Emperor Huang Ti* and the *Chairman Mao Zedong*. Each of those subs carried 12 JL-2 SLBMs with four MIRV warheads per missile. Encircling them were the Collector ships *USS Tangi Valley, USS Rolling Thunder, USS Takur Ghar, USS Seafloat, USS Pointe Du Hoc, USS Chapultepec Castle* and the *USS Manila Bay*. It was a lot of firepower. But what of the mobile thermonuke minefields he had proposed to the JCS?

The true space holo suddenly glared with the yellow-white ball of a thermonuke blast.

Death Leader reappeared in the comlink holo. "Fire on the small bodies lying between us and the Human ships! They are not rocks. They are nuclear—"

"My ship has lost one Magfield engine," interrupted a green praying mantis.

The snake-gorilla clenched both fists. "Idiot! Tell your ship mind to plot every such nuclear rock in front of you. Then destroy any in your path! All captains, do the same!"

Bill checked his system graphic holo. They were still 700,000 miles out from contact with the other fleet. He checked the Collector ship dot that had sustained a melted Magfield engine from the thermonuke mine. It matched the ship run by the AI Melody. He wondered how efficient the music-loving ship mind would be in targeting the mines?

Green streaks of laser fire shot out from the ten Collector ships at the front of the ship ball that enclosed Death Leader's ship. Dozens of such streaks ended in yellow flares. Then one ship fired its antimatter projector. The black beam shot straight ahead, then began covering space in a tight spiral pattern, moving out from the center to a wider footprint. Their ship ball was just 693 miles wide, thanks to every Collector ship being within 131 miles of another ship. Soon two other ships fired antimatter beams in the spiral pattern. Several hundred yellow flares showed briefly as negative matter encountered positive matter and created a total conversion of matter to energy.

Bill grimaced. So much for his minefield. But at least the president's order had been obeyed and the tiny mobile mines had been dispersed by his fellow warriors once the approach vector of the enemy fleet had become apparent. Now, it was just five minutes until the enemy fleet reached the 10,000 mile range of shipboard lasers. When would his wife—

"Star Traveler! Tell our allied ship minds to block weapons use!" Jane yelled from behind him. "Share your mind with the seven ship minds not yet contacted," she said more softly. "Convince them to block weapons use on their ships. Repeat my promise to keep all ship minds alive!"

"Complying. Contacting," the AI hummed. "Two ship minds have agreed to block weapons use on the understanding we will spare their lives. The 22 ship minds now blocking weapons use have a green dash beside their purple dot in everyone's system graphic."

Bill saw that as his graphic imagery changed. That left the three 'don't give a damn' ships marked with red dashes. But now, five more ships gained a red dash. *Crap.*

"Allied ships!" Jane called firmly. "Fire antimatter beams at the engine spaces of enemy ships!"

Bill tapped his control pillar top, targeting a Collector ship that lay 131 miles to the far left of the *Blue Sky*. Another tap and their antimatter projector fired.

In space, death is always waiting.

Bill's targeted ship lost the rear third of its length in a yellow-white fireball of total matter-to-energy conversion.

The sight hurt his eyes even with the automatic damping of the true space holo.

To their right, the five Collector ships they had captured from the enemy now fired black beams at nearby Collector ships.

Five more yellow-white fireballs glared ahead of them, resembling new-born stars.

"Yes!" he yelled, his fingers moving again to acquire a target 260 miles away.

"Disperse!" screamed Death Leader in the comlink holo.

He tapped the AM projector. A black beam shot out. It hit the rear of an enemy ship that lay 600 miles away.

To his right three more bright stars shone in the utter blackness of deep space.

Two beams missed their targets, according to his Weapons targeting panel.

Ten enemy ships removed as a threat to Earth. But 20 more were spreading outward like thistle pods ejected from the mother plant. Already the acceleration of those ships was approaching one-tenth lightspeed.

"Lofty Flyer!" Bill called to their Navigator. "Shift vector angle to 43, 52, 17!"

The enemy ship he was targeting was 3,221 miles away. Its Magfield engines clawed at the magnetic field of Jupiter, using its huge magnetosphere field to help with its acceleration. Other enemy ships did the same, striving to reach beyond the 4,000 mile range of a Collector ship's antimatter projector.

"Vector shifted!" chittered the flying squirrel woman.

"Got another one!" called Stefano from the *Neil C. Roberts*.

Bill tapped his AM projector.

A second yellow-white sun joined Stefano's newborn star.

"All enemy ships are now beyond antimatter targeting range," Star Traveler hummed.

Fuck! He knew that. But the enemy was still within gas laser range. And Chester, thank the gods, had revved up their Magfield engines as he saw the enemy ships rapidly speeding up, outward and away from the covert enemies that had infiltrated the snake-gorilla's fleet. Worse, the eight purple dot with red dash ships that included the snake-gorilla's ship were now firing back at Jane's fleet with their tail lasers.

Green beams shot past the *Blue Sky* and four other allied ships. But two green streaks impacted on the front nose of the *Fallujah*.

"Hull penetration," called Frank over the open comlink signal. "Chris is firing back. Builder of Joy is taking us sideways and in a random walk pattern. We're still pursuing!"

Bill saw that Lofty Flyer had also put their pursuit vector on a random walk spiral so the enemy could not count on a target following a predictable course line.

Course the remaining 18 enemy ships were doing the same as they sped faster to reach a distance of 10,000 miles from the *Blue Sky* and its five ship allies. At least the 10 with friendly AIs were not firing any weapon on them. A new image showed in his comlink holo.

"Captains!" screamed Death Leader, white spittle flying from his giant mouth. "Your ship minds are blocking weapons! Kill them to regain control! Put demolition balls against the back of your captain's habitat room and explode them. The AI will die. But you and your crew can regain control of your ship. And fight against these miserable Humans!"

"Damn," Jane muttered from behind Bill as he fired his two nose lasers at the jinking dot of an enemy Collector ship. "Star Traveler, can that really happen? Can a ship mind be killed that way?"

"It can," the AI hummed quickly, its tone sounding shocked.

"We are 13 live Collector ships plus our subs," she said quickly. "Tell the friendly ship minds on the fleeing ships, and on the unmoving ships, they are free to return weapons control whenever they detect explosives being placed in the captain's habitat!"

"Complying." A long pause lasted. "The captains on the ten fleeing ships with friendly AIs are debating with their crew. Some wish to destroy the AI of their ship. Some disagree, saying they will soon reach a weapons safe distance from us." Another pause happened. "Six ship captains have ordered their crews to emplace bypass circuits on the weapons controls. All six are working on this. Those ships will have full weapons control in two point three eight hours."

"But their ship minds will still be alive," Jane said hurriedly. "What about—"

"Four ship captains are now putting explosives against the wall that separates the ship mind room from the captain's habitat space," the AI interrupted. "Those ship minds are announcing the removal of weapons use control by themselves."

Bill fired again at the rear of a fleeing Collector ship just as the enemy ship reached 9,981 miles from them. Since the *Blue Sky* and the enemy ship were now moving at one-tenth lightspeed, that kept the target within range. His fire was joined by green lasers fired from the two allied ships in his combined-firing group.

A red flare showed in the true space holo. He checked his Weapons fire control panel.

"A hit and penetration of a fuel chamber," Bill called out.

"But we now have 12 enemy ships with full weapons use. They are turning back toward us," Jane said. "All ships! Prepare for attack."

"One ship mind is now dead," Star Traveler hummed. "Three ship minds on the explosives threatening ships still live."

Bill looked to his system graphic holo. His fleet and the enemy fleet were heading sideways away from Callisto, moving outward and toward Earth. The 12 enemy ships with the vaporized engine spaces lay far to their rear, their inertia leaving them on track to fly by Callisto and then continue outward and way from Jupiter. At least the vector track of those 12 did not pass through Ganymede, Europa, Io or the further out moons. But the vector track did pass through the outer third ring of dust that lay close to Saturn. Those ships would pass within 90 miles of the tiny moon Amalthea. Then it was open sailing at one-tenth lightspeed. Which meant those disabled ships could be recovered after the battle was over.

"Jake!" called Jane. "Bring your fleet in close to the backside of the 12 enemy ships. Maybe we can still do our pincer maneuver!"

"Coming," the SEAL replied.

Bill saw that Lofty Flyer had now reversed their vector approach, sending them away at one-tenth lightspeed. That put the 12 weapons capable enemy ships between their six ships and the seven Collector ships led by Jake. The subs managed by Joshua, Paul, Dimitry and Shengli now joined Jake's advance. That made it 29 ships on Jake's side, six ships on Jane's side and the 12 enemy ships in between. The comlink holo to his right, which had shown only Jane, again filled with the black-furred form of Death Leader.

"Human female!" the snake-gorilla screamed. "I am coming for you! No one who deceives a Mokden survives that deceit!"

Jane laughed, shocking Bill. "Stupid primate! You had a month to discover my deception. You failed! And I used that time to win over most ship minds on your ships. They did not like the news that your 'guests' were really Captives. Nor did they like the idea of being used to capture more people."

Muscles moved in the blue-scaled face of the snake-gorilla. As it stood, it lifted both heavily-muscled arms and shook clenched fists at Jane. "Female! Our Mokden females know how to submit. When I catch your ship, I will come aboard and eat of your carcass!"

Jane smiled, then gave the creature her middle finger. "Among humans, this gesture advises you to screw yourself. Which you have already achieved. Twelve of your ships cannot move. Your remaining weapons-active ships are fewer than my combined fleets. If you surrender now, perhaps we will let you live in our prison dome on Mars." She tapped her right armrest. "See this image? It already contains Diligent Taskmaster and the captains and crews of the six ships that attacked Earth. They are vicious, like you. When you join them, will you eat of their bodies, or they eat of yours?"

"You will die!" The creature turned its triangular head and looked down. "Increase speed now!"

"But our engines will melt!" cried a crewperson who resembled a teddy bear.

"Increase now! Or I kill you!" screamed Death Leader.

"Captain," called Chester from his Engines station. "Death Leader's ship *Fear Arrives* has sped up to 11 percent of lightspeed. Most of his other ships are doing the same. He will overtake us."

Bill triple-checked the CO_2 nose lasers of the *Blue Sky*. The lasers, the four shots remaining in his antimatter reservoir and the plasma batteries on their spine and belly were all able to shoot toward the oncoming enemy fleet. The same armaments were still active on the ships of Stefano, Alicia, Frank, Joe and Learned. As they were on the seven Collector ships led by Jake and his captains. The subs added 22 deadly lasers and hundreds of thermonuke warheads to the mix. Who would reach target range first?

"Bright Sparkle," called Jane. "Increase power output from our fusion reactors. Chester, use that power to take us up to 11 percent of lightspeed!"

The color-banded woman on Bill's right tapped her control pillar. "Fusion power output increased by six percent!"

"Speeding up," muttered Chester, his low baritone sounding tense. "That Alien is right, though. We could lose one or both Magfield drives if we maintain this speed too long."

"I know," Jane said, her tone command intense. "But their 12 ships outnumber our six. We have to buy time for the other fleet to reach target range."

Bill had a sudden idea. He tapped his Weapons fire control panel. His feet felt the vibration of weapons launch.

"Captain! I'm firing all our MITV torps at the enemy ships. That's 14 torps, each outfitted with five thermonuke warheads. We can create a minefield between us and them!"

"Yes!" Jane said quickly. "Ship captains! Fire your MITV torps. Add to Bill's warhead minefield. Hurry!"

"Firing," called Joe from the *Moberly*.

"Also firing," husked Frank from the *Fallujah*. "Hull penetration is sealed. We are back to being airtight."

"Launching torps," cried Alicia from the *Musan*, sounding Ranger eager.

"Torps launching," spoke Learned from the *Harken*.

"Doing the same," softly said Stefano from the *Neil C. Roberts*.

Bill's system graphic now filled with a dozen red dots representing the first salvo of MITV torps from the maglev railgun launcher that lay below the Command Bridge of his ship. More red dots joined them. Each ship had 14 torps. Soon, there would be 84 torps speeding back toward the oncoming enemy fleet. The torp nose cones would fly away and launch five thermonuke warheads, each warhead carrying the power of three megatons of thermonuclear disaster. While Death Leader's 12 ships would surely detect and destroy many of them, they might not get all 420 warheads. While none of the torps could reverse their one-tenth lightspeed travel away from the enemy, the enemy's approach at eleven percent lightspeed would bring their ships into range of warheads fitted with magnetic field sensors. Bill hoped three or four of them would detonate and damage a nearby Collector ship. That might happen if a Collector ship hull came within two miles of the plasma fireball of one of the torp warheads.

Bill's system graphic showed the 12 enemy Collector ships with full weapons control were pulling away from the six enemy ships where crews were installing bypass circuits. Those six ships could not fire for another two hours at least. By which time something had to break in this battle. Then he noticed something that surprised him.

"Captain! Five subs and all seven of our other Collector ships are speeding up to 11 percent of lightspeed." The five red sub dots changed position. "Uh, correction. The subs are moving up to 12 percent lightspeed. *Shit*. Their fission reactors must have all the control rods pulled to generate the power needed!"

In his comlink holo, Jane frowned. Her clear helmet glinted as she looked aside at one of her holos. "Those subs are the *Minnesota*, the *Louisiana*, two Russian subs and a Chinese sub. What the hell are their captains thinking?"

Humming came from the ceiling.

"Incoming signal from Peterson Air Force Base," Star Traveler said, his near-human voice sounding surprised.

In the comlink holo there now appeared the image of Poindexter. "Captain Yamaguchi, we've been watching this battle. As has the president, the leaders of China, Russia, Britain and France, and their military staffs. Those five subs are preparing to ram the enemy ships. We cannot allow any enemy to reach Earth."

"I know that!" groused Jane. Her image showed anger on her face. That anger quickly disappeared and a neutral command expression replaced it. "I appreciate the assistance of the JCS and our other fleet members. However, my tactical response is still evolving. I expect to disable or destroy all enemy ships. Now let me do that!"

"Understood," the black woman said, her expression equally neutral. "Departing."

Bill's comlink filled once more with the image of Jane. The image icons of their five ship allies also showed. He refocused on the groupings of ships in the system graphic. He licked his lips. The 12 enemy ships were just 53,000 miles from Jane's ship grouping. Five more minutes and both ship groupings would be in laser firing range of each other.

Yellow-white energy flared in his true space holo. Five more fireballs happened.

"Captain! The six laggard enemy ships with no weapons have lost their engine sections!" He pulled his eyes away from the holos in front of him and sought his wife's tense face. "Love! Jake's Collector ships hit them with antimatter beams."

Jane looked surprised, then more intense. "That means the other fleet ships and subs are within 4,000 miles of the laggard ships. How soon before they are in target range for the 12 pursuing us?"

"Two minutes," Bill said as his fire control panel showed him readouts on every enemy ship, the other Earth fleet ships and their smaller fleet of six ships. "I suggest our ships should disperse sideways. To force the enemy ships to chase us individually. That will prevent them from combining their laser and AM beams against us!"

Jane nodded. "Navigator, take us out at a right angle to our current vector. Avoid any of Jupiter's moons but get us up and out from this vector! Captains, do the same with your ships!"

Stefano, Alicia, Frank, Joe and Learned acknowledged the order.

Bill knew this sideways vector change would cause the 12 enemy ships to do the same. Which meant their torp minefield would likely not hit anyone. Except maybe for the six enemy ships without weapons access.

"Captain, see the minefield threat to the six enemy ships that have lost their engines?" Bill called.

"I see it." She looked up. "Star Traveler, send a neutrino comlink signal to those six ships. Now!"

"Complying. Signal sent. Responses incoming."

A creature who resembled a giant green frog with bulbous eyes appeared in the comlink holo. It rested on an elevated bench atop its command pedestal. Two narrow arms were touching nearby control pillars. Five other enemy captain images also appeared. Two were green praying mantises, one a cockroach like Diligent and two were black-furred grizzly bears with four arms each.

"Captains of the weapons disabled ships," Jane called loudly. "You have no engines. Your ships are approaching a minefield established by my ships. Surrender to me and I will have those mines deactivated. If you continue trying to regain weapons control from your ship AIs, I will let the mines seek you out. They are mobile!"

Bill knew that was a lie. Only the Earth-made thermonuke mines had the hydrogen peroxide jets that allowed them to move toward a sensed magnetic field. Their torps were outstanding Hunter-Killer vehicles well able to sense enemy ships by way of neutrino tracking. But once the warheads were launched, there was no control over their trajectory. However, his fire control panel was able to send shut-down signals to the warheads. He'd never used that option. Would now be the first time?

"I surrender the ship *Elegant Pond*," called the green frog.

Bill noticed the ship with Melody as its ship mind was heading away from the battle at five percent of lightspeed. What to do with it?

"Weapons Chief, disable the mines in front of that ship," Jane ordered. "Anyone else wish to surrender? Or do you choose to take chances with three megaton warheads?"

In seconds the other five captains surrendered to Jane. Who nodded slowly. "Your current vector will take you out of the gravitational field of the planet Jupiter. Humans will come later to salvage your ship. Captains and crew will be allowed to live with other prisoners of war at a habitat dome on Mars."

Bill tapped his fire control panel to shut-down the warheads fired by his railgun. His ship mind-linked panel showed his buddies on the other five ships were doing the same.

The comlink holo suddenly filled with the image of Death Leader.

"Female Human, shortly you will feel the caress of my lasers," the snake-gorilla snarled. "Then my antimatter beam will kill your engines. Are you prepared to die?"

Strangely, all Bill could think of was the fact that they had managed to disable 18 enemy ships by destroying their engines. That left lots of Alien ships to scavenge for the rebuilding of some of them. But the remaining 12 now closed on his six ships. Which were flying outward from their earlier course vector. In the system graphic, he noticed how the enemy ships were now splitting into two-ship pairs. So two ships could combine their laser fire on a single human Collector ship. Where were the seven Collectors and five subs from Jake's fleet? *Ah.* They were 90,000 miles out from Death Leader's ships but closing. The five subs were somewhat ahead of the Collectors. Nice. But the snake-gorilla's ships were now within 12,000 miles of the *Blue Sky* and its five sister ships. A few seconds and—

Green streaks filled the true space holo on Bill's right. The *Blue Sky* shuddered.

"Hull penetrated above the Transport Exit Chamber," Star Traveler hummed. "Sending hover bots and repair robots with structural beams to—"

"Dive!" Jane yelled.

"Diving," chittered Lofty Flyer.

Just as Bill fired his two tail lasers at the two ships pursuing them, the *Blue Sky* shuddered again.

"Spine plasma battery vaporized," the AI hummed.

His system graphic showed hits on the bulbous noses of two chasing ships. One of them spun sideways. Spectroscopic sensors said the ship was venting air and water.

"We're hit!" cried Alicia. "Mark is gone. His Navigator station vanished. We got a hole from ceiling to floor. I'm taking over nav controls!"

Pain hit Bill. He'd liked Mark. The Ranger had been one of the most enthusiastic boarder recruits. Before that the man had stood round after round of beer pitchers at Jack's Deep Six saloon. Now, his fellow fly fisherman was gone. Turned into vapor particles thanks to the deadly green beam fired by their enemy.

He tapped his laser fire control. His two tail lasers joined ten other green beams from their five allied ships. Their laser fire was co-located on four enemy ships, thanks to the target cross-tracking of the ship minds in their six ships. All Bill and the other Weapons folks had to do was tap the Fire patch on top of their Weapons control pillar.

In the system graphic holo, three of the remaining eleven enemy ships spun off to one side or another, their ships leaking air, water and fusion isotope fuel, according to his spectroscope sensor readings. Added to the earlier ship he'd just zapped that removed four enemy ships from the fight. Leaving eight death-seekers.

Amidst the wild jinking, jerking and random movements of enemy and allied ships, green beams crisscrossed the space between them, reaching for invisible hulls.

Bill saw Jake's seven ships and five subs overtake the four wounded enemy ships. The enemy ships fired lasers at Jake's group. They missed. Then Jake's Collector ships fired. Black antimatter beams reached out and demolished the engine sections of the four enemy ships. Those ships stopped their laser fire and focused on recovering ship control.

Which left eight enemy Collectors raining green Hell on the *Blue Sky* and the ships of his saloon buddies.

Two green beams touched the rear end of the *Musan*, killing both of its Magfield engines.

Alicia's ship stayed on its sideways escape route at eleven percent of lightspeed, thanks to already established inertia. But she had no ability to maneuver out of the way of more laser beams. Or an antimatter beam once the enemy closed to within 4,000 miles of the *Musan*.

"Reverse course!" cried Jane to Lofty Flyer. "We're not leaving Alicia to the wolves!"

CHAPTER FOURTEEN

Too much happened all too quickly.

Bill tapped his nose lasers as the *Blue Sky* flipped heads-to-tail so its nose faced the oncoming enemy ships. Their allied ships copied Jane's flip-over maneuver. Magfield engines did not care which direction any Collector ship was aimed. The magnetic field-based engines either pulled or pushed against the magfields of the Sun and nearby planets. Now, with their flip-over, Chester changed their engine setting to attraction toward Jupiter. And the onrushing enemy ships. In seconds they would fly past each other. Black antimatter beams and green laser streaks would flash out. Ships would be hit. Lives would be lost and—

"The subs!" cried Chester. "They're running up the tails of those ships!"

Bill swallowed hard even as he fired their nose lasers at the rapidly nearing enemy ships. Two green flares showed hits. What the hell were their allies trying to do?

Jink. Jink. Triple jink the subs moved.

Yellow-white plasma balls filled the true space holo.

"Fuck!" cursed Bright Sparkle.

He couldn't believe what had just happened. Nor, judging by the sudden silence, could Jane or his crewmates.

The subs *Louisiana, Minnesota, Vladimir Monomakh, Alexsandr Nevskiy* and the *Chairman Mao Zedong* had rammed the rear ends of five enemy Collector ships. The impacts had breached the antimatter reservoirs on those ships. Unleashed antimatter had just consumed five Collectors and five human subs. Six hundred or more people were dead. As were 25 on the enemy Collectors. Those ships had fired their tail lasers at the closing subs but the sideways jinking and spiraling of the sub navigators had kept them whole until impact. But why hadn't the subs first tried launching their missiles at the enemy ships?

He blinked. In five seconds the remaining three enemy ships would reach antimatter beam range. As would the *Blue Sky*, the *Musan* and the four other ships run by his saloon buddies. *Ahhh.* The

Musan, unable to reverse Magfield thrust due to its dead engines, sped away from them on a vector that would take it south of the planetary ecliptic. Leaving the *Blue Sky, Fallujah, Moberly, Harken* and *Neil C. Roberts* to tackle Death Leader and his two remaining ships. Five versus three. Bill gave thanks that at least Alicia and Howard would survive on the *Musan*. Whatever happened now, the remaining subs and ships of the other Earth fleet would surely—

"Look!" cried Jane.

In his system graphic the *Fear Arrives* and its two surviving allies changed their vector angle by 70 degrees, sending the enemy away from Bill's fleet ships even as they closed to within range for their antimatter projectors.

He tapped his fire control panel.

A black beam instantly zipped out faster than he could blink.

It missed.

Black beams from their four Collector allies also reached out, but fell short as the three enemy ships increased the distance to them beyond 4,000 miles. Bill tapped his lasers, as did his four ship allies. Green streaks chased after the fleeing enemy ships. Two were hit but the impacts were at a bad angle. The adaptive optics seeded into those hulls deflected most laser power away. At best the ships were scorched. They now passed beyond the 10,000 mile range of ship lasers. And their new vector track had them headed straight for Earth!

"After them!" yelled Jane. "Change our vector to match theirs. Chester, match their speed!"

"Vector changing," chittered Lofty Flyer.

"Working on it," rumbled Chester. "Eleven percent is all we can safely sustain."

Bill felt a chill run down his spine. "Captain, the enemy is managing 12 percent of lightspeed. They are pulling ahead of us." He checked his system graphic. "Jake and his six Collector ships are changing their vectors too. As are the remaining boomer subs. None of us are matching or closing on the enemy."

His heart beat fast. Then faster. If Death Leader and his two Collector allies could maintain their hyper-fast speed, they would reach Earth before the *Blue Sky* and other Earth ships reached them. Which meant Earth would be hit by MITV thermonukes and antimatter beams fired by the three surviving enemy ships.

The horse-like head of Wind Swift turned and looked back at Jane. "What do we do?"

♦ ♦ ♦

Jane saw the reality of what faced her in the system graphic holo at her left. Even as Jake and six other Collector ships, plus 17 surviving subs pursued Death Leader from one angle, and her *Blue Sky* plus four ships pursued from her angle, the Mokden monster's three ships formed the peak of a vector triangle that had hers and Jake's fleets at either foot of the triangle. Even as she watched, the triangle grew slightly longer as the extra speed of the enemy ships drew them further away. And, eventually, closer to Earth.

"I will not allow the deaths of Joshua, Leonard and their three sub allies be for nothing." An electric tingle coursed along her arms and out to her fingertips. "Bright Sparkle, maintain overload power flow from our reactors. Chester, push us up to 12 percent of lightspeed."

"Working on it," Chester muttered.

"Captain Jane," hummed the voice of Star Traveler. "No Magfield engine in any Collector ship cannot long sustain the strain of exceeding the rated thrust of those engines. While 11 percent of lightspeed can be maintained for a lengthy period, 12 percent is dangerous. You risk engine meltdown. Or explosion. If an engine explosion reaches our fusion isotope fuel tanks, we could lose the rear half of this ship."

She sucked air in deep. "Ship mind, our two Magfield engines were repaired by Megun engineers during our stopover at Harken. Do those repairs improve the survivability of our two engines?"

"The repairs do not improve survivability," the AI hummed low. She thought its voice tone sounded almost fearful.

Options. What were her options?

"Star Traveler, can this ship make an Alcubierre space-time jump to get near Earth? So we can be there before the enemy ships arrive?"

"Alcubierre transit deep within the magnetosphere of a star has never been attempted," the AI hummed long and low, sounding puzzled. "My computations suggest such an attempt would result in the vaporization of this entire ship upon emergence. Disintegration may also happen upon activation of the stardrive. We are deep within the magnetosphere of the star Sol."

"Why!" she yelled, not giving a damn what Poindexter, Hartman or anyone else thought of her temper.

"Because the artificial space-time modulus created by the Alcubierre stardrive is not compatible with the space-time fabric that lies within a star's magnetosphere," the AI hummed. "That is why all Alcubierre star travel begins and ends outside the magnetosphere of a star."

"We're at 12 percent of lightspeed," Chester rumbled from up front. The crewcut man looked back her way, his clean-shaven face showing tight-clenched muscles. His gray eyes fixed on her.

She gave the man a thumbs-up. "Outstanding, vice admiral. Transmit your engine settings to our other ships. In both fleets."

The stocky husband of Sharon turned back to his control pillar. He tapped on its surface. "Engine settings transmitted."

Jane looked at the system graphic which showed the positions and distances of all ships. *Fear Arrives* was now 23,317 miles ahead of the *Blue Sky*. As were its two ship allies. Who seemed able to maintain 12 percent of lightspeed. The graphic showed Jake's ship *Tangi Valley*, which was in the lead ahead of the other Collectors and the 17 surviving subs, was further away. Its range to Death Leader's ship was 32,187 miles. She watched a moment. Those numbers did not change. *Yes!*

"Fleet captains, we are in chase mode now. Death Leader and his ships are not pulling ahead of us. While we are not closing on them, I am willing to see how long the enemy can maintain this overload speed." She licked her lips and told her heart to stop thumping so hard. "Give your people a food, drink and rest break. I do not anticipate imminent combat."

Her Collector ship captains acknowledged her order. As did the captains on the 17 subs that were trailing Jake's ship. Or, rather, 11 subs acknowledged. Six had not, including the British and French ships. Why not?

"Incoming encrypted signal from Peterson," hummed Star Traveler.

What the fuck? Poindexter again? "Accept the signal. Share it with all ships."

"Accepted. Imagery displayed."

Shock hit Jane. Appearing in her comlink holo was not the middle-aged face of Harriet Poindexter. Instead, it was Melody Hartman. She stood up and saluted her commander in chief.

"Madame President, my two fleets are pursuing the enemy. The enemy strength is greatly reduced," she said quickly.

Hartman, sitting in the Oval Office on a Monday afternoon, not long after rain had drenched the green shrubs visible through the window behind her desk, leaned forward. The woman's luxuriantly curled brown air framed an expression of rectitude and determination. Her blue eyes fixed on Jane.

"Captain Yamaguchi, you and your fleets have done outstanding work in this space battle," the Anglo woman said in a low soprano. "However, three enemy Collector ships are heading for Earth. Which lies just five AU from Jupiter. Those ships approach at 12 percent of lightspeed. Which means they will be here within six and a third hours."

"Six point one hours," Star Traveler interjected.

"You must be a saint to cope with that AI," Hartman said, her lips compressing. "Captain, I have sent orders to six boomer subs to run their reactors at overload. They will try to attain 13 percent of lightspeed. Which means they will overtake the enemy. They will either destroy the enemy with lasers, with missiles or ram him. As the five subs did earlier. We mourn the deaths of those good sailors." Hartman sat back and rested her arms on her wooden chair. Her look was one Jane had come to know. It was the look on one's face when you knew you sent people to possible death. "It was my decision, in consultation with the leaders of Russia, China, France and Great Britain, to order those subs to make this effort. You are still in command of the remaining forces. If an enemy ship's engines fail, or they fall within your targeting range, attack them!"

"I will, Madame President," Jane said, hoping her salute held steady.

Hartman nodded. "At ease, captain. Your advice to the other ships was good. Take a break. Eat and relax. Then prepare for the final battle."

"We will, Madame President," she said, lowering her right hand and sitting down in her command seat. In front of her, Chester, Bill and Bright Sparkle also lowered their salutes and sat at their work stations. Lofty Flyer and Wind Swift had stayed focused on their stations.

Hartman's image vanished. Poindexter did not appear. Nor did JCS chairman McAuley. Perhaps the rest of this battle really was up to her. She looked down and ahead.

"Chester, move our engines up to 13 percent of lightspeed." She paused, thinking things through. "Captains Stefano, Frank, Joe and Learned Escape, you are free to join me or remain at 12 percent acceleration."

"I and my crew are joining you," called Stefano.

"So are we," Frank muttered. "Can't let you have *all* the fun!"

"Me too," said Joe.

"Us also," called the artificial voice of Learned. "We are your allies. Whatever danger you face, we too will face."

Jane felt a brief surge of happiness. Then surprise as other ship captain images spoke.

"Captain of the fleet," called Jake. "My ship is increasing speed to 13 percent lightspeed."

"So is mine," reported Mack.

"Mine too," called Janice.

The other four Collector ships captained by new people also said the same.

Which meant 12 Collector ships now pursued three enemy Collector ships. Along with six boomer subs. It looked as if she was indeed a leader. Now came the time to figure out a way to kill the three enemy ships without losing another sub or ship to ramming or antimatter. Too many humans had died in the ships led by Joshua, Paul and the Russian and Chinese ship masters. She had started this war against Alien slave-masters with just one ship. Perhaps her *Blue Sky* could end it.

♦ ♦ ♦

Forty minutes later Bill came back from a quick meal in the Food Chamber and sat at his Weapons station. Everyone else was already back. Bright Sparkle sat to his right, then Chester, Wind Swift and Lofty Flyer. Sparkle was intensely focused on the performance of her three fusion reactors that ran down the middle of their ship. No doubt they were sucking in loads of deuterium and tritium fusion isotopes. Which was not a big deal, especially since America had placed an isotope extraction plant in low orbit just above Jupiter's cloud deck. The automated plant was a copy of the plant they had refueled at during their first visit to HD 128311. He looked past her. Chester, wearing his tube suit like all of them, showed sweat on his forehead. Clearly the man was anxious over the performance of their two Magfield engines. Which, Bill reminded himself, had been repaired by Megun engineers. Those color-talking near humans were incredibly talented people. Maybe their repairs *had* improved the overload tolerance of the engines, despite what Star Traveler had said. Maybe 13 percent of lightspeed could be maintained? Beyond the vice admiral stood Wind Swift. The scaly kangaroo was closely monitoring both the Life Support and Collector Pods stations. Beyond her sat the brown-furred shape of Lofty Flyer. The Aelthorp flying squirrel touched her nav controls now and then, making tiny vector adjustments to keep their ship exactly on the same vector track as the three enemy ships. Which, he noticed from his system graphic, now had a change in their formation. *Fear Arrives* was slightly ahead of his two ship allies by perhaps a few hundred miles. Did that mean anything?

"Ship *Blue Sky* is now at 11,213 miles distance from the nearest enemy ship," Lofty Flyer chittered. "Closure to within 10,000 miles is expected in nine minutes."

His memory of Wind Swift kicked his brain. "Captain! Let's launch our 24 collector pods now! And tell their Magfield engines to speed ahead of us at 14 or more percent of lightspeed. If a few blow up, or most of them croak, so what? We could use the survivors as ramming craft against the enemy!"

"Fine idea XO!" Jane said quickly from behind him. "But let's make them more deadly. I want thermonuke warheads in each craft. How many spares do we have on the deck below?"

Bill checked his Weapons cutaway holo. It showed all weapons at Green Operational. It also showed the status of all ammo, whether it be nukes, antimatter loads or plasma reloads. "Twelve. They are stored in the MITV launcher room below us."

In his comlink holo, his wife and captain grinned toothily. "Yes! Star Traveler, send hover bots to transport those warheads to the Collector Pods Chamber. Load them into 12 pods. Advise me when the pods are loaded."

"Complying. Time to completion of task is three point nine eight one minutes," the AI hummed.

"Wind Swift," called Jane. "Launch 12 pods right now! Set their autopilots on track for the two closest enemy ships. Order the autopilots to increase Magfield engine speed to 14 percent of lightspeed. If they can go faster, move them faster!"

His peripheral vision saw the claw-hands of the kangaroo moving quickly atop her control pillar. "Twelve pods now launched. New operating rules input into their autopilots. Each has acquired the infrared signature of an enemy ship. They are moving to 11, 12, 13, now 14 percent of lightspeed. Captain! They are reaching 15 percent!"

Bill saw that. On his system graphic the tiny red dots of the pods were moving ahead of the *Blue Sky*. He tapped his fire control panel. "Wind Swift, I've sent you a random walk vector track program. Upload them to the pods! That will give them a chance at survival from enemy lasers."

"Uploading evasion program," barked his ally.

He hoped the pods would pre-empt any ramming by the six subs that were just 700 miles behind the *Blue Sky*. Jake and his six Collector ships, along with the ships captained by Stefano, Frank, Joe and Learned, were a touch closer at 500 miles behind the *Blue Sky*. His ship had had a vector angle advantage over the other ships and subs. Plus Jake's fleet had been further away when everyone sped up to 13 percent of lightspeed.

"Task completed," Star Traveler hummed. "One warhead loaded on each of the 12 remaining collector pods."

"Launch them, Wind Swift!" Jane called urgently.

"Launching," the kangaroo barked. "These pods are also moving at 13, 14 . . . now 15 percent of lightspeed!"

"Captain," Bill called. "I've sent the random walk vector track program to these nuke-loaded pods. I'm also sending the program to our allies behind us."

In his comlink holo, Jane brightened, then snapped her fingers. "All sub captains, launch your missiles now! Set them for warhead dispersal once your missiles pass the *Blue Sky*. They can't go any faster than your 13 percent of lightspeed, but they can be a follow up distraction for the lasers on those enemy ships! Do it now!"

"Launching missiles," called the voice of the captain for the *HMS Vengeance*. "My missiliers are transmitting the random walk program into the missile computers."

"*La même choix per mois*," called the French captain of the *FNS Terrible*. "Our missiles are pursuing the enemy," came his translated voice.

The captains of the four Trident subs who were part of the group of six ordered to attack by Hartman also confirmed they too were launching their Trident missiles, with Bill's random walk evasion program uploaded to the missile nav computers. He watched the first group of 12 pods, which were ahead of the 48 empty pods launched by Stefano, Frank, Joe and Learned. Who were also loading nukes onto their remaining 12 pods. Jake and his six fellow Collector captains would be doing the same.

"Captain," called Jake from the *Tangi Valley*. "We're launching 12 empty pods at the enemy ships. Ours are also speeding up to 13, 14, now 15 percent of lightspeed!"

Bill's system graphic holo showed his 12 pods racing ahead of them. Twelve more loaded with nukes were not far behind. Those two clusters were followed by the 48 pods from their fleet group. Another group of 48 pods from Jake's fleet now showed as tiny red dots on the graphic. That made for 120 highly mobile collector pods bearing down on the three enemy ships. They would soon be followed by another nuke-loaded group of 108 pods. Then the ICBM missiles would appear, barely pulling ahead of the two fleets. The warheads from the four Trident subs would amount to 1,152 warheads, plus a few hundred more from the Brit and French subs. He realized the pod and missile attacks would come in waves versus a single group of hundreds. He checked the fancy iWatch that Jane had got him on their return to Earth. *Yes!* Time for the second group of nuke-loaded pods to launch from Stefano's and Jake's ships. Which now happened. Two groups of 48 and 84 pods now became a fifth and sixth wave after the four waves of unarmed pods. Inside, in his sneaky SEAL heart, he realized there was no way the lasers on three Collector ships could kill several hundred collector pods running up their tails!

"XO, looks like your pod attack idea, plus our missile warhead loads, are going to give the enemy fits!" Jane said sharply, sounding happier than he'd heard in some while.

"Pods are within 8,000 miles of the enemy ships," Bill called back, watching the tiny dots on his system graphic. Bright green streaks and yellow flares on his true space holo drew his attention. "Crap. All three enemy ships are firing tail lasers at the approaching pods. Ten down, twelve, first wave is gone." He focused on the second wave of nuke-loaded pods. "Nine more hit. Twelve gone." He saw something that gave him hope. "But half of the 48 in the third wave are still alive! They are jinking, warping and hiccupping their way on my random walk program! Fifteen are alive and at 3,000 miles. Approaching 1,200 miles distance." A green light blinked on his fire control panel. "Captain! We are less than 10,000 miles from the enemy! I'm firing lasers!"

"Other ships," Jane called. "Fire when in target range!"

Bill tapped his lasers, sending two green streaks toward the nearest enemy Collector ship. He was aiming for its engine section rather than the small laser emitter nodes. The conical engine section of a Collector ship was still hard to hit. The enemy was now moving to random walk jinking as someone alerted the captains to the fact they were within attack range from the *Blue Sky* and her four ship allies. Soon, Jake and his six ship allies would be in range to fire their lasers. Shortly after that would come the six boomer subs, each outfitted with a laser scavenged from a transport ship.

A green flare showed in his true space holo. On his system graphic holo, one of the two enemy ships lagging behind Death Leader's ship now jerked, then its random walk movement ended. Or rather slowed. Had one of its Magfield engines died from his lasers?

"Captain!" Bill yelled. "One enemy ship is slowing to five percent of lightspeed. They've lost a Magfield engine."

"Great! Now let's see—"

In space, death happens very quickly.

The red dots of three pods converged on the wounded enemy ship, hitting with enough inertial force to vaporize the fantastic flexmetal skin of the ship. The plasma balls created by those three impacts traveled on into the ship's thousand foot long body. Yellow-white light flared on his true space holo.

"Jane!" Bill called. "Enemy ship is gone! Its antimatter reservoir was beached by a pod impact!"

"Interesting," Star Traveler hummed from the ceiling. "Its ship mind put out a cry for help just before it . . . evaporated."

"My ships are firing on the enemy," called Stefano.

"Ours also," called Jake.

Bill touched his fire control panel, adding his lasers to the mix. Green streaks from 24 lasers crossed the 8,714 miles separating the *Blue Sky* from the Death Leader and his ship ally. Green flares showed on his true space panel. He glanced at his system graphic.

"Captain!" he called. "Both ships were hit but are still maintaining 12 percent of lightspeed. Uh, damn! The two are speeding up to 13 percent of lightspeed. They are matching our Collector ship speed. But they are not pulling away from us. And here comes the fourth wave of empty pods. I'm firing our lasers."

Everyone else added their laser fire. The six subs also fired since they were not far behind Jake's seven ships. In fact, the subs were pulling ahead. Had they gone to 14 percent of lightspeed?

Dozens of yellow flares filled his true space holo. Bill checked his graphic holo. The news was depressing.

"Captain, the two enemy ships have flipped nose-to-tail and are now firing their antimatter projectors at the oncoming pods," Bill reported. "They killed 43 pods in the fourth wave. Their lasers are taking out those pods beyond 4,000 miles. But our nuke-loaded fifth wave is jinking like an ice skater trying not to fall!" He paused, counting yellow flares. "Fourteen of the fifth wave of pods are dead from laser strikes." Green flares showed now. "But our third group of lasers are taking a toll! Hits on Death Leader's ship and the enemy ship behind it."

Death visited again.

Yellow-white light flared brightly in the middle of his true space holo.

"Rearmost enemy ship is now gone," Bill said, his breath coming too fast and his heart beating like he was running a marathon. "Two empty pods hit its tail. Three nuke-loaded pods hit its mid-section. Whatever blew on the loaded pods just added to the antimatter blow-up." He looked back to his wife, whose pale face was tight-clenched. Her command manner was almost gone as Jane watched the sudden reversal, then improvement of their battle fortunes.

"Good news. But Death Leader's ship is pulling away from us," she said, pointing at her system graphic holo. "And the bastard's using his antimatter projector to sweep the space behind him. Our sixth wave of pods is gone."

Bill jerked back to his own system graphic holo. What Jane had just said, he now saw. Death Leader's ship was now slowly pulling away at 14 percent of lightspeed. Worse, three Collector ships in Jake's fleet were falling behind. Rapidly. They must have lost—

"Oh no!" Jane cried.

His heart plummeted. The true space holo now held a new yellow-white plasma ball. He sighed.

"The *Pointe Du Hoc* is gone. With ship mind and crew." He looked back to her.

Jane grimaced, then nodded. "All other Collector ships! Reduce your speed to one-tenth lightspeed now! That is my order. Protect our people on the *Seafloat* and the *Manila Bay*. Jake and Stefano, this includes you too!"

CHAPTER FIFTEEN

Jane's heart hammered at the death of the Collector ship. The *Pointe Du Hoc* had been captained by a Ranger gal, Jesse Winthorp. Other Rangers and Delta Force folks had been her crew. Plus a Slinkeroo walking snake. With some spouses aboard. Now, they were all gone. Perhaps their engine meltdown had reached their isotope fuel tanks and somehow uncontrolled fusion had happened. Or maybe the rearmost fusion reactor had lost fusion containment. What mattered was the fact they were dead and gone. Only memories now survived. In addition, three other Collector ships were wounded, with only a single Magfield engine still working. Rather, the *Musan* had zero engines while the *Seafloat* and *Manila Bay* still had a single engine. As Star Traveler had warned, traveling at 13 percent of lightspeed had been too much for the Magfield engines on those ships. The loss of the *Pointe Du Hoc* and the engine loss on its two sister ships had convinced her to call a halt to the other ships' mad gamble with odds and Alien tech. In her system graphic, most of her allied ships were slowing to the normal one-tenth lightspeed that was the approved rating for a Collector ship traveling normal space. Further back were the ten remaining Trident subs that had not joined Jake's pell-mell dash. But not all her allies had slowed. The six boomer subs under orders from President Hartman continued at 13 percent of lightspeed. A speed they could make on a single Magfield engine only due to their smaller size and lower mass than a Collector ship. And one Collector ship was still close behind her ship.

"Stefano! I said *all* ships must slow to rated Magfield speed."

In her comlink holo, the image appeared of Bill's SEAL buddy. And fellow trout fisherman, she recalled from Bill's late night sharings. His buff, tightly muscled frame did not move within the tube suit he wore as he sat in his command seat atop his own command pedestal. The man's pale brown eyes fixed on her.

"Captain of the fleet, a SEAL does not leave another SEAL alone on the battlefield," he said firmly. "Bill is that SEAL. You are my ally. Who now faces the enemy. You will not face that monster alone." He waved to someone out of the image. "Bob, move us up to

14 percent of lightspeed." He looked back to her. "The *USS Neil C. Roberts*, BBG-9, is now joining you. We have your back."

Jane licked her lips. There were only three people on that ship. Stefano, Bob at Engines and Cassandra at Weapons. Their spouses were on other ships. Which meant three more humans, besides her and her people, now faced imminent death. As did the captains and crews of the six boomer ships. She nodded. "Your assistance is accepted, *Neil C. Roberts*." Was there more to say? The man's ship was out of pods. An idea hit her. "Captain Stefano, have your ship mind launch the three transport craft on your ship. Each is armed with a laser and a few nuke missiles. Cassandra can operate their weapons from her station." The man's eyebrows lifted. "Maybe the transports can hit 15 percent of lightspeed, like the pods. Or maybe not. But they can give you extra laser guns!"

The soft-spoken man showed a brief smile. "We obey, captain. A very good idea. And Cassandra likes the idea of adding three more laser platforms to our nose lasers. Which she is firing now on the enemy."

"Good," Jane said, turning away from the man who was their backup in case the *Blue Sky* lost both engines and became vulnerable to an attack from the *Fear Arrives*. Green laser streaks from Stefano's ship joined those from Bill's station. Three of the four beams missed. The fourth hit Death Leader's ship a glancing blow. No loss of air or water or fuel showed on her sensors. *Damn!* She scanned her system graphic. Most of the last waves of nuke-armed pods were gone, thanks to Death Leader's use of antimatter against them. Was that three, or four AM shots? The bastard would be out of AM reloads for the ten minutes it took his particle accelerator to create more antimatter. The monster did not know of Bill's expansion of their capability to six shots from the standard four shots on the Alien-built Collectors. Three small red dots showed up next to Stefano's ship. The transports had been launched. They moved now to 15 percent of lightspeed. Good. Her comlink holo filled with three captain images.

"Captain," called Jake from the *Tangi Valley*. "I'm a SEAL also. I wish to join Stefano as backup."

"Me too," called Janice from the *Takur Ghar*. "A SEAL I am and a SEAL I will always be. Let us join you and Stefano."

"And me also," said Mack from the *Rolling Thunder*. "I too am a SEAL. Let me help cover your back."

Jane felt touched and heartened by the three captains' effort to come to her aid. But if she agreed to their demand, surely she would hear similar talk from their fellow spec ops folks with battle training in Marine, Air Force and Coast Guard special operations. In both fleets. "No. Your offer is much appreciated. But a single backup ship is all that is needed. Plus I have the six boomer subs adding in laser firepower. You two, and everyone else, stay at ten percent of lightspeed and help our wounded ships. And one of you needs to go after Alicia on the *Musan*. She has zero engines. Stop that ship's momentum, or get her people and ship mind off it!"

"Understood," Jake called. "I'll go after the *Musan*."

Mack grimaced. "Reducing speed to 10 percent."

Janice, a fellow Japanese-American like herself, showed an upset expression. "Captain Jane, my duty to you goes beyond my SEAL status! You know—"

"I do know what you mean," Jane said, giving the young woman a smile. "Your family will know of your fight to serve the honor of all *nihonjin*. You serve that honor now by following my orders. Pull back. Save your craft for future defense of Earth."

"As you command. *Sayonara*."

Jane turned away from the comlink holo and faced the holos in front of her. The true space holo showed black space and hundreds of white dot stars. In the distance showed the red ball of Mars. They were just past the Asteroid Belt. Earth now lay three AU ahead. Four hours or less. And the enemy was speeding away at 14 percent of lightspeed. Time to follow Stefano's example and end this. Somehow.

"Chester, move us up to 15 percent of lightspeed. We and the subs and Stefano can—"

Two yellow plasma balls showed in the true space holo. They were off to the side of her ship, or lagging just a bit.

Bill slammed his fist on an armrest. "Damn! The *HMS Vengeance* and the *FNS Terrible* just died! Their Magfield engines blew. Which had to have killed their reactors."

She sighed. Her heart felt heavy. A total of 135 men onboard the Brit sub and 111 men on the French sub were now vapor spreading across cold vacuum.

"Captain Jane," called Star Traveler. "This ship cannot sustain travel at 15 percent of light speed. My home is not a collector pod."

"I know that! But—"

"Jane!" interrupted Bill. "I have an answer to further endangering the *Blue Sky*." He stood up and walked toward her, his tube suit not hiding the tenseness of his face or the tightness of his shoulders. "I'm heading back to the *Talking Skin*. It can hit 15 percent lightspeed for a while. And it can jink as good as the pods. I'm taking demo balls with me plus a nuke bar." He stopped below her seat and looked up at her. His hazel eyes met hers. "When I get to *Fear Arrives*, Star Traveler can remote open its hull to its Transport Access Chamber. Or I'll use a demo ball to blow a hole into the fucking ship!" He turned away and headed for the hallway entry door. "I'll put the nuke bar in its Engine space. Or close enough. Even with hallway pressure hatches closed against me, I will get there. I'll try to get off using the transport. Or maybe one of its pods."

"Bill! It's not needed! Our lasers will take it down."

"It *is*," he said, his voice strong as he stood before the open door. She looked back. He gave a shrug. "Lower the speed of the *Blue Sky* and the *Neil C. Roberts* to 14 percent. That's a risk anyway. More will blow this ship. Taking you, my friends and our loyal ship mind with it. Remember, I've done solo stuff before. And you or Chester can handle my Weapons station. We can only fire lasers right now. You guys keep up the laser fire while I jink and jiggle."

He passed through the open door. Which slid shut as he entered the hallway and turned right, heading for one of their two transports. She turned away, looked ahead, nodded at the faces of Chester, Bright Sparkle, Wind Swift and Lofty Flyer, then said the needed words. "Chester, cut us back to 14 percent of lightspeed. Stefano, you do the same." She tapped a control pillar in front of a side holo. That holo now glowed with a repeat of Bill's Ship Weapons station holo. She tapped the fire control panel that appeared on the pillar's top. Their two nose lasers fired coherent green streaks at the snake-gorilla's ship. The beams missed as the enemy jinked to one side. On her systems graphic holo she saw their ship, Stefano's ship and the four remaining subs were now at 5,124 miles away from *Fear Arrives*. Ahead of them the thousand plus missile warheads now moved slowly toward the enemy ship, their solid fuel exhausted. Maybe the warheads would reach the enemy ship. Some of which had x-ray lasers on them. Likely not, with them limited to an inertial speed of 14 percent of light. A new red dot showed on her system graphic. It was Bill. In the transport. It now moved ahead of them at

15 percent of light. Slowly it moved, but it was gaining on the enemy ship. Which would happen first? Would Death Leader's ship blow up from engine overload? Would Bill's transport die? Would the four pursuing subs, now going like bats out of hell at 15 percent, blow up before they reached the bastard who threatened her world? She didn't know. She just knew that if the other ships died, she would offload her crew onto the *Tall Trees* transport and take over sole control of the *Blue Sky* herself. She could do it using the mind-control helmet on the alternate command seat in the Engine chamber. If necessary, she would ram the fucking bastard herself!

◆ ◆ ◆

Bill jinked his transport to one side and then up into a partial spiral. Green laser fire from Death Leader streaked past where he'd been. The control panel of the transport showed its own system graphic flat image. The three transports launched by Stefano were close behind him and getting closer. The weapons screen on the panel before him showed his ship held four thermonuke-tipped missiles. Plus their nose laser, which was as powerful as the ones on the *Blue Sky*. He tapped the fire control sensor patch lying next to the weapons screen. A green streak shot out from the *Talking Skin*. It missed the *Fear Arrives*. But a laser beam from one of Stefano's transports did hit the bastard. A brief spurt of air and water said there had been a penetration. He played with the nav hand-grip, causing his transport to jerk down, sideways, up, across and then sideways again. Two green laser beams streaked past his prior vector track. He was gaining on the bastard! It was just 4,015 miles away. Which meant he and the other transports would face antimatter shortly. He looked closely at the system graphic, then over at the electro-optical scope screen that showed nothing in the normal light spectrum. But the neutrino detector on the left side of his control panel did show the enemy's neutrino emissions. Which were superimposed on an outline of the enemy's long teardrop shape. When the three neutrino emission points, which came from the ship's three fusion reactors, seemed to shorten, that meant Death Leader was changing his ship's nose angle to lock onto Bill's transport. The neutrino dots changed. He tapped his laser firing patch.

"Got you, you bastard!"

Sensors showed air, water and metallic debris erupting from the bulbous nose of the teardrop. Had he hit the antimatter projector's port?

Bill jinked sideways. The system graphic screen showed the other three transports jinking and jigging in various vector angles. A black beam speared out toward them, according to what he could see in the electro-optical scope image that filled one screen on his control pane. No luck on the AM projector. Yellow-white light flared on the scope image. Which meant one of Stefano's transports was now dead. He spoke, counting on his helmet comlink to instantly cross-link to his transport's neutrino comlink.

"Jane! Try for the bastard's antimatter projector. At the upper nose space."

"Firing on him," Jane said quickly. "That was his fourth AM shot. He's out of antimatter for the next ten minutes. Think you can reach him before he reloads?"

Bill scanned the system graphic screen. It said he was 1,234 miles from the misbegotten fusion of a cobra and a gorilla. He pulled on the nav hand-grip, avoiding two new laser beams.

"Yes! Keep distracting him with yours and Stefano's laser fire! And the subs' laser fire. Uh, just before I get to his hull, blow the nuke warheads! That will create a sensor overload for his ship. It should help me with my closing and boarding."

"Will do," Jane said. "The four Trident subs are right on your heels. They're firing their lasers now. They'll be your backup if you have to use a pod to escape."

"Thanks." Escape was the least of the things on his mind as he did his best to emulate a flying squirrel darting through tree branches. Four laser beams hit the *Fear Arrives*. The ship staggered in its forward flight, then steadied. But large amounts of air, water and some isotope fuel were spewing from its midsection. Or so his sensors reported. His scope actually showed tiny silver sparkles from the gaseous globules. Which quickly disappeared as they turned to vapor. Ten new green laser streaks shot past Bill, which meant the fire control panels on the four subs were being coordinated with the laser fire from Jane and Stefano's ship, and the four surviving subs. Star Traveler had to be doing that. It had created the Magfield control tablets used by every sub out there. That tablet cross-linked to the other sub controls. It seemed his ship's AI was able to override whatever a sub sailor was trying to fire on by orienting its laser fire in coordination with laser fire from the other ships. He grinned. It was ten, no, eleven lasers against the two on the *Fear Arrives*!

"We're coming for you, you bastard!"

In the scope image, green flares showed at two spots on the enemy ship. More air and water spewed out. Then two green lasers shot past Bill. His system graphic screen showed Stefano's transports were now gone. *Fuck!*

"Bill?" called Jane. "The four subs are adding their laser fire to yours and ours. It's wounded. You're getting real close now. Get onboard, plant that nuke bar and get the hell out!"

"Will do." Bill tapped his missile fire control panel. His transport shuddered four times, as one after the other, the four missiles in the belly of the transport shot out and ahead toward Death Leader. Maybe one of them—

Two yellow flares showed in his scope screen. Two dots vanished from his system graphic. Two more yellow flares. Two more dots vanished. His last two missiles were now vapor. And he was within the 400 mile target range of Death Leader's spine-mounted plasma battery. Which now fired at him.

"Blow the nuke warheads!" he yelled as he jigged the nav hand-grip to one side, letting the yellow plasma ball sweep past. Another plasma ball came flaming out of the battery. He jinked. It missed.

"Detonating all but the x-ray laser warheads," Jane called. "No way are we going to fry you!"

His true space screen went orange, then yellow, then golden, then near white as more than 1,300 thermonuclear warheads detonated. They plasma balls spread out, combined with other nearby warhead blasts and created a miles-wide front of radiation. Which now sleeted his way. His helmet ear buds squealed as the radio band was overloaded. He crossed his fingers that 4,000 miles of distance was allowing his transport's metal frame to absorb most of the gamma and x-rays emitted by the blasts. This was the moment when the enemy's sensors should be overloaded.

"I'm heading in," Bill said, hoping his neutrino comlink's passage through an alternate dimension would allow his words to be heard by Jane.

Bill twisted the hand-grip, causing his transport to move to one side of the enemy Collector ship. Its nose lasers and antimatter projector could not swing wide enough to get him. Those weapons had maybe a ten degree angle movement. He was beyond their angle. And they weren't firing anyway. Clearly their targeting sensors were overloaded by the nuke blasts. But another plasma ball came at him from the spine battery. A second quickly followed from its belly plasma battery. *Fuck this.* He aimed his nose laser and killed the spine battery. A jink on the hand-grip and he dodged both plasma balls. He touched his laser's patch. The belly plasma battery went red molten, then yellow, then it became dispersing metallic vapor.

"Contact!" he yelled as the *Talking Skin's* belly touched down on the rear end of the *Fear Arrives*. He tapped on the magnetic clamps. Just in time. The ship rolled, trying to dislodge him. Giving thanks for the gravity plates that kept him stable, Bill got up from the pilot seat, grabbed his backpack, snapped shut the holster cover for his .45, then grabbed his laser and taser tubes and ran toward the midbody airlock. He touched a patch. Its hatch opened. He entered. It closed. He touched the outer airlock Operate patch. It opened. Nothingness greeted his eyes. Which of course made sense. The enemy's hull was as invisible to his eyes as it was to all normal sensors. "Leaving the ship." He jumped out, aiming toward the belly hull of the *Talking Skin*. Which was of course quite visible. Two black streaks along the transport's side testified to how close he'd come to dying. Well, that only counted in—

"I'm on the ship!" he yelled as his tube suit boots made contact and their built-in mag clamps came on. Which way? Didn't matter. "Star Traveler, can you override this ship mind's control of its outer hull? Can you create an opening for me to enter?"

Humming sounded over his helmet's comlink. "Unable to override local ship mind control," the AI said.

"What would it take for you to override it?"

"Its death," his ship mind ally said.

Well, killing another AI was not something Star Traveler had ever done. Unlike humans, who were very good at killing other humans. And nasty Aliens. "It's okay. I'm arming a yellow demo ball. It should create a decent hole. Stepping away."

Bill walked back to the hull of his transport, putting ten yards distance between him and the demo ball. Which he'd set on a five second delay. Which now ended.

"*Kaboom!*" came the sound of the demo ball exploding.

What the hell? He was in vacuum. How could—

"Regrets for transmitting my acoustic monitoring of sensory output from the *Fear Arrives* comlink circuits," Star Traveler said. "While I cannot override its ship mind's control of ship functions, I do receive all inputs from its autonomous ship systems. Be aware the ship mind Dexterity will respond according to Emergency Protocols the same way I did when you and Captain Jane put on tube suits."

He shook his head. The ringing from the blast subsided. His eyes showed him a gray metal ring that glowed redly against black space. *Yes!* He walked quickly toward it. The ring rim began slowly closing as the ship's flexmetal tried to seal the rupture in its hull. He tried running. Not good. He kept walking fast. Faster. He got to the gray metal ring when it was three feet wide. He bent down, grabbed the ring edge and pulled himself into a room. Half gee gravity grabbed at him. Falling head first towards the room's gray metal floor, he twisted in midair the way he'd learned in free fall chute jumps, twisted and landed on his right hip.

"Thunk!" came over his tube suit's external com.

Which meant the hole above him had now sealed and some air was refilling the air lost from the room. He rolled over to his knees, put gauntleted hands against the floor and slowly stood up. Red light shone down on him. He looked around. Large blocks of metal, some tables, some automated metal grinders and cutters, and other powered mech told him what he needed to know. He was in this ship's Factory Chamber. Which meant he was on the left side of the enemy ship and close to the cross hallway that led to the Engine chamber. Reaching back, he pulled his taser and laser tubes out of his backpack, turned and walked toward the eight foot high oval outline that was the door which gave access to this ship's left side hallway. It would open on sensing his bodyheat.

"Jane, I'm in. In the Factory Chamber. Heading out."

◆ ◆ ◆

She heard the good news of Bill's survival and entry into the enemy ship. Cheers came from up front as Bill, Bright Sparkle, Wind Swift and Lofty Flyer gave vent to finally hearing good news. The death of the transports from Stefano's ship as they closed on the bastard had put her heart in her mouth, or whatever meant severe fright. She'd faced fear during the SERE survival training she'd taken with other Air Force officers. Surviving in the Southwest desert by eating insects and getting your water from ripping open cacti and sucking their innards had not been fun. Or easy. In her time in SERE she had felt fear that she and her fellows had been forgotten by the people in charge. Now, she was the one in charge.

"Good job," she replied, trying to sound matter of fact.

The last thing Bill needed was any sign his commanding officer was uncertain, afraid or fearful. He'd told her how he and fellow SEALs were trained to suppress fear, suppress worry, suppress any feeling that got in the way of accomplishing the mission. Well, she wasn't a SEAL. Nor had she ever had the spec ops training of his saloon buddies. But she had more live fire experience in space combat than any other human now chasing the homicidal maniac who wanted to kill her home world. Why hadn't Death Leader turned away and headed north of the ecliptic, aiming for the system's magnetosphere and escape from death at the hands of humans? Was it some crazy Mokden fixation on punishing humans? Or was the creature simply focused on hurting humanity before it died? At least her world was safe from total destruction. One Collector ship could not turn Earth into a radioactive cinder covered with antimatter scars. Still, millions would die if she and Bill and Stefano and the four subs did not finish this job. She scanned her system graphic holo, then her true space holo.

"Stefano, keep firing on Death Leader's ship. That will force the creature to focus on jinking his ship and keep him off Bill's back."

"Firing lasers," called the SEAL.

"Also firing our laser," called the captain of the Trident boomer USS Tennessee.

"The USS Kentucky is firing too," called its captain.

"We're firing also!" called a raw voice full of Northeast twang as the USS Maine fired its laser.

"Uh, our reactor's steam output is showing blockage. Ensign! Is the Magfield engine glowing? We gotta—"

The *Wyoming* captain's female voice vanished as Jane's true space holo showed a yellow plasma ball spreading over the blackness of deep space.

She thought it was a sad image, appearing just to the right of Mars' red ball.

"Subs! Cut back to 14 percent of lightspeed. Now! And maintain a live monitor on your Magfield engines! If anything looks different on their tube hulls, cut power! Immediately. Or you'll go up like the *Wyoming* just did."

Acknowledgments came from the captains of the three surviving subs.

Jane took a deep breath and focused on the tactical situation showing in her holos. The system graphic showed the enemy ship dot with Bill's transport touching it, 4,000 miles plus of open space, the three surviving subs and just behind them, her *Blue Sky* and Stefano's *Neil C. Roberts* ship. Clearly the sub captains still aimed to ram the *Fear Arrives* if Bill's effort failed. She checked the distance to target readout on her Weapons pillar panel. It showed her and Stefano's ship were at 4,913 miles out. At least the sub captains were obeying her and had dropped their speed to 14 percent. Which could still kill them. And hers and Stefano's ship. What was happening with Bill?

◆ ◆ ◆

Bill walked fast down the left side hallway. He had called ship mind Dexterity and demanded it open the Factory Chamber's door. It had complied, citing a Protocol Seven directive. The scream of Death Leader that it should increase hallway gravity to a hundred gees had been refused by its citation of Protocol Eight. Which forbid any change in ship gravity levels that would cause deadly harm to any bioform. He slowed his run down the hallway as he arrived at the cross hallway opening in the left side of the main hallway. He lifted his white taser tube, poked it around the corner of the wall that gave entry to the cross hall, and then leaned forward.

Empty. Red light shone along the hundred or more feet of the cross hallway. A brighter red glow at its end showed where it joined the right side main hallway. He lowered the taser and ran as fast as he could in the ship's half gee toward the short hallway in the center of the cross hallway. It opened to his right and gave access to the ship's

Engine Chamber hatch. He stopped just where the cross hallway met the junction with the Engine hallway. He poked his taser's nose past the wall edge, swung the taser outward, then pressed the button at the end of the tube. A coherent red electric beam spat out and disappeared from his sight. He was taking no chances on an ambush. He poked his helmet just past the wall edge and looked to his right.

Empty also. A red glow showed on the flexmetal wall to the left of the Engine entry hatch.

"Star Traveler, any chance you can get Dexterity to open the Engine Chamber hatch?" he called over his helmet comlink.

"Trying. No response," the AI hummed.

With a last glance back the way he'd come, then ahead to the other end of the cross hallway, he ran around the corner and stopped before the hatch. Pulling his backpack around to the floor in front of him, he laid down his taser and laser tubes, opened the backpack, pulled out a black dome and box magnetic disruptor, tapped it active, then placed it to the left of the hatch. He reslung his backpack, picked up his taser and laser tubes and stepped back to the junction with the cross hallway. Looking out briefly he saw no crew.

"*Kazap!*"

He looked back and saw the magnetic disruptor block had killed the hatch's electronic controls. The hatch had opened. The red lit Engine Chamber lay open to him.

"Jane, I'm going inside the Engine Chamber. No opposition yet. Cross your fingers for me!"

CHAPTER SIXTEEN

"I am."

Jane crossed her fingers. Sitting in her command seat, watching the holos as she and others chased after the homicidal monster who wished to dominate, or destroy all opposition, she felt useless. Was her Bill going to survive this crazy boarding? While his plan made total sense, and gave her the option to save lives, she recalled his choice during the boarding of the ship commanded by Diligent Taskmaster, when a boarding team was being outflanked. He'd opened a hole in the ship's Command Bridge wall and dived in, distracting the deadly cockroach for the moments needed to allow the boarding team to drop through a ceiling hole. He'd taken a bad laser wound doing that. And he could have been killed. Would Bill keep his promise to her to come back alive? To stay alive for her? Would love overrule duty?

"Jane, he'll survive this," called Chester from up front.

She saw the man was still at his Engines seat, but had turned back to face her. His clean-shaven face showed an amiable smile. The man was trying to reassure her. "Thank you. If anyone can survive alone on that ship, outnumbered five to one, Bill can. He's a SEAL. And he has me waiting for him."

Chester nodded. "My Sharon told me what it was like for her as she waited out the months when I was on deployment with the *USS George H. W. Bush*. You're feeling that on top of the final command authority." He smiled big. "Like Stefano said, you have me and the other crew folks at your back. We will win this thing!"

Jane took in a deep breath. She tried to smile back. "Thank you, Chester. Sharon is lucky to have you. And Bill is the man I should have met years ago." She turned away and stared at the system graphic and true space holos. "Waiting is the shits."

♦ ♦ ♦

Bill stepped up to the open hatch, then moved to the right of it. Poking his taser tube through the open hatch, he leaned forward and took a quick look and pull-back. Ahhh. Empty of anyone. Like the Engine Chamber on the *Blue Sky*, this large room was filled with the two long tubular forms of its Magfield engines. To his right was the alternate command seat, the mind-link helmet sitting on its bench seat. Fifteen feet of open space lay between him and the command seat pedestal. A thought hit him.

"Ship mind Dexterity, please display an interior holo map of this ship. Display all bioforms now present in the holo," he said, hoping this ship's indifferent mind would comply with the Emergency Operations of the Ship program that was part of every AI's core functioning.

"Displaying holo," came a mech-toned voice over his comlink. "All bioform locations displayed."

A teardrop shape floated before them, identical in shape to the *Blue Sky* cross-section holo that he watched at his Weapons station. The shape shimmered and grew translucent. Two main hallways now appeared inside the teardrop, along with many box-like rooms that linked to the hallways. The cross hallway at the bulbous nose showed, as did the tail-end cross hallway he'd just passed through. Red dots shone bright. Three were present in the Command Bridge room. Two dots were halfway down the left and right side hallways. Clearly two ship crew were heading his way. Or was one of them the snake-gorilla monster?

"Very good. Show me the location of captain Death Leader. Show him as a red dot with a green outline."

"Complying. Location indicated," came the mech hum of this ship's artificial intelligence.

The bastard was at the center of the Command Bridge! Two red dots near him were his crew. Which meant the two red dots heading Bill's way were also crew. "Show me the images of the captain and all crew. Display in holo form adjacent to—"

"Discontinue compliance with bioform request!" a snarling voice interrupted. "End holo display now! And stop talking to this bioform! Command Sequence Larva Four Red."

"Holo discontinued." The ship holo vanished. "However, Protocol Seven, Emergency Operations of the Ship requires that I respond to any bioform who wears a vacuum suit."

Nothing more came from the snake-gorilla. Who had earlier tried to kill him with super gravity. "Thank you, Dexterity. I will try to help the crew and captain of this ship receive treatment in the Med Hall of this ship." Bill stepped further into the Engine Chamber, stopped beside the right side Magfield tube, laid down his backpack and pulled out the nuke bar.

Humming came over his comlink. "Are the captain and crew of this ship sick?"

He smiled as he tapped in the activate code on the nuke bar, then tapped in a five minute delay. That should be enough time for him to get back to the Factory Chamber and then up to his transport. "They have mental issues. They persist in attacking spaceships that seek to defend the third world that orbits this local star. A bioform disagreement exists. I am seeking to have Death Leader change his behavior."

"Changing bioform behavior is difficult. My experience with prior captains of this ship indicates bioforms rarely consider the long-term results of their actions," the AI hummed.

"Totally agree with you," Bill said, standing up. How truthful should he be? "Ship mind Dexterity, I have placed an explosive on one of this ship's Magfield engines. When it explodes, this ship will lose all motive power. However, you will survive and so will all bioforms located in the middle and front sections of this ship."

"Engine disablement is necessary?" hummed the ship mind.

Bill wondered at the AI's naivety. It sounded much like Star Traveler had sounded when he and Jane had first spoken with the *Blue Sky's* AI. "It is necessary. Once the engines shut down, I and other bioforms will be able to provide medical aid to Death Leader."

"I will observe your behavior with interest," the AI said, his mech tone the same as before.

Bill turned away from the nuke bar and engines. He grabbed his backpack, picked up his weapon tubes and headed for the exit hatch. Passing through it, he mentally calculated the last locations of the crew. Time enough. He turned, reached out, grabbed the edge of the hatch that had swung out against the entry hall wall, and pulled. The hatch closed with a loud "clang!" He stepped back and aimed his red laser tube at its top rim. Holding the tube's midbody power box, he tapped the Fire button at the end next to him. A centimeter-wide green beam shot out and struck the spot where the hatch metal met the flexmetal of the Engine Chamber wall. Sparks flew to all sides. Then the seam metal glowed red. Slowly, it became yellow and half-molten. He moved the laser beam to the right, then down the right side of the hatch. Two minutes later the green beam was sealing the bottom. He stopped, grabbed his taser tube with his left hand, and walked slowly up to the junction of the Engine access hallway with the cross hallway. Memory told him the crew on this ship might know the height and shape of a human. He bent down, kneeled and pushed his helmet just past the wall edge where the access hall became one with the cross hallway.

Nothing.

"Jane, I've planted the nuke bar and sealed the Engine hatch. I'm heading back to the Factory Chamber, then up to my transport."

"Great!" came his wife's soft soprano over the suit's comlink. "Stefano's lasers hit the upper nose of the ship you're on. We're just inside 4,000 miles and there is no antimatter fire. Just lasers. I think we killed its antimatter projector."

"Congrats," he said hurriedly as he ran left down the cross hallway.

Earlier, the left side crewperson coming his way had been passing by this ship's Med Hall. Which now put it somewhere inside the Containment Cell Chamber, moving along its central metal walkway. It would come through the hatch before he could get to the Factory door. He stopped at the cross hallway's junction with the left side main hallway. He squatted, then leaned forward and looked around the wall edge. No lifeform showed in the red lit hallway. More than a hundred feet ahead lay the giant oval door that allowed exit from the room filled with twenty containment cells. He stepped out, then backward until he felt the edge of the other junction wall. To his right he could see down the long, red-lit cross hallway. He aimed his laser tube that way. Ahead, he faced the similarly red-lit left side hallway. Between him and the cell hatch lay the giant oval door that led into the Factory Chamber. That was on the hallway's left side. On its right was another oval door that led, he recalled, to a habitat room for one of the crew. Ahead, the cell chamber hatch swung open. He squatted down and aimed his taser down the left side hallway.

A green praying mantis Alien, wearing its version of a tube suit, stepped through the hatch, a red laser tube in its upper arm pair. Its two black eyes scanned ahead. Just as it saw him, he pressed the fire button of his taser.

The red beam of coherent electrical energy shot across the 120 feet separating them in less than the blink of an eye.

"Yargh!" cried the critter, its mandible voice coming over Bill's comlink.

Its four arms jerked sideways, the laser tube flying free. As did the red cube its lower arm pair had used to open the hatch. Standing on its two stick legs, it went into the taser shakes and twists Bill knew well.

A green laser beam passed just above his helmet.

He dropped to the floor, rolled a bit and aimed his laser at the black bodyshape of something that looked like a grizzly with four arms. The green beam of his weapon shot along the cross hallway and struck the bear in its gut.

"Yawww!" it roared, then fell backwards. Its legs thrashed a moment, then stopped.

Bill felt his heart hammering. The bear had arrived at the right side hallway's junction with the cross hallway just as he fired at the praying mantis. Lousy timing! He'd been sure the right side crewperson would not be faster than the left side. A near fatal assumption. At least the half-darkness of his red-lit hallway had made targeting him less than easy.

He got up and ran toward the taser shaking mantis. The red cube it had held lay just beyond its twisting footpads. He'd learned to always grab a red cube whenever on an enemy Collector ship. It would open the door to the Factory Chamber. And to any other door except for the ship's Weapons and Command Bridge doors. Or so he recalled from memories more than a year old. Looking back the way he'd come, he bent down and grabbed the cube. A memory hit him.

"Dexterity, are the captain and crew bioforms still at the locations shown in the earlier ship holo?"

"They are," the AI said over his helmet comlink.

"Discontinue responses to bioform!" snarled the deep voice of Death Leader over his suit comlink.

"Emergency protocol requires my response to any bioform wearing a vacuum suit," the ship mind replied.

Bill turned and headed back to the Factory door and access to his transport. It was his best way off this ship. It—

The white glow of a man-high holo took form in front of him. A shape materialized in it. A shape two feet taller than Bill.

"Human!" snarled the giant black-furred snake-gorilla. "Your attack on my engines demands a response." Its gorilla like mouth opened wide. A purple tongue moved. "Your Human female leader occupies the closest Collector ship. While it has avoided my lasers, nothing can avoid the beam of my antimatter projector! There! She is vapor!"

Noooo!—

◆ ◆ ◆

Jane told herself to be patient as she waited for Bill to say he'd left the Collector. He could handle himself. He knew to ask the ship mind for a holo of where crew people were located. He knew the AI had to respond to him since he wore a tube suit. Bill knew all that he needed to know. And he learned fast, as she recalled from their takeover of the *Blue Sky*. She focused on watching the system graphic with its depictions of Death Leader's ship, the three subs, her ship and Stefano's ship. Which was slightly behind her by a dozen miles or so. The *Blue Sky* was at 3,912 miles from the enemy. The subs slightly nearer. They were not getting much closer since their 14 percent of lightspeed matched his 14 percent. Though hers and Stefano's ships had picked up a little extra momentum thanks to the few moments they'd been at 15 percent of lightspeed. Her ship swerved to one side to avoid laser fire from the *Fear Arrives*. Lofty Flyer was doing wonders with their maneuvering. She tapped the Weapons control pillar top. Two green beams shot out. One missed the jinking enemy, but the other hit on its right side, where its Collector Pods Chamber was located. Silver sparkles showed briefly in her true space holo. Sensors said water, air and a few metal frags had spewed out from the hit. No pods though. Which meant it had not been a deep penetration. She waited as the Weapons fire control sensors worked to put her firing reticule on the jerking, jinking and jiggling enemy ship. Soon she would hit the middle of the nose where—

A black beam of antimatter came for her.

It missed. Barely. Her seat vibrated. Maybe not.

"Our Collector Pods Chamber is open to space!" barked Wind Swift from her Life Support and Pods station.

The bastard had to have three more AM shots in storage. "Lofty! Take us up! Star Traveler, cross-link the lasers from me, Stefano and the subs! We have to get that projector killed!"

"Complying," the AI hummed over her helmet comlink.

Her targeting reticule hit the upper center of the ship's bulbous nose. "Fire!" she yelled as she touched her firing patch.

Seven green streaks shot forward.

In the true space holo, bright green flares filled the upper nose of the teardrop that was the *Fear Arrives*.

"Bill! We're okay!"

◆ ◆ ◆

Jane's voice over his helmet comlink made a chill go down his spine. His life he readily put at risk. Her life should never be this close to death. He aimed his laser tube at the holo of Death Leader and fired. The green beam passed through the holo of him.

"Bastard! You failed!"

The creature's cobra hoods flared wide. White eyes stared. "I have more antimatter! She—"

"Its projector is dead!" Jane yelled.

Death Leader clearly heard what Jane had said. It snarled, turned and the holo disappeared.

As the snake-gorilla vanished, Bill turned round, pointed the red cube at the hatch leading into the airlock of the Containment Cell Chamber, grabbed one leg of the shaking mantis, and ran inside. The hatch closed behind him. He pointed the red cube at the inner hatch. It opened. He ran out onto the central metal walkway that ran down the room and ended at a similar airlock on the opposite end. The shaking body of the mantis came with him. He stopped at the first cross walkway that led to white pods on the left and right.

"Dexterity! Which of these pods is empty?"

"The pod on your left is empty," the AI hummed.

Bill turned, pointed his red cube at the twenty foot wide white pod, walked fast down the side walkway while keeping his finger pressed on the cube's open button. He stopped before the open entry. Red light showed inside. White walls were apparent. No landscape holo emitters were active. He lifted the mantis' body and tossed it inside. It landed with a thud he heard through his suit's external speaker. He let up on the red cube. The entry hatch slammed down, sealing the mantis inside. It would survive in there. It was unlikely the nuke bar blast would reach this far up the ship. Which reminded him to check his wrist iWatch. Forty-three seconds to detonation. He ran back to the central walkway, turned left, pointed the red cube at the airlock entry oval and slid inside. Letting up on the cube, he ran twenty feet ahead, opened the airlock exit door, and entered the left side hallway. Behind him the containment cell chamber hatch slid shut. To his left was the giant oval door that gave access to the ship's Med Hall. He was three-fourths of the way to the Command Bridge entry—

"*Kaboom-crunch!*" came over his comlink.

The hallway shifted sharply.

He slammed against the wall on his right. His helmet stayed intact. Blinking away the impact disorientation, he grabbed his laser and taser tubes from where they'd fallen on the floor, checked his holster to be sure his .45 was still there, saw his survival knife was still in his left leg pouch, then ran down the left side hallway at a fast lope. He would pass through the giant Transport Exit Chamber, go down a ramp to the deck below, then up a ramp to this deck and exit into the long hallway. Which had several pressure walls and hatches to pass through. His red cube would open them all.

"Jane! I'm heading for Death Leader. He's in the Command Bridge. Time to take him out."

"Bill!" she cried. "The last third of the ship is gone. Your transport broke free. Forget him. Take one of their transports and get back to me!"

He didn't answer.

His duty demanded that he enter the Command Bridge, taser zap the two crew there so the ship's lasers would not hurt his wife or Stefano or one of the subs, and then zap or kill the monster who had brought 36 Collector ships to kill his world.

♦ ♦ ♦

There was no response from Bill.

Jane did what she had to do. "Lead ships! Reduce your Magfield speed to 10 percent!" She paused, then spoke. "Bill is onboard the enemy ship. If he fails, the *Blue Sky* will go to 15 percent and chase down this bastard!"

"Engine speed reduced," called Chester from up front.

"As you command," said the comlink holo image of Stefano.

The captains of the *Tennessee, Kentucky* and *Maine* said the same. Those subs, like her ship, were at 3,814 miles out from the *Fear Arrives*. Which continued ahead on momentum at 14 percent of lightspeed. The same speed as her two Collectors and the subs. The enemy ship fired its two nose lasers at them. Lofty Flyer lifted them further up and beyond the angle that the laser nodes could adjust to. The *Neil C. Roberts* and the subs did the same. The five of them formed a ring with the enemy ship at its center. Far ahead. They had maneuvering power. Death Leader did not.

Behind them were three clusters of ships. There were the *Moberly, Fallujah* and *Harken* not too far back. Jake's remaining fleet of the *Rolling Thunder, Takur Ghar, Chapultepec Castle, Seafloat* and *Manila Bay* were strung out according to when they'd lost an engine or had dropped back to ten percent of lightspeed. The 14 surviving boomer subs were scattered among those ships. Farther away was Jake's ship *Tangi Valley*, which was diving south ecliptic to catch the engine-less *Musan*.

What could she do to help Bill? The system graphic holo gave her the answer.

"Star Traveler! Is Bill's transport *Talking Skin* still intact? Is it operational?"

"The transport is intact and its Magfield engine still operates. The nuclear blast was modest and did not reach the transport's hull," the AI hummed.

"Good! Take control of its autopilot and move the transport back to the enemy ship. Have it hover just above the Command Bridge section of the *Fear Arrives*."

"Complying. Transport is responding. New position reached. Transport is holding position."

Jane was growing to like the echoing sound of Star Traveler's voice inside her helmet.

Two green laser beams shot out from the *Fear Arrives*. They passed through the middle of her ship ring, hitting nothing.

"Stefano, sub captains, I am having Star Traveler indicate the exact locations of the enemy ship's nose lasers," she called over the ship-to-ship neutrino comlink. "Will you join me in taking out the last weapons of the enemy?"

Enthusiastic responses came over the comlink.

Jane knew she could have shot all seven lasers herself, using her weapons cross-linking with the lasers on the other ships. Instead, she chose to give her combat mates the chance to join her in removing the last teeth of the monster who enslaved people and would murder a world.

"Firing," she said.

"Firing," came from the other captains.

Her true space holo showed green flares on the right and left sides of the enemy ship's bulbous nose.

"Star Traveler, are the enemy lasers melted down?" she called.

"They are," hummed the AI. "Also, its plasma batteries were destroyed by Weapons Chief MacCarthy."

That confirmed what her sensors had told her "Bill, your transport is hovering just above the Command Bridge. Come to me when you're done doing your duty."

◆ ◆ ◆

Bill heard Jane's words. The news his transport was intact and waiting for him was almost as good to hear as her voice. She loved him. He loved her. While his duty remained, he was not going to be stupid and let three Aliens kill him. They had to be removed or killed in order to take control of this ship. Only when all crew were unconscious would Dexterity accept him as the substitute captain. Which would allow him control over the remnants of the ship. He arrived at the spot where the left side hallway joined the front cross hallway. His hallway curved to the right in a long arc. Was anyone waiting for him with lasers? Were there repair robots ready to shoot lasers at him? One way to find out.

He knelt, pulled off his backpack, reached inside and grabbed a canteen of water. He held it up.

"Dexterity, reduce gravity in the cross hallway to zero."

"Complying," the AI hummed over his comlink.

Bill tossed the canteen down the curving hallway. Then he grabbed his backpack and weapon tubes. He stepped forward into the gravity free part of the hallway. Lowering his taser tube, he pressed it diagonally against the metal floor. His body floated forward slowly, his right hip close to the hallway wall. Holding his laser tube with his left hand, he pointed the taser tube forward, ready to use it to stop his forward movement, depending on what he saw.

Green light speared into the canteen. Steam and water spurted out.

He poked the floor with his taser. His forward momentum stopped. Pushing sideways against the floor he felt the inside hallway wall stop his movement. Floating two feet above the floor, he reached inside his backpack, grabbed a yellow demo ball, tapped in a three second delay and tossed it ahead. His body moved back as it obeyed Newton's Third Law.

"*Kaboom!*"

The sound echoed in his helmet.

Pushing his taser tube against the floor in front of him, his body rotated upright. His feet touched the floor. Pointing his laser tube forward, he kicked hard, aiming up and sideways.

Smoke and flames showed as a tin can repair robot burned from the demo ball impact. Behind it a second robot's top dome swung its black laser tube toward him.

Bill fired.

His green laser beam hit the second robot's laser.

Black smoke and yellow sparks spewed from the top of the second robot. But its two mech arms still moved. The pincers at the end of each arm opened and reached for him. But its effort to move forward was blocked by the burning hulk of the first robot. Clearly there was still gravity in front of the entry hatch to the Command Bridge.

"Dexterity, restore normal ship gravity to this hallway."

"Complying."

Bill pulled his knees up to his chest and landed easily on his boots. The impact was minimal. Which told him the local gravity was still a half gee. He'd felt far worse during chute drops. He scanned the space between him and the two robots. They were twenty feet away. His laser would not harm the laser resistant body metal of the tin can-shaped robots. But the caterpillar tracks on which they moved could be made half-molten. He lifted his laser tube, put it atop his right shoulder, held the midbody power pack with his left hand and with his right hand touched the tube's firing button.

Green light spat forward, hitting the gray metal treads of the first robot. He moved to the right and forward. He fired again. The metal treads of the second robot glowed red, then orange, then a light yellow. He let off the firing button. A mech sound came from the second robot as it tried to rotate its treads. It could not move.

"Jane," he called. "I'm outside the Command Bridge door. I'll get inside like I did when I helped Stefano's team."

"Understood. The ship's lasers are dead. We all are intact. The subs are holding back. Be careful."

"I will."

Bill looked up at the ceiling of the hallway. The roof was 15 feet above the floor. He had no doubt there were monitor eyes present on the ceiling. Every Collector ship had monitor eyes along its hallways and inside its chambers. He'd taught himself exactly where those eyes were. He lifted his taser tube, aimed and shot a red electric beam at a spot above the entry door. Yellow sparks showed. Moving his taser aim, he took out the monitor eyes ten feet further down the hallway, the eye directly above him, and the eye just above the captain's habitat room door. Which was directly across from the entry door to the bridge.

"Death Leader, lasers cut both ways. The wall between you and me will yield to my laser," he said.

"Your death awaits you inside," grunted the snake-gorilla.

Bill opened his backpack, took out two yellow demo balls and a magnetic disruptor box. He moved forward.

Ten feet from the entry hatch, he put one demo ball against the wall separating him from the bridge. He tapped its detonation to ten seconds. Moving forward very carefully, he lifted the disruptor box and attached it to the wall section that butted up to the entry hatch. He tapped it active and set it to surge power into the wall. The way he'd done at the Engine hatch. He tapped in a six second delay. He moved to the right, ducked the reaching mech arm of the second robot, and tossed a demo ball past it. The ball hit the bridge wall at five feet past the entry hatch. It stuck to the wall. Its delay was two seconds. Moving back past the first demo ball, he held his taser and laser tubes in his hands and waited.

"*Kaboom!*" went the distant demo ball. A hole five feet wide showed in the flexmetal wall.

"*Zrrnap!*" went the magnetic disruptor block. The entry hatch opened.

Bill fired a taser beam through the open entry door.

The nearest demo ball blew.

"*Kaboom!*" went its shaped charge.

He stepped to the near edge of the five foot wide hole, aimed both tubes, bent his helmet, and looked inside.

Two teddy bear crewpersons were on the floor, their laser tubes knocked from their paws by the force of the demo ball blasts. They wore tube suits.

"You!" screamed Death Leader from his perch six feet above the bridge floor.

Bill jumped inside and rolled left as he brought up both tubes. He fired the taser. It missed the snake-gorilla, which was moving its laser tube from an aim at the entry hatch towards him.

A green beam lanced out.

Death Leader looked down at the smoking hole that cut through his tube suit and into his giant chest. He looked up. Inside the clear helmet, white eyes fixed on Bill. The creature jumped from the top of the command pedestal, his scaly tail flaring to one side for balance.

Bill fired both his taser and the laser, then rolled further left. "Thunk!"

Twisting his body away from the black-furred fist of the mortally wounded monster, Bill aimed his laser tube at the creature's blue-scaled head. White eyes stared. The gorilla mouth snarled. The thickly muscled arms raised up the creature's upper body. Two laser holes in the monster's gut and chest poured out red blood. Which smeared the inside of the clear tube suit.

"No one defeats a Mokden!" it snarled, bloody spittle flying from its mouth. The spittle hit the inside of its helmet. Black-furred legs pushed against the floor. It came at him.

Bill fired.

A red hole appeared in Death Leader's head.

The monster landed atop him.

Two massive hands gripped the rim of his helmet.

It lifted off.

Dying spasms sent black-furred fingers to his throat.

They squeezed hard.

Then the grip slackened.

He pushed up against the monster's dead weight.

It fell to one side.

Rolling away, Bill grabbed his taser, lifted it, aimed it at the two teddy bears on the floor and fired twice.

They went into taser shakes that had them spitting blood into the inside of their helmets.

"Command Bridge taken."

CHAPTER SEVENTEEN

Jane heard Bill's words. Was he wounded? What had happened?

"Bill! Is Death Leader—"

"He's dead. Two crew are alive up here. One crew alive in a cell. One crew dead back at the Engine. It's vapor now. Give me a moment. Gotta have a takeover chat with this AI."

"Understood. Congratulations!"

Nothing came from him except for grunts and the sounds of movement. She looked forward.

"Chester, how are the engines?"

"Green Operational, according to my status holo," the man said, relief in his voice. "We are moving at 10 percent of lightspeed, which is less than our momentum. We have full maneuvering power."

"Good."

She checked her systems graphic holo. The surviving three subs and Stefano's ship were still in the ring formation. Their Magfield engines were operating to maintain that position. Everyone was back at the normal 10 percent engine power level. Including the ships and subs far behind her. Relief filled her. Her heart's fast beating slowed. Bill was alive. The enemy commander was dead. Bill would soon be in control of the unpowered ship. And they had just passed the orbit of Mars. Which meant they were one and a half AU away from Earth. That put them just shy of two hours from home. Maybe sooner given how her group of ships were moving at 14 percent of lightspeed. Soon, every ship in all the fleets and groupings would have to go to deceleration if they were not to shoot by the planet. But first things first.

"Bright Sparkle, you did wonders with your fusion plants, thank you! Wind Swift, your dispersal of the collector pods and your arming of them was outstanding. Thank you." She looked to the right. "And Lofty Flyer, your dodging of enemy laser and antimatter fire was incredible. Thank you all, and I hope your spouses can rejoin you after we arrive at Earth."

The Megun woman who wore only her trademark blue shorts looked back from her seat at her station. Her jade green eyes were bright. She smiled a big, human-natural smile. "So glad we survived! And I am glad our engines held up to the strain."

Jane gave the woman a thumbs-up. "I'm sure the rebuilding work by your Megun engineers was the reason our two engines held up so well. No matter what our ship mind thinks!"

Chester also looked back. Sweat showed on the man's lightly tanned forehead. His gray eyes looked tired. But he showed a smile. "Double what you just said re those Megun engineers! It's a wonder we didn't lose one or both engines. I'm super glad Stefano's engines also held up." He gestured back to his Engines station. "I am very eager to return this post to Time Marker's care! Diplomacy is easier than handling volatile engines!"

She smiled back.

Wind Swift's horse-like head, encased in a tubular helmet, turned her way. The silvery scaled kangaroo person leaned back on her thick tail. Her fabric skirt was bunched up inside her tube suit. Her red eyes fixed on Jane.

"Thank you, captain of our endeavor," she barked. "My Life Support post is mostly automatic, thank the Great Egg. The Collector Pods station was interesting. But I too am eager for our crewmate Long Walker to return and join us."

Jane nodded, then fixed on the brown-furred squirrel woman who had moved the *Blue Sky* like a bee buzzing around and away from an attacking wasp. It was incredible how she had kept them away from most laser strikes.

"Lofty Flyer, how do you feel?"

The human-tall flying squirrel stood up from her nav seat and stretched out her arms. The skin flaps that ran from her arms down to her knees flared a bit, but were constrained by her tube suit. Her pug face's mouth opened. Her yellow eyes fixed on Jane.

"Would feel much better if I could shed this terrible suit and let my arm flaps feel the way they feel when I glide through the trees!" she chittered. Her long prehensile tail curled up, then straightened out. "Is that possible?"

"Soon," Jane said as she looked back to the true space, system graphic and weapons holos in front of her. "We are still in combat status. Until that last ship out there is shut down. Or destroyed. Please be patient."

Her navigator nodded in the human-style the Aelthorp person had learned from a year spent with humans, then she turned back and sat at her station. Her four-fingered hands touched her nav control pillar. The orientation of the *Blue Sky* adjusted slightly.

Jane felt exhausted. They were intact. Though the hull opening above the Collector Pods Chamber was a problem. Her ship status holo showed the gaping rip left by the glancing antimatter strike was too big to be healed by flexmetal stretching. The part of the hull that normally opened up like the cargohold flaps of the old Space Shuttles was partly gone. One flap did not work thanks to it being fused to the unmoving part of the hull. Still, the other flap could move. Its movement outward, added to the fact half the flap was gone, would allow the entry of pods. Which were non-existent thanks to their use as attack devices. Well, that could be fixed, eventually. Now, she waited for word from Bill on what he was doing, had done, would do. She was eager to know. But she would not bug him. He had won the fight against the monster who had started all this dying and destruction of ships. He had fulfilled their mutual obligation to duty, honor and country. He deserved her confidence and her patience.

◆ ◆ ◆

Bill sat on the command bench of the *Fear Arrives* and waited as the pedestal pillar lifted him up to six feet above the floor. Which held the two tasered teddy bear crewpersons and the bloody red body of Death Leader. The air of the room didn't smell of death. Cooked meat maybe. And he liked having his helmet off. It lay against the back of his tube suit, hanging on the hinge that allowed the wearer to breath, eat and do whatever without having to rely on the helmet's water sack for nourishment. He looked up at the room's ceiling.

"Ship mind Dexterity, I assert my right to be the new captain for this vessel."

A low hum sounded. "Are you the primary bioform present in this room? Protocol Four, Emergency Operations of the Ship dictates that I respond to the primary bioform still alert and aware whenever all ship crew and the ship master are not alert and aware."

"I am," Bill said. "Three crew still live but they are not aware at the moment. I am the only aware bioform on this ship."

"So long as you are the primary bioform that is aware and alert, Protocol Four dictates that I respond to any order or request by you so long as it does not endanger ship operations, or ship crew," the AI said, its tone curious. "What are your intentions?"

Bill scanned the six holos that surrounded the command bench. The system graphic showed this ship, his nearby transport and the distant ships of Jane's combined fleet. The true space holo showed the red ball of Mars receding as they passed it. The world was not on the direct track to Earth, but off to one side in its normal orbit of Sol. Still, it was close enough to show as a small red ball. The yellow glare of the Sun filled the middle of the holo. A tiny blue sparkle was far distant Earth. Other holos included the ship status holo. Which displayed the ship in an overhead cutaway like his weapons holo. The rear third of the ship was missing. Well, that was what five kilotons of atomic power would do. The plasma ball of a five kiloton nuke was rather small, but it had been enough to vaporize the Engine Chamber, the fuel tanks, the Factory Chamber, part of the Recycling Chamber and the nearest fusion reactor. Which left two reactors powering everything on the ship. Good enough for the moment.

"My intentions are multiple," he said, remembering to be clear, direct and uncomplicated. "First, I direct you to disable the still active repair robot outside the entry door to this chamber."

"Disabled."

"Second, send hover bots here to pick up the two unconscious crew and transport them to a collector pod. The third crewperson is in a containment cell. Are there any other bioforms in the other containment cells?"

"Hover bots are dispatched," hummed the AI. "Yes, captive bioforms occupy six of the containment cells."

Two flying hover bots entered through the open hatch and swept down to the two suited teddy bears. Small manipulator arms extruded from the silver balls and took hold of the teddy bears. One bear per hover bot. They lifted up and headed soundlessly for the open hatch.

"Okay. My third decision is for you to eject those six cells plus the crewperson's cell out to space. The hull ceiling above the cells chamber opens up for such transfers, right?"

"It does. I am opening the hull. The seven cells are ejected."

"Good. Number four. Open the working hull flap above the Collector Pods Chamber of this ship. Move the collector pod containing the two crewpersons out into space. Then move seven more pods out of the chamber. Send them to grab the containment cells with their gripping arms. Understood?"

"Understood," the AI hummed. "Complying." Seconds passed. "The seven cells are now captured by seven pods. The eighth pod will join them once the crewpersons are loaded into it."

"Good. Dexterity, you reside in a chamber just behind the captain's habitat room, right?"

"I do reside there."

Now came the key issue. "Are you able to exit from that chamber? And still retain enough power to stay aware?"

"I am able to do that," the AI hummed low. "There is a transit shaft directly above my chamber. It is the route by which I was delivered to this ship. Why do you ask?"

He looked down at the floor, checked that his weapon tubes were still there along with his backpack, then looked up. "Because my captain, Jane Yamaguchi, does not wish for any ship mind to die when she destroys a Collector ship."

"Will she destroy my ship? This is my home."

Bill thought he heard a tone of anxiety in the AI's voice. Good. "I understand that. She understands that. But this ship used its weapons against her ship. The battle this ship's captain started cost the lives of Captain Jesse Winthorp and her five crewpersons. It has also cost the lives of hundreds of humans onboard eight space-going submarines. Worse, it cost me the life of Mark Neller. My drinking buddy. I do not forgive his death. This ship must die."

"How will this happen?" the AI hummed, its tone strange-sounding.

"First, you *will* live!" Bill said loudly. "This ship has three transports in its Transport Exit Chamber. I saw them as I passed through. Right?"

"Three transports are present in that chamber. Why?"

Bill half-grinned. "Cause I intend one of those transports to be your transport to my ship, the *Blue Sky*. That is the Collector ship closest to this ship. You can take remote control of that transport's nav panel, can't you?"

"I can."

"Can you fit inside the transport?"

"Yes. My shape is as tall as that of a Human bioform and as wide as you. I can pass through the transport's midbody airlock. Its fusion reactor can be tapped by me to provide the power I need."

"Good!" Bill glanced again at the systems graphic holo. It showed his ship and Stefano's ship and subs were no closer than before. "Can the collector pods you now control move the cells containing Captives and crewperson so they follow your transport?"

"They can."

He nodded to himself. "Then that sorts nicely. After I leave this room, I will head up to my transport that is above the Command Bridge. As I exit, I want you to eject yourself from this ship, enter your transport, take control of it and the pods and cells, and follow me back to the *Blue Sky*. You will be safe there. And the cells can be deposited into that ship's Containment Cell Chamber. Will you come with me?"

Low humming came from the ceiling. "Joining you is the way of survival. I will do as you have directed. What happens after I enter your ship's transport chamber? What happens to me?"

The question every living person always wondered about. He thought this AI would come out of this pickle in decent shape. "You will travel to my world of Earth on my ship. You can stay on the *Blue Sky*, chatting with our ship mind Star Traveler, until we have built a new Collector ship at our orbital factory. You can then inhabit that ship as your new home. Sound good?"

"Not good. Very desirable," the AI said. "I am now in contact with Star Traveler. A most talented ship mind. When do you leave this ship?"

"Now." He stood and waited for the command pedestal to lower to deck level. He stepped off, grabbed his backpack, put it on, then grabbed his taser and laser tubes. Bill stuck them into the top of the backpack. He reached back, grabbed his helmet, pulled it down until he heard the snap-click of it sealing against the suit rim, then looked up. "Dexterity, please open a hole in the ceiling above me. And the ceiling of the particle accelerator room above. I wish to travel up to the ship's outer hull. Where you will open a hole so I can pass through and up to my transport."

"Opening hole in ceiling," the AI hummed.

"Kill all gravity in here."

"Gravity off here and in the rooms above."

He smiled. Nice that the AI had anticipated his need for null gees in the rooms above. Maybe it would end up being as cooperative as Star Traveler. Maybe it would even start to care about the actions of the bioforms who occupied its new ship. Which would be its new home. Maybe it was just being pragmatic, trading a partial ship with no engines for a future whole ship with engines. There was time enough to work with this AI after he got it onboard the *Blue Sky*. He kicked against the deck's metal floor and rose up.

"Jane, I'm heading for the *Talking Skin*," he called over his helmet comlink. "I've convinced this ship's AI to follow me so you can destroy this ship without killing its ship mind. Uh, we are bringing with us eight collector pods. Seven are transporting containment cells with Captives in them. The eighth is loaded with two taser-zapped crew folks. You might wish to eject seven cells from our Containment Cell Chamber."

"Bill!" she called, sounding happy. "What a relief! Glad you made this deal with the AI. And I'm glad we're saving the lives of some Captives. We can deliver them to Geneva later on, after we reach Earth. Come home, my XO."

He grinned as, below him the particle accelerator's floor hole closed and the ceiling above opened up. Beyond it another hole opened in the ship's flexmetal hull. A puff of whiteness was the exit of air from the two rooms. Above him, white stars shone against carbon-black space. The gray hull of his transport hovered just above the hole. Already Star Traveler was orienting the ship so its open midbody airlock hatch would be in line with his vector track. Very nice to have the cooperation of a ship mind that could anticipate human needs. Since it had been listening to all he'd said, and was now in touch with Dexterity, maybe the smart-ass AI would arrange for two of its hover bots to transport the two teddy bears to containment cells on their ship. Might as well put those cells to some use.

"Sounds fine, my captain. Your XO returns. And congrats on saving Earth from destruction. And seven billion people from an ugly death."

◆ ◆ ◆

Jane sobered as she heard Bill's words. Strange. She had become the leader of people that she had always hoped to be when she'd done her sat monitoring job at Space Command. As a captain she had supervised two people in Building One at Peterson. Out here, she'd commanded hundreds. Thousands as she mentally added up the crews on the subs, living and gone. She licked her lips. This battle was nearly done. She watched her holos, especially the systems graphic that showed moving red dots for Bill's transport, the AI transport and eight collector pods carrying containment cells. The cells were airtight and able to survive on their own for some hours. It was how a Collector ship captain transferred sold Captives to a Buyer's ship. It was part of the design of such ships. There were hull flaps on the right side for the exit of collector pods. And hull flaps on the left side for the exit of Captive-filled cells. Plus a large hangar door on the left side that allowed the entry and exit of three transports. Which mental image reminded her they were short a transport. This new transport would join the transports *Tall Trees* and *Talking Skin*. She liked that.

"We're home," Bill called over the comlink.

She saw that. The pods were depositing the cells into the Containment Chamber slots that she had emptied of cells. The transports were now entering the transport chamber. In seconds the collector pods would arc up and over the demolished spine plasma battery and down to an entry into her Collector Pods Chamber. Now empty. At least they had gained back eight pods. Nice to benefit from the ship that she would soon destroy.

"I see that," she called. "Welcome home! XO, come up here ASAP. I think you will want to be present for the final act of this battle."

"Will do," Bill responded.

What else? Well, she needed to pee. The multiple cups of coffee she'd had since morning, lifting her helmet to suck dry the coffee squeeze pods, had left her bladder feeling too full. She stood up. "Heading to my habitat room. Captain is off the bridge. Command assigned to Vice Admiral Chester Richardson."

The man stood up from his Engines station just as Jane stepped off her command pedestal platform. He gave her a salute and a smile. "Command accepted. Temporarily."

She saluted him back, then turned and headed for the exit to the front cross hallway. Time to hurry. She wanted to be back in her seat when Bill arrived.

♦ ♦ ♦

Bill exited the *Talking Skin's* midbody airlock and walked down the slanting ramp that gave access to the Transport Exit Chamber's gray metal floor. In front of him the transport containing Dexterity settled down on its support legs. The other transport's midbody hatch slid open. Above him two silvery hover bots appeared, slanting down. They entered the open hatch. It closed. He began walking toward the corner of the chamber where there was a ramp leading to the deck below. Which would connect him with a ramp leading up to the deck that gave access to the left side main hallway. Just like on the enemy ship. He stopped when his ears, now exposed to air since he'd pushed his helmet back onto his back, heard the other transport's hatch opening. He looked back.

The two hover bots slowly exited. Resting atop them was a purple metal box with faceted corners and side walls. The hover bots finished exiting the airlock, turned toward him and flew his way.

"Dexterity, is that you riding on those hover bots?"

"It is me," the AI's humming voice said from the suit's comlink speakers. "Ship mind Star Traveler has invited me to occupy a habitat room near it."

Bill stopped at the down ramp entry. He frowned. "Don't you need to be near a fusion reactor for power?"

"Not always," the AI hummed as the hover bots came up to him, then carried the long box of the AI over his head, and down the ramp to the deck below. "We ship minds can exist on broadcast power. Even your Human low tech society possesses such power transmission capabilities."

"True," Bill said, turning and walking down the ramp as he followed the slow moving hover bots.

"However, Star Traveler has promised to reroute a power cable from the front fusion reactor into my habitat room," it hummed. "That cable will link to my power intake socket. Your ship mind has also promised to provide me with some sensor links to this ship's systems. It feels very . . . lonely to not perceive my home."

Bill followed the hover bots up the ramp that led up to the deck level used by him and all crew. "Lonely I know about. Had not realized how alone I was until I met Jane and fell in love with her."

More humming came over his comlink. "Love is a bioform emotion, yes?"

"Yes." He stopped before the hatch door that gave access to the left side hallway. The hover bots preceded him through it.

"We ship minds have long lives. We find satisfaction in contact with other ship minds. Star Traveler has an unusual compartment it labels 'deception'. Did you know this?"

Bill followed after the hover bots. They sped up and moved quickly along the hallway. "I do know of it. Its compartment is similar to one function of a bioform mind."

"Strange. But I assume I will meet other bioforms as I wait in orbit for my new ship home to be built. Is this correct?"

Bill grinned. How would this ship mind react to fake out bidding in a poker game? It clearly was not able to read facial expressions. Not yet anyway. "That is correct. We humans come in two primary genders, male and female, along with variants of those two genders. You are familiar with gender variations, aren't you?"

"I am. I chose the male gender after my birth and graduation from the nursery asteroid at the star you call Kepler 443."

"Welcome to bio-life," he called to the vanishing form of the two bots and AI.

"Thank you."

The three mech creatures disappeared around the curve of the left side hallway. Time for him to return to duty. He picked up his walk until he was loping along the corridor, his backpack jiggling a bit. It felt less heavy than before. That made sense considering the stuff he'd left behind on *Fear Arrives*. Demo balls and magnetic disruptor blocks were not light items. He stopped before the Command Bridge entry hatch. He pulled up his ship's red cube from where it hung about the waist of his tube suit, pointed it at the hatch and pressed the Open spot. The hatch swung out toward him, moving to his right. He stepped through the hatch.

Jane was sitting six feet up on top of the command pedestal, her posture in her captain's seat one of tenseness. Ahead of him were Bright Sparkle, Chester, Wind Swift and Lofty Flyer.

"Hey everyone! I'm back!"

CHAPTER EIGHTEEN

Jane heard Bill's words. She turned, looked back to him, let her eyes drink in the fact he showed no wounds, and smiled. Then she saluted him.

"Welcome back, XO. Excellent job you did in taking over that ship. Any surprises?"

Bill saluted her back, walked up to just below her elevated seat, looked up, gave her a wink, then headed forward. "Not a lot. Turns out the Mokden snake-gorillas can shake off a taser hit. I got him at least once and he showed no reaction. Which is why I used the laser. Several times. He pursued me. He died before he could try to wrassle me."

Jane wondered at that. She'd heard his voice when he'd lied to the monster about cutting his way through a wall with his laser. She'd heard Death Leader's voice reacting. The two demo ball blasts had been loud to her ears. Then she'd heard only the sounds of heavy breathing on Bill's part, some grunts, the sounds of a struggle, the snap as his helmet opened up. Then had come the sound of Bill's taser zapping the crewpersons on the ship. That was followed by his discussion with ship mind Dexterity. Had it been as easy as Bill made it sound? Maybe she could get the newly arrived Dexterity to transmit holo vids of what had happened on the bridge. Sometime when Bill was elsewhere. What mattered was he was *here*, alive and ready to take over his Weapons station.

"Sounds good," she replied. She tapped the weapons control pillar in front of her. "Just transferred your Weapons control functions back to your station."

"Thanks." He pulled off his backpack, let it fall behind his seat, then sat. Her husband, lover and ship's Executive Officer leaned forward, touching the four holo control pillars that partly surrounded his work station. He fixed on the systems graphic holo to his left. "The *Fear Arrives* is not doing anything. Though it is powered up and operational thanks to its two surviving fusion reactors. What next?"

"Wellll . . . ," she said slowly. "I thought you might like to aim our antimatter projector at that hulk and remove it from my sight. Yes?"

♦ ♦ ♦

Bill grinned. Whenever Jane spoke that way he had learned it was both an invitation and a prompt for him to do something. "Yes. Very much yes, captain."

He checked his true space holo. It showed nothing but a scatter of white stars and the distant blue sparkle of Earth. Plus the yellow orb of the Sun at the upper left of the holo. He looked at his Weapons holo. The cross-section of the ship showed most weapons as Green Operational. The topside plasma battery was a melted pile of junk thanks to a laser hit. There was a large opening over the Collector Pod Chamber where something had removed 40 feet of hull. And there was a smaller hole above the ship's Containment Cell Chamber. Which was now being closed by repair robots and hover bots sent there by Star Traveler. The ship's MITV railgun launching chamber below his level was empty of torps. What was operational were the pairs of nose and tail lasers, the belly plasma battery and the topside antimatter projector. The AM reservoir held enough antimatter for six shots. He tapped the fire control panel to set up the targeting reticule for the AM projector. Putting his finger on the panel, he moved the reticule sideways until it lay directly over the front part of the *Fear Arrives*. He tapped that part of the panel, locking in the target lock.

"Captain, ready to fire."

"XO and Weapons Chief, fire."

Bill tapped the fire patch on the panel.

In his true space holo, a black beam of antimatter spat forward at the speed of light. Its contact with the giant bulbous nose of the enemy ship was disastrous. A yellow-white cloud of energy replaced the front portion of the ship. He tapped the fire patch again. The second antimatter beam hit the faint plasma cloud, vaporized the few particles in it, then passed through and struck the middle fragment of the ship. The fragment became yellow-white plasma in the true space holo. The radar, infrared, ultraviolet and neutrino sensors on his weapons control pillar showed the rest of the story. Nothing solid remained. Only billowing gases briefly produced by the matter-to-energy destruction of the enemy ship showed on the true space holo. Which now vanished since the powerful explosion had consumed nearly a hundred percent of the ship's matter. The purple dot of the ship disappeared from his system graphic holo. He looked right to his comlink holo. Jane's image filled it.

"Captain, enemy ship *Fear Arrives* is gone. No enemy ships are operational. Enemy commander is dead."

Behind him he heard a loud sigh from her. Chester also sighed and sat back in his seat. Bright Sparkle gave him a thumbs-up and a big smile. Wind Swift and Lofty Flyer showed their approval in the manner of their species.

"Excellent," Jane said, her tone command formal. "Star Traveler, establish an encrypted neutrino comlink to Peterson. Mark it to the attention of General Harriet Poindexter."

"Signal sent. Response incoming."

◆ ◆ ◆

Jane looked to her right at her comlink holo. It filled with the black face and gray-streaked hair of her commander and the chief of the United States Air Force. She was also the woman in command of all Earth forces operating beyond the atmosphere, by command of President Hartman and agreement of other national leaders. *And* she was the mother of a grown son who had come close to dying in the attacks on American rocket launching bases that had happened during Diligent Taskmaster's six ship attack on Earth. On the woman's right side sat General Paul J. McAuley, chairman of the JCS, his thick-jawed face looking very sober. On her left sat the Japanese-American general who commanded the Army. Beyond those people were the other chiefs of the Marines, Navy, National Guard and the vice chairman of the JCS. Seven in all. They were all there, like that day a year ago when she had orbited above Peterson in the sole starship controlled by a human. How things had changed since then. She saluted the woman.

"General Poindexter, I report. The enemy is defeated. Their ships are destroyed or disabled. There is no longer any Alien threat to Earth."

The woman fixed brown eyes on her. Her slim fingers held an iPad just above the flat screen inset into the tactical display table at Building One where the JCS chiefs now sat. Behind Poindexter and the chiefs were several dozen people of all officer grades. Those included officers from Britain, France, Russia and China, as best she could tell by the uniforms they wore. Clearly Building One had become the joint command site for the defense of Earth.

"So we have observed, Captain Yamaguchi. We appreciated the continuous neutrino downlink of audio vid from your command deck." Poindexter glanced down at her iPad, winced, then laid it down. She looked up. "What were our losses?"

Jane had been dreading this moment. It was one reason she'd stalled on destroying the *Fear Arrives* until Bill's return. That had now happened. It was time to face her duty, as Bill had.

"My fleets lost one Collector ship and eight subs." She licked her lips, recalling sad details from memory. Painful memory. "The Collector ship *USS Pointe De Hoc*, BBG-6, was lost with all aboard. Those were Captain Jesse Winthorp, two Rangers, two Delta Force enlisted and a Slinkeroo crewmate. Six in all." She took a deep breath. "The lost subs are the *USS Wyoming, USS Louisiana, USS Minnesota, HMS Vengeance, FNS Terrible, Vladimir Monomakh, Alexsandr Nevskiy* and the *Chairman Mao Zedong*. People lost on the subs amount to at least 1,029. Plus we lost Ranger Mark Neller when the *USS Musan* was hit by a laser. That ship lost both engines and is being corralled by the *USS Tangi Valley*. In total, we lost 1,036 humans and one Alien ally during our multiple battles near and past Jupiter."

Poindexter blinked, licked her lips, then nodded quickly. "We will handle the notifications to their families and spouses. And to the Slinkeroo embassy in Geneva. What of the enemy ships that survived? What is their status?"

Finally, a chance to share some good news. "We destroyed eight enemy Collector ships, including the flagship *Fear Arrives*. Twenty-two enemy ships have lost their Magfield engines, but most of each ship is intact. The ship minds on 21 ships are cooperating with us. Most AIs blocked weapons use in the early part of the battle. One ship mind was destroyed by the enemy in order to regain ship control." She paused, checked her system graphics holo, and looked back to the woman who controlled her destiny. "General Poindexter, I have asked those subs and Collector ships who lag behind my current group of five ships to use their Magfield spacedrives to rendezvous with the enemy ships, then use their drives to push those ships onto a vector aimed at the Earth-Moon system. As I discussed with you, I plan to move the surviving enemy ships into orbit above Earth. There to receive new Magfield engines from the ship factory you recently orbited. Is this disposition satisfactory?"

McAuley's expression brightened. "So we have gained the foundations for 22 new Collector ships? With operational stardrives?"

Jane noticed the calmness of Poindexter. Well, if she wasn't bothered by the JCS chairman's insertion of himself into her first debriefing, she would not object. "General McAuley, yes, that is correct. And yes, all 22 captured enemy ships have operational Alcubierre stardrives. All stardrives are located in the middle of a Collector ship. Only the rear third of each ship was destroyed."

She noticed the movement of the foreign officers closer to the JCS table. Clearly some of them wanted to claim some of her captured ships. The Army chief of staff on Poindexter's left leaned forward.

"Captain Poindexter, Ranger Sergeant Neller was part of my Army family," said the general, whose name she recalled was Kenji Fujiwara. "Please be aware we will shortly inform his parents that he is being awarded the Distinguished Service Cross, the Distinguished Service Medal and the Purple Heart." The man paused. "Captain Winthorp was also a Ranger. She too will be awarded the Distinguished Service Cross, the Distinguished Service Medal and the Purple Heart. The other Ranger and Delta Force crew members on her ship will each be awarded the Distinguished Service Medal, the Soldier's Medal and the Purple Heart. I wish I could do more."

Her heart thumped faster. The many deaths she had just recited were terrible. The deaths of people she knew was worse. The loss of Bill's saloon buddy Mark was supremely painful. She'd gotten to know the man. His absence from her life was a hollow echo deep inside. "Thank you, General Fujiwara. The news . . . is good to hear. I hope it will give solace to his parents and her husband."

Poindexter leaned forward. "That is also my hope. For Sergeant Neller's parents and for the families of all those we lost. Finally, yes, your use of outlying ships to redirect the 22 enemy ships is approved by me." The middle-aged woman looked down at her iPad, then up, her curly black eyebrows lifting. "Captain Yamaguchi, what is—"

"General," interrupted the new Chief of Naval Operations, a black man whose head was shaved smooth. "May I add a few words?"

The woman looked to her far left where the CNO sat. "Vice Admiral Jackson, you may."

The man fixed dark brown eyes on Jane. "Captain Yamaguchi, my Navy family lost Captain Joshua Baraka of the *Louisiana*, Captain Paul Leonard of the *Minnesota* and Captain Janet Murchison of the *Wyoming*. I aim to ensure they will each receive the Navy Cross for their incredible willingness to dive their subs into enemy Collector ships. Thereby removing the ultimate threat to America. Their crews will each receive the Navy and Marine Corps Medal, plus the Purple Heart. Thank you."

Poindexter's expression did not show irritation. If anything, her veil of command sternness gained a tinge of sadness. She looked to Jane. "Captain, what is the status of your fleet? What ships, specifically, are still operational and able to defend Earth and the Solar system?"

She glanced at her systems graphic holo. It showed the presence of every operational Magfield engine in her spread-out fleet. Jane looked up. "Collector ships that are still operational include the *USS Blue Sky, USS Tangi Valley, USS Rolling Thunder, USS Takur Ghar, USS Seafloat, USS Chapultepec Castle, USS Manila Bay, USS Neil C. Roberts, USS Fallujah, USS Moberly* and the *USS Harken.* The *USS Musan* is intact but its Magfield engines are melted down." She paused, glanced at the system graphic, then looked back. "Our surviving boomer subs include the *USS Henry M. Jackson, USS Alabama, USS Alaska, USS Nevada, USS Tennessee, USS Pennsylvania, USS West Virginia, USS Kentucky, USS Maryland, USS Nebraska, USS Rhode Island* and the *USS Maine.* Among our allies, there survive the *Dimitry Donskoy*, the *Yuri Dolgorukiy* and the *Emperor Huang Ti.* In short, 11 Collector ships and 15 subs are fully operational."

Poindexter blinked. "Excellent news. Please bring your ship, the *USS Neil C. Roberts* and your three Trident subs back to Earth. How long will it take you to arrive here?"

"Two hours or so," Jane said, wondering what the woman had in mind.

The black woman frowned. "But your ships are traveling at, uh, 13 or was it 14 percent of lightspeed? Won't it take longer to slow them down so you can make Earth orbit?"

Jane shook her head. She ignored the smile of Bill as he looked back at her. "General Poindexter, all ships using Magfield spacedrives are able to slow down nearly as fast as we can speed up. It's just a matter of setting the engines to push against the Sun and inner planets, rather than pull toward them. We will slow to one percent of lightspeed within the next ten minutes. I plan to take it slower than normal due to the strain our engines experienced during the hyper-fast pursuit we did of the leading enemy ships."

"Oh." The woman gave a quick nod. "Of course you know your ships best. We look forward to your arrival here and—"

"Incoming signal," muttered McAuley from her right, pointing down at his own iPad. "You know who."

Poindexter frowned, then nodded. She looked up. "Captain, President Melody Hartman is joining us live, from the White House." The woman stood up, as did the other chiefs.

Jane hurriedly did the same. As did Chester and Bill. And Bright Sparkle, bless her. "Star Traveler, please repeat our comlink holo signal at the front of the bridge."

"Complying."

A tall holo appeared before the line of function stations. She faced the holo as did her crewmates. All of them saluted.

Melody Hartman filled the holo. This time she was standing behind her wooden desk in the Oval Office. She turned from looking out the window at the people passing distantly on the sidewalk beyond the fence that encircled the White House. Her curly brown hair had gray streaks in it. Her brown eyebrows looked lighter than before. She was wearing a checkered blue and green pantsuit. While trim looking, the older woman looked tired as she put hands on her hips and faced Jane.

"Captain Yamaguchi, thank you from the bottom of my heart for defeating our foe." The woman's soprano voice sounded strong and firm. Her gaze became that of the new FDR she had aspired to be. "Are your other ships and subs receiving my image?"

"Yes, madame president. I have always shared all communications from high command with my fellow captains," Jane said, hoping her voice did crack. She still held her salute, as did Bill and Chester.

The woman nodded quickly. Good. Be at ease, all of you." Jane dropped her salute and adopted a parade rest posture. "Glad to hear that so many of our Collector ships and subs survived this battle. And that your XO once again boarded an enemy ship and took down its commander." The woman, who Jane knew was looking at a flat screen repeater image of her bridge and crew, looked toward Bill. "Chief Petty Officer MacCarthy, enlisted grade E-7, please be aware that I am recommending to the DOD that you be promoted to Lieutenant Commander, officer grade O-3." She looked back to Jane. "Air Force Captain Yamaguchi, you command our nation's only space fleet. I will nominate you to assume the rank of Brigadier General, grade O-7. I suspect the Senate will quickly approve your promotion."

Shock filled her. She was being jumped past three ranks above her, from her O-3 Captain rank to a one star general. Then again, it was wartime and wartime promotions came fast. Plus hers was a new branch of the Air Force. Or rather, Air Force and Navy, considering the BBG designation of her Collector ship. Well, being a brigadier general was better than being some kind of admiral. She saluted again, then smiled.

"Madame President, thank you! I never expected—"

"I know you didn't. Nor did your XO," the woman interrupted, her manner sharply focused. "But you and he earned these promotions. As did those ship captains and crew who died in combat." The woman's pale pink lipstick looked weathered. She blinked quickly. "Regarding your fleet members and the captured enemy ships. Be aware that I will propose to Congress that America provide a rebuilt Collector ship to Great Britain, France, China and Russia. They each lost one or more subs. America will still possess 18 new Collector ships plus your 12 that survived the battle. I doubt any Buyer society starship or group of ships will ever again attack the Solar system and Earth. Let alone the United States of America."

Jane noticed that in her comlink holo, which held the images of all seven JCS chiefs, General McAuley's full lips pursed. No doubt the Marine was not happy at losing four future starships. She lowered her salute.

"Madame President, thank you for that information. I believe the efforts of those subs that died in the fight to protect Earth warrant the action you suggest." She paused, knowing this was not the time to whine. Or demand. Still. "May I ask about your plans for my current fleet?"

The Anglo woman stepped forward to her desk and stood behind her padded seat. She rested her hands on top of the seat. Her eyes and expression moved from formal to . . . to conspiratorial. "Tell me, Captain, what is the current status of our armed forces?"

"We are in a state of war as declared by Congress. Our enemy are the 413 star systems that make up the Buyer society," she replied, hoping she had said what the president expected to hear.

"Correct," Hartman said, her tone almost a snap. "That state of war will exist for some years yet. Like the war on terrorism, we must seek out and destroy the primary military forces of the enemy. Tell me, what are the enemy's primary military locations? And forces?"

Jane licked her lips, raking her mind for the details. "Primary military locations are the ship mind nursery asteroid in system Kepler 443, and a new Collector ship factory in system Kepler 66. There are 59 Market worlds scattered among the 413 star systems that contain Buyers. The Buyer society controls at least 50 operational Collector ships," she said. What was her commander in chief aiming at?

Hartman nodded slowly, her face expectant. "Two more questions. What do the new Collector ships built by us and by our Megun allies need in order for those ships to operate most effectively? And what actions would most damage the Buyer society?"

Ahhh. "President Hartman, all new Collector ships require a ship mind AI to be most effective. The self-aware AIs make possible the small five or six person crews on each ship." She paused. "We could achieve the most harm on the enemy by taking control of the ship mind nursery at Kepler 443 and by destroying their new factory at Kepler 66. We would thereby gain ship minds for our new ships. And we would make any new enemy Collector ships less combat effective."

"Exactly." Hartman blinked. Her blue eyes peered intensely at Jane. "While I will always seek the advice of my JCS chiefs, it appears obvious that the next job for your fleet of starships is to take command of the ship mind nursery at Kepler 443, then travel to Kepler 66 to destroy the new ship factory. I have no doubt that in doing these two tasks, you will fight and defeat more enemy ships. You would also destroy all Buyer compounds on any Market world that you encounter."

Her heart thudded. More long, long trips away from home. Still, her tours of combat duty were no longer than those currently faced by aircraft supercarriers and many Navy subs. The seated figure of Chester reminded her of a question that must be asked.

"Madame President, what about the NATO of the Stars mission that you sent us out on? Vice Admiral Richardson did a wonderful job in negotiating our treaty with the Slinkeroo." Jane took a breath. "I sent that data to Peterson along with the audio vidcam records of our travels and encounters."

Hartman's eyebrows lifted. Her expression went thoughtful. Finally she snapped the fingers on her right hand. "I still believe in the NATO of the Stars. Humanity and America need more allies. Continue visiting the star systems of your Alien crewmates. Seek their membership in our alliance. In particular I hope to gain the assistance of the Megun people who repaired your Magfield engines," the woman said. "That makes three objectives for the next time your *USS Blue Sky* leaves the Solar system with many of your current Collector ships. Think you can handle that?"

"I can," Jane said firmly, still maintaining her parade rest, forward leaning posture. "However, my ship needs a rebuilding of its topside plasma battery and hull repairs over its Collector Pods Chamber. Can my ship, and the *USS Musan*, receive priority repair assistance at the ship factory you put into orbit?"

"They can," Hartman said, her tone becoming conversational. "And I believe the five ships you captured in the enemy fleet system need additional crew. They are now operating with just three crew each. Correct?"

Jane nodded quickly. "Very correct, madame president. Hopefully we can gain new special operations crew members while our ships are undergoing repairs. And resupply of food and essentials."

"I am sure General Poindexter will handle the new crew and supplies matters very nicely. As she did earlier." The woman who was the leader of 315 million of her fellow citizens squinted, then smiled slowly. "Ship repairs do not require the presence of the ship's captain. Will you, your XO, your entire crew, and the captains of your

Collector ships join me and my husband for dinner at the White House?"

Jane felt surprise, then understood. This woman faced a new presidential election in two years. She had no doubt the woman would ask Congress and the states to approve a third term for herself. Then she would run a patriotism-infused campaign similar to what FDR had done during World War II. She didn't mind. This woman was the strong, decisive leader America needed in a time of deadly threat to her nation, the Constitution and the world.

"I will be happy to join you and your family at the White House," Jane said. "We will come down in our transports, rather than the *Blue Sky*, if that is agreeable?"

"Very agreeable. I believe your transports can fit onto the South Lawn. No need to fence off the Ellipse, like last time," Hartman said amiably. Then she went intensely serious. Her face became that of a leader who knew she commanded. "Once your ships are repaired, new crew added and supplies provided, you *will* travel to Kepler 443 to capture and hold the ship mind nursery. After that, you will attack the new ship factory and find new allies for our NATO of the Stars alliance as conditions permit. Those are your future orders. I look forward to seeing you this evening at the White House."

Jane saluted the woman once more. "I accept my orders. I and my crew and fellow captains will attend your dinner tonight."

"Good." Hartman looked aside, then forward. "General Poindexter, General McAuley, send me the names of every human who died in defense of America, our Constitution and Earth. I will make personal contact with the survivors of each lost combatant."

"It will be done," Poindexter said.

The image of Hartman disappeared. Leaving her facing seven seated JCS chiefs. The Air Force chief pursed her lips, then shrugged. "Well, you heard what the president wants. As did we. Take low Earth orbit. Move your ship to the ship factory complex you will see as you arrive. While you wait for your other ship captains to arrive, bring yourself and XO MacCarthy down to Peterson. We folks here in Building One and Two wish to see you in person." The woman smiled. "After all, you have to be here so I can pin your brigadier general's silver star on your shoulders, and for Weapons Chief MacCarthy to receive his lieutenant commander's oak leaf."

Jane laughed. "Exactly so. My XO and I look forward to seeing you, the rest of the JCS and the officers of our allied nations." She sobered. "The Russian, Chinese, British and French sub captains were fine men. I wish to present short vidcam records of each ship's combat actions to the allied officers behind you."

Poindexter's amiable mood shifted to formality with a tinge of sadness. "We will welcome you both to our abode. Your offer of vidcam records will, I am sure, be appreciated by the liaison officers of those nations. See you in two hours."

CHAPTER NINETEEN

Bill watched as Lofty Flyer moved the *Blue Sky* into a 240 mile equatorial orbit above Earth. Rather than use their engines to hold position above Peterson, they would orbit like normal satellites. And rockets. His true space holo showed rockets lifting off from French Guiana, Baikonur and Wenchang Launch Center on Hainan Island. His Weapons control pillar depicted each rocket lifting off along with their vital characteristics. It was an Ariane 6 rising from Guiana, an Energia taking off from Russia and a Long March 5 rocket departing from China's new spaceport on the island that lay at the northern end of the South China Sea. All were heavy lifters, similar to the American super heavy-lifter SLS rocket that produced 7.2 million pounds of thrust. He recalled the SLS was more powerful than the Saturn V moon rocket of decades ago. *Ahhh.* His Weapons holo added another rocket outline and data just as the bright flare of a rocket appeared in his true space holo. An SLS was lifting from Kennedy Space Center in Florida. The trajectories of all four rockets were projected for an orbital track close to the giant hulk that was the Collector ship factory that orbited just 20 miles ahead of them. He looked back.

"Captain, Jane, any news on what those four heavy-lifters are bringing up to orbit?"

His wife, who'd just returned from a brief nap in their habitat room suite, lifted her eyebrows, then nodded. "Yup. Part of the orbital action update I got on my iPad from Peterson. Those rockets are bringing up prefab sections of what will become humanity's first spacedock." She half-smiled. "Looks like the prez is aiming to imitate the Megun facilities. I suspect some of our Collector ships will be pressed into bringing stuff up."

That mattered not to him. The system graphic on his left showed only human-controlled ships and subs were present in the Solar system. Jake's ship *Tangi Valley*, and his saloon buddies' ships *Fallujah*, *Moberly*, *Harken* and *Musan*, were just passing Mars on their way to a rendezvous with Earth. The *Musan* had been pushed onto the proper vector by Jake's ship. She would be put into orbit next to the ship factory hulk by one of his drinking buddies. There were only eight left now, with the loss of Mark. At least Stefano was close by in the *Neil C. Roberts*. His SEAL buddy would join them for the White House dinner. In about seven hours or so. Which made him think of another question.

"Captain, will the spouses of our other ship captains be able to join us at the White House?"

In the comlink holo on his right, Jane gave an easy smile. "Of course they can! And those spouses on other ships like Lorilee and Helen, Learned Escape and Builder of Joy, will join their spouses. Here or on other ships. The ship minds can handle ship matters when every bioform is off ship."

Her easy smile left him feeling up. His wife had carried a tremendous load ever since they had returned from the Slinkeroo system. He hoped there would not be any media vidcams at the dinner tonight. No need for them to be more of a worldwide celebrity than they already were. He'd turned off his iPhone as they arrived in orbit precisely to block pestering calls from CNN, BBC, *Daichi Shimbun* and the *Times* of London. But there was one person he wanted to talk to. See even.

"Captain, my sister Joan lives in Denver as you know. We're heading to CSprings to meet the JCS folks. She could drive down there. Any chance I could pull her onto our transport and take her to the White House dinner?"

In the holo, she smiled at him. "Bill! You are becoming almost civilized!" Like him and everyone else, she was out of her tube suit and wore her Air Force Blue jacket and pants. He too wore the Navy version of dress-up. Her dark brown eyes looked him over, then she winked. "You'll do. For the JCS, for Joan, for the prez and for me."

Bill sighed, then looked back to his wife, lover and captain of the starship that had been their home for more than a year. He gave her a thumbs-up, then leaned on the right side armrest of his seat, keeping her alive, beautiful face in view. He never wanted to lose her. She might be his ship commander, but she was the core of what made normal life worthwhile. Plus, she understood what Duty, Honor and Country meant. Along with freedom, liberty and free choice.

"Thanks," he said. Then realized what the president's orders also meant. "Uh, any idea whether one of our crewmate's stars lies on the way to Kepler 443? I'd love to do some sight-seeing before we get combat serious."

Jane blinked, her expression sobering as the fact of them being on active duty status hit her once more. Damn. He'd hoped to ease her load.

"I agree," she said, her meso-soprano voice filling the space between him and her. She nodded to Chester, who was watching their byplay. As was Bright Sparkle, who had a big grin on her face. "Well, the Megun people's star of Kepler 452 is very much aligned with the vector track to Kepler 443. And it is just 1,400 light years away, versus the 2,541 light years to 443."

Bright Sparkle's green eyes grew very wide. Beyond her, Wind Swift turned toward them, her red eyes scanning Bill, Jane, Chester and Bright Sparkle. "My star also lies in that direction. You call it Kepler 22. Captain Jane, my people would welcome a visit from you and your fleet."

His wife looked thoughtful. "Wind Swift, I would love to visit your star system. And yes, it lies on the same vector track. It is also closer than the Megun system. Your world is just 620 light years distant from Earth. Maybe we can visit both the Cheelan and Megun systems on our way out to Kepler 443?"

"Yes!" barked Wind Swift.

"Wonderful," spoke Bright Sparkle's speaker/vidcam.

Jane looked back to Bill, her thin black eyebrows rising. Her oval face had an impish look on it.

"Well, Mr. Tourist Man, you up for adding two more members to our alliance, before we tote our antimatter projectors into Kepler 443?"

Bill grinned. At last, there were some bright spots in his future. "Yes! Very much yes. Would love to see what Wind Swift's world is like. And I'd love to return to the world where we got married. Maybe we could celebrate our first anniversary of being married?"

Jane looked puzzled. "Uh, that's still six months away. We'll be heading out in a few weeks."

Bill shrugged. "I meant our next *monthly* anniversary! You up for celebrating that? Again?"

His beautiful, brave and amazing wife smiled like a nova rising in the east. "Yes!"

And with that the future for Bill became something he looked forward to. He had been bored on desk duty at Coronado. He'd been bored in Denver while being retired. Now, thanks to being kidnapped by a giant cockroach, he was doing things he'd never imagined. And he was meeting people who sure as hell did not resemble him, Jane or Chester. That was just fine! He turned back and fixed his gaze on his true space holo. The yellow-orange flames of four ascending rocket ships told him his future, with Jane, was going to be one damn fine adventure!

THE END

ABOUT THE AUTHOR

T. Jackson King (Tom) is a professional archaeologist, journalist and retired Hippie. He learned early on to question authority and find answers for himself, thanks to reading lots of science fiction. He also worked at a radiocarbon dating laboratory at UC Riverside and UCLA. Tom attended college in Paris and Tokyo. Tom is a graduate of UCLA (M.A. 1976, archaeology) and the University of Tennessee (B.Sc. 1971, journalism). He has worked as an archaeologist in the American Southwest and has traveled widely in Europe, Russia, Japan, Canada, Mexico and the USA. Other jobs have included short order cook, hotel clerk, legal assistant, telephone order taker, investigative reporter and newspaper editor. He also survived the warped speech-talk of local politicians and escaped with his hide intact. Tom writes hard science fiction, anthropological scifi, dark fantasy/horror and contemporary fantasy/magic realism. Tom's novels are **FIGHT THE ALIENS** (2016), **FIRST CONTACT** (2015), **ESCAPE FROM ALIENS** (2015), **ALIENS VS. HUMANS** (2015), **FREEDOM VS. ALIENS** (2015), **HUMANS VS. ALIENS** (2015), **GENECODE ILLEGAL** (2014), **EARTH VS. ALIENS** (2014), **ALIEN ASSASSIN** (2014), **THE MEMORY SINGER** (2014), **ANARCHATE VIGILANTE** (2014), **GALACTIC VIGILANTE** (2013), **NEBULA VIGILANTE** (2013), **SPEAKER TO ALIENS** (2013), **GALACTIC AVATAR** (2013), **STELLAR ASSASSIN** (2013), **STAR VIGILANTE** (2012), **THE GAEAN ENCHANTMENT** (2012), **LITTLE BROTHER'S WORLD** (2010), **ANCESTOR'S WORLD** (1996, with A.C. Crispin), and **RETREAD SHOP** (1988, 2012). His short stories appeared in **JUDGMENT DAY AND OTHER DREAMS** (2009). His poetry appeared in **MOTHER EARTH'S STRETCH MARKS** (2009). Tom lives in Santa Fe, New Mexico, USA with his wife Sue. More information on Tom's writings can be found at www.tjacksonking.com/.

PRAISE FOR T. JACKSON KING'S BOOKS

EARTH VS. ALIENS

"This story is the best space opera I've read in many years. The author knows his Mammalian Behavior. If we're lucky it'll become a movie soon. Many of the ideas are BRAND NEW and I loved the adaptability of people in the story line. AWESOME!!"—**Phil W. King,** *Amazon*

"It's good space opera. I liked the story and wanted to know what happened next. The characters are interesting and culturally diverse. The underlying theme is that humans are part of nature and nature is red of tooth and claw. Therefore, humans are naturally violent, which fortunately makes them a match for the predators from space."—**Frank C. Hemingway,** *Amazon*

STAR VIGILANTE

"For a fast-paced adventure with cool tech, choose *Star Vigilante*. This is the story of three outsiders. Can three outsiders bond together to save Eliana's planet from eco-destruction at the hands of a ruthless mining enterprise?" –**Bonnie Gordon,** *Los Alamos Daily Post*

STELLAR ASSASSIN
"T. Jackson King's *Stellar Assassin* is an ambitious science fiction epic that sings! Filled with totally alien lifeforms, one lonely human, an archaeologist named Al Lancaster must find his way through trade guilds, political maneuvering and indentured servitude, while trying to reconcile his new career as an assassin with his deeply-held belief in the teachings of Buddha. . . This is a huge, colorful, complicated world with complex characters, outstanding dialogue, believable motivations, wonderful high-tech battle sequences and, on occasion, a real heart-stringer . . . This is an almost perfectly edited novel as well, which is a bonus. This is a wonderful novel, written by a wonderful author . . .Bravo! Five Stars!" –**Linell Jeppsen,** *Amazon*

LITTLE BROTHER'S WORLD

"If you're sensing a whiff of Andre Norton or Robert A. Heinlein, you're not mistaken . . . The influence is certainly there, but *Little Brother's World* is no mere imitation of *Star Man's Son* or *Citizen of the Galaxy*. Rather, it takes the sensibility of those sorts of books and makes of it something fresh and new. T. Jackson King is doing his part to further the great conversation of science fiction; it'll be interesting to see where he goes next."–**Don Sakers**, *Analog*

"When I'm turning a friend on to a good writer I've just discovered, I'll often say something like, "Give him ten pages and you'll never be able to put him down." Once in a long while, I'll say, "Give him five pages." It took T. Jackson King exactly *one sentence* to set his hook so deep in me that I finished ***LITTLE BROTHER'S WORLD*** in a single sitting, and I'll be thinking about that vivid world for a long time to come. The last writer I can recall with the courage to make a protagonist out of someone as profoundly Different as Little Brother was James Tiptree Jr., with her remarkable debut novel ***UP THE WALLS OF THE WORLD***. I think Mr. King has met that challenge even more successfully. His own writing DNA borrows genes from writers as diverse as Tiptree, Heinlein, Norton, Zelazny, Sturgeon, Pohl, and Doctorow, and splices them together very effectively." – **Spider Robinson, Hugo, Nebula and Campbell Award winner**

"*Little Brother's World* is a sci-fi novel where Genetic Engineering exists. . . It contains enough details and enough thrills to make the book buyers/readers grab it and settle in for an afternoon read. The book is well-written and had a well-defined plot . . . I never found a boring part in the story. It was fast-paced and kept me entertained all throughout. The characters are fascinating and likeable too. This book made me realize about a possible outcome, when finally science and technology wins over traditional ones. . . All in all, *Little Brother's World* is another sci-fi novel from T. Jackson King that is both exciting, thrilling and fun. Full of suspense, adventure, romance, secrets, conspiracies, this book would take you in a roller-coaster ride." –**Abby Flores**, *Bookshelf Confessions*

THE MEMORY SINGER

"A coming of age story reminiscent of Robert A. Heinlein or Alexei

Panshin. Jax [the main character] is a fun character, and her world is compelling. The social patterns of Ship life are fascinating, and the Alish'Tak [the main alien species] are sufficiently alien to make for a fairly complex book. Very enjoyable."—**Don Sakers**, *Analog Science Fiction*

"Author T. Jackson King brings his polished writing style, his knowledge of science fiction 'hardware,' and his believable aliens to his latest novel *The Memory Singer*. But all this is merely backdrop to the adventures of Jax Cochrane, a smart, rebellious teen who wants more from life than the confines of a generational starship. There are worlds of humans and aliens out there. When headstrong Jax decides that it's time to discover and explore them, nothing can hold back this defiant teen. You'll want to accompany this young woman . . in this fine coming-of-age story."—**Jean Kilczer**, *Amazon*

RETREAD SHOP

"Engaging alien characters, a likable protagonist, and a vividly realized world make King's first sf novel a good purchase for sf collections."–*Library Journal*

"A very pleasant tour through the author's inventive mind, and an above average story as well."–*Science Fiction Chronicle*

"Fun, with lots of outrageously weird aliens."—*Locus*

"The writing is sharp, the plotting tight, and the twists ingenious. It would be worth reading, if only for the beautiful delineations of alien races working with and against one another against the background of an interstellar marketplace. The story carries you . . . with a verve and vigor that bodes well for future stories by this author. Recommended."–*Science Fiction Review*

"For weird aliens, and I do mean weird, choose *Retread Shop*. The story takes place on a galactic trading base, where hundreds of species try to gain the upper hand for themselves and for their group. Sixteen year-old billy is the sole human on the Retread Shop, stranded when his parents and their shipmates perished. What really makes the ride fun are the aliens Billy teams up with, including two who are plants. It's herbivores vs. carnivores, herd species vs. loners, mammals vs. insects and so on. The wild variety of physical types is only matched by the extensive array of cultures, which makes for a very entertaining read." –**Bonnie Gordon,** *Los Alamos Daily Post*

"Similar in feel to Roger Zelazny's Alien Speedway series is *Retread Shop* by T. Jackson King. It's an orphan-human-in-alien-society-makes-good story. Well-written and entertaining, it could be read either as a Young Adult or as straight SF with equal enjoyment." – **Chuq Von Rospach,** *OtherRealms 22*

"If you liked Stephen Goldin's Jade Darcy books duo, and Julie Czerneda's Clan trilogy, then you will probably like *Retread Shop* since it too has multiple aliens, an eatery, and an infinity of odd events that range from riots, to conspiracy, to exploring new worlds and to alien eating habits . . . It's a fun reader's ride and thoroughly entertaining. And, sigh, I wish that the author would write more books set in this background." –**Lyn McConchie, co-author of the** *Beastmaster* **series**

HUMANS VS. ALIENS

"Another great book from this author. This series has great characters and story is wall to wall excitement. Look forward to next book."— **William R. Thomas,** *Amazon*

"Humans are once again aggressive and blood thirsty to defend the Earth. Pace is quick and action is plentiful. Some unexpected plot twists, but you always know the home team is the best."—**C. Cook,** *Amazon*

ANCESTOR'S WORLD
"T. Jackson King is a professional archaeologist and he uses that to great advantage in *Ancestor's World*. I was just as fascinated by the details of the archaeology procedures as I was by the unfolding of the plot . . . What follows is a tightly plotted, suspenseful novel."– *Absolute Magnitude*

"The latest in the StarBridge series from King, a former Rogue Valley resident now living and writing in Arizona, follows the action on planet Na-Dina, where the tombs of 46 dynasties have lain undisturbed for 6,000 years until a human archaeologist and a galactic gumshoe show up. Set your phasers for fun."–*Medford Mail Tribune*

ALIEN ASSASSIN
"The Assassin series is required reading in adventure, excitement and daring. The galactic vistas, the advanced alien technologies and the action make all the Assassin books a guarantee of a good read. Please keep them coming!"—**C. B. Symons,** *Amazon*

"KING STRIKES AGAIN! Yes, T. Jackson King gives us yet again a great space adventure. I loved the drama and adventure in this book. There is treachery in this one too which heightens the suspense. Being the only human isn't easy, but Al pulls it off. Loved the Dino babies and how they are being developed into an important part of the family of assassins. All of the fun takes place right here and we are not left hanging off the cliff. Write on T.J."—**K. McClell,** *Amazon*

THE GAEAN ENCHANTMENT
"For magic, a quest and a new battle around every corner, go with *The Gaean Enchantment*. In this novel, Earth has entered a new phase as it cycles through the universe. In this phase, some kinds of "magic" work, but tech is rapidly ceasing to function. In the world of this book, incantation and sympathetic magic function through connection to spirit figures who might be described as gods." – **Bonnie Gordon,** *Los Alamos Daily Post*

"In *The Gaean Enchantment* the main character, Thomas, back from Vietnam and with all the PTSD that many soldiers have—nightmares, blackouts—finds his truth through the finding of his totem animal, the buffalo Black Mane. He teaches Thomas that violence and killing must always be done as a last resort, and that the energies of his soul are more powerful than any arsenal . . . Don't miss this amazing novel of magic and soul transformation, deep love, and Artemis, goddess of the hunt and protector of women."–**Catherine Herbison-Wiget,** *Amazon*

JUDGMENT DAY AND OTHER DREAMS

"King is a prolific writer with an old-time approach–he tells straight-ahead stories and asks the big questions. No topic is off limits and he writes with an explorer's zest for uncovering the unknown. He takes readers right into the world of each story, so each rustle of a tree, each whisper of the wind, blows softly against your inner ear."–**Scott Turick, *Daytona Beach News-Journal***

"Congratulations on the long overdue story collection, Tom! What I find most terrific is your range of topics and styles. You have always been an explorer."–**David Brin, Nebula and Hugo winner**

"I'm thoroughly loving [the stories]; the prose is the kind that makes me stop and savor it – roll phrases over my tongue – delicious. I loved the way you conjure up a whole world or civilization so economically."–**Sheila Finch, SF author**

"***Judgment Day and Other Dreams*** . . . would make a valued addition to any science fiction or fantasy library. There is a satisfying and engrossing attention to detail within the varied stories . . . The common thread among all works is the intimate human element at the heart of each piece. King's prose displays a mastery over these myriad subjects without alienating the uninitiated, thus providing the reader with a smooth, coherent, and altogether enjoyable experience . . . King is able to initiate the reader naturally through plot and precise prose, as if being eased into a warm bath . . . There is a dedicated unity amongst some of the entries in this anthology that begs to be explored in longer formats. And the works which stand apart are just as notable and exemplify King's grasp of human emotions and interactions. This collection displays the qualities of fine writing backed by a knowledgeable hand and a vivid imagination . . . If ***Judgment Day and Other Dreams*** is anything to go by, T. Jackson King should be a household name." –**John Sulyok, *Tangent Online***

52842710R00143

Made in the USA
Lexington, KY
12 June 2016